Kog and Sardak suddenly howled. The table between us flung upwards. Samos and I, buffeted, stumbled back. The dark lantern, scattering flaming oil, struck a wall to the side of the room. I saw the eyes of the two creatures glinting like fiery copper plates.

With a cry of rage Sardak hurled the great Kur spear. It shattered half through the wall some forty feet behind us.

With a titanic beating of wings the two tarns, the creatures mounted on them, took flight from the ruins. I staggered back in the wind from the wings. I half shut my eyes against the dust and debris which struck against my face. The flames from the burning oil leaped almost horizontally backwards, torn and lashed by the wind. Then they burned again, as they had a moment before.

I saw the creatures mounted on the tarns, silhouetted against one of Gor's three moons, fleeing over the marshes. **"They have escaped,"** said Samos.

SAVAGES
OF GOR

John Norman

DAW BOOKS, INC.

DONALD A. WOLLHEIM, PUBLISHER

1633 Broadway, New York, NY 10019

FIRST PRINTING, MARCH 1982

1 2 3 4 5 6 7 8 9

 DAW TRADEMARK REGISTERED
U.S. PAT. OFF. MARCA
REGISTRADA. HECHO EN U.S.A.

PRINTED IN U.S.A.

CONTENTS

1

KOG AND SARDAK;

THE PARLEY IN THE DELTA

"How many are there?" I asked Samos.

"Two," he said.

"Are they alive?" I asked.

"Yes," he said.

At the second Ahn, long before dawn, the herald of Samos had come to the lakelike courtyard of my holding in many-canaled Port Kar, that place of many ships, scourge of Thassa, that dark jewel in her gleaming green waters. Twice had he struck on the bars of the sea gate, each time with the Ka-la-na shaft of his spear, not with the side of its broad tapering bronze point. The signet ring of Samos of Port Kar, first captain of the council of captains, was displayed. I would be roused. The morning, in early Spring, was chilly.

"Does Tyros move?" I asked blond-haired Thurnock, that giant of a man, he of the peasants, who had come to rouse me.

"I think not, Captain," said he.

The girl beside me pulled the furs up about her throat, frightened.

"Have ships of Cos been sighted?" I asked.

"I do not think so, Captain," said he.

There was a sound of chain beside me. The chain had moved against the collar ring of the girl beside me. Beneath the furs she was naked. The chain ran from the slave ring at

7

the foot of my couch, a heavy chain, to the thick metal collar fastened on her neck.

"It is not, then, on the business of Port Kar that he comes?" I had asked.

"I think perhaps not, Captain," said Thurnock. "I think that the matters have to do with business other than that of Port Kar."

The small tharlarion-oil lamp he held illuminated his bearded face as he stood near the door.

"It has been quiet," I said, "for too long."

"Captain?" he asked.

"Nothing," I said.

"It is early," whispered the girl next to me.

"You were not given permission to speak," I told her.

"Forgive me, Master," she said.

I threw back the heavy furs on the great stone couch. Quickly the girl pulled up her legs and turned on her side. I, sitting up, looked down at her, trying to cover herself from the sight of Thurnock. I pulled her then beneath me. "Ohh," she breathed.

"You will grant him, then, an audience?" asked Thurnock.

"Yes," I said.

"Oh," said the girl. "Ohh!"

Now, as she lay, the small, fine brand high on her left thigh, just below the hip, could be seen. I had put it there myself, at my leisure, once in Ar.

"Master, may I speak?" she begged.

"Yes," I said.

"One is present," she said. "Another is present!"

"Be silent," I told her.

"Yes, my Master," she said.

"You will be there shortly?" asked Thurnock.

"Yes," I told him. "Shortly."

The girl looked wildly over my shoulder, toward Thurnock. Then she clutched me, her eyes closed, shuddering, and yielded. When again she looked to Thurnock she did so as a yielded slave girl, pinned in my arms.

"I shall inform the emissary of Samos that you will be with him in moments," said Thurnock.

"Yes," I told him.

He then left the room, putting the small tharlarion-oil lamp on a shelf near the door.

I looked down into the eyes of the girl, held helplessly in my arms.

"What a slave you made me," she said.

"You are a slave," I told her.

"Yes, my Master," she said.

"You must grow accustomed to your slavery, in all its facets," I told her.

"Yes, my Master," she said.

I withdrew from her then, and sat on the edge of the couch, the furs about me.

"A girl is grateful that she was touched by her Master," she said.

I did not respond. A slave's gratitude is nothing, as are slaves.

"It is early," she whispered.

"Yes," I said.

"It is very cold," she said.

"Yes," I said. The coals in the brazier to the left of the great stone couch had burned out during the night. The room was damp, and cold, from the night air, and from the chill from the courtyard and canals. The walls, of heavy stone, too, saturated with the chilled, humid air, would be cold and damp, and the defensive bars set in the narrow windows, behind the buckled leather hangings. On my feet I could feel the dampness and moisture on the tiles. I did not give her permission to draw back under the covers, nor was she so bold or foolish as to request that permission. I had been lenient with her this night. I had not slept her naked on the tiles beside the couch, with only a sheet for warmth, nor naked at the foot of the couch, with only a chain for comfort.

I rose from the couch and went to a bronze basin of cold water at the side of the room. I squatted beside it and splashed the chilled water over my face and body.

"What does it mean, my Master," asked the girl, "that one from the house of Samos, first captain in Port Kar, comes so early, so secretly, to the house of my Master?"

"I do not know," I said. I toweled myself dry, and turned to look upon her. She lay on her left elbow, on the couch, the chain running from her collar to the surface of the couch, and thence to the slave ring fixed deeply in its base. Seeing my eyes upon her she then knelt on the surface of the couch, kneeling back on her heels, spreading her knees, straightening her back, lifting her head, and putting her hands on her thighs. It is a common kneeling position for a female slave.

"If you knew, you would not tell me, would you?" she asked.

"No," I said.

"I am a slave," she said.

"Yes," I said.

"You had me well," she said, "and as a slave."

"It is fitting," I said.

"Yes, Master," she said.

I then returned to the couch, and sat upon its edge. She then left the couch, that she might kneel on the tiles before me. I looked down at her. How beautiful are enslaved women.

"Perhaps," I said, "you might speculate on what business brings the emissary of Samos of Port Kar to my house this morning?"

"I, Master?" she asked, frightened.

"Yes," I said. "You once served Kurii, the Others, the foes of Priest-Kings."

"I told all that I knew," she exclaimed. "I told all in the dungeons of Samos! I was terrified! I held back nothing! I was emptied of information!"

"You were then valueless," I said.

"Except, perhaps, as I might please a man as a slave," she said.

"Yes," I smiled.

Samos himself had issued the order of enslavement on her. In Ar I had presented the document to her and shortly thereafter, as it pleased me, implemented its provisions. She had once been Miss Elicia Nevins, of Earth, an agent of Kurii on Gor. Then, in Ar, a city from which once I had been banished, I had caught and enslaved her. In those compartments which had been her own in Ar she had become my capture, and had been stripped and placed in my bonds. In her own compartments, then, at my leisure, I had branded her and locked on her fair throat the gleaming, inflexible circlet of bondage. Before the fall of darkness, and my escape, I had had time, too, to pierce her ears, that the full degree of her degradation and slavery, in the Gorean way of thinking, be made most clear.

To Gorean eyes the piercing of the ears, this visible set of wounds, inflicted to facilitate the mounting of sensual and barbaric ornamentations, is customarily regarded as being tantamount, for most practical purposes, to a sentence of irrevocable bondage. Normally ear-piercing is done only to the lowest and most sensuous of slaves. It is regarded, by most Goreans, as being far more humiliating and degrading to a woman than the piercing of a girl's septum and the consequent fastening on her of a nose ring. Indeed, such an aperture does not even show. Some slave girls, of course, are fixed for both. Their masters, thus, have the option of ornamenting their lovely properties as they please. It might be mentioned that nose rings are favored in some areas more than in others, and by some peoples more than others. On behalf of the nose ring, too, it should be mentioned that among the Wagon Peoples, even free women wear such rings. This, however, is unusual on Gor. The nose ring, most often, is worn by a slave.

These rings, incidentally, those for the ears and for the nose, do not serve simply to bedeck the female. They also have a role to play in her arousal. The brushing of the sides of the girl's neck by the dangling ornament is, in itself, a delicate stimulation of a sensitive area of her body, the sides of her neck beneath the ears; this area is quite sensitive to light touches; if the earring is of more than one piece, the tiny sounds made by it, too, can also be stimulatory; accordingly, the earring's feel and movement, and caress, and sometimes sound, persistent, subtle and sensual, functioning on both a conscious and subliminal level, can often bring a female to, and often keep her indefinitely in, a state of incipient sexual readiness. It is easy to see why free women on Gor do not wear them, and why they are, commonly, only put on low slaves. Similar remarks hold, too, of course, for the nose ring, which touches, lightly, the very sensitive area of a girl's upper lip. The nose ring, too, of course, makes clear to the girl that she is a domestic animal. Many domestic animals on Gor wear them.

The girl kneeling before me, once Elicia Nevins, once the lofty, beautiful and proud agent of Kurii, now only my lovely slave, reached for my sandals. She pressed them to her lips, kissing them, and then, head down, began to tie them on my feet. She was quite beautiful, kneeling before me, performing this lowly task, the heavy iron collar and chain on her neck.

I wondered what the emissary of Samos might wish.

"Your sandals are tied, Master," said the girl, lifting her head, kneeling back.

I regarded her. It is pleasant to own a woman.

"Of what are you thinking, Master?" she asked.

"I was thinking," I said, "of the first time that I put you to my pleasure. Do you recall it?"

"Yes, Master," she said. "I have never forgotten. And it was not only the first time that you put me to your pleasure. It was the first time that any man had put me to his pleasure."

"As I recall," I said, "you yielded well, for a new slave."

"Thank you, Master," she said. "And while you were waiting for darkness, to escape the city, whiling away the time, you made me yield again and again."

"Yes," I said. I had then, after the fall of darkness, deeming it then reasonably safe, bound her naked, belly up, over the saddle of my tarn and, eluding patrols, escaped from the city. I had brought her back to Port Kar, where I had thrown her, a bound slave, to the feet of Samos. He had had her put in one of his girl dungeons, where we had interrogated her. We had learned much. After she had been emptied of information she might then be bound naked and thrown to the urts in the canals, or, perhaps, if we wished, kept as a slave. She was comely. I had had her hooded and brought to my house. When she was unhooded she found herself at my feet.

"Are you grateful that you were spared?" I asked.

"Yes, Master," she said, "and particularly that you have seen fit to keep me, if only for a time, as your own slave."

Nothing so fulfills a woman as her own slavery.

After I had used her, I had put her with my other women. Most of these are available to my men, as well as to myself.

"A girl is grateful," she said, "that this night you had her chained to your slave ring."

"Who is grateful?" I asked.

"Elicia is grateful," she said.

"Who is Elicia?" I asked.

"I am Elicia," she said. "That is the name my Master has seen fit to give me."

I smiled. Slaves, no more than other animals, do not have names in their own right. They are named by the Master. She wore her former name, but now only as a slave name, and by my decision.

I stood up, and drew about me one of the furs from the couch. I went to the side of the room and, with a belt, belted the fur about me. Also, from the wall, from its peg, I took down the scabbard with its sheathed short sword. I removed the blade from the scabbard and wiped it on the fur I had belted about me. I then reinserted the blade in the scabbard. The blade is wiped to remove moisture from it. Most Gorean scabbards are not moisture proof, as this would entail either too close a fit for the blade or an impeding flap. I slung the scabbard strap over my left shoulder, in the Gorean fashion. In this way the scabbard, the blade once drawn, may be discarded, with its strap, which accouterments, otherwise, might constitute an encumbrance in combat. On marches, incidentally, and in certain other contexts, the strap, which is adjustable, is usually put over the right shoulder. This minimizes slippage in common and recurrent motion. In both cases, of course, for a right-handed individual, the scabbard is at the left hip, facilitating the convenient and swift across-the-body draw.

I then went again to the side of the fur-strewn, great stone couch, at the side of which, on the tiles, chained by the neck, knelt the beautiful slave.

I stood before her.

She lowered herself to her belly and, holding my ankles gently with her hands, covered my feet with kisses. Her lips, and her tongue, were warm and wet.

"I love you, my Master," she said, "and I am yours."

I stepped back from her. "Go to the foot of the couch," I told her, "and curl there."

"Yes, Master," she said. She then, on her hands and knees, crawled to the foot of the couch and, drawing up her legs, curled there on the cold tiles.

When I went to the door, I stopped and looked back, once, at her. She, curled there on the cold, damp tiles, at the foot of the couch, the chain on her neck, regarded me.

The only light in the room was from the tiny tharlarion-oil lamp which, earlier, Thurnock had placed on the shelf near the door.

"I love you, my Master," she said, "and I am yours."

I then turned about and left the room. In a few Ahn, near dawn, men would come to the room and free her, and then, later, put her to work with the other women.

"How many are there?" I asked Samos.

"Two," he said.

"Are they alive?" I asked.

"Yes," he said.

"This seems an unpropitious place for a meeting," I said. We were in the remains of a half-fallen, ruined tarn complex, built on a wide platform, at the edge of the rence marshes, some four pasangs from the northeast delta gate of Port Kar. In climbing to the platform, and in traversing it, the guards with us, who had now remained outside, had, with the butts of their spears, prodded more than one sinuous tharlarion from the boards, the creature then plunging angrily, hissing, into the marsh. The complex consisted of a tarn cot, now muchly open to the sky, with an anterior building to house supplies and tarn keepers. It had been abandoned for years. We were now within the anterior building. Through the ruined roof, between unshielded beams, I could see patches of the night sky of Gor, and one of her three moons. Ahead, where a wall had mostly fallen, I could see the remains of the large tarn cot. At one time it had been a huge, convex, cage-like lacing of mighty branches, lashed together, a high dome of fastened, interwoven wood, but now, after years of disrepair, and the pelting of rains and the tearings of winds, little remained of this once impressive and intricate structure but the skeletal, arched remnants of its lower portions.

"I do not care for this place," I said.

"It suits them," said Samos.

"It is too dark," I said, "and the opportunities for surprise and ambush are too abundant."

"It suits them," said Samos.

"Doubtless," I said.

"I think we are in little danger," he said. "Too, guards are about."

"Could we not have met in your holding?" I asked.

"Surely you could not expect such things to move easily about among men?" asked Samos.

"No," I granted him.

"I wonder if they know we are here," said Samos.

"If they are alive," I said, "they will know."

"Perhaps," said Samos.

"What is the purpose of this parley?" I asked.

"I do not know," said Samos.

"Surely it is unusual for such things to confer with men," I said.

"True," granted Samos. He looked about himself, at the delapidated, ramshackle building. He, too, did not care overly much for his surroundings.

"What can they want?" I wondered.

"I do not know," said Samos.

"They must, for some reason, want the help of men," I speculated.

"That seems incredible," said Samos.

"True," I said.

"Could it be," asked Samos, "that they have come to sue for peace?"

"No," I said.

"How can you know that?" asked Samos.

"They are too much like men," I said.

"I shall light the lantern," said Samos. He crouched down and extracted a tiny fire-maker from his pouch, a small device containing a tiny reservoir of tharlarion oil, with a tharlarion-oil-impregnated wick, to be ignited by a spark, this generated from the contact of a small, ratcheted steel wheel, spun by a looped thumb handle, with a flint splinter.

"Need this meeting have been so secret?" I asked.

"Yes," said Samos.

We had come to this place, through the northeast delta gate, in a squarish, enclosed barge. It was only through slatted windows that I had been able to follow our passage. Any outside the barge, on the walkways along the canals, for example, could not have viewed its occupants. Such barges, though with the slats locked shut, are sometimes used in the transportation of female slaves, that they may not know where in the city they are, or where they are being taken. A similar result is obtained, usually, more simply, in an open boat, the girls being hooded and bound hand and foot, and then being thrown between the feet of the rowers.

I heard the tiny wheel scratch at the flint. I did not take my eyes from the things at the far end of the room, on the floor, half hidden by a large table, the area open behind them leading to the ruined tarn cot. It is not wise to look away from such things, if they are in the vicinity, or to turn one's back upon them. I did not know if they were asleep or not. I guessed that they were not. My hand rested on the hilt of my sword. Such things, I had reason to know, could move with surprising speed.

The wick of the fire-maker was now aflame. Samos, carefully, held the tiny flame to the wick of the now-unshuttered dark lantern. It, too, burned tharlarion oil.

I was confident now, in the additional light, that the things were not asleep. When the light had been struck, with the tiny noise, from the steel and flint, which would have been quite obvious to them, given the unusual degree of their auditory acuity, there had been only the slightest of muscular contractions. Had they been startled out of sleep, the reaction, I was confident, would have been far more noticeable. I had little doubt they were, and had been, from the first, clearly and exactly aware of our presence.

"The fewer who know of the warrings of worlds, the better," said Samos. "Little is to be served by alarming an unready populace. Even the guards outside do not understand, clearly, on what business we have come here. Besides, if one had not seen such things, who would believe stories as to their existence? They would be regarded as mythical or stories of wondrous animals, such as the horse, the dog and griffin."

I smiled. Horses and dogs did not exist on Gor. Goreans, on the whole, knew them only from legends, which, I had little doubt, owed their origins to forgotten times, to memories brought long ago to Gor from another world. Such stories, for they were very old on Gor, probably go back thousands of years, dating from the times of very early Voyages of Acquisition, undertaken by venturesome, inquisitive creatures of an alien species, one known to most Goreans only as the Priest-Kings. To be sure, few Priest-Kings, now, entertained such a curiosity nor such an enthusiastic penchant for exploration and adventure. Now, the Priest-Kings had become old. I think that perhaps one is old only when one has lost the desire to know. Not until one has lost one's curiosity, and concern, can one be said to be truly old.

I had two friends, in particular, who were Priest-Kings, Misk, and Kusk. I did not think that they, in this sense, could ever grow old. But they were only two, two of a handful of survivors of a once mighty race, that of the lofty and golden Priest-Kings. To be sure, I had managed, long ago, to return the last female egg of Priest-Kings to the Nest. Too, among the survivors, protected from assassination by the preceding generation, there had been a young male. But I had never learned what had occurred in the Nest after the return of the egg. I did not know if it had been viable, or if the male had been suitable. I did not know if it had hatched or not. I did not know if, in the Nest, a new Mother now reigned or not. If this were the case I did not know the fate of the older generation, nor the nature of the new. Would the new generation be as aware of the dangers in which it stood as had been the last? Would the new generation understand, as well as had the last, the kind of things that, gigantic, shaggy and dark, intertwined, lay a few feet before me now? "I think you are right, Samos," I said.

He lifted the lantern now, its shutters open.

We viewed the things before us.

"They will move slowly," I said, "that they may not startle us. I think that we, too, should do the same."

"Agreed," said Samos.

"There are tarns in the tarn cot," I said. I had just seen one move, and the glint of moonlight off a long, scimitarlike beak. I then saw it lift its wings, opening and shutting them twice. I had not detected them earlier in the shadows.

"Two," said Samos. "They are their mounts."

"Shall we approach the table?" I asked.

"Yes," said Samos.

"Slowly," I said.

"Yes," said Samos.

We then, very slowly, approached the table. Then we stood before it. I could see now, in the light of the lantern, that the fur of one of the creatures was a darkish brown, and the fur of the other was almost black. The most common color in such things is dark brown. They were large. As they lay, together, the crest of that heap, that living mound, marked by the backbone of one of them, was a few inches higher than the surface of the table. I could not see the heads. The feet and hands, too, were hidden. I could not, if I had wished, because of the table, have easily drawn the blade and struck at them. I suspected that the position they had taken was not an accident. Too, of course, from my point of view, I was not displeased to have the heavy table where it was. I would not have minded, in fact, had it been even wider. One tends to be most comfortable with such things, generally, when they are in close chains, with inch-thick links, or behind close-set bars, some three inches in diameter.

Samos set the lantern down on the table. We then stood there, not moving.

"What is to be done?" asked Samos.

"I do not know," I said. I was sweating. I could sense my heart beating. My right hand, across my body, was on the hilt of my sword. My left hand steadied the sheath.

"Perhaps they are sleeping," whispered Samos.

"No," I said.

"They do not signal their recognition of our presence," said Samos.

"They are aware we are here," I said.

"What shall we do?" asked Samos. "Shall I touch one?"

"Do not," I whispered, tensely. "An unexpected touch can trigger the attack reflex."

Samos drew back his hand.

"Too," I said, "such things are proud, vain creatures. They seldom welcome the touch of a human. The enraged and bloody dismemberment of the offender often follows upon even an inadvertent slight in this particular."

"Pleasant fellows," said Samos.

"They, too," I said, "like all rational creatures, have their sense of propriety and etiquette."

"How can you regard them as rational?" asked Samos.

"Obviously their intelligence, and their cunning, qualifies them as rational," I said. "It might interest you to know that, from their point of view, they commonly regard humans as subrational, as an inferior species, and, indeed, one they commonly think of in terms little other than of food."

"Why, then," asked Samos, "would they wish this parley?"

"I do not know," I said. "That is, to me, a very fascinating aspect of this morning's dark business."

"They do not greet us," said Samos, irritably. He was, after all, an agent of Priest-Kings, and, indeed, the first captain of the council of captains, that body sovereign in the affairs of Port Kar.

"No," I said.

"What shall we do?" he asked.

"Wait," I suggested.

We heard, outside, the screaming of a predatory ul, a gigantic, toothed, winged lizard, soaring over the marshes.

"How was this rendezvous arranged?" I asked.

"The original contact was made by a pointed, weighted message cylinder, found upright two days ago in the dirt of my men's exercise yard," said Samos. "Doubtless it was dropped there at night, by someone on tarnback."

"By one of them?" I asked.

"That seems unlikely," said Samos, "over the city."

"Yes," I said.

"They have their human confederates," he said.

"Yes," I said. I had, in my adventures on Gor, met several of the confederates of such creatures, both male and female. The females, invariably, had been quite beautiful. I had little doubt that they had been selected, ultimately, with the collar in mind, that they might, when they had served their purposes, be reduced to bondage. Doubtless this projected aspect of their utility was not made clear to them in their recruitment. She who had once been Miss Elicia Nevins, now the slave Elicia in my holding, chained now nude by the neck to my slave ring, had been such a girl. Now, however, instead of finding herself the slave of one of her allies, or being simply disposed of in a slave market, she found herself the slave of one of her former enemies. That, I thought, particularly on Gor, would give her slavery a peculiarly intimate and terrifying flavor. It was an Ahn or so until dawn now. Soon, doubtless, she would be released from the ring. She would be supervised in relieving and washing herself. Then she would be put with my other women. She then, like the others, after having been issued her slave gruel, and after having finished it, and washed the wooden bowl, would be assigned her chores for the day.

We heard, again, the screaming of the ul outside the building. The tarns in the tarn cot moved about. The ul will not attack a tarn. The tarn could tear it to pieces.

"We have been foolish," I said to Samos.

"How so?" asked Samos.

"Surely the protocols in such a matter, from the point of view of our friends, must be reasonably clear."

"I do not understand," said Samos.

"Put yourself in their place," I said. "They are larger and stronger than we, and quite possibly more ferocious and vicious. Too, they regard themselves as more intelligent than ourselves, and as being a dominant species."

"So?" asked Samos.

"So," said I, "naturally they expect not to address us first, but to be first addressed."

"I," asked Samos, "first speak to such as they, I, who am first captain in the high city of Port Kar, jewel of gleaming Thassa?"

"Correct," I said.

"Never," said he.

"Do you wish me to do so?" I asked.

"No," said Samos.

"Then speak first," I said.

"We shall withdraw," said Samos, angrily.

"If I were you," I said, "I do not think I would risk displeasing them."

"Do you think they would be angry?" he asked.

"I expect so," I said. "I do not imagine they would care to have been fruitlessly inconvenienced by human beings."

"Perhaps I should speak first," said Samos.

"I would recommend it," I said.

"They it is, after all," said he, "who have called this meeting."

"True," I encouraged him. "Also, it would be deplorable, would it not, to be torn to pieces without even having discovered what was on their minds?"

"Doubtless," said Samos, grimly.

"I can be persuasive," I admitted.

"Yes," agreed Samos.

Samos cleared his throat. He was not much pleased to speak first, but he would do it. Like many slavers and pirates, Samos was, basically, a good fellow.

"Tal," said Samos, clearly, obviously addressing this greeting to our shaggy confreres. "Tal, large friends."

We saw the fur move, gigantic muscles slowly, evenly, beginning to stir beneath it. As they had lain it would have been difficult to detect, or strike, a vital area. Sinuously, slowly, the two creatures separated and then, slowly, seemed to rise and grow before us. Samos and I stepped back. Their heads and arms were now visible. The light reflected back, suddenly, eccentrically, from the two large eyes of one of them. For an instant they blazed, like red-hot copper disks, like those of a wolf or coyote at the perimeter of a firelit camp.

I could now, the angle of the lighting being different, see them, blinking, as the large, deep orbs they were. I could see

the pupils contracting. Such creatures are primarily nocturnal. Their night vision is far superior to that of the human.
Their accommodation to shifting light conditions is also much
more rapid than is that of the human. These things have been
selected for in their bloody species. When the eyes of the
creature had reflected back the light, the light, too, had suddenly reflected back from its fangs, and I had seen, too, the
long, dark tongue move about on the lips, and then draw
back into the mouth.

The creatures seemed to continue to grow before us. Then
they stood erect before us. Their hind legs, some eight to ten
inches in width, are proportionately shorter than their arms,
which tend to be some eight inches in width at the biceps and
some five inches, or so, in width at the wrist. Standing as they
were, upright, the larger of the two creatures was some nine
feet tall, and the smaller some eight and a half feet tall. I
conjecture the larger weighed about nine hundred pounds and
the smaller about eight hundred and fifty pounds. These are
approximately average heights and weights for this type of
creature. Their hands and feet are six digited, tentaclelike and
multiply jointed. The nails, or claws, on the hands, are usually filed, presumably to facilitate the manipulation of tools
and instrumentation. The claws, retractable, on the feet are
commonly left unfiled. A common killing method for the
creature is to seize the victim about the head or shoulders,
usually with the teeth, and, raking, to disembowel it with the
tearing of the clawed hind feet. Other common methods are
to hold the victim and tear away the throat from between the
head and body, or to bite away the head itself.

"Tal," repeated Samos, uneasily.

I looked across the table at the creatures. I saw intelligence
in their eyes.

"Tal," repeated Samos.

Their heads were better than a foot in width. Their snouts
were two-nostriled, flattish and leathery. Their ears were
large, wide and pointed. They were now erected and oriented
towards us. This pleased me, as it indicated they had no immediate intention of attacking. When such a creature attacks
the ears flatten against the sides of the head, this having the
apparent function of reducing their susceptibility to injury.
This is a common feature of predatory carnivores.

"They do not respond," said Samos.

I did not take my eyes from the creatures. I shrugged. "Let

us wait," I said. I was uncertain as to what alien protocols the creatures might expect us to observe.

The creatures stood upright now but they could function as well on all fours, using the hind legs and the knuckles of the hands. The upright carriage increases scanning range, and has probably contributed to the development and refinement of binocular vision. The horizontal carriage permits great speed, and has probably contributed, via natural selections, to the development of olfactory and auditory acuity. In running, such creatures almost invariably, like the baboon, have recourse to all fours. They will normally drop to all fours in charging, as well, the increased speed increasing the impact of their strike.

"One is a Blood," I said.

"What is that?" asked Samos.

"In their military organizations," I said, "six such beasts constitute a Hand, and its leader is called an Eye. Two hands and two eyes constitute a larger unit, called a "Kur" or "Beast," which is commanded by a leader, or Blood. Twelve such units constitute a Band, commanded again by a Blood, though of higher rank. Twelve bands, again commanded by a Blood, of yet higher rank, constitute a March. Twelve Marches is said to constitute a People. These divisors and multiples have to do with, it seems, a base-twelve mathematics, itself perhaps indexed historically to the six digits of one of the creature's prehensile appendages."

"Why is the leader spoken of as a Blood?" asked Samos.

"It seems to have been an ancient belief among such creatures," I said, "that thought was a function of the blood, rather than of the brain, a terminology which has apparently lingered in their common speech. Similar anachronisms occur in many languages, including Gorean."

"Who commands a People?" asked Samos.

"One who is said to be a 'Blood' of the People, as I understand it," I said.

"How do you know that one of these is a 'Blood,'" asked Samos.

"The left wrist of the larger animal bears two rings, rings of reddish alloy," I said. "They are welded on the wrist. No Gorean file can cut them."

"He is then of high rank?" asked Samos.

"Of lower rank than if he wore one," I said. "Two such

rings designate the leader of a Band. He would have a ranking, thusly, of the sort normally accorded to one who commanded one hundred and eighty of his fellows."

"He is analogous to a captain," said Samos.

"Yes," I said.

"But not a high captain," said Samos.

"No," I said.

"If he is a Blood, then he is almost certainly of the steel ships," said Samos.

"Yes," I said.

"The other," said Samos, "wears two golden rings in its ears."

"It is a vain beast," I said. "Such rings serve only as ornaments. It is possible he is a diplomat."

"The larger beast seems clearly dominant," said Samos.

"It is a Blood," I said.

There was a broad leather strap, too, running from the right shoulder to the left hip of the smaller of the two creatures. I could not see what accouterment it bore.

"We have greeted them," said Samos. "Why do they not speak?"

"Obviously we must not yet have greeted them properly," I said.

"How long do you think they will remain tolerant of our ignorance?" asked Samos.

"I do not know," I said. "Such creatures are not noted for their patience."

"Do you think they will try to kill us?" asked Samos.

"They have already had ample opportunity to attempt to do so, if that were their intention," I said.

"I do not know what to do," said Samos.

"The occasion is formal, and we are dealing with a Blood," I said, "one doubtless from the steel ships themselves. I think I have it."

"What do you recommend?" asked Samos.

"How many times have you proffered greetings to them?" I asked.

Samos thought, briefly. "Four," he said. " 'Tal' was said to them four times."

"Yes," I said. "Now, if one of these beasts were to touch the hand, or paw, of another, the hand, or paw, of each being open, indicating that weapons were not held, that the touch was in peace, at how many points would contact be made?"

"At six," said Samos.

"Such creatures do not care, usually, to be touched by humans," I said. "The human analogy to such a greeting then might be six similar vocal signals. At any rate, be that as it may, I think the number six is of importance in this matter."

Samos then held up his left hand. Slowly, not speaking, he pointed in succession to four fingers. He then held the small finger of his left hand in his right hand. "Tal," he said. Then he held up the index finger of his right hand. "Tal," he said again.

Then, slowly, the smaller of the two creatures began to move. I felt goose pimples. The hair on the back of my neck stood up.

It turned about and bent down, and picked up a large shield, of a sort adequate for such a creature. It lifted this before us, displaying it, horizontally, convex side down. We could see that the shield straps were in order. It then placed the shield on the floor, to the side of the table, to their left. It then went back and again bent down. This time it brought forth a mighty spear, some twelve feet in length, with a long, tapering bronze head. This, with two hands, holding it horizontally, across its body, it also displayed, lifting it ceremoniously upwards and towards us, and then drawing it back. It then put the spear down, laying it on the floor, to their left. The shaft of the spear was some three inches in diameter. The bronze head might have weighed some twenty pounds.

"They honor us," said Samos.

"As we did them," I said.

The symbolism of the creature's action, the lifting of weapons, and then the setting aside of them, was clear. This action also, of course, was in accord with the common Gorean convention in proposing a truce. That the creatures had seen fit to utilize this convention, one of humans, was clear. I found this a welcome accommodation on their part. They seemed concerned to be congenial. I wondered what they wanted. To be sure, however, it was only the lighter colored, and smaller, of the two creatures, that with rings in its ears, which had performed these actions. It might, indeed, be, for most practical purposes, a diplomat. The larger creature, the Blood, had stood by, unmoving. Yet clearly these actions had been performed in its presence. This, then, was sufficient evidence of their acceptance on its part. I noted, the sort of thing a warrior notes, that the spear had been placed to their left, and that its head, too, was oriented to their left. It was thus placed, and oriented, in such a way that the Blood, which stood on the left, from their point of view, if it favored the right hand, or paw, as most such creatures do, rather like humans, could easily bend down and seize it up.

"I see they have not come to surrender," said Samos.

"No," I said. The shield straps, which had been displayed to us with the shield, the shield held convex side down, had not been torn away or cut, which would have rendered the shield useless. Similarly the shaft of the spear had not been broken. They had not come to surrender.

The lips of the smaller of the two creatures drew back, exposing the fangs. Samos stepped back. His hand went to the hilt of his sword.

"No," I said to him, quietly. "It is trying to imitate a human smile."

The creature then detached, from the broad strap which hung diagonally about its body, from its right shoulder to the left hip, an instrumented, metallic, oblong, boxlike device, which it placed on the table.

"It is a translator," I said to Samos. I had seen one in a complex, some years earlier, in the north.

"I do not trust such creatures," said Samos.

"Some of them, specially trained," I said, "can understand Gorean."

"Oh," said Samos.

The smaller of the two creatures turned to the larger. It said something to him. The speech of such creatures resembles a succession of snarls, growls, rasps and throaty vibrations. The noises emitted are clearly animal noises, and, indeed, such as might naturally be associated with a large and powerful, predatory carnivore; yet, on the other hand, there is a liquidity, and a precision and subtlety about them which is unmistakable; one realizes, often uneasily, that what one is listening to is a language.

The larger one inclined its huge, shaggy head, and then lifted it. The tips of two long, curved fangs, in the position of the upper canines, protruded slightly from its closed mouth. It watched us.

The smaller of the two creatures then busied itself with the device on the table.

Lowering the head is an almost universal assent gesture, indicating submission to, or agreement with, the other. The dissent gesture, on the other hand, shows much greater variety. Shaking the head sideways, among rational creatures, may be taken as a negation of assent. Other forms of the nonassent gesture can be turning the head away from the other, sometimes with a gesture of the lips, indicating distaste, or even of ejecting an unwanted substance from the mouth, backing away, or lifting the head and extending the neck, sometimes baring the fangs and tensing the body, as in a variation on the bristling response.

"To be sure," I said, "it is extremely difficult for them to speak Gorean, or another human language." It was difficult for them, of course, given the nature of their oral cavity, throat, tongue, lips and teeth, to produce human phonemes. They can, however, sometimes in a horrifying way, approximate them. I shuddered. I had, once or twice, heard such creatures speaking Gorean. It had been disconcerting to hear human speech, or something resembling human speech, emanating from such a source. I was just as pleased that we had a translator at our disposal.

"Look," said Samos.

"I see," I said.

A small, conical, red light began to glow on the top of the machine.

The slighter of the two monsters then drew itself up. It began to speak.

We understood, initially, of course, nothing of what it said. We listened to it, not moving, in the dim, pale-yellowish, flickering light of the unshuttered dark lantern, amidst the dark, dancing shadows in that abandoned tarn complex.

I remember noting the glinting of the golden rings in its ears, and the moistness of saliva about its dark lips and on its fangs.

"I am Kog," came from the translator. "I am below the rings. With me is Sardak, who is within the rings. I speak on behalf of the Peoples, and the chieftains of the Peoples, those who stand above the rings. I bring you greetings from the Dominants, and from the Conceivers and Carriers. No greetings do I bring you from those unworthy of the rings, from the discounted ones, the unnamed and craven ones. Similarly no greetings do I bring you from our domestic animals, those who are human and otherwise. In short, honor do I do unto

you, bringing you greetings from those who are entitled to
extend greetings, and bringing you no greetings from those
unworthy to give greetings. Thus, then, do I bring you greetings on behalf of the Peoples, on behalf of the ships, and the
Steel Worlds. Thus, then, do I bring you greetings on behalf
of the cliffs of the thousand tribes." These words, and word
groups, came forth from the translator, following intervals
between the creature's inputs. They are produced in a flat,
mechanical fashion. The intonation contours, as well as
meaningful tonal qualities, pitches and stresses, from which
one can gather so much in living speech, unfortunately, tend
to be absent or only randomly correlated in such a formal,
dessicated output. Similarly the translation, it seems, is often
imperfect, or, at least, awkward and choppy. Indeed, it takes
a few moments before one can begin to follow the produc-
tions of such a machine coherently but, once this adjustment
is made, there is little difficulty in comprehending the gist of
what is being conveyed. In my presentation of the machine's
output I have, here and there, taken certain liberties. In particular I have liberalized certain phrasings and smoothed out
various grammatical irregularities. On the other hand, given
the fact that I am conveying this material in English, at two
removes from the original, I think that the above translation,
and what follows, is not only reasonably adequate in a literal
sense, but also conveys something, at least, of the flavor of
the original. On the other hand, I do not claim to understand
all aspects of the translation. For example, I am unclear on
the ring structure and on the significance of the references to
tribal cliffs.

"I think, Samos," I said, "you are expected to respond."

"I am Samos," said Samos, "and I thank you for your
cordial and welcome salutations."

Fascinated, Samos and I listened to what was, with one exception, a succession of rumbling, throaty utterances emanating from the machine. The machine apparently accepted and
registered Gorean phonemes, and then scanned the phonemic
input for those phoneme combinations which expressed
Gorean cognitive units, or morphemes. In this way, morphemes, *per se*, or linguistic cognitive units, at least as com-
prehended units, do not occur in the machine. With a human
translator sound is processed, and understood morphemically,
which understanding is then reprocessed into the new phonemic structures. With the machine the correlation is simply be-

tween sound structures, *simpliciter,* and it is the auditor who supplies the understanding. To be sure, a linguistic talent of no mean degree is required to design and program such a device. We did hear one Gorean word in the translation. That was the name 'Samos'. When the machine encounters a phoneme or phonemic combination which is not correlated with a phoneme or phoneme combination in the new language it presents the original input as a portion of the new output. For example, if one were to utter nonsense syllables into the device the same nonsense syllables, unless an accident or a coincidence occurred, would be played back.

The creatures, then, heard the name of Samos. Whether they could pronounce it or not, or how close they could come to pronounce it, would depend on the sound and on the capacity of their own vocal apparatus. This is different, it should be noted, with the names of the two creatures, 'Kog' and 'Sardak'. These names were given in Gorean phonemes, not in the phonemes of the creatures' own language. In this case, of course, this made it clear that these two names, at least, had been programed into the machine. The machine, doubtless, had been altered to be of aid to two particular individuals in some particular mission. Presumably Samos and I could not have pronounced the actual names of the creatures. 'Kog' and 'Sardak', however, doubtless correlated in some fashion, given some type of phonemic transcription found acceptable by the creatures, with their actual names. There was probably, at least, a syllabial correlation.

"I bring you greetings," said Samos, "from the Council of Captains, of Port Kar, Jewel of Gleaming Thassa."

I saw the lips of the two creatures draw back. I, too, smiled. Samos was cautious, indeed. What would the Council of Captains know of such creatures, or of the warrings among worlds? He had not identified himself as being among the party of those forces arrayed against the ravaging, concupiscent imperialism of our savage colleagues. I myself, whereas I had served Priest-Kings, did not regard myself as being of their party. My lance, in such matters, so to speak, was free. I would choose my own wars, my own ventures.

"I bring you greetings, too," said Samos, "from the free men of Port Kar. I do not bring you greetings, of course, from those who are unworthy to greet you, for example, from our slaves, who are nothing, and who labor for us, and whom we use for our sport and pleasure."

Kog briefly inclined his head. I thought Samos had done rather well. Slaves on Gor are domestic animals, of course. A trained sleen in a sleen market will usually bring a higher price than even a beautiful girl sold naked in a slave market. This is doubtless a function of supply and demand. Beautiful female slaves are generally cheap on Gor, largely as a result of captures and breedings. It is not unusual, in most cities, for a prize tarsk to bring a higher price than a girl. The girls understand this, clearly, and it helps them to understand their place in the society.

"I speak on behalf of the Peoples, on behalf of the Steel Worlds," said Kog.

"Do you speak on behalf of all the Peoples, on behalf of all the Steel Worlds?" asked Samos.

"Yes," said Kog.

"Do you speak on behalf of all of those of the Peoples, of all of those of the Steel Worlds?" asked Samos. This, I thought, was an interesting question. It was, of course, subtly different from the preceding question. We knew that divisions as to tactics, if not ultimate objectives, existed among parties of such creatures. We had learned this in the Tahari.

"Yes," said Kog, unhesitantly.

When Kog had made his response to the question I was, by intent, watching not him but the other of the two creatures. Yet I saw no flicker of doubt or uneasiness in his eyes, nor any incipient lifting of the broad ears. It did, however, draw its lips back slightly, observing my attention. It had apparently found my attempt to read its behavioral cues amusing.

"Do you speak on behalf of Priest-Kings?" asked Kog.

"I cannot," said Samos.

"That is interesting," said Kog.

"If you would speak with Priest-Kings," said Samos, "you must go to the Sardar."

"What are Priest-Kings?" asked Kog.

"I do not know," said Samos.

Such creatures, I gathered, had no clear idea of the nature of Priest-Kings. They had not directly experienced Priest-Kings, only the power of Priest-Kings. Like burned animals they were wary of them. Priest-Kings, wisely, did not choose to directly confront such creatures. Not a little of the hesitancy and tentativeness of the militaristic incursions of such creatures was, I suspected, a function of their ignorance of, and fear of, the true nature and power of the remote and mysterious denizens of the Sardar. If such creatures should come to clearly understand the nature of the Priest-Kings, and the current restrictions on their power, in virtue of the catastrophic Nest War, I had little doubt but what the attack signals would be almost immediately transmitted to the steel worlds. In weeks the silver ships would beach on the shores of Gor.

"We know the nature of Priest-Kings," said Kog. "They are much like ourselves."

"I do not know," said Samos.

"They must be," said Kog, "or they could not be a dominant life form."

"Perhaps," said Samos. "I do not know."

The larger of the two creatures, during this exchange, was watching me. I smiled at him. Its ears twitched with annoyance. Then again it was as it had been, regal, savage, distant, unmoving and alert.

"Can you speak on behalf of the men of the two worlds?" asked Kog. This was a reference, doubtless, to the Earth and Gor.

"No," said Samos.

"But you are a man," said Kog.

"I am only one man," said Samos.

"Their race has not yet achieved species unification," said the larger of the two creatures, to his fellow. His remark, of course, was picked up by the translator and processed, as though it had been addressed to us.

"That is true," said Kog. I wondered, hearing this, if the beasts, either, had achieved species unification. I was inclined to doubt it. Such creatures, being territorial, individualistic and aggressive, much like men, would not be likely to find the bland idealisms of more vegetative organisms interesting, attractive or practical. Logical, and terrible, they would not be likely to find the fallacy of the single virtue, the hypothesis of social reductivism, alluring.

All creatures are not the same, nor is it necessary that they should be. Jungles may be as appealing to nature as gardens. Leopards and wolves are as legitimately ingredient in the order of nature as spaniels and potatoes. Species unification, I suspected, would prove not to be a blessing, but a trap and a bane, a pathology and curse, a societal sanitarium in which the great and strong would be reduced to, or must pretend to be reduced to, the level of the blinking, the cringing, the creeping and the tiny. To be sure, values are involved here, and one must make decisions. It is natural that the small and weak will make one decision, and the large and strong another. There is no single humanity, no single shirt, no correct pair of shoes, no uniform, even a gray one, that will fit all men. There are a thousand humanities possible. He who denies this sees only his own horizons. He who disagrees is the denier of difference, and the murderer of the better futures.

"It is unfortunate," said Sardak, speaking to Kog, "that they have not achieved species unification. Else, once the Priest-Kings are disposed of, it would be easier to herd them to our cattle pens."

"That is true," said Kog.

What Sardak said seemed to me, too, likely to be true. Highly centralized structures are the most easily undermined and subverted. Cutting one strand of such a web can unravel a world. One hundred and eighty-three men once conquered an empire.

"Can you speak on behalf of the Council of Captains, of Port Kar?" asked Kog.

"Only on matters having to do with Port Kar, and then after a decision of the council, taken after consultation," said Samos. This was not exactly correct, but it was substantially correct. It seemed to me a suitable answer, under the circumstances. The creatures, of course, would not be familiar with council procedures.

"You do, however, have certain executive powers, do you not?" inquired Kog. I admired the creatures. Clearly they had researched their mission.

"Yes," said Samos, guardedly, "but they are not likely to be involved in matters of the sort with which we are here likely to be concerned."

"I understand," said Kog. "On behalf of whom, then, do you speak?"

"I speak," said Samos, rather boldly I thought, "on behalf of Samos, of Port Kar, on behalf of myself."

Kog snapped off the translator and turned to Sardak. They conversed for a moment in their own tongue. Kog then snapped the translator back on. This time, almost instantly, the small, conical red light began to glow.

"It is sufficient," said Kog.

Samos stepped back a bit.

Kog turned away, then, to a leather tube and, with his large, furred, tentaclelike digits, with their blunted claws, removed the cap from this tube.

I suspected that the two creatures did not believe Samos when he protested to them that he could speak only on behalf of himself. At the least they would be certain that he would be significantly involved in the affairs of Priest-Kings. They would seem to have little alternative, then, to dealing with him.

From the long, leather tube, Kog removed what appeared to be a large piece of closely rolled, soft-tanned hide. It was very light in color, almost white, and tied with string. There was a slight smell of smoke about it, probably from the smoke of the turl bush. Such hides may be waterproofed by suspending them from, and wrapping them about, a small tripod of sticks, this set over a small fire on which, to produce the desiderated smoke, the leaves and branches of the turl bush are heavily strewn.

Kog placed the roll of hide on the table. It was not rawhide, but soft-tanned hide, as I have suggested. In preparing rawhide the skin, suitably fleshed, is pegged down and dried in the wind and sun. The hide may then, without further ado, be worked and cut. This product, crude and tough, may be used for such things as shields, cases and ropes. Soft tanning a hide, on the other hand, is a much more arduous task. In soft tanning, the fleshed hide must be saturated with fats, and with oils and grease, usually from the brains of animals. These are rubbed into the hide, and worked into it, usually with a soft flat stone. The hide is then sprinkled with warm water and tightly rolled, after which it is put aside, away from the sun and heat, for a few days. This gives the time necessary for the softening ingredients, such as the fats and oils, to fully penetrate the leather. The skin is then unrolled and by rubbing, kneading and stretching, hand-softened over a period of hours. The resulting product ranges from tan to creamy white, and may be worked and cut as easily as cloth.

"You are familiar, are you not," asked Kog, with one known as Zarendargar?"

"Who is Zarendargar?" asked Samos.

"Let us not waste one another's time," said Kog.

Samos turned white.

I was pleased that, outside, on the platform of this anterior building of the tarn complex, there were several guards. They were armed with crossbows. The iron bolts of these devices, weighing about a pound apiece, were capable of sinking some four inches into solid wood at a range of some twenty yards. To be sure, by the time the guards might be summoned into the building Samos and I might be half eaten.

Kog looked closely at Samos.

"Zarendargar," said Samos, "is a well-known commander of the steel worlds, a war general. He perished in the destruction of a supply complex in the arctic."

"Zarendargar is alive," said Kog.

I was startled by this pronouncement. This seemed to me impossible. The destruction of the complex had been complete. I had witnessed this from pasangs across the ice in the arctic night. The complex would have been transformed into a radioactive inferno. Even the icy seas about it, in moments, had churned and boiled.

"Zarendargar cannot be alive," I said. It was the first time I had spoken to the beasts. Perhaps I should not have spoken, but I had been in the vicinity of the event in question. I had seen the explosion. I had, even from afar, been half blinded by the light, and, moments later, half staggered by the sound, the blast and heat. The shape, height and awesomeness of that towering, expanding cloud was not something I would ever forget. "Nothing could have lived in that blast," I said, "nor in the seas about it."

Kog looked at me.

"I was there," I said.

"We know," said Kog.

"Zarendargar is dead," I said.

Kog then unrolled the hide on the table. He arranged it so that Samos and I could easily see it. The hair rose up on the back of my neck.

"Are you familiar with this sort of thing?" asked Kog of Samos.

"No," said Samos.

"I have seen things like it," I said, "but only far away, on another world. I have seen things like it in places called museums. Such things are no longer done."

"Does the skin seem to you old," asked Kog, "faded, brittle, cracked, worn, thin, fragile?"

"No," I said.

"Consider the colors," said Kog. "Do they seem old to you? Do they seem faded to you?"

"No," I said. "They are bright, and fresh."

"Analysis, in virtue of dessication index and molecular disarrangement, suggests that this material, and its applied pigments, are less than two years old. This hypothesis is corroborated by correlation data, in which this skin was compared to samples whose dating is known and independent historical evidence, the nature of which should be readily apparent."

"Yes," I said. I knew that such beasts, on the steel worlds, possessed an advanced technology. I had little doubt but what their physical and chemical techniques were quite adequate to supply the dating in question to the skin and its paints. Too, of course, the nature of their historical evidence would be quite clear. To be sure, it would be historical data at their disposal, and not mine. I had no way of knowing the pertinent facts. That such beasts, on this world, carried primitive weapons was a tribute to their fear of Priest-Kings. Carrying such weapons they might be mistaken for beasts of their race who now, for all practical purposes, were native to Gor, beasts descended from individuals perhaps long ago marooned or stranded on the planet. Priest-Kings, on the whole, tend to ignore such beasts. They are permitted to live as they will, where they may, on Gor, following even their ancient laws and customs, providing these do not violate the Weapons Laws and Technology Restrictions. To be sure, such beasts usually, once separated from the discipline of the ships, in a generation or two, lapsed into barbarism. On the whole they tended to occupy portions of Gor not inhabited by human beings. The Priest-Kings care for their world, but their primary interest is in its subsurface, not its surface. For most practical purposes life goes on on Gor much as though they did not exist. To be sure, they are concerned to maintain the natural ecosystems of the planet. They are wise, but even they hesitate to tamper with precise and subtle systems which have taken over four billion years to develop. Who knows what course a dislodged molecule may take in a thousand years?

I looked at Kog and Sardak. Such creatures, perhaps thousands of years ago, had, it seemed, destroyed their own world. They now wanted another. The Priest-Kings, lofty and golden, remote, inoffensive and tolerant, were all, for most practical purposes, that stood between the Kogs and Sardaks, and the Earth and Gor.

"This is," said Kog, to Samos, "a story skin."

"I understand," said Samos.

"It is an artifact of the red savages," said Kog, "from one of the tribes in the Barrens."

"Yes," said Samos.

The Red Savages, as they are commonly called on Gor, are racially and culturally distinct from the Red Hunters of the north. They tend to be a more slender, longer-limbed people; their daughters menstruate earlier; and their babies are not born with a blue spot at the base of the spine, as in the case with most of the red hunters. Their culture tends to be nomadic, and is based on the herbivorous, lofty kaiila, substantially the same animal as is found in the Tahari, save for the wider footpads of the Tahari beast, suitable for negotiating deep sand, and the lumbering, gregarious, short-tempered, trident-horned kailiauk. To be sure, some tribes do not have the kaiila, never having mastered it, and certain tribes have mastered the tarn, which tribes are the most dangerous of all.

Although there are numerous physical and cultural differences among these people they are usually collectively referred to as the red savages. This is presumably a function of so little being known about them, as a whole, and the cunning, ruthlessness and ferocity of so many of the tribes. They seem to live for hunting and internecine warfare, which seems to serve almost as a sport and a religion for them. Interestingly enough most of these tribes seem to be united only by a hatred of whites, which hatred, invariably, in a time of emergency or crisis, takes precedence over all customary conflicts and rivalries. To attack whites, intruding into their lands, once the war lance has been lifted, even long-term blood enemies will ride side by side. The gathering of tribes, friends and foes alike, for such a battle is said to be a splendid sight. These things are in virtue of what, among these peoples, is called the Memory.

"The story begins here," said Kog, indicating the center of the skin. From this point there was initiated, in a slow spiral,

to be followed by turning the skin, a series of drawings and
pictographs. As the skin is turned each marking on it is at the
center of attention, first, of course, of the artist, and, later, as
he follows the trail, of the viewer. The story, then, unantici-
pated, each event as real as any other, unfolds as it was lived.

"In many respects," said Kog, "this story is not untypical.
These signs indicate a tribal camp. Because of the small number of lodges, this is a winter camp. We can also tell this
from these dots, which represent snow."

I looked at the drawings. They were exactly, and colorfully
done. They were, on the whole, small, and precise and delicate, like miniatures. The man who had applied the pigments
to that hide canvas had been both patient and skillful. Too,
he had been very careful. This care is often a feature of such
works. To speak the truth is very important to the red savages.

"This jagged line," said Kog, "indicates that there is hunger
in the camp, the sawing feeling in the stomach. This man,
whom we take to be the artist, and whom we shall call Two
Feathers, because of the two feathers drawn near him, puts
on snowshoes and leaves the camp. He takes with him a bow
and arrows."

I watched Kog slowly turn the skin. The drawings are first
traced on the skin with a sharp stick. Many of them are then
outlined in black. The interior areas, thusly blocked out, may
then be colored in. The primary pigments used were yellows,
reds, browns and blacks. These are primarily obtained from
powdered earths, clays and boiled roots. Blues can be obtained from blue mud, gant droppings and boiled rotten
wood. Greens can be obtained from a variety of sources, including earths, boiled rotten wood, copper ores and pond al-
gae. The pigments, commonly mixed with hot water or glue,
are usually applied by a chewed stick or a small brush, or
pen, of porous bone, usually cut from the edge of the kailiauk's shoulder blade or the end of its hip bone. Both of these
bones contain honeycombed structures useful in the smooth
application of paint.

"This man travels for two days," said Kog, pointing to two
yellow suns in the sky of the hide. "On the third day he finds
the track of a kailiauk. He follows this. He drinks melted
snow, held in his mouth until it is warm. He eats dried meat.
On the third day he builds no fire. We may gather from this
he is now in the country of enemies. Toward the evening of

the fourth day he sees more tracks. There are other hunters, mounted on kaiila, who, too, are following the kailiauk. It is difficult to determine their number, for they ride single file, that the prints of one beast may obscure and obliterate those of another. His heart is now heavy. Should he turn back? He does not know what to do. He must dream on the matter."

"Surely," said Samos, "it could be only a coincidence."

"I do not think so," said Kog.

"This hide," said Samos, "could be nothing but the product of the crazed imagination of an ignorant savage. It might, too, be nothing more than the account of a strange dream."

"The organization and clarity of the account suggests rationality," said Kog.

"It is only the story of a dream," said Samos.

"Perhaps," said Kog.

"Such people do not distinguish clearly between dreams and reality," said Samos.

"They distinguish clearly between them," said Kog. "It is only that they regard both as real."

"Please, continue," I said.

"Here, in the dream," said Kog, indicating a series of pictographs which followed a small spiral line, "we see that the kailiauk invites the man to a feast. This is presumably a favorable sign. At the feast, however, in the lodge of the kailiauk, there is a dark guest. His lineaments are obscure, as you can see. The man is afraid. He senses great power in this dark guest. The kailiauk, however, tells the man not to be afraid. The man takes meat from the hands of the dark guest. It will be his ally and protector, the kailiauk tells him. He may take it for his medicine. The man awakens. He is very frightened. He is afraid of this strange medicine. The dream is strong, however, and he knows it cannot be repudiated. Henceforth he knows his medicine helper is the mysterious dark guest."

"From where," asked Samos, "does this man think he obtained this medicine helper?"

"Surely the man will think he obtained it from the medicine world," said Kog.

"It seems an interesting anticipatory dream," I said.

"Surely the dream is ámbiguous," said Samos. "See? The lineaments of the dark guest are unclear."

"True," I said. "Yet something of its size, and of its

awesomeness, and force, particularly within a lodge, seems evident."

"You will also notice," said Kog, "that it sits behind the fire. That is the place of honor."

"It could all be a coincidence," said Samos.

"That is quite true," I said. "Yet the matter is of interest."

"Other explanations, too, are possible," said Samos. "The man may once have seen such things, or heard of them, and forgotten them."

"That seems to me quite likely," I said.

"But why, in the dream, in this dream," asked Samos, "should the dark guest appear?"

"Possibly," I said, "because of the man's plight, and need. In such a situation a powerful helper might be desired. The dream, accordingly, might have produced one."

"Of course," said Samos.

"Considering the events of the next day," said Kog, "I think certain alternative explanations might be more likely. This is not, of course, to rule out that the man, in his quandary, and desperate straits, might not have welcomed a powerful ally."

"What do you suggest?" I asked.

"That he, earlier, during the day, saw sign of the medicine helper, but only in the dream interpreted it."

"I see," I said.

"Even more plausibly, and interestingly," said Kog, "I suspect that the dark guest, in that moonlit snow, actually appeared to the man. The man, hungry, exhausted, striving for the dream, betwixt sleeping and waking, not being fully aware of what was transpiring, saw it. He then incorporated it into his dream, comprehending it within his own conceptual framework."

"That is an interesting idea," I said.

"But it is surely improbable that the paths of the man and the helper should cross in the vast, trackless wastes of the snowbound Barrens," said Samos.

"Not if both were following the kailiauk," said Kog.

"Why would the helper not have eaten the man?" I asked.

"Perhaps," said Kog, "because it was hunting the kailiauk, not the man. Perhaps because if it killed a man, it was apprehensive that other men would follow it, to kill it in turn."

"I see," I said.

"Also," said Kog, "kailiauk is better than man. I know. I have eaten both."

"I see," I said.

"If the helper had visited the man," said Samos, "would there not have been prints in the snow?"

"Doubtless," said Kog.

"Were there prints?" asked Samos.

"No," said Kog.

"Then it was all a dream," said Samos.

"The absence of prints would be taken by the man as evidence that the helper came from the medicine world," said Kog.

"Naturally," said Samos.

"Accordingly the man would not look for them," said Kog.

"It is your hypothesis, however," conjectured Samos, "that such prints existed."

"Of course," said Kog, "which then, in the vicinity of the camp, were dusted away."

"From the point of view of the man, then," said Samos, "the dark guest would have come and gone with all the silence and mystery of a guest from the medicine world."

"Yes," said Kog.

"Interesting," said Samos.

"What is perfectly clear," said Kog, "is how the man viewed the situation, whether he was correct or not. Similarly clear, and undeniably so, are the events of the next day. These are unmistakably and unambiguously delineated." Kog then, with his dexterous, six-jointed, long digits, rotated the skin a quarter of a turn, continuing the story.

"In the morning," said Kog, "the man, inspired by his dream, resumed his hunt. A snow began to fall." I noted the dots between the flat plane of the earth and the semicircle of the sky. "The tracks, with the snow, and the wind, became obscured. Still the man pressed on, knowing the direction of the kailiauk and following the natural geodesics of the land, such as might be followed by a slow-moving beast, pawing under the snow for roots or grass. He did not fear to lose the trail. Because of his dream he was undaunted. On snowshoes, of course, he could move faster through drifted snow than the kailiauk. Indeed, over long distances, in such snow, he could match the speed of the wading kaiila. Too, as you know, the kailiauk seldom moves at night."

The kailiauk in question, incidentally, is the kailiauk of the
Barrens. It is a gigantic, dangerous beast, often standing from
twenty to twenty-five hands at the shoulder and weighing as
much as four thousand pounds. It is almost never hunted on
foot except in deep snow, in which it is almost helpless. From
kaiilaback, riding beside the stampeded animal, however, the
skilled hunter can kill one with a single arrow. He rides close
to the animal, not a yard from its side, just outside the hooking
range of the trident, to supplement the striking power of his
small bow. At this range the arrow can sink in to the
feathers. Ideally it strikes into the intestinal cavity behind the
last rib, producing large-scale internal hemorrhaging, or
closely behind the left shoulder blade, thence piercing the
eight-valved heart.

The hunting arrow, incidentally, has a long, tapering point,
and this point is firmly fastened to the shaft. This makes it
easier to withdraw the arrow from its target. The war arrow,
on the other hand, uses an arrowhead whose base is either
angled backwards, forming barbs, or cut straight across, the
result in both cases being to make the arrow difficult to ex-
tract from a wound. The head of the war arrow, too, is fastened less securely to the shaft than is that of the hunting
arrow. The point thus, by intent, if the shaft is pulled out, is
likely to linger in the wound. Sometimes it is possible to
thrust the arrow through the body, break off the point and
then withdraw the shaft backwards. At other times, if the
point becomes dislodged in the body, it is common to seek it
with a bone or greenwood probe, and then, when one has
found it, attempt to work it free with a knife. There are cases
where men have survived this. Much depends, of course, on
the location of the point.

The heads of certain war arrows and hunting arrows differ,
too, at least in the case of certain warriors, in an interesting
way, with respect to the orientation of the plane of the point
to the plane of the nock. In these war arrows, the plane of
the point is perpendicular to the plane of the nock. In level
shooting, then, the plane of the point is roughly parallel to
the ground. In these hunting arrows, on the other hand, the
plane of the point is parallel to the plane of the nock. In level
shooting, then, the plane of the point is roughly perpendicular
to the ground. The reason for these different orientations is
particularly telling at close range, before the arrow begins to

turn in the air. The ribs of the kailiauk are vertical to the ground; the ribs of the human are horizontal to the ground.

The differing orientations may be done, of course, as much for reasons of felt propriety, or for medicine purposes, as for reasons of improving the efficiency of the missile. They may have some effect, of course, as I have suggested, at extremely close range. In this respect, however, it should be noted that most warriors use the parallel orientation with respect to both their war and hunting points. It is felt that this orientation improves sighting. This seems to me, too, to be the case. The parallel orientation, of course, would be more effective with kailiauk, which are usually shot at extremely close range, indeed, from so close that one might almost reach out and touch the beast. Also, of course, in close combat with humans, if one wishes, the perpendicular alignment may be simply produced; one need only turn the small bow.

"Toward noon," said Kog, slowly turning the hide, "we see that the weather has cleared. The wind has died down. The snow has stopped falling. The sun has emerged from clouds. We may conjecture that the day is bright. A rise in temperature has apparently occurred as well. We see that the man has opened his widely sleeved hunting coat and removed his cap of fur."

"I had not hitherto, before seeing this skin," said Samos, "realized that the savages wore such things."

"They do," said Kog. "The winters in the Barrens are severe, and one does not hunt in a robe."

"Here," said Samos, "the man is lying down."

"He is surmounting a rise," said Kog, "surmounting it with care."

I nodded. It is seldom wise to silhouette oneself against the sky. A movement in such a plane is not difficult to detect. Similarly, before entering a terrain, it is sensible to subject it to some scrutiny. This work, whether done for tribal migrations or war parties, is usually done by a scout or scouts. When a man travels alone, of course, he must be his own scout. Similarly it is common for lone travelers or small parties to avoid open spaces without cover, where this is possible, and where it is not possible, to cross them expeditiously. An occasional ruse used in crossing an open terrain, incidentally, is to throw a kailiauk robe over oneself and bend down over the back of one's kaiila. From a distance then, particularly if one holds in one's kaiila, one and one's mount may be mistaken for a single beast, a lone kailiauk.

Scouts are sometimes called sleen by the red savages. The sleen is Gor's most efficient and tenacious tracker. They are often used to hunt slaves. Too, the scout, often, in most tribes, wears the pelt of a sleen. This pelt, like a garment which is at one time both cowl and cape, covers both the head and back. It is perhaps felt that something of the sleen's acuity and tenacity is thus imparted to the scout. Some scouts believe that they become, when donning this pelt, a sleen. This has to do with their beliefs as to the mysterious relationships which are thought to obtain between the world of reality and the medicine world, that, at times, these two worlds impinge on one another, and become one. To be sure, from a practical point of view, the pelt makes an excellent camouflage. It is easy, for example, to mistake a scout, on all fours, spying over a rise, for a wild sleen. Such animals are not uncommon in the Barrens. Their most common prey is tabuk.

"And this, you see," said Kog, turning the hide, "is what he saw on that bright and thawing morning."

"It is what he said he saw," said Samos.

In the declivity below the rise there lay a slain kailiauk, dark in the snow. There could be no mistaking what, alert, huge, catlike, like a larl, crouched behind the kailiauk.

"You see?" asked Kog.

"The dark guest," said Samos.

"Clearly delineated," said Samos.

"Yes," said Kog, "seen clearly now, in its own form."

I could not speak.

"Surely this is only the product of the imagination of the artist," said Samos.

"Too, there are five riders of the kaiila, with kaiila lances, between the kailiauk and the dark guest, and the man."

"These are the other hunters, those whose tracks were found, those who had also been following the kailiauk," said Samos.

"Yes," said Kog.

The kaiila lance is used in hunting kailiauk as well as in mounted warfare. It is called the kaiila lance because it is designed to be used from kaiilaback. It is to be distinguished in particular from the longer, heavier tharlarion lance, designed for use from tharlarionback, and often used with a lance rest, and the smaller, thicker stabbing lances used by certain groups of pedestrian nomads. The kaiila lance takes, on the whole, two forms, the hunting lance and the war lance. Hunting lances are commonly longer, heavier and thicker than war lances. Too, they are often undecorated, save perhaps for a knot of the feathers of the yellow, long-winged, sharp-billed prairie fleer, or, as it is sometimes called, the maize bird, or corn bird, considered by the red savages to be generally the first bird to find food.

The point of the hunting lance is usually longer and nar-rower than that of the war lance, a function of the depth into which one must strike in order to find the heart of the kail-iauk. The shafts of the kaiila lances are black, supple and strong; they are made of tem wood, a wood much favored on Gor for this type of purpose. Staves for the lances are cut in the late winter, when the sap is down. Such wood, in the long process of smoking and drying over the lodge fire, which con-sumes several weeks, seasoning the wood and killing any in-sects which might remain in it, seldom splits or cracks. Similarly, old-growth wood, or second-growth wood, which is tougher, is preferred over the fresher, less dense first-growth, or new-growth, wood.

After drying the shafts are rubbed with grease and straightened over the heat of a fire. Detailed trimming and shaping is accomplished with a small knife. A rubbing with sandstone supplies a smooth finish. The head, of metal, or of bone or stone, with sinew or rawhide, and also sometimes with metal trade rivets, is then mounted on the lance. Lastly, grips, and loops, and decorations, if desired, are added. The sinew and rawhide, before being bound on the lance, are soaked with hot water. The heated water releases a natural glue in these substances, and the water itself, of course, pro-duces a natural shrinking and contraction in drying. The mounting, thus, is extremely solid and secure. The tarn lance, it might be mentioned, as is used by the red savages who have mastered the tarn, is, in size and shape, very similar to the kaiila lance. It differs primarily in being longer and more slender. These lances are used in a great variety of ways, but the most common method is to thrust one's wrist through the wrist loop, grasp the lance with the right hand, and anchor it beneath the right arm. This maximizes balance, control and impact. With the weight of a hurtling kaiila behind the thrust such a lance can be thrust through the body of a kailiauk. To be sure, the skillful hunter will strike no more deeply than is necessary, and his trained kaiila will slow its pace sufficiently to permit the kailiauk to draw its own body from the lance. This permits the lance to be used again and again in the same hunt.

"Notice the manner in which the lances are held by the mounted hunters," said Kog.

"The first one," said Samos, "has his lance in the attack position."

"He, then, will be the first to die," I said.

"Of course," said Kog.

One of the other mounted hunters held his lance in his right hand, its butt resting on his thigh. From this position he could rapidly bring the lance to the attack position. He was, accordingly, the second fellow with whom the man must deal. A third mounted hunter held the lance across his body, it resting in the crook of his left arm. He was the third fellow to reckon with. The other two mounted hunters still wore their lances in their shoulder loops, slung across their back. They might be saved to last.

"The man removes his bow from the fringed, beaded bow case," said Kog. "He strings the bow." The bow, of course, is left unstrung until it is ready to be used. This conserves the resilience of the wood and the tightness and strength of the sinew string. "From his quiver," said Kog, "he extracts six arrows. Three he holds, with the bow, in his left hand. One he fits to the string. Two he holds in his mouth."

"The first mounted hunter is prepared to attack," said Samos.

"The man, on his snowshoes, descends the slope between himself and his enemies," said Kog, "his arrow to the string."

The range and striking power of the small bow, while not negligible, do not compare with that of the peasant bow, or long bow. The red savage, accordingly, whenever possible, attempts to maximize the possibilities of an effective hit by decreasing the distance between himself and the target. This fits in, incidentally, with his glorification of close combat.

The most highly regarded battle exploit among most tribes, for which the highest honors are accorded, is not to kill an armed enemy but to touch or strike one with the open hand. The more danger and risk that is involved in a deed, on the whole, the greater is the concomitant glory of accomplishing it. Killing the enemy, thus, in the heraldry of the red savages, ranks far beneath the besting of the enemy, and in a way that supposedly demonstrates one's greater prowess and courage. It is thus understandable that touching an armed enemy with the open hand counts among most tribes as a first coup. The second and third man to accomplish such a deed would then receive second coup and third coup. Killing an enemy with a bow and arrow from ambush, on the other hand, might be counted as only a fifth or seventh coup.

Needless to say, the counting of coup, which is reflected in the feathers and adornments to which one is entitled, is a matter of great importance to the red savages. Indeed, there are also, in many tribes, practical considerations which also become involved in these matters. For example, it is unlikely that one can advance within a tribe, or become a leader or chieftain, unless one has frequently counted coup. Too, in many tribes, a man who has not counted coup is not permitted to mate. In other tribes, such a man, if he is over twenty-five, is permitted to mate, but he is not allowed to paint his mate's face. Thus will her shame before the other women be made clear.

The institution of counting, or tallying, coup has several obvious effects on the structure and nature of the society of the red savages. In particular, it tends, on the whole, to arrange social hierarchies in such a way that the society is oriented toward aggressiveness and warfare, features which tend to protect and preserve, in an almost natural harmony and balance, delicate relationships between food supplies, territories and populations. Viewed in this manner tribal warfare may be seen as an example of intraspecific aggression, with its attendant consequences in decentralizing and refining diverse populations. Too, if one regards these things as of any interest, the counting of coup and intertribal warfare lends color, excitement and zest to the lives of the red savages. They live in a world in which danger is not unknown. Surely they could live otherwise, but they have not chosen to do so. They live with the stars and the winds, and the kaiila and kailiauk. They have not chosen to revere the fat-bellied, beer-drinking gods of more sedentary peoples. Too, of course, it should be noted that the counting of coup tends, statistically, to ensure that it is the stronger and healthier, the more alert, the more intelligent and sharper-sensed who will reproduce themselves. This is in marked contrast to certain societies where it is the healthiest and finest who are sent off to war while the inferior and defective remain behind in safety, making money and multiplying themselves.

In most tribes, incidentally, a man who refuses to go on the warpath is put in women's clothes and given a woman's name. He must then live as a woman. Henceforth he is always referred to in the female gender. Needless to say, she is never permitted to mate. Sometimes she must even serve the members of a warrior society, as a captive female.

Interestingly enough, whites stand outside the coup structure. This is something that few of them will object to. It seems they are simply not regarded, on the whole, as being suitable foes, or foes worthy enough to stand within the coup structure. It is not that the red savages object to killing them. It is only that they do not take pride, commonly, in doing so. Similarly a man of the high cities would not expect to be publicly rewarded for having speared a tarsk or slain an urt. Accordingly the red savage will seldom go out of his way to slay a white person; he commonly sees little profit in doing so; in killing such a person, he is not entitled to count coup.

"The man, now," said Kog, "is not fifty feet from the mounted hunters. In the soft snow he has descended the slope silently."

"Surely the dark guest, as we may call him, that crouching behind the kailiauk, has seen him."

"Of course," said Kog, "but he has given no sign."

"No sign," I said, "which was read by the mounted hunters."

"Yes," said Kog. His lips drew back, over his fangs. There are always signs. It is only a question of their detectability. They are as small, sometimes, as the dilation of a pupil.

"The bow is drawn," said Kog.

The small bow has many advantages. High among these is the rapidity with which it may be drawn and fired. A skilled warrior, in the Gorean gravity, can fire ten arrows into the air, the last leaving the bow before the first has returned to the earth. No Gorean weapon can match it in its rate of fire. At close range it can be devastating. Two further advantages of the small bow that might be mentioned are its maneuverability and its capacity to be concealed, say beneath a robe. It can be easily swept from one side of the kaiila to the other. In this type of combat, incidentally, it is not unusual for the warrior to shield himself behind the body of his racing kaiila, and, circling the enemy, rise up, suddenly, to fire over the animal's back or, sometimes, from beneath its neck. A heel over the animal's back and a fist in its silken neck hair, or an arm thrust through a leather throat loop, provide the leverage needed for these feats.

To be sure, these folk are superb riders. A child is often put on kaiilaback, its tiny hands clutching the silken neck, before it can walk. Sometimes a strap dangles back for a few feet from the throat loop. This is to be seized by the warrior who may have been struck from his mount, either to recapture the beast or, using the strap, being pulled along, with the momentum of the racing steed, to vault again to its back. This strap, incidentally, is used more often in hunting than in warfare. It could be too easily grasped by an enemy on foot, with the result of perhaps impeding the movement of the kaiila or even causing it to twist and fall. Needless to say, it is extremely dangerous to fall from one's kaiila in hunting kailiauk, because one is often closely involved with numerous stampeding beasts, or the given beast one is pursuing may suddenly turn on one.

In hunting kailiauk the hunters usually scatter about, each selecting his own animals. Accordingly, one's fellows are seldom close at hand to rescue one. This is quite different from mounted warfare, where one's fellows are usually quite close and ready, in an instant, to sweep one up or help one to regain one's mount. The red savage does not take an industrial or arithmetical approach to warfare. He would rather rescue one comrade than slay ten of the enemy. This has to do with the fact that they are members of the same tribe and, usually, of the same warrior society. They will have known one another almost all of their lives; as children and boys they have played together and watched the kaiila herds in the summer camps together; they may even have shared in their first kailiauk hunt; now, as men, they have taken the warpath together; they are comrades, and friends; each is more precious to the other than even a thousand coups.

This explains some of the eccentricities of tribal warfare; first, actual war parties, though common, are formed less often than parties for stealing kaiila; in this sport the object is to obtain as many kaiila as possible without, if possible, engaging the enemy at all; it is a splendid coup, for example, to cut a kaiila tether strap which is tied to the wrist of a sleeping enemy and make off with the animal before he awakens; killing a sleeping enemy is only a minor coup; besides, if he has been killed, how can he understand how cleverly he has been bested; imagine his anger and chagrin when he awakens; is that not more precious to the thief than his scalp; in actual warfare itself large-scale conflicts almost never occur. The typical act of war is the raid, conducted usually by a small group of men, some ten to fifteen in number, which enters enemy country, strikes, usually at dawn, and makes away, almost as soon as it came, with scalps and loot; sometimes, too, a woman or two of the enemy is taken; men of most tribes are fond of owning a woman of the enemy; male prisoners are seldom taken; because of their camaraderie and the sporting aspect of their warfare a group of red savages will usually refuse to follow even a single enemy into rock or brush cover; it is simply too dangerous to do so; similarly the red savages will almost never engage in a standing fight if they are outnumbered; often, too, they will turn their backs on even an obvious victory if the costs of grasping it seem too high; sometimes, too, a large number of red savages will retreat before an unexpected attack of a small number of enemies; they prefer to fight on their own terms and at times of their own choosing; too, they may not have had time to make their war medicine.

"Even with the small bow," said Samos, "surely he cannot expect to best five men."

"It does not seem likely," I admitted.

"He conceives himself to be in the presence of the medicine helper," said Kog. "He is undaunted."

"Turn the hide," I said.

The creature rotated the hide on the heavy table, in the light of the unshuttered dark lantern.

"The first of the mounted hunters is dead," said Kog, "he who had had the lance in the attack position. The kaiila of the others, however, have bolted."

I nodded. I had feared this. The lofty, silken kaiila is an extremely alert, high-strung beast.

"The second mounted hunter, he who had held the lance ready, is thrown from the kaiila to the snow. The man must, thus, in the instant, change his aim to the third mounted rider, he who held the lance across his body. He fells him.

The dark guest acts. He leaps across the body of the slain kailiauk. He seizes the man who had fallen to the snow."

I did not care to look at that picture.

"We may conjecture that the hunter in the snow has screamed," said Kog. "The two other hunters, with their lances across their backs, bolt away. In the distance they turn to regard the kailiauk, the dark guest, the man. The dark guest leaps to the carcass of the kailiauk, its blood red in the snow. Nearby, in the snow, lies he who had been the second mounted hunter. His lance is broken. His body has been half bitten through. The dark guest throws back his head, scratches at his chest, lifts his clawed hands, challenges the other two mounted hunters. The blood of the second hunter is red about his jaws and on the matted fur of his chest. The other two hunters take their leave. Now the dark guest and the man are alone, with the kailiauk, with three riderless kaiila. The dark guest again crouches behind the kailiauk. The man puts away his bow and arrows. The dark guest invites him to the feast."

"The story is an interesting invention," said Samos.

"Turn the hide," I said to Kog.

"The dark guest has left," said Kog. "The man cuts meat from the kailiauk."

Kog again turned the hide.

"The man returns to his camp," said Kog. "He returns with three kaiila, on one of which he rides. The other two are burdened with meat from the kailiauk. Now there will not be hunger in his camp. He returns, too, with the hide of the kailiauk, rolled before him, and three scalps. He will make a shield."

Again Kog turned the hide.

"This is the shield that he will make," said Kog, indicating the last picture on the hide. This last picture was much larger than the other pictures. It was some seven or eight inches in diameter.

"I see," I said.

"The shield bears, clearly delineated, the visage of the dark guest, the medicine helper."

"Yes," I said.

"Do you recognize the picture?" asked Kog.

"Yes," I said, "it is Zarendargar, Half-Ear."

"You cannot be sure," said Samos.

"We, too, believe it to be Zarendargar, whom some humans call Half-Ear," said Kog.

"He is, then, alive," I said.

"It would seem so," said Kog.

"Why have you shown us the picture?" I asked.

"We wish your help," said Kog.

"To rescue him from the Barrens?" I asked.

"No," said Kog, "to kill him."

"This is preposterous," said Samos. "This entire story is naught but the fantasy of a savage."

"You will note," said Kog, "that the story is unfolded on this hide."

"So?" asked Samos.

"It is kailiauk hide," said Kog.

"So?" asked Samos.

"The red savages depend for their very lives on the kailiauk," said Kog. "He is the major source of their food and life. His meat and hide, his bones and sinew, sustain them. From him they derive not only food, but clothing and shelter, tools and weapons."

"I know," said Samos. "I know."

"In their stories they revere him. His images and relics figure in their medicine."

"I know," said Samos.

"Further, they believe that if they are unworthy of the kailiauk, he will go away. And they believe that this once happened, long ago."

"So?" asked Samos.

"So," said Kog, "they do not lie on the hide of the kailiauk. It would be the last place in the world that they would choose to lie. On the hide of the kailiauk one may paint only truth."

Samos was silent.

"Beyond this," said Kog, "note that the image of the dark guest appears on the shield."

"I see," said Samos.

"It is a belief of the red savages that if they are unworthy, or do not speak the truth, that their shield will not protect them. It will move aside or will not turn the arrows and lances of enemies. Many warriors claim to have seen this happen. The shields, too, are made of the hide of the kailiauk, from the thick hide of the back of the neck, where the skin and musculature are thick, to support the weight of the trident and turn the blows of other tridents, especially in the spring buffetings, attendant upon which follows mate selection."

"I shall accept," said Samos, "that the artist is sincere, that he believes himself to be telling the truth."

"That much is undeniable," said Kog.

"But the whole thing may be only the faithful report of a vision or dream."

"The portion of the skin pertinent to the dream, or vision," said Kog, "is clearly distinguished from the portion of the skin which purports to be concerned with real events. Further, we find little reason to believe that the artist could have been, or would have been, mistaken about the nature of those events, at least in their broad outlines."

"The dark guest may not be Zarendargar," said Samos. "The resemblance may be only a coincidence."

"We do not find that a likely possibility," said Kog. "The distances and the times, and the dating of this skin, the details of the representation, all these things, suggest that it is Zarendargar. Similarly fellows of our species, or their descendants, lapsed into barbarism, seldom roam the Barrens. There is too little cover and the heat in the summer is too severe."

"The story on the hide takes place in the winter," said Samos.

"That is true," said Kog, "but game, in the Barrens, is scarce in the winter. Too, the land is too open, and tracks are difficult to conceal. Our people prefer wintering in forested or mountainous areas."

"They will normally seek out such areas," I said.

"Yes," said Kog.

"It is your assumption, then," I said, "that Zarendargar is in hiding."

"Yes," said Kog, "in the unlikely and dangerous terrain of the Barrens."

"He knows that he will be sought?" I asked.

"Yes," said Kog. "He knows that he has failed."

I recalled the destruction of the vast supply complex in the Gorean arctic.

"I met Zarendargar," I said. "It does not seem to me likely that he would be hiding."

"How then would you explain his presence in the Barrens?" inquired Kog.

"I cannot," I said.

"We have searched for him for two years," said Kog. "This hide is our first clue."

"How did you come by this hide?" I asked.

"It was received in trade," said Kog. "It came, eventually, to the attention of one of our agents. Thence it was transported to the steel worlds."

"It does not seem the sort of thing with which the artist would willingly part," I said.

"Quite possibly not," said Kog.

I shuddered. The artist, doubtless, had been slain, his body left stripped and mutilated in the customary manner of the red savages. The object, then, through trade channels, would have come, I supposed, to one of the high cities, perhaps Thentis, the nearest of the large cities to the Barrens.

"We seek Zarendargar," said Kog. "We are his appointed executioners."

Yet there was something puzzling to me in these matters. I could not fully understand what it was. For one thing, I doubted that Zarendargar was in hiding. Yet, otherwise, I could not explain his presence in the Barrens. Too, I was not fully confident that the artist was dead. He impressed me as a competent and resourceful warrior. The skin, on the other hand, had apparently been traded. I was troubled by these things. I did not understand them.

"His crime was failure?" I asked.

"It is not tolerated on the steel worlds," said Kog, "not in one who is above the rings."

"Doubtless he received a fair trial," I said.

"Judgment was pronounced in accord with the statutes of the steel worlds," said Kog, "by the high council, composed of seventy-two members elected from among the representatives of the thousand cliffs."

"The same council was both judge and jury?" I asked.

"Yes," said Kog, "as is the case in many of your own cities."

"Zarendargar was not present at this trial," I said.

"If the presence of the criminal were required," said Kog, "it would make it impossible, in many cases, to pass judgment."

"That is true," I said.

"A limitation on judicial proceedings of such a sort would be intolerable," said Kog.

"I see," I said.

"Was evidence submitted in support of Zarendargar?" I asked.

"In a case of this sort, evidence against the court is inadmissible," said Kog.

"I see," I said. "Who, then," I asked, "spoke on behalf of Zarendargar?"

"It is wrong to speak on behalf of a criminal," said Kog.

"I understand," I said.

"Due process of law, as you may see," said Kog, "was strictly observed."

"Thank you," I said, "my mind is now satisfactorily relieved on the matter."

Kog's lips drew back over his fangs.

"Even so," I asked, "was the vote unanimous?"

"Unanimity constitutes an impediment to the pursuit of expeditious and efficient justice," said Kog.

"Was the vote unanimous?" I asked.

"No," said Kog.

"Was the vote close?" I asked.

"Why do you ask?" asked Kog.

"I am curious," I said.

"Yes," said Kog, "interestingly, it was."

"Thank you," I said. I knew there were factions among these creatures. I had learned this, clearly, in the Tahari. Too, I suspected some of the council, even if they were not of the party of Zarendargar, would have recognized his value to the steel worlds. He was doubtless one of the finest of their generals.

"There is no division here," I said, "between the political and the judicial."

"All law exists to serve the interests of the dominant powers," said Kog. "Our institutions secure this arrangement, facilitate it and, not unimportantly, acknowledge it. Our institutions are, thus, less dishonest and hypocritical than those of groups which pretend to deny the fundamental nature of social order. Law which is not a weapon and a wall is madness."

"How do we know that you are truly appointed to fulfill the edict of the council?" I asked.

"Do you doubt the word of one who is of the Peoples?" asked Kog.

"Not really," I said. "I was just curious about your credentials."

"You could not read them if we displayed them," said Kog.

"That is true," I said. I was truly amazed at the patience which the creatures exhibited. I knew they were short-tempered, even with their own kind. Yet Samos and I had not been attacked. They must need something desperately.

"I swear to you on the rings of Sardak," said Kog, putting his paw on the two rings of reddish alloy on the left wrist of Sardak.

"That is good enough for me," I said, magnanimously. I had not the least idea, of course, of the significance of this gesture on the part of Kog, but I gathered, under the circumstances, that its import must be rather weighty. Sardak was, I was sure, Kog's Blood, or leader. If Kog swore falsely I gathered that it would then be up to Sardak to kill him. Sardak, however, did not move.

"You are doubtless who you say you are," I admitted.

"Even if we were not," said Kog, "we could still do business."

"Business?" I asked.

"Surely," said Kog. "We are met here in the interest of our mutual profit."

"I do not understand," I said.

"Zarendargar is a dangerous enemy to human beings," said Kog. "He is a proven foe of Priest-Kings. He is your enemy. How fortunate, then, that we may conjoin our efforts in this matter. What a rare, welcome and felicitous coincidence do we here encounter. It is in your interest to have Zarendargar killed, and it is our business to kill him. Let us, thus, pool our forces in this common enterprise."

"Why do you wish our help in this matter?" I asked.

"Zarendargar is in the Barrens," said Kog. "This is a large and perilous country. It teems with red savages. To enter such a country and find him it seems to us useful to enlist the help of human beings, creatures of a sort which the red savages will understand to be of their own kind, creatures with whom they might be expected, for a price, to be cooperative. They are superb trackers, you must understand, and may find the search stimulating. Too, they may wish to rid their country of something as dangerous as Zarendargar."

"They would hunt him down like an animal, and slay him?" I asked.

"Presumably," said Kog. "And, humans, you see, would be useful in dealing with them."

"I see," I said.

"What is your answer?" said Kog.

"No," I said.

"Is that your final decision?" asked Kog.

"Yes," I said.

Kog and Sardak suddenly howled. The table between us flung upwards. Samos and I, buffeted, stumbled back. The dark lantern, scattering flaming oil, struck a wall to the side of the room. "Beware, Samos!" I cried. I stood ready with the sword in the guard position. Kog hesitated, tearing at the boards with his clawed feet.

"Guards!" cried Samos. "Guards!" Burning oil was adhering to the ruined wall to our right. I saw the eyes of the two creatures glinting like fiery copper plates. Sardak reached down and seized up the huge spear which Kog had earlier placed to the side. "Beware, Samos!" I cried.

Guards, with crossbows, rushed into the room, behind us. With a cry of rage Sardak hurled the great spear. It missed Samos and shattered half through the wall some forty feet behind us. Kog hurled the shield towards us and, like a great, shallow, concave bowl, it skimmed through the air, between us, and broke boards loose near the roof behind us. "Fire," cried Samos to his men. "Fire!"

With the titanic beating of wings the two tarns, the creatures mounted on them, took flight from the ruins of the tarn cot. I staggered back in the wind from the wings. I half shut my eyes against the dust and debris which struck against my face. The flames from the burning oil on the wall to my right leaped almost horizontally backwards, torn and lashed by the wind. Then they burned again, as they had a moment before. I saw the creatures mounted on the tarns, silhouetted against one of Gor's three moons, fleeing over the marshes. "They have escaped," said Samos.

"Yes," I said. They had restrained themselves as long as they had been able to. What a titanic effort of will must have been necessary for them, creatures so ferocious and savage, to have controlled themselves as long as they had. They had done particularly well considering the numerous provocations to which, deliberately, I had subjected them, to test the depth of their commitment to their mission and the depth of their need of human help.

"Look at this," said one of Samos' men, working loose the great spear from the wall.

"And this," said another, lifting up the huge shield.

Samos' men examined the spear and shield.

"Forget what you have seen here this night," said Samos.

"What were they?" asked one of Samos' men, standing beside me.

"We call them Kurii, Beasts," I said.

2

I WILL GO TO THE BARRENS

"It was a trick," said Samos, "to lure you into the Barrens, where they might have slain you with impunity."

Samos and I rode inside the squarish, covered barge in which we had earlier come to the tarn complex in the marshes. It was now shortly after dawn. We were making our way through the canals of Port Kar. Here and there, on the walks at the edges of the canal, men were moving about. Most were loading or readying small boats, or folding nets. I saw, through the small, slatted window near me, a slave girl drawing water from the canal, with a rope and bucket.

"Surely so elaborate a hoax would not have been necessary if our destruction had been their only end in view," I said.

"Perhaps," said Samos.

"They might have attacked us almost immediately in the tarn complex, and presumably have made good their escape," I said.

"True," said Samos. It was unlikely that we could have adequately defended ourselves against a sudden onslaught of such foes at that short a distance.

I saw a man outside on the walk, a few yards away, mending a net. Ovoid, painted floats lay beside him. On my knees, rolled, was the hide which had been displayed to us by Kog and Sardak in the tarn complex. We had retrieved it from the burning complex. Too, at our feet, dented, but still operational, as we had determined, was the boxlike translator. We had left the burning complex behind us in the marshes, its smoke ascending in the gray light of the morning. The huge shield and spear we had discarded in the marshes. The less evidence of such things about the better, we speculated, for men.

"Do you think you should have gone with them?" asked Samos.

"No," I said.

"It could, of course," said Samos, "have been a portion of their plan that if Zarendargar had been successfully destroyed, they might then turn on you."

"Yes," I said, "or I on them."

"That possibility would not be unlikely to occur to such creatures," said Samos.

"No," I said.

"You do not feel you should have gone with them," said Samos.

"No," I said.

"What do you think they will do now?" asked Samos.

"They will go to the Barrens," I said.

"They will hunt Zarendargar," said Samos.

"Of course," I said.

"Do you think they will attempt to enlist the aid of men?" asked Samos.

"Doubtless," I said.

"It is easy for me to understand why they came first to us," said Samos.

"Of course," I said. "Our aid might prove invaluable. Too, they would expect us to be as eager, as zealous, as they, to bring about the destruction of Zarendargar. The venture, presumably, would be one which would be in our common interest, one in which we could find a mutual profit."

"It would also be easier for them to approach us than many men," said Samos, "for, from our wars, such as they, and their nature and intelligence, are not unknown to us."

"That is true," I said.

"They will have difficulty recruiting efficient aid," said Samos, "for few white men are allowed to tread the Barrens, and those who are permitted to encroach upon their fringes are normally permitted to do so only for purposes of trade."

"I think it is fair to assume," I said, "that they do not have an agent in the Barrens. If they had had such an agent, then it is unlikely they would have approached us in the first place. Similarly the Barrens would seem to be an unlikely, desolate and profitless place in which to have placed an agent."

"They must obtain new recruits," said Samos.

"That seems likely," I said.

"We have their translator," said Samos.

"That is unimportant," I said. "Doubtless they have another among their stores."

"What of the red savages themselves?" asked Samos.

"Few red savages live outside of the Barrens," I said, "and those who do would presumably be as unfamiliar with them as would be anyone else in their circumstances."

"What of the red savages of the Barrens?" asked Samos.

"Such would have to be approached at their own risk," I said. "From the hide we saw that the mounted hunters were apparently preparing to charge Zarendargar when they were interrupted by the man's attack."

"But the translator," said Samos.

"A bewildering complexity of tribal languages is spoken in the Barrens," I said, "most of them unintelligible to native speakers of the others. I find it hard to believe that their translators would be prepared to deal with any one of those languages, let along several of them."

"Zarendargar is then perhaps safe," said Samos.

"Not at all," I said. "Kurii are tenacious. With or without human aid we may be sure that they will not rest until they have found their quarry."

"Zarendargar, then, is doomed," said Samos.

"Perhaps," I said.

I glanced again outside the barge, through the now-opened slats of the small window. On a gently inclined slope of cement leading down to the canal, the water lapping at her knees, there knelt a slave girl doing laundry. She wore her steel collar. Her tunic came high on her thighs. It is thought desirable for a female slave to work long hours at menial tasks. I smiled to myself. It is pleasant to own a woman, absolutely, in the Gorean fashion.

"It is your belief, then," said Samos, "that the skin is genuine."

"Yes," I said, "and from what I know of the red savages, I would conjecture that this skin is from the very beast whose image is portrayed upon it."

"Ai," said Samos. "Perhaps!"

"I think it is more than likely," I said.

"I pity Zarendargar," said Samos.

"He would not appreciate the sentiment," I said.

I moved on the low wooden bench, one of several aligned perpendicularly to the interior port wall of the inclosed barge. There was a similar set of benches aligned identically against the starboard wall.

"These benches are uncomfortable," I said to Samos. My legs were cramped.

"They are designed for women," said Samos.

There was room for five women on each bench. With my heel I kicked some light, siriklike slave chains back under the bench. Such chains are too light for a man, but they are fully adequate for a woman. The primary holding arrangements for women on the benches, however, are not chains. Each place on the bench is fitted with ankle and wrist stocks, and for each bench there is a plank collar, a plank which opens horizontally, each half of which contains five matching, semi-circular openings, which, when it is set on pinions, closed, and chained in place, provides thusly five sturdy, wooden inclosures for the small, lovely throats of women. The plank is thick and thus the girls' chins are held high. The plank is further reinforced between each girl with a narrowly curved iron band, the open ends of which are pierced; this is slid tight in its slots, in its metal retainers, about the boards, and secured in place with a four-inch metal pin, which may or may not be locked in place. Each girl is held well in her place, thusly, not only by the ankle and wrist stocks, which hold her ankles back and her wrists beside her, but by the plank collar as well.

"We are passing a market," said Samos. "You had better close the window slats."

I glanced outside. The smell of fruit and vegetables, and verr milk, was strong. I also heard the chatter of women. Dozens of women were spreading their blankets, and their wares, on the cement. There are many such markets in Port Kar. Men and women come to them in small boats. Also, of course, sometimes the vendors, too, will merely tie up their boats near the side of the canal, particularly when the space on the cement is crowded. The markets, thus, tend to extend into the canal itself. The only fully floating market authorized by the Council of Captains occurs in a lakelike area near the arsenal. It is called the Place of the Twenty-Fifth of Se'Kara, because of the monument there, rising from the water. On the twenty-fifth of Se'Kara in Year One of the Sovereignty of the Council of Captains, the year 10,120 C.A., Contasta Ar, from the Founding of Ar, a sea battle took place in which the fleet of Port Kar defeated the fleets of Cos and Tyros. The monument, of course, commemorates this victory. The market forms itself about the monument. That year, incidentally, is also regarded as significant in the history of Port Kar because it was in that year that, as it is said, a Home Stone consented to reside within the city.

"Please," said Samos.

I looked at the benches. Most of them were smooth, and, on many, the dark varnish was all but worn off. Slave girls are normally transported nude.

"Please," said Samos.

"I'm sorry," I said. I closed the window slats by moving one of the slats. They can be most easily closed, of course, by moving the narrow, vertically mounted, central wooden lever, but this lever, as would be expected, is on the outside. The window is designed to be opened and shut from the outside. Too, it can be locked shut, and normally is, from the outside, when cargo is within. As I have earlier indicated the slave girl is normally transported in total ignorance of her destination. Keeping a girl in ignorance is commonly thought useful in her control and management. Too, it helps her keep clearly in mind that she is a slave. Curiosity is not becoming in a Kajira is a common Gorean saying. The girl learns quickly that it is not her business to meddle in the affairs of her master but, rather, to be beautiful, and serve him, abjectly and totally.

"I do not wish too many to know of our early morning journey," said Samos.

I nodded. We were well known in Port Kar. There was little point in provoking the populace to idle speculations.

"We are passing another market," I said.

"Verr milk, Masters!" I heard called. "Verr milk, Masters!"

I opened the slats a tiny crack. I wished to see if she were pretty. She was, in her tunic and collar, kneeling on a white blanket, spread on the cement, with the brass container of verr milk, with its strap, near her, and the tiny brass cups. She was extremely lightly complexioned and had very red hair. "Verr milk, Masters," she called. Slaves may buy and sell in the name of their masters, but they cannot, of course, buy and sell for themselves because they are only animals. It is rather for them to be themselves bought and sold, as the masters might please.

"Will you make a report of this morning's business to the Sardar?" I asked.

"A routine report of all such contacts is to be made," said Samos.

"Do you expect the Sardar to take action?" I asked.

"No," said Samos.

"That, too, is my speculation," I said.

"It is their custom in most such matters to let matters take their course."

"True," I said.

"Are you interested?" asked Samos.

"I was curious to hear your view," I said. "It coincides with mine, as I had thought it would."

"Why do you ask?" asked Samos.

"I was curious," I said.

"Oh," said Samos.

We rode together for a time in silence, toward my holding, through the canals.

"I met Zarendargar, in the north," I said.

"That is known to me," said Samos.

"He impressed me as a fine commander, and a good soldier," I said.

"He is a terrifying and dangerous enemy," said Samos. "Men and Priest-Kings would be well rid of him. Let us hope that the beasts we met this morning will be successful in their quest."

I looked again through the tiny crack in the slats. It was near the sixth Ahn. Small boats now moved about on the canal. Most were propelled by the swaying movement of a steering oar. Some, larger boats and light galleys, such as might be used in the Tamber Gulf or, abroad, on Thassa, were being rowed from thwarts. These vessels were singly or doubly ruddered. In negotiating the canals their long, sloping yards were lowered, being then fully or partially inboard, in either case being aligned with the keel. This was in accord with an ordnance of Port Kar.

"The Council of Captains must meet in two days," said Samos. "It is proposed that the Sa-Tarna quay in the south harbor be extended. What division of this will be borne by public expense remains moot. Too, if this license be granted, an exploitable precedent may be set. Already there is talk among the merchants in rep-cloth and the lumber and stone merchants."

We were now passing an open slave market. The merchant was chaining his girls on the broad, tiered, cement display shelves. One girl lay on her stomach, on her elbows, her head down, the heavy iron collar on her neck visible beneath her hair; a short, weighty chain of thick dark links connected this collar, by its collar ring, to a wide, stout ring, anchored deeply in the cement, almost beneath her chin; the chain was no more than six inches long; I gathered that she was being disciplined; another girl, a blonde, sat on her shelf with her knees drawn up, her ankles crossed, her arms about her knees; I saw her chain descend from her collar, disappear behind her right leg, and then re-emerge from behind her right thigh, thence running to the ring to which she was attached; another girl, a long-haired brunet, on all fours, faced me, with glazed eyes, seemingly uncomprehendingly regarding the inclosed barge as it passed by in the canal; she had just been chained; it is common to put a woman on all fours for neck chaining; the slaver stepped away from her; neck chaining, incidentally, is common in a market for female slaves, as it is for she-sleen; several girls, standing, awaited their chaining, in turn, on the tiers; I could see the small, incisive brand marks on their left thighs, high, just below their left hips; they were in ankle coffle, their left ankles chained together; more than one of them shaded her eyes against the morning sun; it would be a long day for most of them, chained in the sun, on the hard, granular surfaces of the hot cement shelves.

"These issues," said Samos, "are subtle and complex."

The women were chained nude, of course, for that is the way that slave girls are commonly displayed for their sale, particularly in low markets, and, indeed, even in a private sale from one of the purple booths in the courtyard of a rich slaver there will come a time when the slave, even an exquisite, high slave, must put aside her silks and be examined raw, as though she were a common girl. The Gorean male is a practiced and wary buyer. He wishes to see, fully and clearly, and preferably at his own pace, and leisure, what it is for which he is considering putting out his hard-earned money.

"I think that I would favor granting the license," said Samos, "but that I would also insist on the restriction of the subsidy to such an amount that an attack by every mercantile subcaste in Port Kar on the public coffers will not be encouraged. That seems to me reasonable. The various subcastes, it seems to me, should be expected, on the whole, to rely on their own resources. Direct council support, for example, has never been petitioned by the Slavers."

I considered the Barrens. They are not, truly, as barren as the name would suggest. They are barren only in contrast, say, with the northern forests or the lush land in river valleys, or the peasant fields or meadows of the southern rain belts. They are, in fact, substantially, vast tracts of rolling grasslands, lying east of the Thentis mountains. I have suspected that they are spoken of as the Barrens not so much in an attempt to appraise them with geographical accuracy as to discourage their penetration, exploration and settlement. The name, then, is perhaps not best regarded as an item of purely scientific nomenclature but rather as something else, perhaps a warning. Also, calling the area the Barrens gives men a good excuse, if they should desire such, for not entering upon them. To be sure, the expression 'Barrens' is not altogether a misnomer. They would be, on the whole, much less arable than much of the other land of known Gor. Their climate is significantly influenced by the Thentis mountains and the absence of large bodies of water. Prevailing winds in the northern hemisphere of Gor are from the north and west. Accordingly a significant percentage of moisture-laden air borne by westerly winds is forced by the Thentis mountains to cooler, less-heated air strata, where it precipitates, substantially on the eastern slopes of the mountains and the fringes of the Barrens. Similarly the absence of large bodies of water in the Barrens reduces rainfall which might be connected with large-scale evaporation and subsequent precipitation of this moisture over land areas, the moisture being carried inland on what are, in effect, sea breezes, flowing into low-pressure areas caused by the warmer land surfaces, a given amount of radiant energy raising the temperature of soil or rock significantly more than it would raise the temperature of an equivalent extent of water.

The absence of large bodies of water adjacent to or within the Barrens also has another significant effect on their climate. It precludes the Barrens from experiencing the moderating effects of such bodies of water on atmospheric temperatures. Areas in the vicinity of large bodies of water, because of the differential heating ratios of land and water, usually have warmer winters and cooler summers than areas which are not so situated. The Barrens, accordingly, tend to be afflicted with great extremes of temperature, often experiencing bitterly cold winters and long, hot, dry summers.

"Another possibility," Samos was saying, "would be a loan to the Sa-Tarna merchants, at a reduced rate of interest. Thus we might avoid the precedent of a direct subsidy to a subcaste. To be sure, we might then encounter resistance from the Street of Coins. Tax credits would be another possible incentive."

At the edge of the Thentis mountains, in the driest areas, the grass is short. As one moves in an easterly direction it becomes taller, ranging generally from ten to eighteen inches in height; as one moves even further east it can attain a height of several feet, reaching as high as the knees of a man riding a kaiila. On foot, it is easier to become lost in such grass than in the northern forests. No white man, incidentally, at least as far as I know, has ever penetrated to the eastern edge of the Barrens. Certainly, as far as I know, none has ever returned from that area. Their extent, accordingly, is not known.

"The issues are complicated," said Samos. "I do not know, truly, how I should cast my vote."

Tornadoes and booming, crashing thunder can characterize the Barrens. In the winter there can be blizzards, probably the worst on Gor, in which snows can drift as high as the mast of the light galley. The summers can be characterized by a searing sun and seemingly interminable droughts. It is common for many of the shallow, meandering rivers of the area to run dry in the summer. Rapid temperature shifts are not unusual. A pond may unexpectedly freeze in En'Kara and, late in Se'Var, a foot or two of snow may be melted in a matter of hours. Sudden storms, too, are not unprecedented. Sometimes as much as twelve inches of rain, borne by a southern wind, can be deposited in less than an hour. To be sure, this rain usually runs off rapidly, cutting crevices and gullies in the land. A dry river bed may, in a matter of minutes, become a raging torrent. Hail storms, too, are not infrequent. Occasionally the chunks of ice are larger than the eggs of vulos. Many times such storms have destroyed flights of migrating birds.

"What do you think?" asked Samos.

"I once shared paga with Zarendargar," I said.

"I do not understand," said Samos.

We felt the barge turn slowly in the canal. Then we heard oars being drawn inboard on the starboard side. The barge, then, gently, struck against a landing, moving against the leather coils tied there.

"We are at my holding," I said.

I rose from the low bench and went to the door and opened it, emerging near the stern of the barge. Two of my men were holding mooring ropes, one from the bow of the barge and one from the stern. I climbed to the rail of the barge and ascended from thence to the surface of the landing.

Samos, below me, came to the interior threshold of the cabin door.

"It has been an interesting morning," he said.

"Yes," I said.

"I shall see you at the meeting of the Council in two days," he said.

"No," I said.

"I do not understand," said Samos.

"Zarendargar is in great danger," I said.

"We may rejoice in that," said Samos.

"The Death Squad is already on Gor," I said.

"It would seem so," said Samos.

"How many do you think there are?" I asked.

"Two," said Samos.

"Surely," I said, "there would be more." I did not think only two Kurii would be sent to dispatch one such as Zarendargar.

"Perhaps," said Samos.

"I once shared paga with Zarendargar," I said.

Samos stepped forth onto the deck of the barge, at the stern. He looked up at me, startled. It seemed no longer was he concerned that our camaraderie of the morning might be noted. "What madness do you contemplate?" he whispered.

"Surely Zarendargar must be warned," I said.

"No!" said Samos. "Let him be slain as expeditiously as possible!"

"I do not think, in such a case, Kurii are inclined to slay expeditiously," I said.

"It is none of your affair," said Samos.

"Those affairs are mine which I choose to make mine," I said.

"White men are not even allowed in the Barrens," said Samos.

"Surely some must be," I said, "if only to effect the graces and utilities of trade."

I looked over the low roof of the barge's cabin to the canal beyond. A hundred or so feet away there was the small boat of an urt hunter. His girl, the rope on her neck, crouched in the bow. This rope is about twenty feet long. One end of it is tied on her neck and the other end is fastened on the boat, to the bow ring. The hunter stood behind her with his pronged urt spear. These men serve an important function in Port Kar, which is to keep down the urt population in the canals.

At a word from the man the girl, the rope trailing behind her, dove into the canal. Behind the man, in the stern, lay the bloody, white-furred bodies of two canal urts. One would have weighed about sixty pounds, and the other, I speculate, about seventy-five or eighty pounds. I saw the girl swimming in the canal, the rope on her neck, amidst the garbage. It is less expensive and more efficient to use a girl for this type of work than, say, a side of tarsk. The girl moves in the water which tends to attract the urts and, if no mishap occurs, may be used again and again. Some hunters use a live verr but this is less effective as the animal, squealing, and terrified, is difficult to drive from the side of the boat.

The slave girl, on the other hand, can be reasoned with. She knows that if she is not cooperative she will be simply bound hand and foot and thrown alive to the urts. This modality of hunting, incidentally, is not as dangerous to the girl as it might sound, for very few urts make their strike from beneath the surface. The urt, being an air-breathing mammal, commonly makes its strike at the surface itself, approaching the quarry with its snout and eyes above the water, its ears laid back against the sides of its long, triangular head. To be sure, sometimes the urt surfaces near the girl and approaches her with great rapidity. Thus, in such a situation, she may not have time to return to the boat. In such a case, of course, the girl must depend for her life on the steady hand and keen eye, the swiftness, the strength and timing, the skill, of the urt hunter, her master. Sometimes, incidentally, a master will rent his girl to an urt hunter, this being regarded as useful in her discipline. There are very few girls who, after a day or two in the canals, and then being returned to their masters, do not strive to be completely pleasing.

"You need not warn Zarendargar," said Samos. "He knows

he will be sought. That we have, in effect, on the authority of one of the very beasts to whom we spoke this morning."

"He may not know that the Death Squad has landed on Gor," I said. "He may not know that they are aware of his general location. He may not know with whom it is that he will be dealing."

"These things are his concern," said Samos, "not yours."

"Perhaps," I said.

"Once," said Samos, "he sent you forth upon the ice, to be slain by another Kur."

"He did his duty, as he saw it," I said.

"And now you would render him succor?" asked Samos.

"Yes," I said.

"He might slay you, instantly, if he saw you," said Samos.

"It is true he is an enemy," I said. "That is a risk I must take."

"He may not even recognize you," said Samos.

"Perhaps," I said. This was, I supposed, a danger. Just as human beings often found it difficult to distinguish among various Kurii, so, too, many Kurii, apparently, often found it difficult to distinguish among various human beings. On the other hand, I was confident that Zarendargar would know me. I had no doubt but what I would recognize him. One does not forget a Kur such as Half-Ear, or Zarendargar, one who stood above the rings, a war general among the Kurii.

"I forbid you to go," said Samos.

"You cannot do that," I said.

"In the name of Priest-Kings," he said, "I forbid you to go."

"My wars are my own," I said. "I choose them as I please."

I looked beyond Samos to the boat and urt hunter in the canal. The girl climbed, shivering, into the bow of the boat, the wet rope on her neck. In the bow of the boat, crouching there, nude and shivering, she coiled, in careful circles, in the shallow, wooden rope bucket beside her, the central length of the rope, that between her neck and the bow ring. Only then did she reach for the thick woolen blanket, from the wool of the hurt, and clutch it, shuddering, about her. Her hair, wet, was very dark against the white blanket. She was comely. I wondered if she were being rented out for discipline, or if she belonged to the urt hunter. It was not easy to tell.

Most Gorean slave girls are comely, or beautiful. This is easy to understand. It is almost always the better looking women who are taken for slaves, and, of course, in breeding slaves, it is commonly only the most beautiful of female slaves who are used, these usually being crossed, hooded, with handsome male silk slaves, also hooded. The female offspring of these matings, needless to say, are often exquisite. The male offspring, incidentally, and interestingly, to my mind, are often handsome, strong and quite masculine. This is perhaps because many male silk slaves are chosen to be male silk slaves not because they are weak or like women, but because they are not; it is only that they are men, and often true men, who must serve women, totally, in the same fashion that a slave female is expected to serve a free master. To be sure, it is also true, and should be admitted in all honesty, that many male silk slaves are rather feminine; some women prefer this type, perhaps because they fear true men; from such a silk slave they need not fear that they may suddenly be turned upon, and tied, and taught to be women. Most women, however, after a time, find this type of silk slave a banality and a bore; charm and wit can be entertaining, but, in time, if not conjoined with intellect and true masculine power, they are likely to wear thin.

The feminine type of male silk slave, incidentally, for better or for worse, is seldom selected for breeding purposes. Gorean slave breeders, perhaps benighted in this respect, prefer what they take to be health to what they think of as sickness, and what they take to be strength to what they deem weakness. Some female slaves, incidentally, have a pedigreed lineage going back through several generations of slave matings, and their masters hold the papers to prove this. It is a felony in Gorean law to forge or falsify such papers. Many Goreans believe that all women are born for the collar, and, that a woman cannot be truly fulfilled as a woman until a strong man puts it on her, until she finds herself reduced to her basic femaleness at his feet.

In the case of the bred female slave, of course, she has been legally and literally, in anyone's understanding, bred to the collar, and in a full commercial and economic sense, as a business speculation on the part of masters. The features most often selected for by the breeders are beauty and passion. It has been found that intelligence, of a feminine sort, as opposed to the pseudomasculine type of intelligence often found in women with large amounts of male hormones, is commonly linked, apparently genetically, with these two hitherto mentioned properties. There are few male slaves with long pedigrees. Goreans, though recognizing the legal and economic legitimacy of male slavery, do not regard it as possessing the same biological sanction as attaches to female slavery. The natural situation, in the mind of many Goreans, is that the master set/slave relation is one which ideally exists between man and woman, with the woman in the property position. Male slaves, from time to time, can receive opportunities to win their freedom, though, to be sure, usually in situations of high risk and great danger. Such opportunities are never accorded to the female slave. She is totally helpless. If she is to receive her freedom it will be fully and totally, and only, by the decision of her master.

"You are, then, seriously, considering going to the Barrens?" asked Samos.

"Yes," I said.

"You are a foolish and stubborn fellow," said Samos.

"Perhaps," I said. I lifted the roll of kailiauk hide I carried. "May I keep this?" I asked.

"Of course," said Samos.

I handed it to one of my men. I thought it might prove useful in the Barrens.

"You are fully determined?" asked Samos.

"Yes," I said.

"Wait," he said. He went back to the door of the inclosed cabin and re-entered it. In a moment he re-emerged, carrying the boxlike translator which we had brought from the tarn complex. "You may need this," said Samos, handing it to one of my men.

"Thank you, Samos," I said.

"I wish you well," he said.

"I wish you well," I said. I turned away.

"Wait!" he said.

I turned back to face him.

"Be careful," he said.

"I will," I said.

"Tarl," he said, suddenly.

I turned back to face him, again.

"How is it that you could even think of doing this?" he asked.

"Zarendargar may need my assistance," I said. "I may be able to aid him."

"But why, why?" he asked.

How could I explain to Samos the dark affinity I shared with one whom I had met only in the north, and long ago, with one who, clearly, was naught but a beast? I recalled the long evening I had once spent with Zarendargar, and our lengthy, animated conversations, the talk of warriors, the talk of soldiers, of those familiar with arms and martial values, of those who had shared the zest and terrors of conflict, to whom crass materialisms could never be more than the means to worthier victories, who had shared the loneliness of command, who had never forgotten the meanings of words such as discipline, responsibility, courage and honor, who had known perils, and long treks and privations, to whom comfort and the hearth beckoned less than camps and distant horizons.

"Why, why?" he asked.

I looked beyond Samos, to the canal beyond. The urt hunter, with his girl and boat, rowing slowly, was taking his leave. He would try his luck elsewhere.

"Why?" asked Samos.

I shrugged. "Once," I said, "we shared paga."

3

I RECEIVE INFORMATION;
I WILL TRAVEL NORTHWARD

"Perhaps this one?" asked the merchant.

"I am trying to locate the whereabouts of a trader, one called Grunt," I said.

The blond-haired girl, nude, kneeling, shrank back against the cement wall. Her small wrists were bound tightly behind her, to an iron ring fastened in the wall.

"She is not without her attractions," said the merchant.

"Do you know where this fellow, Grunt, may be found?" I asked.

Another girl, also blond, a long chain on her neck, also fastened to a ring in the wall, had crept to my feet. She then lowered herself to her belly before me. She held my right ankle in her small hands and began to lick and kiss softly at my feet. I felt her mouth and small, warm tongue between the straps on my sandals. "Please buy me, Master," she whispered. "I will serve you helplessly and well." The difference between slave girls are interesting. The first girl was a fresh capture, clearly. She had not yet even been branded. The other girl, clearly, had already known the touch of a master.

"I think he has ventured north, along the perimeter," said the merchant.

"Buy me, I beg you, Master!" whispered the girl at my feet.

I looked to the girl kneeling at the wall. Swiftly she put down her head, reddening.

"That one," said the man, indicating the girl at the wall, "was formerly free. She was taken only five days ago. Not yet, as you note, is her thigh even marked."

"Why not?" I asked. Usually a girl is marked within hours of her capture. It is usually felt that, after her capture, there is little point in permitting any possibility that she might be confused with a free woman.

"I want her deeply and cleanly branded," he said. "An iron master travels among several of the smaller border towns. He is good at his business and has an assortment of irons, ranging from lovely and delicate to rude and brutal."

I nodded. It was not unusual for the border towns, along the eastern edge of the Thentis mountains, to be served by itinerant tradesmen and artisans. There was often too little work for them to thrive in a given town but an ample employment for their services and goods in a string of such towns. Such tradesmen and artisans commonly included some five to ten towns in their territory.

"Do not fret, little beauty," said the man to the girl. "You will soon be properly marked."

The girl lifted her head, and looked at me.

"You see," said the man, "she is already curious as to the touch of a man."

"I see," I said.

"What sort of brand would you like, little beauty?" asked the man. "Have no fear. Whatever brand you wear, I guarantee, will be unmistakable and clear."

She looked up at him. With the back of his hand he lashed her head to the side.

She then looked up at him, again, frightened. Blood was at her lip. "Whatever brand you wish for me, Master," she said.

"Excellent," said the man. He turned to me. "That is her first, full, verbal slave response. She has had, of course, other sorts of slave responses and behaviors before this, such things as squirmings, strugglings, cringings, pain and fear, and behavioral presentations and pleadings, making herself pretty and holding herself in certain ways, presenting herself as a helpless, desirable female, trying to provoke the interest of attractive men."

The girl looked at him with horror, but I saw, in her eyes,

that what he had said was true. Even unbranded, she was already becoming a slave.

"Please, Master. Please, Master," begged the girl at my feet.

"What sort of brand would you like, my dear?" asked the man of the girl at the wall. "Have no fear. I am now permitting you to express a preference. I shall then, as it pleases me, accept your preference, or reject it."

Her lip, now swollen, trembled.

"Would you like a lovely and feminine brand," he asked, "or a rude and brutal brand, one fit for a pot girl or a tendress of kaiila?"

"I am a woman, Master," she said. "I am feminine."

I was pleased to hear this simple confession from the girl, this straightforward, uncompromising admission of the reality of her sex. How few of the women of my old world, I thought, could bring themselves, even to their lovers, to make this same, simple admission. What a world of difference it might make to their relationships, I speculated. Yet this admission, nonverbally, was surely made, and even poignantly and desperately, by many women of my old world, despite the injunctions and conditionings against honesty in such matters enjoined by an antibiological, politicized society. I hoped that upon occasion, at least, these admissions, these declarations, these cries for recognition and fulfillment, whether verbal or nonverbal, might, in his kindness, be heeded by a male.

It is an interesting question, the relation between natural values and conditioned values. To be sure, the human infant, in many respects, seems to be little more than a *tabula rasa*, a blank tablet, on which a society, whether sensible or perverted, may inscribe its values. Yet the infant is also an animal, with its nature and genetic codings, with its heritage of eons of life and evolution, tracing itself back to the combinations of molecules and the births of stars. Thus can be erected conflicts between nature and artifice, whether the artifices be devised or blind. These conflicts, in turn, produce their grotesque syndromes of anxiety, guilt and frustration, with their attendant deleterious consequences for happiness and life. A man may be taught to prize his own castration but somewhere, sometime, in the individual or in the maddened collectivity, nature must strike back. The answer of the fool is the answer he has been taught to give, the answer he must continue to defend and beyond which he cannot see, an answer historically deriving from an *ethos* founded on the macabre superstitions and frustrated perversions of lunatics, an answer now co-opted to serve the interests of new, grotesque minorities who, repudiating the only rationale that gave it plausibility, pervert it to their own ends. The sludge of Puritanism, with its latent social power, bequeathed from one generation to the next, can serve unaccustomed masters. The only practical answer to these dilemmas is not continued suppression and censorship, but a society, a world, in which nature is freed to thrive. It is not a healthy world in which civilization is nature's prison. Nature and civilization are not incompatible. A choice need not be made between them. For a rational animal each can be the complement and enhancement of the other. For too long has the world been under the domination of the grotesque and insidious. One fears mostly they may begin to believe their own lies. They think they herd sheep. It is possible, unbeknownst to themselves, they walk with wolves and lions.

The merchant regarded the girl at the wall. Under his gaze she straightened herself. "Yes," he said. "I see that you are feminine. Accordingly, you will be appropriately branded."

"Thank you, Master," she said.

"It will be the common Kajira mark," he said, "indicating that you are beautiful, but only another slave girl."

"Thank you, Master," she said. I thought the cursive Kef, sometimes referred to as the staff and fronds, beauty subject to discipline, would look well upon her thigh.

"I am already branded, Master," said the girl at my feet. She looked up at me. It was true. She wore the Kef high on her left thigh, just under the hip. This is the most common brand site for a Gorean slave girl.

"She bellies to you," said the man. "She likes you."

"Perhaps you have warned her that if she does not belly to the first man in the market she is to be whipped," I smiled.

"No," chuckled the man, "but it is true that I have denied her the touch of a man for two days." The sexual relief of a slave girl, like her clothing and her food, is also something under the total command of the master.

The girl whimpered in frustration. "No, Master," she wept. "You are the sort of man to whom I would belly naturally. To see you is to want to belly myself before you."

"Master," said the girl at the wall, addressing me, "if I were not bound, I, too, would belly myself before you."

"Excellent!" said the merchant. "This is the first time she has spoken so. Apparently you are the sort of man she regards as a desirable master."

I said nothing. A girl in a market knows she is to be sold. Accordingly she will often try to influence a man she finds attractive to buy her. If he does not buy her, she knows she may be bought by one who is worse. Most girls, of course, prefer to be bought by a man who is exciting and attractive to them, one whom they would find irresistible, one whom they would desire to serve, rather than by one who is gross and disgusting to them. To be sure, as slave girls, they would have to serve either perfectly. The decision as to whether the girl is to be purchased or not, is, of course, in the final analysis, totally the man's. In this respect the girl must wait, and is absolutely helpless. In this respect she has as little personal control over her fate as an inanimate, displayed object in an emporium on Earth.

The girl at the ring pulled against the bonds on her small wrists, leaning toward me. The girl at my feet looked up at me. I felt the chain on her neck across my right foot.

"Have they names?" I asked the merchant.

"No," said the merchant, "I have not yet named them."

"The trader, Grunt," I said, "you speculate has ventured northward?"

"Yes," said the man.

I kicked back the girl at my feet. Whimpering, she crawled back to the wall, where she lay curled at its foot, watching me. The other girl, fastened by the wrists to the ring, shrank back against it. She looked at me with horror and fear, but, also, with another expression in her eyes, as well, one of fascination and awe. I think then she realized a little better than before what it might be to be a slave. She would be subject to discipline. Our eyes met. I saw in her eyes that she now realized that she, like any other slave girl, was, and would be, under total masculine domination. She shuddered, and looked down. I saw her tremble with fear and pleasure. I saw that she, properly trained, would make some man a superb slave.

"The next town northward is Fort Haskins," I said. This lay at the foot of the Boswell Pass. Originally it had been a trading post, maintained by the Haskins Company, a company of Merchants, primarily at Thentis. A military outpost, flying the banners of Thentis, garrisoned by mercenaries, was later established at the same point. The military and strategic importance of controlling the eastern termination of the Boswell Pass was clear. It was at this time that the place came to be known as Fort Haskins. A fort remains at this point but the name, generally, is now given to the town which grew up in the vicinity of the fort, primarily to the west and south. The fort itself, incidentally, was twice burned, once by soldiers from Port Olni, before that town joined the Salerian Confederation, and once by marauding Dust Legs, a tribe of red savages, from the interior of the Barrens. The military significance of the fort has declined with the growth of population in the area and the development of tarn cavalries in Thentis. The fort now serves primarily as a trading post, maintained by the caste of Merchants, from Thentis, an interesting recollection of the origins of the area.

"It will be my conjecture," said the man, "that he whom you seek, the trader, Grunt, is bound not for Fort Haskins, but for Kailiauk."

"Ah," I said. I should have guessed that. Kailiauk is the easternmost town at the foot of the Thentis mountains. It lies almost at the edge of the Ihanke, or Boundary. From its outskirts one can see the markers, the feathers on their tall wands, which mark the beginning of the country of the red savages.

"I trust that you do not desire to kill him," said the man.

"No," I smiled.

"You do not wear the garb of the dark caste, nor do you have the black dagger painted upon your brow."

"I am not an Assassin," I said.

"Grunt is a peculiar fellow, and secretive, but, I think, inoffensive."

"I do not wish him harm," I said. "And I thank you for your help."

"Are you on foot?" asked the man.

"Yes," I said. I had sold my tarn two days ago and begun to make my way northward on foot. The Kurii from whom we had obtained the story hide must, in turn, have obtained it from an operative somewhere in this area. I thought to attract less attention on foot than as a tarnsman.

"If you wish to contact Grunt, I advise you to do so

promptly. It is En'Kara, and he will soon be entering the Barrens."

I attempted to press a tarsk bit into his hand, but he pushed it back.

"I have done nothing," he smiled.

"My thanks," I said. I turned to go.

"Fellow," said he.

"Yes?" I said, turning again to face him.

"A slave wagon is leaving on the north road at noon," he said. "It could take you as far as Fort Haskins."

"My thanks!" I said.

"It is nothing," he said.

I glanced again at the two blond slave girls. I glanced first at the one kneeling by the wall, her wrists bound to the ring behind her. In her bonds, she had learned she was a woman. It is difficult for a woman, stripped and bound, and owned by a man, not to be aware of her femininity. These symbols of, and expressions of, nature, are not hard to read. She understands them, and fully and well. I glanced then to the other girl, she lying by the wall, looking at me, the chain on her neck. Her psychophysiological distress, that of a slave girl, was clearly almost intolerable. Perhaps her master would give her to one of his attendants for the night. The desperation of her needs might then, for a time, be assuaged, until, in a few Ahn, irresistibly and compellingly, they would again arise within her. I glanced then again to the first girl. I smiled. She, too, once properly branded and collared, would come to know such needs. She, too, internally and subjectively, would come to know what it was, fully, to be a female slave.

"I wish you well," I said to the man.

"I wish you well," he said.

I then turned, and left.

4

WE SEE SMOKE;

WE ENCOUNTER SOLDIERS

I thrust my shoulder against the giant wooden wheel of the slave wagon.

I heard, ahead, the crying out of the driver, the snapping of his long whip over the backs of the two draft tharlarion harnessed to the wagon. "Pull, lazy beasts!" he cried.

Knee deep in the mire I thrust, slipping, against the thick wooden wheel.

The wheel moved and the wagon, groaning, creaking, lurched upward and rolled forward.

I waded about the wagon and then attained the graveled surface and, running, caught up with the wagon, and drew myself up to the wagon box, beside the driver.

"Why do you wish to find Grunt?" asked the driver, a young man with shaggy hair, cut short across the base of his neck.

"I am searching for something which may be in the Barrens," I said.

"Stay out of them," warned the young man. "It can be death to enter them."

"Grunt comes and goes, as I understand it," I said.

"Some, merchants and traders, are permitted, by some of the tribes," said the young man.

"Of all," I said, "I have heard that he is most welcome in the Barrens, and travels furthest within them."

"That may be true," said the fellow.

"Why is that, I wonder," I said.

"He speaks some Dust Leg, and some of the talk of other tribes," said the fellow. "Too, he knows sign."

"Sign?" I asked.

"Hand talk," said the young man. "It is the way the red savages of different tribes communicate among one another. They cannot speak one another's languages, you know."

"I would suppose not," I admitted.

Hand sign, I suspected, was the key to the capacity of the tribes to unite and protect their territories against outside encroachment, that and what they called the Memory.

"Various traders, I suspect, know Hand Sign," I said.

"Several," said the young man.

"But, too, he knows some of the tribal languages," I said.

"Not so much," said the young man. "A few words and phrases. The savages come sometimes to the trading points. We learn something of one another's talk. Not much."

"Communication is largely conducted in Sign, then," I said.

"Yes," said the young man. He stood then and cracked the whip again over the backs of the tharlarion. Then, again, he sat down.

"If various traders know Sign and some, too, have some smattering of some of these languages, what makes Grunt so special? Why is it he alone who is permitted to venture so deeply into the Barrens?"

"Perhaps the savages feel they have nothing more to gain from Grunt," laughed the young man.

"I do not understand," I said.

"You will," he said.

"Can we see the boundary from here?" I asked. We were now at the crest of a hill.

"Not clearly, but it is out there," he said, pointing to our right. "See," he asked, "the low hills, the grassy hills, at the horizon?"

"Yes," I said.

"They are on the other side of the boundary," he said.

"When do we arrive at Fort Haskins?" I asked him.

"Tomorrow morning," he said. "We will camp tonight."

"Master," said a soft, feminine voice, from behind us, timidly, "may a lowly slave speak?"

"Yes," said the young man.

The wagon carried ten girls. The common Gorean slave

wagon has a long bed, surmounted with a rectangular frame, usually covered with blue-and-yellow canvas. A long, solid, heavy metal bar, hinged near the front, and locked in place at the rear, runs the length of the bed. The girls enter the wagon at the rear, crawling, their ankles chained, the bar between their legs. When the bar is locked in place their ankles, thus, are chained about it. This arrangement, while providing perfect security, permits them considerable latitude of movement. They may, for example, sit, or kneel or lie in the wagon bed, confined only by the chaining on their ankles. Here, however, near the perimeter, such luxuries were seldom available. The wagon on which I rode had, obviously, originally been intended for the transportation of sleen. It was little more than a sleen cage, of heavy, wooden poles, lashed together, its rear gate fastened with a chain and padlock, set on a flat wagon bed. Because of the nature of the cage the girls imprisoned within it were bound hand and foot.

"Our bonds are cruelly tight, Masters," said the girl. "We beg that they may be loosened, if only slightly."

The young man turned about, angrily, on the wagon box, and regarded the girl, who shrank back, on her knees, bound hand and foot, behind the bars.

"Be silent, Slave Girl," he said.

"Yes, Master!" she said.

"Rejoice that I do not stop the wagon and haul you out, each of you, and give you ten lashes apiece," he said.

"Yes, Master!" said the girl, struggling to move back on her knees from the bars.

"Yes, Master. Yes, Master!" said several of the other girls.

The young man then turned about, and gave his attention to the road and the tharlarion.

I smiled. The men of the perimeter do not pamper their slaves. Indeed, not even a blanket had been thrown into the wagon bed to soften the blows of the springless cart, or to shield the flesh of the bound beauties from the splintery roughness of the sturdy planks on which they rode. It is common, of course, both in civilized areas and along the perimeter, to transport female slaves nude.

"It is interesting," I said, "that you do not have an armed escort."

"You are not a highwayman, are you?" he asked.

"No," I said.

"Women are generally cheap along the perimeter," he said.

"Why should this be?" I asked. That seemed to me surprising.

"The perimeter has been stable for over a century," he said. "Accordingly women are generally no more scarce here than elsewhere."

"But why should they be cheap?" I asked.

"The savages," he said. "They raid in the south and sell in the north. They raid in the north and sell in the south."

I nodded. The perimeter was thousands of pasangs long. There were various outlying farms, and many settlements and villages.

"Do they sell all the items garnered in their flesh harvests?" I asked.

"No," he said. "They take some with them, back into the Barrens."

"What do they do with them there?" I asked.

"I do not know," laughed the young man. "Doubtless they put them to good use."

"Doubtless," I agreed. The red savages, I had no doubt, could find many useful employments for helpless, white female slaves.

"At what time tomorrow morning should we arrive at Fort Haskins?" I asked.

"I am scheduled to deliver my freight to Brint, the Slaver, at half past the ninth Ahn," he said. "You may, of course, wish to leave the wagon before that."

I nodded. It would be pointless to stay longer than necessary with the wagon. I would stay with it until it reached its destination only if that destination lay on the road to Kailiauk.

"What is to be done with these slaves?" I asked. "Are they to be sold in Fort Haskins?"

"I think they are to be shipped west over the Boswell Pass," he said, "to Thentis and, from thence, to be distributed to western markets."

"They had better be given something to wear," I said, "if they are to be carried over the pass."

"They will be tied in hides," said the young man. "Because the trading hides are cheap in places like Fort Haskins and Kailiauk."

"There is another reason, a recent reason, why girls are so cheap in this area," said the young man.

"What is that?" I asked.

"Barbarians," he said.

"Barbarians?" I asked.

"Yes," he said, "unskilled, untrained, raw, luscious little beasts, many of whom can speak almost no Gorean."

"Where do they come from?" I asked.

"I do not know," he said. "The source for their delivery seems to be somewhere in the vicinity of Kailiauk. They are not good for the market."

This information intrigued me. The delivery points for slavers in league with Kurii shifted about on the surface of Gor. This practice, doubtless, was intended to aid them to elude detection by Priest-Kings.

"Are these barbarians commonly shipped west over the Boswell Pass?" I asked.

"Almost never," said the young man. "They are generally taken south and, apparently, transported over the southern passes."

This new information confirmed my suspicions that these girls were indeed the fruits of slaving on Earth. If they were transported over the Boswell Pass they might, eventually, come to the attention of Clark of Thentis, a slaver of Thentis, who had rendered services to Priest-Kings.

"Interesting," I said. The vicinity of Kailiauk, with its nearness to the Barrens, seemed a remote and useful place for a delivery point. Too, this might explain how the story hide might have come to the attention of Kurii. They might have an agent in Kailiauk, or in its vicinity.

"It is said that such barbarians, properly tamed and trained, make excellent slaves," said the young man.

"I am glad to hear that," I said.

"But I would not want to own one," said the young man.

"Have you ever owned one?" I asked.

"No," he said.

"Then you should not speak so soon," I said.

"That is true," he said, laughing.

I myself thought the young man did not know what he was missing. Earth girls, brought to Gor after years of sexual starvation on Earth, finding themselves suddenly subjected to total masculine domination, finding themselves absolute slaves, even to the market and the whip, the brand and the collar, the touch of an insolent master, finding themselves given no choice but to release and manifest their deepest and most beautiful, most profound, most hitherto hidden female nature, often made the most grateful, rapturous and perfect of slaves.

"Still," said the young man, "they are not good for the market."

"That may be true," I said. It seemed to me not unlikely that an influx of barbarian females, in a given area, at a given time, might depress prices. To be sure, the slavers in league with the Kurii usually distributed these girls throughout various markets. This made the females more difficult to trace back to their delivery points and, of course, tended, on the whole, to improve the prices one could receive for them.

"It will soon be time to camp," said the young man.

"The slaves, I trust," I said, jerking my head back toward the lovely, bound inmates of the wagon, "are on their slave wine."

"Yes," laughed the young man.

"Please, Master," begged the girl who had spoken earlier to the young man, "when we camp, tie my neck to a tree and untie my ankles. I desire to serve you."

"No, I!" cried another girl. "I!" cried another.

The young man laughed. He saw the girls desired to placate him. But, too, of course, to be honest, he was a handsome fellow, and they were bound female slaves. Carting such freight about does not pay high wages but there are fringe benefits connected with such work. If the girls are not virgins such a teamster commonly has his pick of the load.

"My neck, too, can be tied to a tree and my ankles, too, can be untied, Master," said another of the girls, addressing me. She was a luscious blonde. I slapped the wood of the wagon box with pleasure.

"Look!" said the young man, suddenly, pointing to our right. "Smoke!" Amost at the same moment he rose to his feet and cracked his long whip over the backs of the tharlarion. Grunting, they increased their lumbering pace. Twice more he cracked his whip. The girls in the back were suddenly quiet. I gripped the edge of the wagon box. To our right, in a long, sloping valley, some two or three pasangs from the road, there were three narrow, slowly ascending columns of smoke.

"Faster! Har-ta!" cried the young man to the tharlarion.

"Surely we must stop," I said. "Perhaps we can render assistance."

"It is too late," he said, "by the time you can see the smoke. Everyone there, by now, would be dead, or taken."

One of the girls in the back cried out in fear. Naked, bound slaves, they were absolutely helpless.

"Nonetheless," I said, "I must make inquiries."

"You will do so then by yourself," said the young man.

"Agreed," I said. "Stop the wagon."

"Riders!" said the young man. Ahead, on the road, there was a rolling cloud of dust. He jerked the tharlarion back. Grunting they scratched at the gravel of the road. They tossed their snouts in the nose straps. The young man looked wildly about. He could not turn the wagon on the narrow road. The girls screamed, squirming in their bonds.

"They are soldiers," I said. I stood on the wagon box, shading my eyes.

"Thank the Priest-Kings!" cried the young man.

In moments a troop of soldiers, lancers and crossbowmen, mounted on kaiila, reined up about us. They wore the colors of Thentis. They were covered with dust. Their uniforms were black with sweat and dirt. The flanks of their prancing kaiila were lathered with foam. They snorted and, throwing back their heads, sucked air into their lungs. Their third lids, the transparent storm membranes, were drawn, giving their wild, round eyes a yellowish cast.

"Dust Legs," said the officer with the men. "The road is closed. Whither are you bound?"

"Fort Haskins," said the young man.

"You cannot remain here, and it would be dangerous to go back," said the officer. "I think you are best advised to proceed to Fort Haskins as quickly as possible."

"I shall do so," said the young man.

"It is unusual, is it not, for the Dust Legs to be on the rampage?" I asked. I had understood them to be one of the more peaceful of the tribes of the Barrens. Indeed, they often acted as intermediaries between the men of the settlements and the wilder tribes of the interior, such as the Yellow Knives, the Sleen and Kaiila.

"Who are you?" asked the officer.

"A traveler," I said.

"We do not know what has stirred them up," said the officer. "They have taken no life. They have only burned farms, and taken kaiila."

"It is perhaps a warning, of some sort," I said.

"It would seem so," said the officer. "They did not, for example, attack at dawn. They came openly, did their work unhurriedly, and withdrew."

"It is very mysterious," I said.

"They are a peaceful folk," said the officer, "but I would be on my way, and with dispatch. Sleen or Kaiila may be behind them."

One of the girls in the back whimpered in terror.

The officer, slowly, rode around the wagon, looking through the wooden bars at our bound cargo. The girls shrank back under his gaze, bound, inspected slaves.

"I would be on my way as soon as possible," said the officer. "I would not expect even Dust Legs to resist this cargo."

"Yes, Captain!" said the young man. The officer took his mount to the side and the soldiers, too, drew their kaiila to one side or the other. The young man then stood up, shaking the reins with one hand and cracking the whip with the other. "Move, move, you beasts!" he cried. The tharlarion lumbered into motion and the slack was taken up in the traces, and the wagon, creaking, lurched ahead. The girls were as quiet as tiny, silken field urts in the presence of forest panthers, being conducted in their cage between the ranks of the soldiers.

In a few Ehn we were more than a pasang down the road. It was lonely, and dark.

There was whimpering, and sobbing, behind us.

"The slaves are terrified," I said.

"We shall not camp," said the young man. "We shall press on through the night. I shall stop only, from time to time, to rest the tharlarion."

"That is wise," I said.

"It is not like the Dust Legs," he said.

"That, too, would be my understanding of the matter," I said.

5

I THROW STONES ON
THE ROAD TO KAILIAUK

I stepped aside, to the side of the road. It had rained early this morning. The road was still muddy. The men, some afoot, some on kaiila, with the clank of weapons and the rattle of accouterments, filed past me. I looked into the eyes of some of them. They were mercenaries. Yet they belonged to no mercenary company I recognized. Doubtless they had been hired here and there. They wore various uniforms, and parts of uniforms, and carried an assortment of weapons. Some of them, I suspected, might even be men without a Home Stone. They were moving northward, as I was. They, like I, I speculated, were bound for Kailiauk. I took it there were about a thousand of them. This was unusually large for a Gorean mercenary force. It would require a considerable amount of money to hire and sustain such a force.

In the center of the road, approaching, between, and with, the lines, drawn by two tharlarion, was an ornately carved, high, two-wheeled cart. An officer, a bearded fellow with a plumed cap, perhaps the captain of the mercenary company, rode beside this cart. On a curule chair, fixed on the high cart, under a silken canopy, proud and graceful, bedecked with finery, garbed in the ornate Robes of Concealment, veiled, sat a woman. Chained by the neck to the side of the cart, clad in rags, was a red youth.

"Hold!" said the woman, lifting her small, white-gloved hand as the cart drew near to me.

"Hold!" called the officer, turning his kaiila and lifting his hand.

"Hold! Hold!" called other officers.

The lines stopped. The woman lowered her hand.

She regarded me. "Tal," she said.

"Tal, Lady," said I to her.

With one hand, nonchalantly, she freed her outer veil. Her features, then, were concealed but poorly by the second veil, little more than a wisp of diaphanous silk. She did this, apparently, that she might speak to me more easily. She smiled. I, too, smiled, but inwardly. A master might have given such a veil to a slave, as a joke. She was a vain woman. She wished me to see that she was stunningly beautiful. I saw that she might make an acceptable slave.

"I see that you carry a sword," she said.

"Yes, Lady," said I.

"Who are you?" she asked.

"A traveler, a swordsman," I said.

"This is the Lady Mira, of Venna," said the bearded officer. "I am Alfred, captain of this company, mercenary of Port Olni." Venna is a resort town west of the Voltai, north of Ar. Port Olni is located on the north bank of the Olni River. It is a member of the Salerian Confederation.

"Apparently you do not wish to reveal your name," said the woman.

"The name of a lowly fellow, such as myself," I said, "could surely be of no interest to so fine a lady."

"Are you a bandit?" she asked.

"No, Lady," said I.

"Can you use the blade hung at your hip?" she asked.

"After a fashion, Lady," I said.

"We are hiring swords," she said.

"My thanks, Lady," I said. "I do not wish to take fee."

"Draw your weapon," said the officer.

I drew the blade quickly, smoothly, and stepped back. When a Gorean tells you to draw your blade, it is generally not wise to spend a great deal of time discussing the matter. He may have something in mind.

"Attack him," said the officer to one of the men nearby.

Our blades had not crossed twice before the point of my sword was at the fellow's throat.

"Do not kill him," said the officer hastily.

I resheathed my blade and the fellow, white-faced, backed away.

"A silver tarsk a month," said the officer. This was a handsome sum. I was sure it was more than most of the men about me were receiving.

"Whither are you bound, Captain," I asked, "and on what business!"

"We are going to Kailiauk, and are then going to enter the Barrens," he said. "There are tribes to be subdued."

"I do not understand," I said.

"Surely you have heard of the depredations which took place yesterday?" he asked.

"Your forces were surely assembled before yesterday," I said.

He laughed. I supposed such forces might indeed enter the Barrens and wreak some havoc, perhaps falling upon some Dust-Leg villages. Too often it seems it is the peaceful and innocent who are slaughtered. In this a lesson may be found that it may not be prudential to be either too peaceful or too innocent. One does not survive with wolves by becoming a sheep. That is only a short-cut to destruction.

"There are thousands of savages in the Barrens," I said.

"These men are professionals," he said. "One such mercenary is worth a thousand half-naked savages."

I heard laughter about me.

"They will flee," he said, "at the very sound of our drums."

I said nothing.

"Too long has the perimeter held," he said. "We shall advance it, to the east. The banners of civilization are in our grasp."

I smiled. I wondered if barbarisms were civilizations which were not one's own.

"Are you going to take a woman into the Barrens?" I asked. "Surely you can surmise what the red savages would do with such a woman?"

"I am perfectly safe, I assure you," laughed the Lady Mira. I wondered what she would feel like if she found herself naked and bound with rawhide, lying at the feet of lustful warriors.

"The Lady Mira is of the Merchants," said the officer. "She has been empowered to negotiate hide contracts with the conquered tribes."

"Who is this?" I asked, indicating the red youth, in rags, chained by the neck to the side of the cart.

"Urt, a Dust Leg, a slave," said the officer. "We purchased him in the south. He can speak with Dust Legs, and knows sign."

The boy looked at me, with hatred.

"How long was he a slave?" I asked.

"Two years," said the officer.

"From whom was he originally purchased?" I asked.

"Dust Legs," said the officer.

"It seems unlikely they would sell one of their own tribe," I said.

"They are savages," said the officer.

"You are not a Dust Leg," I said to the boy.

He did not respond to me.

"You will trust your translations to such a fellow?" I asked.

"Our clearest speech," said the officer, "will be with steel."

"You have many men," I said. "Your expedition must be very expensive. Had it been mounted by several cities I think I would have heard of it. Whence comes the gold for these numerous and manifold fees?"

The officer looked at me, angrily.

"We are sustained by the merchant council of Port Olni," said the woman. "Our papers are in order."

"I see," I said.

"Seldom," said the officer, "have I seen steel move as swiftly, as deceptively, as yours. My offer stands. Rations and a silver tarsk, one for each month of service."

"Rations, and a golden tarsk," said the woman, looking down at me. Over her veil of light silk her eyes shone. She had made the offer without consulting the officer. She had obviously much authority and power. I wondered what she would look like, if reduced to helpless bondage.

"My thanks, Lady," I said. "But I am in my own service."

"A position might be found for you, even in my intimate retinue," she said.

"I am in my own service," I said.

"Move on!" she called, lifting her gloved hand, and sitting angrily back in the curule chair.

I stepped to the side of the road.

"Forward!" called the officer, lifting his arm. The lady looked at me, angrily, her gloved hands now clutching the

arms of the curule chair. Then she lifted her head and looked
directly ahead. "Ho!" called the officer. His arm fell. The
lines of mercenaries then moved forward, with the wagon in
their midst, northward, toward Kailiauk. I withdrew to the
side and sat in some shadows, among rocks, to observe the
lines. I estimated the number of men, and, carefully, counted
the supply wagons. My conjectures were warranted. Considering the game presumably available in the Barrens there were
several more wagons in the lines than would have seemed
called for.

When the lines and wagons had passed I emerged from
the rocks and, at a distance, followed them toward Kailiauk.

The merchants of Port Olni, of course, would not be sus-
taining the enormous expense of such an expedition. They
were not intimately involved in the hide traffic and, if they
had been, as merchants, their procedures, initially, at any rate,
would have been mercantile and not military. They would
surely have tried, at least in the beginning, to work through
local traders or, say, Dust Legs themselves. I had, in my
mind, no doubt as to what source on Gor had both the motivation and resources to mount such an expedition. Similarly
I had little doubt as to who were the occupants of certain of
the closed wagons in the lines.

On the road to Kailiauk I threw back my head and
laughed heartily. I, Tarl Cabot, had been approached by
agents of Kurii, and asked to take fee! I had little doubt that
Kog and Sardak, and others like them, scratched impatiently,
and twisted, uncomfortably, anxious to get on with their
work, in wagons ahead of me. Such close confinements, vol-
untary and self-imposed, would surely be almost intolerable
for them. I admired their discipline. I hoped that it would
hold out. It was nice to know where they were.

I bent down and picked up a rock, and tossed it ahead of
me, down the road. Then I continued on again, toward Kailiauk.

One additional thing I had noted about the forces ahead of
me. There had been no slave wagons in the lines, nor,
chained in throat coffle, trudging in the dust behind the supply wagons, any slave girls. That I took to be the doing, and
a tribute to the power, of the Lady Mira of Venna. As a free
woman she doubtless hated slave girls, the lascivious, shameless sluts who drove men wild with such desire for them.
Too, doubtless it pleased her vanity to be the only woman

among so many men. I had seen her features, concealed by
only a wisp of silk. I wondered what she might look like in
dancing silk and a steel collar, perhaps kneeling before me,
the shadow of my whip falling across her body. I thought
then she might not seem so proud, not as a humbled, owned
slave. The Kurii, I granted them, almost always chose female
agents of incredible beauty. This is so, I gather, that when
they have served their serious purposes, there is always something else that may be done with them.

I spun another rock down the road, after the lines and
wagons.

I should not have demonstrated the skill with the sword
that I had, I supposed. Indeed, I had resolved, as a part of a
disguise, to pretend to only modest skill with the weapon,
unless it proved necessary to do otherwise. As soon as the
two blades had touched, however, I had seen what could be
done, and had done it. The matter was reflexive as much, or
more, than rational. The steel, as is often the case, had
seemed to think for itself. But I did not regret what I had
done. I chuckled. Let them see, said I to myself, the skill of
one who had once trained in the martial courts of Ko-ro-ba. I
laughed. I wondered what these agents of Kurii would think
if they had known that Tarl Cabot had been in their midst.
But they would have no reason to suppose him in the vicinity
of the Barrens. They would know only that they had encountered one who, obviously, was not unaccustomed to steel.

Once again I thought of the Lady Mira of Venna. Yes, I
thought, she would look well, like any other beautiful
woman, stripped and collared, crawling to the feet of a man.

6

KAILIAUK

I looked down into the broad, rounded, shallow pit, leaning over the waist-high wooden railing. In the pit, about five feet below the surface of the ground, there were nineteen girls. They wore wrist and ankle shackles, their wrists having some six inches of play and their ankles some twelve inches of play. They were also chained together by the neck. None of them stood, for such a girl, in such a pit, is not permitted to stand, unless given an express order to do so. The pit was muddy, for it had rained in the morning. They looked up, some of them who dared to do so, at the men looking down at them, from about the circular railing, assessing their quali- ties as females. Did they look into the eyes of their future masters? They had not yet even been branded.

"Barbarians," said the fellow next to me.

"Clearly," I said.

"There are two other pits," said the fellow. "Did you see them?"

"Yes," I said. "I have already perused their contents." It is pleasant to see naked, chained women, either slaves or those soon to be slaves.

I had spent a night on the road and had arrived in Kail- iauk, hungry and muddy, yesterday, shortly after the tenth Ahn, the Gorean noon. Indeed, I had heard the striking of the time bar, mounted on the roof of the Administrator's store, as I had approached the town's outskirts. In Kailiauk, as is not unusual in the towns of the perimeter, the Adminis- trator is of the Merchants. The major business in Kailiauk is the traffic in hides and kaiila. It serves a function as well, however, as do many such towns, as a social and commercial center for many outlying farms and ranches. It is a bustling town, but much of its population is itinerant. Among its permanent citizens I doubt that it numbers more than four or five hundred individuals. As would be expected it has several inns and taverns aligned along its central street.

Its most notable feature, probably, is its hide sheds. Under the roofs of these open sheds, on platforms, tied in bundles, are thousands of hides. Elsewhere, here and there, about the town, are great heaps of bone and horn, often thirty or more feet in height. These deposits represent the results of the thinnings of kailiauk herds by the red savages. A most common sight in Kailiauk is the coming and going of hide wagons, and wagons for the transport of horn and bones. The number of kailiauk in the Barrens is prodigious, for it affords them a splendid environment with almost no natural enemies. Most kailiauk, I am sure, have never seen a man or a sleen.

The Barrens are traversed by a large number of herds. The four or five best-known herds, such as the Boswell herd, he for whom the Boswell Pass is named, and the Bento herd and the Hogarthe herd, named after the first white men who saw them, number, it is estimated, between two and three million beasts. The tremors in the earth from such a herd can be felt fifty pasangs away. It takes such a herd two to three days to ford a river. It has occasionally happened that enemy tribes have preyed on such a herd at different points and only afterwards, to their chagrin and amusement, realized their proximity to one another. Besides these major herds there are several smaller, identifiable herds numbering in the hundreds of thousands of animals. Beyond these, as would be expected, there are many smaller herds, the very numbers of which are not even calculated by the red savages themselves, herds which often range from a few hundred to several thousand animals.

It is speculated that some of these smaller herds may be subherds of larger herds, separating from the major herd at certain points during the season, depending on such conditions as forage and water. If that is the case then the number of kailiauk may not be quite as large as it is sometimes estimated. On the other hand, that their numbers are incredibly abundant is indubitable. These herds, too, interestingly enough, appear to have their annual grazing patterns, usually describing a gigantic oval, seasonally influenced, which covers many thousands of pasangs. These peregrinations, as would be expected, tend to take a herd in and out of the territory of given tribes at given times. The same herd, thus, may be hunted by various tribes without necessitating dangerous departures from their own countries.

The kailiauk is a migratory beast, thusly, but only in a rather special sense. It does not, for example, like certain flocks of birds, venture annually in roughly linear paths from the north to the south, and from the south to the north, covering thousands of pasangs in a series of orthogonal alternations. The kailiauk must feed as it moves, and it is simply too slow for this type of migration. It could not cover the distances involved in the times that would be necessary. Accordingly the herds tend not so much to migrate with the seasons as to drift with them, the ovoid grazing patterns tending to bend northward in the summer and southward in the winter. The smell of the hide sheds, incidentally, gives a very special aroma to the atmosphere of Kailiauk. After one has been there for a few hours, however, the odor of the hides, now familiar and pervasive, tends to be dismissed from consciousness.

"Some of them are quite pretty," said the fellow next to me, looking down into the pit, his elbows on the railing.

"Yes," I said. We stood within the compound of Ram Seibar, a dealer in slaves. It is a reasonably large compound, for he also handles kaiila. It is, I would estimate, something over three hundred feet square, or, say, a bit less than a tenth of a pasang square. It contains several slave pits but only three were now occupied. It also contains several larger and smaller wooden structures, primarily holding areas, barracks for men and various ancillary buildings. The entire compound is enclosed by a wooden palisade. On the largest building, the main sales barn, about seventy feet wide and a hundred and twenty feet in length, there flies the pennon of Seibar, a yellow pennon on which, in black, are portrayed shackles and a whip.

"Do you know Grunt, the trader?" I asked the fellow.

"Yes," said he.

"Is he in the vicinity?" I asked.

"I do not know," said the man.

I had sought this fellow in the various inns and taverns of Kailiauk. I could find no one who seemed to know of his whereabouts. Indeed, I had begun to despair of finding him.

This morning, at the Five Horns stables, in Kailiauk, I had bought two kaiila. Bridles, a saddle, various sorts of gear, supplies, and trading goods, too, I had purchased in the town, at the store of Publius Crassus, of the Merchants, who is also Kailiauk's Administrator. Too I had purchased a short bow, modeled on the sort used by the savages, fit for clearing the saddle, and a quiver of twenty sheaf arrows.

In my opinion one of the mistakes of the white cavalries of the perimeter areas was their reliance on the crossbow, which is primarily an infantry weapon. It does, of course, have various advantages. It has considerable striking power, it may be kept ready to fire almost indefinitely, and, for most men, it is easier to fire with accuracy from the saddle than the straight bow. It will also, at short ranges, penetrate most of the hide shields used by the red savages.

Its major disadvantage is its slowness in rate of fire. The cavalry crossbow does have an iron stirrup in which the rider, without dismounting, may insert his foot, thus gaining the leverage necessary for drawing the cable back with both hands. If the rider is right handed he usually inserts his right foot in the stirrup and leans to the right in drawing the cable; this procedure is reversed, of course, usually, if the rider is left handed. While this procedure permits the rider to reload without dismounting and tends to improve, at some cost to striking power, the bow's rate of fire, it still provides, in my opinion, no adequate compensation for the loss of rapidity of fire. I think it not unlikely that the red savage could discharge three to five shafts in the time a single quarrel could be set in the clumsier weapon. In my opinion, if the crossbow, of the lighter, more quickly loading type, had proved to be a superior missile weapon in the typical combats practiced in the Barrens the red savages would have had recourse either to it, or to something analogous to it. But they have not.

I opted, accordingly, taking them for my authorities in the matter, for a weapon similar in design to theirs, one which had, apparently, proven its usefulness in the abrupt, sudden and fierce engagements characteristic of war on the vast grasslands of the Barrens. Unable to find Grunt, I feared I must enter the Barrens alone. Already, early this morning, the Lady Mira of Venna, and Alfred of Port Olni, with their mercenaries, had left Kailiauk.

The fellow leaning on the rail turned to look at me. "Why do you wish to find Grunt?" he asked.

"I wish to enter the Barrens," I said.

"It is madness to do so," said he.

I shrugged.

"It is unfortunate you did not come to Kailiauk a month ago," he said.

"Why is that?" I asked.

"Settlers, armed, with two hundred wagons, crossed the Ihanke," he said. "Men, women, children. There must have been seven or eight hundred of them. You could have accompanied them. There is perhaps safety in such numbers."

"Perhaps," I said. Such a party, however, I knew must travel slowly. Also, it would be impossible to conceal its trails and movements.

"You are a big fellow," he said, "and seem quick, and strong. Why did you not sign articles with the troops who left this morning?"

I did not respond to him.

"It was the largest mercenary band ever to leave Kailiauk," he said. "You should have gone with them."

"Perhaps," I said.

"I'm chained! I'm chained!" wept one of the girls in the pit below. She knelt, nude, in the mud. With her small hands, her tiny wrists in their close-fitting manacles, she seized the chain attached to the collar on her neck. She jerked it twice against the back of her neck. It cut at the back of her neck. "I'm chained," she wept, disbelievingly. "Where am I? What has become of me? Where are my clothes? Who are these men? How is it that they dare to look at me? In what place do I find myself?"

"They cannot even speak Gorean," said the man beside me.

"Barbarians," I said.

"Yes," he said. The girl had spoken in English. This had confirmed my surmise as to their origin. I had come to Seibar's market out of curiosity. I had heard he was the major dealer in Kailiauk for barbarian slaves. I did not know, but I suspected that he himself was not in league with Kurii, but merely purchased wholesale lots of such girls from one or more of their agents. Such girls, I gathered, from my conversations with the teamster with whom I had ridden to Fort Haskins, were sold at various points along the perimeter. I had, earlier in the afternoon, on one of my purchased kaiila, scouted the terrain north and south of Kailiauk. In my ride I had come to one place, sheltered among small hills, in which I had found scorched grass and several, rounded six-inch-deep impressions in the earth. It had been there, I speculated, that one of the steel ships of the Kurii had landed. Also there were wagon tracks leading away from the area, toward Kailiauk. I was less fortunate, at various small camps and outlying farms, in obtaining information as to the possible whereabouts of a white trader named Grunt. I did not approach the Ihanke, nor did I wish to do so, if possible, until I knew exactly what I was doing. I did not know, for example, even if it were guarded or not.

"Even if such girls understood Gorean," said the fellow next to me, amused, "they could probably not even understand what was required of them. They probably do not even know the hundred kisses."

"They could be taught," I said.

"That is so," he laughed.

"Stand aside, Gentlemen, if you would," said a voice near us, that of a slaver's man.

We stepped back and he, from a basket, hurled an assortment of scraps, such as crusts of bread and rinds of fruit, into the muddy pit. It was the refuse, the garbage, I gathered, from a meal of the slaver's men.

In the pit the girls regarded the refuse with horror. Then I saw the small, chained hand of one reach forth toward a piece of roll. She picked it up and thrust it in her mouth. Another girl then reached to a bit of fruit. Another then snatched at a gravy-sopped wedge of yellow Sa-Tarna bread. Then, in an instant, in their chains, they scrambled in the mud after the garbage, twisting and shrieking, caught and restricted in their chains, scratching, and rolling and fighting, for the least of the tidbits cast to them by a free man.

"They are slaves," said the man near me, as we returned to the railing.

"Yes," I said. Too, I saw that their education had begun.

"There is better stock inside, I hear," said the man, "hidden away until the time of the sale, some even in the barbarian garments in which they were captured."

"That is interesting," I said.

"But they, too," said the man, "will learn to take food on their belly."

"Of course," I said. Then I turned away from the railing. I was angry that I had not been able to locate Grunt, the trader. In the morning, with or without him, I would enter the Barrens.

7

GINGER

"Barbarians! Barbarians for sale!" called the fellow, standing on the circular wooden platform, outside the opened gate of the large, palisaded enclosure.

From within I saw a nude woman, her hands tied behind her back, being dragged forth, each arm in the charge of a slaver's man.

"Barbarians for sale!" called the fellow on the platform. He was a gross, corpulent fellow, and wore a long, opened, soiled shirt of blue-and-yellow silk. His leather trousers were fastened with a wide, triply buckled belt. To this belt was fastened a substantial, beaded sheath, apparently containing a stout, triangular-bladed dagger. He wore, too, kaiila boots, with belled, silver heel points, kaiila goads. In his hand there was a long, supple kaiila quirt of black leather, about a yard in length. His hair was bound back with strands of twisted, blue-and-yellow cloth. His caste, even in the town of Kailiauk, was that of the slavers.

The woman, her hands tied behind her, each arm in the rude grasp of a slaver's man, was thrust to the height of the platform, beside the corpulent fellow.

"In addition to our usual stock of fine merchandise," called the corpulent fellow, "we have just received a new lot of barbarians!"

These would be the same girls of whom I had seen several this afternoon, in the slave pits within the compound. I had come again, in the evening, after supper, to the compound of Ram Seibar. I thought I might look in on some of the sales.

Afterwards I might go to a tavern, to have a cup of paga and see if I could rent a girl to take to my room for the night, to return her in the morning.

"They have not yet been picked over," said the man. "This little plum, juicy with pleasures for a master," he said, indicating the girl on the platform with him, with a gesture of his kaiila quirt, "is one of the sorriest of the lot." This, in my opinion, was not true. I thought she would have ranked rather high among the girls. To be sure, the most luscious merchandise, presumably to be sold rather late in the evening, had probably not even been put in the pits.

"Display her, Lads," said the fellow. The two slaver's men thrust the woman forward, toward the crowd, and bent her backwards. She whimpered.

"And this is one of the worst of the lot," said the fellow. The two slaver's men turned the woman first to one side, and then to the other. "Meat so fresh that it has not yet even been marked!" said the fellow. "That is enough, Lads," he said. They then turned the woman about and dragged her down the steps and back into the compound. "If you would see more," said the man to those of us gathered about, about the outdoor platform, "you must come within. Within you may buy her, and others like her, from the side blocks. Too, even more luscious merchandise you may seek from the central block in open bidding!" I wondered if the woman knew that she was, in all likelihood, to be soon branded. In most Gorean cities it is illegal to offer an unbranded woman in a public sale. This is presumably in deference to the delicacy and sensibilities of free women. The brand draws a cataclysmic gulf between the Gorean free woman, secure in her arrogance, beauty and caste rights, and the stripped, nameless, rightless slaves, suitably vended as the mere lovely beasts they are in the flesh markets of this primitive, gorgeous world. Unbranded women, of course, may be sold privately, for example, as fresh captures to slavers or, say, to men who have speculated that they might find them of interest.

"Barbarians! Barbarians for sale!" now continued to call the fellow on the wooden platform outside the gate to the compound of Ram Seibar. "In addition to our usual stocks of fine merchandise, we have just received a new lot of barbarians. They have not yet been picked over. They will be put up for sale within the Ahn. Step within, Noble Gentlemen, and examine our offerings. Patronize the house of Ram Seibar! Free drinks! No purchase necessary!"

I felt a small tugging at my sleeve, and then felt my arm delicately held. I felt a soft cheek pressed against my arm. "Master," whispered a voice. I looked down, and the girl, with loose, auburn hair, looked up. She smiled. "Accompany me to Randolph's tavern," she said. "I will give you much pleasure." About her throat, narrow, sturdy and closely fitting, was a steel collar. I stepped back, that I might see her better. She wore a short, fringed, beaded shirtdress. This came high on her thighs. It was split to her waist, well revealing the sweetness and loveliness of her breasts. It was belted upon her with a doubly looped, tightly knotted rawhide string. Such a string is more than sufficient, in its length, and in its strength and toughness, to tie a woman in a number of ways. She was barefoot. About her left ankle there was, about two inches high, a beaded cuff, or anklet. Her garb was doubtless intended to suggest the distinctive, humiliating and scandalously brief garment in which red savages are sometimes pleased to place their white slaves. One difference, however, must surely be noted. The red savages do not use steel collars. They usually use high, beaded collars, tied together in the front by a rawhide string. Subtle differences in the styles of collars, and in the knots with which they are fastened on the girls' necks, differentiate the tribes. Within a given tribe the beading, in its arrangements and colors, identifies the particular master. This is a common way, incidentally, for warriors to identify various articles which they own.

"It is my hope that Master will find Ginger pleasing," she said.

"Ginger?" I asked.

"Master?" she asked.

"Are you a barbarian?" I asked.

"Once, Master," she whispered. "But I have been trained. I am no longer a stranger to my collar."

"Watch out!" cried a man.

"Oh!" cried the girl. I seized her and pulled her from the place where she stood. Two kaiila thundered past.

"Make way!" we heard. "Make way!" There was then the thudding of the clawed pads of kaiila, several of them, almost upon us. "Ho! Ho!" called their drovers, riding behind them, swirling their coiled rawhide ropes in the air. I and the others backed against the wall of the compound of Ram Seibar. The kaiila, perhaps a hundred to a hundred and fifty of them, thundered past. I did not think such beasts should be run through the streets, but it sometimes pleases their drovers to do so. It had happened more than once since I had been in Kailiauk. The kaiila were presumably from the northern ranches and would be sold in Kailiauk, and in the towns to the south.

"It is needless for that to be done in that fashion," said a fellow near me. "There are shorter routes to the corrals and the wired pastures."

"Individuals are sometimes injured," said another man.

"The tavern girls live in terror of them," said another fellow.

I looked down at the girl in my arms. I saw that what he had said was true. This pleased me. It was fitting that slave girls lived in terror of free men.

"They do not come that often to Kailiauk," said a fellow, cheerfully.

"When they come," said another, "it is with a thirst for paga and the wenches of the taverns."

"Who can blame them?" said another.

The kaiila ranches, I supposed, were remote, desolate places. Land which is suitable for farming, and in proximity to towns, is seldom, along the perimeter, put to the uses of grazing.

"They are generally good fellows," said another man.

"They spend their money freely," added another.

"That is a point in their favor," said another.

"A point in our favor," said another.

"Some are dangerous and cruel," said another man.

"Let us hope there will be no killings," said another.

Killings among such men, hot-tempered and aflame with paga, I supposed might occur not infrequently. Too often, I suspected, a suspicion of cheating at stones or disks, or a dispute over a slave, might lead to the flash of steel, the sudden movement of a knife.

"You saved me, Master," said the girl, holding to me.

"Perhaps to some extent," I said, "I have protected the investment of your master." It is well to help a slave keep clearly in mind that she is only an article of property.

"He had me cheaply," she smiled.

"Perhaps I should not have bothered," I said.

"But I am worth more now," she said.

"Oh?" I said.

"Return with me to the tavern of Randolph," she said. "I will show you." She then pressed her body against me, closely and lasciviously, and helplessly, in the manner of the female slave, that of the woman who knows herself completely subject to the will of men. She then put her arms about my neck and, standing on her toes, lifting her lips to mine, kissed me. I then, by the arms, held her from me. "You kiss well, Slave," I told her. "Thank you, Master," she said.

"Is it true that you are a barbarian?" I asked.

"Yes, Master," she said. "I was sold, even, from the house of Ram Seibar."

"When?" I asked.

"Eighteen months ago," she said.

"You are now no stranger to your collar," I said. The kiss of a slave girl is unmistakable.

"No, Master," she said.

"The central street seemed busy tonight," I said. "I find it hard to believe that you have been sent forth to solicit business, the evening being such as it is, for the tavern of Randolph."

She looked at me, suddenly, frightened.

The fellow on the platform, at that time, began again to address the crowd. "Barbarians! Barbarians for sale!" he called. "Enter now. The sales begin in a few Ehn. Buy at the house of Ram Seibar! Barbarians for sale, cheap and pretty!"

"Solicit elsewhere," I told her.

"Please, Master," she said.

"If you do not wish to use her," said a fellow standing nearby, "do you mind my taking her?"

"Of course not," I said.

"Lead me to the tavern of Randolph," said the man to the girl.

"Master!" said the girl to me.

"Do you dawdle to obey, Slave?" inquired the man.

"No, Master," she cried, turning white, "no!"

"Precede me," he said.

"Yes, Master," she said.

"As a slave girl," he said.

"Yes, Master!" she said. With a sob she began to precede him, and as a slave girl.

"Barbarians for sale! Barbarians for sale, cheap and pretty!" called the fellow on the platform.

I then went through the gate and entered the compound of Ram Seibar.

8

GRUNT

I turned my attention from the apparently lovely young woman, though she was fully clothed, who was strung up by the wrists near the central block. Her ankles had also been crossed and bound, a slaver's trick to accentuate the sweet curvatures of her hips and legs. A thong also ran from over the bonds on her ankles to an iron ring a few inches below her feet. This tends to prevent undue movement on the rope.

A distinction must be drawn between the side blocks and the central, or main, block, in a vending area. I shall describe the situation, specifically, as it exists in the sales barn of Ram Seibar. It is not untypical of the arrangements in many such places, particularly in outlying areas. To be sure, there is, it seems, from market to market, and from city to city, an almost infinite variety of ways in which women may be, and are, displayed and sold. This is not surprising since the institution of female slavery, on Gor, is both extremely successful and quite ancient.

In the central hall of the sales barn of Ram Seibar, which is open to the public, there are twenty-one blocks. Twenty of these are subsidiary blocks, or side blocks. These occur, aligned, ten to a side, along the walls, to the left and right, as one enters. They are spaced rather evenly, in order not to suggest distinctions among them. Too, they are placed a few feet out from the walls. At one's convenience, then, one may walk entirely about them. They are about a yard high and five feet in diameter. In the center of each there is an iron ring. The central block, which must be ascended by stairs, lies at the far end of the hall as one enters, opposite the door. It is about seven or eight feet in height and some twenty feet in diameter. Girls are seldom auctioned from the side blocks. Occasionally fixed prices are set on them. If this is the case the price is usually written on their body, either with a grease pencil or a lipstick. Usually, however, of course, they find themselves being bargained for. The girl usually hopes that her master will pay enough for her to convince him that she is of at least minimal value, and will not pay so much that he will be angry with the merchant, for in such a case he is almost certain to take his dissatisfaction out on her lovely hide. "Side-block girl," in the argot of the slave girl, like "pot girl" and "kettle-and-mat girl," is a term of disparagement. It must be admitted there is more prestige in being auctioned from a major, or central, block than there is in being casually purchased from a side block. One might as well be sold off a slaver's public shelf, in a city, or out of a cage, or kneeling in the mud outside a village, from a "slaver's necklace." To be sure, a girl who is once sold off a side block may, in time, her femininity blossoming under the discipline of the whip and the harsh tutelage of masters, become a treasure, a slave so beautiful and desirable that men will pay fortunes to have her at their feet.

I wandered over to the left wall to look at some of the side blocks.

"I shall take this one," I heard a fellow say, and so simply was the girl sold. She was one of the few girls on whom Ram Seibar had set a fixed price. It was written on her back in lipstick, forty copper tarsks. She was one of the few who had been freshly branded. Her wrists were crossed and bound before her, in cruel loops of rawhide, and, by a tight loop encircling her body, cutting into her flesh, held tightly before her. This was to prevent her from tearing at the brand. Her cheeks were stained with tears. She, like the other girls on the side blocks, was fastened on her block. Uniformly they wore collars and chains, the chains some five feet in length and attached to the block rings. She saw money change hands. She knew she had been sold. She looked at her master, and shuddered. She saw that he was handsome.

When one girl was sold from a block a new one was put in her place.

"How can you sell an unbranded woman?" asked a fellow of a slaver's man, indicating a freckled, fairly complexioned, red-haired barbarian kneeling frightened on a nearby block, the palms of her hands down on the wood. The black iron of her collar, and the chain, contrasted nicely with the lightness and texture of her skin.

"Is she worth fifty tarsks to you?" asked the slaver's man.

"Yes," said the fellow, slowly.

Immediately the slaver's man removed a long piece of rawhide, about four feet in length, from his belt. He took the girl's hands behind her, and, crossing them, with one end of the rawhide, fastened them tightly together. He then looped the rawhide about her belly, jerked it tight, and tied it to her bound wrists. The girl looked behind herself, frightened, her hands fastened closely at the small of her back. With a key he opened the girl's collar and placed it, with its chain, on the block. He then seized the girl by the arms and slid her from the block, into the waiting arms of an attendant. "Fifty tarsks for this freckled, little she-tarsk," he said. "This will be the buyer," he said, indicating the fellow who had expressed an interest in the girl. The attendant nodded and, throwing the girl over his shoulder, left.

"Pick her up in ten Ehn, at the front entrance," said the slaver's man to the prospective buyer. "She will be branded."

The man nodded, and turned away.

I smiled to myself at the artifice involved in this transaction. The sale, technically, would not take place until after the young woman was branded. I watched her being carried out through a side entrance. I wondered if she knew she were being carried to the iron. This lot of barbarians, which I guessed as being in the neighborhood of seventy or eighty girls, had been, as nearly as I could determine, delivered only last night or this morning. Even now the majority of them had not been marked. This was a function, of course, of the brief amount of time they had been in the possession of Ram Seibar. It takes time to bring an iron to branding heat and the iron, of course, its head sinking and searing, burning, into the girl's flesh, marking her, loses heat rapidly. A given iron, accordingly, must be reheated before being reapplied. This situation is further complicated by the fact that the iron, normally, is cleaned following each application, a procedure which further reduces its heat. The cleaning is important for the precision and clarity of the next marking. Thus, in effect, each girl is marked with a new, fresh iron.

The most common brand site in a Gorean slave girl is the

outer side of the left thigh, closely beneath the hip. In this brand site the identificatory mark is thus placed high enough to be covered by the brief cloth of a common slave tunic and is available for convenient and immediate inspection if the tunic is lifted. The time it takes to brand several women can be reduced by the common expedient of heating several irons, but most iron masters will not work with more than two or three irons at a given time. Similarly, in a given house, normally only one fellow, at a time, attends to the branding. The rapidity with which the girls were being placed on sale, incidentally, is not unusual at the perimeter. This is, I think, in part a response to buyer pressure and, in part, the result of an unwillingness on the part of most perimeter slavers to devote time, or much time, to such niceties as diet, exercise and training. They reason, I suppose, that the master can manage, feed and train the girl, once he owns her, according to his own pleasures.

"I shall take this one," said a short, stocky, broad-shouldered fellow, in a wide-brimmed hat. "She has strong legs. Have her branded and put with the others."

The slaver's man nodded. They did not even discuss price. I gathered that a limited-lot price must have been agreed upon earlier, perhaps with Ram Seibar himself. The slaver's man did not seem hesitant to deal with him. I gathered he was well known in the area. He had bought more than one girl. Though the girls he purchased were comely, he did not seem, particularly, to be interested in that. He seemed to be buying them for some other reason.

As one girl, a branded one, was sold from a block down the way another girl, a blonde, was brought forward and flung on her hands and knees on the vacated block. A slaver's man then locked the collar on her, with its chain, running to the block ring. She looked about herself, frightened. A fellow reached forth to touch her thigh. She struck at his hand and scrambled back. "Don't! Don't!" she cried, in English. Almost instantly a slaver's man, a whip raised, was upon her. The men about the block stepped back, watching, as she, on her side, and twisting, writhed under her lashing. The slaver's man then folded back the blades of the whip, under their clip, and hooked the whip, by its butt ring, on his belt. He then knelt her on the block, posing her. When the fellow again reached forth to touch her she did not resist. She had learned that she was the sort of woman whom men might touch when and as they pleased.

She contrasted interestingly with another girl, an auburn-haired girl, on the next block. The auburn-haired girl, cooperatingly and without the least resistance, assumed various postures and attitudes, following the indications of the various men about her block. She even permitted herself, without the least resistance, to be posed, and by hand, for their interest. She knelt now on the block, back on her heels, her knees spread, her back straight, her head back, her hands behind the back of her head. I had little doubt but what the situation of both of these girls would become even more clear to them once they were branded.

"Noble Sirs!" called a voice, that of the fellow in the soiled blue-and-yellow shirt who had, earlier, been advertising the sale outside the compound. "Noble Sirs," he called. "We are ready for the final auction of the evening!"

This announcement was greeted with a murmur of interest and the men in the hall began to move toward the front of the room, to the vicinity of the central block. It was near the central block that the fully clothed, apparently lovely young woman was strung up by the wrists. She, it seemed, had been saved for last. During the course of the evening, from time to time, at irregular intervals, some fifteen or sixteen girls had been offered, in open bidding, to the crowd. Some of these, at least initially, had been clothed, though often in little other than panties and a brassiere. I had stayed to see this woman sold for I was curious to see if she was as beautiful as the delicate lineaments of her face suggested. She was a fair-skinned, slender, willowy girl. She appeared to be sweetly breasted, with a small waist and lovely, flaring hips, doubtless nestling a luscious love cradle. She had small wrists and ankles. They would look well in shackles. I saw that her eyes, when she opened them, in pain and terror, to look out on the crowd, were blue. Her hair was red, and bound back, rather severely, with a ribbon. She squirmed a moment in the bonds, and then hung still, near the central block. Her body, from what I could see of it, and judge of it, showed promise. It might prove adequate, I speculated, even for that of a pleasure slave.

I glanced back, and particularly to the left, at some of the side blocks. The side blocks were now deserted, the men having drifted forward, except by their occupants, now forgotten, kneeling or crouching upon them, their necks in their collars, fastened by their chains to the block rings. I smiled to myself. Some of the merchandise looked angry; no longer were they the centers of attention; they, though naked and chained, and on slave blocks, had been simply put from mind; they must remain behind, alone, precisely where they were, chained, while masters chose to ignore them, bestowing their attention on an item of at least temporarily greater interest. Already the merchandise was exhibiting the vanity of slaves. But let them rest content for, when the auction was done, men doubtless would drift back to their perusal; they would then be again subjected to the close scrutiny of masters; they would then be examined again, and closely, to see if they might be of any interest.

"I believe we are ready to proceed," called the gross, corpulent fellow in the soiled blue-and-yellow shirt. With his kaiila quirt he indicated the suspended girl. "We have here the last item to be put up for auction this evening, a fair-skinned, red-haired barbarian beauty."

"We do not know if she is a beauty or not," called a man. "Strip her!"

"But I hasten to assure you," continued the slaver's man, giving no heed to the fellow's enthusiastic contribution, "that the market will remain open for yet another Ahn following this auction. You are then invited to reconsider with an eye for prospective purchase the trinkets and baubles strewn forth for your delectation upon our side blocks."

"On with it!" cried a man. "Let us see her!"

"We have saved this barbarian beauty for last," said the slaver's man. "She will make a fitting conclusion to the auctions of this evening, such a splendid evening at the house of Ram Seibar! Behold her! Is your interest not whetted?"

I could see, by glancing around, that the interest of several of the men was indeed whetted.

"Even clothed," laughed the auctioneer, "is your interest not whetted?"

"That it is!" laughed more than one man.

"Let us see her!" called another.

That the woman was being sold last in the auctions does not indicate, *per se*, that she was the most beautiful. On the other hand, it was undeniable that she was quite beautiful. Several of the girls I had seen auctioned off during the course of the evening, incidentally, had been quite extraordinary.

This woman, at any rate, was surely among the most beautiful. Some of the girls auctioned earlier had also been presented to the buyers initially clothed, to one extent or the other, their clothing then being removed, sometimes sardonically and ceremoniously, during the course of their sale. This was the only woman, however, who had been presented before the buyers strung up by the wrists.

"A fair-skinned, red-haired barbarian beauty," called the auctioneer, "highly intelligent, exquisitely refined and of delicate sensibilities, a woman on her own world doubtless of class and station—but on this world, our world of Gor, only a meaningless piece of slave meat, a girl who will learn to wear a collar, a girl who will learn to serve and obey, a girl who will learn to please, a girl who will learn that she belongs, and rightfully, to men!"

"Let us see her!" called more than one man.

The auctioneer signaled to an attendant who, from a side of the hall, brought forth a shallow copper bowl, some two feet in diameter, filled with slender cylinders of oil-impregnated wood. In a moment, with a fire-maker, of flint and steel, he had ignited this wood. The girl looked at it. I do not think, at that time, she clearly understood its significance.

"Let us see her!" called a man.

"But, of course!" called the auctioneer. He hung the long, black kaiila quirt on his belt.

The woman looked out on the crowd, miserably. She did not understand, fully, I am sure, what was going to be done to her. She was a barbarian, her freedom only recently terminated. She spoke no Gorean. She had been brought into the hall and strung up so cruelly by the wrists only after the completion of the earlier auctions. Too, I had little doubt that her masters had kept her ignorant of their occurrence. She knew little more than the fact that she was being displayed before men, though for what reason and to what end, I conjectured, she scarcely dared speculate.

"Shall we begin?" inquired the auctioneer of the crowd. "Shall we see if she is any good?"

"Yes! Yes!" shouted more than one man. I smiled to myself. The auctioneer knew his business.

"But first," said the auctioneer, "behold the absurdity of these garments. They seem to be a cross between the garments of a free woman and those of a slave." Most obviously, from what I could see, the woman wore an attractive office dress, of a sort which is often implicitly prescribed, particularly by female executives, for subordinate female employees regarded as too feminine to be considered for the executive class. "That is very pretty, Jane. I like to see you wear things like that." "Yes, Miss Tabor." This is also a useful way, of course, for the female executive to make it clear to their male colleagues that such women, unlike themselves, are only females.

It was a long, brown, white-flecked, shirred shirtdress, of some soft, smooth synthetic material, of mid-calf length. It had small, red, round buttons securing the long, exciting frontal closure and appearing, too, at the cuffs. It also had a brown, white-flecked, matching tie belt. About her throat was a single string of pearls, doubtless simulated, or they would have been removed from her by her first captors. She wore stockings or pantyhose. On her feet were black, shiny, high-heeled dress sandals, each secured, apparently, by a single, narrow black ankle strap. The fact that she was dressed as she was led me to believe that the woman worked in business and that she had been taken by the slavers on her way home from work. I think she could forget about the office. In the future she would have other duties.

"Are these the garments of a free woman or of a slave?" asked the auctioneer.

"Of a slave," shouted men. "Remove them!"

The Goreans probably regarded them as the garments of a slave because of their smoothness and prettiness. Too, the shirred quality of the dress would permit it to move, and swirl, excitingly about her body, if she chose to move in certain ways. Too, the lower portions of her calves and her pretty ankles were revealed by the dress. That she wore slave garments was probably also suggested to them by the transparency and sheerness of the coverings on her legs and, of course, from the Gorean view, her footwear, so slight and pretty, with the black ankle straps, was such that it would be likely to be affected only by a woman begging for the collar.

"She came to us this way," said the auctioneer. "I myself have not yet seen her."

"Let us see her," called a man.

"I wonder if she is any good," said the auctioneer.

"Begin!" "Begin!" shouted men.

"Of course!" laughed the auctioneer. He then went to the suspended girl and, thrusting up the ropes on her ankles, unbuckled the narrow, ankle-encircling black straps of her high-heeled dress sandals. He drew them from her feet and held them up, together, in his right hand. "Note the straps," he said. "We are familiar with such straps, are we not?"

Several of the men laughed. They resembled the small black straps, buckled, with which one occasionally binds the wrists and ankles of slaves, before, or while, one amuses oneself with them.

He then drew the large, triangular-bladed knife from the beaded sheath on his belt and slashed the straps and uppers of the sandals, discarding them then in the flaming copper bowl at the side.

"She has pretty feet," he said. He then resheathed his dagger and, extending his hand, locked his fingers about the string of pearls on the girl's throat. She cried out as he jerked them from her neck. "She has a pretty neck, too," he said, bending her head back by the hair.

"Yes," said a man.

He then released her hair and, stepping forward, again addressed himself to the crowd. "Doubtless some Master will soon find something more suitable with which to enclose that lovely neck than a string of pearls," he speculated.

There was laughter.

"Further," said the auctioneer, lifting the pearls, "these pearls have been examined. They are false. She wore false pearls."

There was an ugly response in the crowd. Goreans have a rather primitive sense of honesty.

"What should be her punishment?" asked the auctioneer.

"Slavery!" said several.

"She is already a slave," said the auctioneer, "though perhaps she does not yet know it."

"Let the man who buys her then pay her back," said a man, "punishing her well, and lengthily, for her fraud."

"Is that agreeable?" asked the auctioneer.

"Yes," said several.

"I am better than she is," said a feminine voice beside me. I felt my arm being gently taken. I looked down. I recalled her. I had encountered her outside the compound of Ram Seibar, before the sale. She was a barbarian slave, and a tavern girl. Her name was Ginger. "I thought you were occupied," I said. She nibbled at my sleeve. "He kept me for

Ahn," she said, murmuringly, poutingly. "He made me serve him well."

"Excellent," I said.

"I am not now occupied, Master," she said.

"Do not listen to her, Master," purred a voice from my other side. "Come with me, rather, to Russell's tavern. I will make your night a delight." I looked to my left. A dark-haired girl was there. She, too, obviously, was a tavern girl, but she was garbed quite differently from Ginger. The taste or business sense of their masters, I gathered, differed. Slaves, of course, are garbed precisely as their masters please. "I, too, am a barbarian," she said. "I am Evelyn."

She wore a black, tight, off-the-shoulder bodice and a short, black, silk skirt, decorated with red thread and ruffles, and stiffened with crinoline. A black ribbon choker was placed behind the steel collar on her throat. A red ribbon, matching the decorations on her skirt, was in her hair. She had not been permitted stockings or footwear. Such things are normally denied the Gorean slave girl. Her costume, like that of Ginger, the short, fringed, beaded shirtdress of tanned skin, with the beaded anklet, intended to resemble the garb in which red masters sometimes saw fit to clothe their white female slaves, if permitting them clothing, suggested its heritage of other times and other places. Most Gorean garments, of course, of the sorts worn by humans, trace back to terrestrial antecedents. I looked at the white bosom of Evelyn, lifted, shaped and confined in the tightness of the bodice, for the interest of masters. What man, I wondered, would not wish to unlace or tear away that bodice, to subject its treasures, like the woman herself, to the ravishments of his mouth and hands.

"Pay her no attention, Master," said Ginger. "Come with me to the tavern of Randolph."

"No, with me, to the tavern of Russell," said Evelyn.

"Surely you two have sneaked in here," I said. I did not think Ram Seibar would wish girls soliciting in his hall, particularly during the course of a sale.

"The worst that would happen is that we would be whipped from the room," said Evelyn.

"But across the calves," said Ginger. "That hurts."

"Yes," said Evelyn, shuddering. I gathered they had, more than once, been thusly speeded from the hall by wrathful attendants.

"Release me!" cried the suspended girl, hanging by her wrists, before the crowd.

"No," she said, "no!" The tie belt on her dress had then been jerked loose, its ends dangling, supported by their loops, beside her hips.

"No," she said, "no, no!" But one by one, slowly, the auctioneer's knife was cutting the buttons from the long, frontal closure of her dress. "What do you want?" she cried. "What are you doing?" Then the last button had been cut away. "What do you think I am? What are you doing to me?" she cried. The sides of the dress were then brushed back.

"I do not think she is pretty," said Ginger.

"No, I do not either," said Evelyn. "You may even be prettier than she."

"I am beautiful," said Ginger. "It is you who might even, possibly, be prettier than she, my man-hungry little slave slut."

"Man hungry?" said Evelyn. "I have heard how you bite your chains, how you whine to be released at night."

"It is no secret in Kailiauk," said Ginger, "the fingernail scratches in your kennel!"

"I cannot help it if men have released my slavery," said Evelyn, tears in her eyes.

"They, too, have released my slavery," said Ginger, "and fully."

"I am more helplessly passionate than you," said Evelyn.

"No, you are not," said Ginger.

"It is well known in Kailiauk that I am a better slave than you," said Evelyn.

"I am a better slave than you," said Ginger, "Slave Slut."

"No, you are not, Slave Slut," hissed Evelyn.

"Be silent, Slave Sluts," I said.

"Yes, Master," said Ginger.

"Yes, Master," said Evelyn.

Beneath the dress the girl was wearing a full, knee-length slip of white silk. The dress, then, by cutting with the knife, and ripping, was removed from her. It, too, was then thrown on the flames, following the dress sandals and pearls.

I saw, then, that the slip had small, over-the-shoulder straps. These were severed and then, cutting and ripping from the back, the auctioneer loosened the slip. It could now, at his least convenience, be removed from the girl. At the left knee it had a deep cocktail slit. This interested me, suggesting that the girl might have good slave potential. This slit, affording an exciting glimpse of the girl's calf and lower thigh, was, of course, drawn to the attention of the audience by the auctioneer.

I wondered why the two tavern girls, Ginger and Evelyn, had sought me out. Obviously there were many men in Kailiauk. Indeed, at this time of the evening, it seemed strange to me that they would even be absent from the tavern. Surely this was the time of the evening when they might be expected to be applying themselves to the business of making a living for their masters, performing exquisitely, chained, in their alcoves. I dismissed the matter from my mind.

"No," begged the suspended girl, "please, don't!"

The slip was then lifted away from her body.

"A silver tarsk," said a man.

"Excellent," said the auctioneer.

This seemed to me an unusually high bid for a raw, untrained barbarian slave, particularly as an opening bid. On the other hand, I had noted that girls seemed to bring high prices in Kailiauk. Several of the girls had gone from the side blocks, for example, for prices ranging between thirty and fifty copper tarsks. In certain other markets these girls, in their current state of barbarity and ignorance, might have brought as little as seven or eight tarsks apiece. These prices, of course, were a function of context and time. In Kailiauk there are many affluent fellows, rich from the trade in hide and horn, and the traffic in kaiila. Furthermore, this close to the perimeter, only a few pasangs from the Ihanke, far from the normal loci of slave raidings, and slave routes, female slaves, particularly beautiful ones, are not abundant. Accordingly men, coming in from surrounding areas, are willing to pay high to have one in their blankets.

The girl now wore a brassiere, a garter belt and stockings. Too, beneath the narrow garter belt, in what was perhaps an indication of charming reserve, I could see silken panties.

"She is not really ugly," said Ginger.

"No," said Evelyn.

The girl watched in horror as the remains of her silken slip was cast upon the flames, causing them to spring up anew. Her Earth clothing, before her very eyes, piece by piece, was being destroyed. It was thus being made clear to her that she was making a transition to a new reality.

"No," she said, "please, no."

The auctioneer freed her stockings from the hooks and buttons on the four garter straps. In a moment the auctioneer had drawn the stockings from her legs, slipping them underneath the ropes on her ankles and discarding them in the flames. Then, after viewing her for a moment, he stepped behind her. He undid the two-hook back closure on the garter belt. This article of clothing, too, then, in a moment, was cast into the flames. She then hung before us clad only, save for the ribbon binding back her hair, in her brassiere and panties.

"Undo her hair!" called a man.

"Yes!" called another man.

I smiled to myself. Yes, it was the exact time for the woman's hair to be unbound. The hair of slave girls, incidentally, unless shaved or shortened as a punishment, is usually worn long. There is more, cosmetically, which can be done with long hair and such hair, too, is often useful in the performance of intimate duties for her master. Too, of course, it can be balled and thrust in her mouth, for use as a gag, either, say, when one does not wish to hear her for a time, or, perhaps, if one wishes, to silence her cries in the throes of her submission spasms. Too, of course, she may be bound with it.

"Of course," said the auctioneer. He then untied the hair ribbon which had bound her red hair back so primly. He threw it in the fire. He then fluffed her hair and brought it forward, over her shoulders. He then brushed it back, behind her back, and smoothed it. He turned her on the rope, to the left and right, that men might see the cut and fall of the hair against her back. It was pretty. Then the auctioneer turned her so that she was, again, helplessly, exposed frontally to the crowd.

"She is really quite pretty," said Ginger, irritatedly.

"Yes," agreed Evelyn.

"But not as pretty as I," said Ginger.

"At least not so pretty as I," said Evelyn.

I smiled. I had little doubt the suspended girl would bring a higher price than either of them, though they both were, admittedly, obviously full and desirably luscious slaves.

"Two silver tarsks," said a man.

"Excellent," said the auctioneer.

The girl looked out on the crowd with fear and misery. Doubtless she hoped, against hope, that she had now been adequately displayed to the crowd. Surely the brutes would not dare go further. That she had been brought clothed into the hall surely argued that her dignity and pride would continue to be respected, at least to the degree that she was now concealed. Too, had the fellow attending to her not now paused in his abusive, insolent labors? But then she glanced to the side blocks. There there were women, much like herself; they, fixed in place, wearing collars and chains, she could not help but note, were absolutely naked. But she, surely, was different from them! She was finer, and more delicate. Anyone could see that! Then she hung, relieved, in the ropes. The auctioneer was conferring with an attendant, to the side. Her ordeal, as she conceived it, was now concluded. The exposure and disgrace which had been visited upon the other girls was not to be her lot. She was better. She was different.

The attendant, to whom the auctioneer had been addressing himself, took his exit.

But did the girl not know that she was not different? Did she not know that she, too, was only a slave?

"I wonder if she is beautiful," said Ginger.

"As she is now clad, it is not difficult to speculate on the matter," said Evelyn.

"Why don't they take off her clothes, so we can see," said Ginger.

"Yes," said Evelyn.

I smiled to myself. These girls, at any rate, understood something of the nature of a Gorean market.

"Were you a side-block girl?" asked Ginger.

"No," said Evelyn. "I was auctioned."

"I, too," said Ginger.

"Were you brought in naked?" asked Evelyn.

"Yes," said Ginger.

"I was, too," said Evelyn.

"Do you think that they think she is better than us?" asked Ginger.

"Perhaps," said Evelyn. "Men are fools."

"No!" cried the suspended girl, suddenly. "Don't! Please!"

The auctioneer was behind her.

"No!" she cried. "I am a virgin! I have never been seen by men!"

"No!" she cried.

Her breasts were lovely.

Would the last vestige of her modesty not be permitted her?

"No," she pleaded. "Please, no!"

"No!" she cried, and then hung, helpless and sobbing, in the ropes.

I saw that the stripped slave was beautiful.

"Three tarsks," said a man.

"Three five," said another. This was a bid of three silver tarsks and fifty copper tarsks. There are one hundred copper tarsks to one silver tarsk in Kailiauk. The ratio is ten to one in certain other cities and towns. The smallest Gorean coin is usually a tarsk bit, usually valued from a quarter to a tenth of a tarsk. Gorean coinage tends to vary from community to community. Certain coins, such as the silver tarsk of Tharna and the golden tarn of Ar, tend, to some extent, to standardize what otherwise might be a mercantile chaos. This same standardization, in the region of the Tamber Gulf and south, along the shore of Thassa, tends to be effected by the golden tarn of Port Kar. Coin merchants often have recourse to scales. This is sensible considering such things as the occasional debasings of coinages, usually unannounced by the communities in question, and the frequent practice of splitting and shaving coins. It is, for example, not unusual for a Gorean coin pouch to contain parts of coins as well as whole coins. Business is often conducted by notes and letters of credit. Paper currency, however, in itself, is unknown.

"Four!" called out another man.

"Five!" cried out another.

"But, Gentlemen," called the auctioneer, turning the girl on the rope, turning her left thigh to the crowd, "restrain your bids! Can you not see that she has not yet even been branded?"

"Mark her! Mark her!" called more than one man.

On the height of the central block I saw two attendants sliding out a branding rack. Another, its handles wrapped in heavy cloth, carried out a cylindrical, glowing brazier, from which protruded the handles of two irons. He placed this near the branding rack. At the same time the auctioneer freed the ankles of the girl from the ropes. He then freed the end of her wrist rope from its ring and the rope, sliding through the overhead ring, loosened. As it did so the attendant to whom the auctioneer had earlier addressed himself, now returned, supported the girl. I did not think she could stand. When the rope permitted it he lifted her in his arms. Her weight was nothing for him. The auctioneer then jerked the remainder of the rope through the overhead ring. The attendant then carried the girl, the rope trailing beside him, to the height of the central block. There, with the help of another fellow, he lowered her into the heavy rack, and spun shut the sturdy vises on her left and right thighs. She had been carried to the rack naked, her wrists bound before her. She winced, unable to move her thighs, dismayed doubtless at the perfect tightness with which they were held. Her wrists were then freed of the rope and taken behind her where they were fastened to a sturdy metal pole, a portion of the rack, by dangling slave bracelets.

The fellow who had carried in the brazier now drew forth, holding it with two gloves, an iron. It was white hot.

The girl regarded it, wild-eyed.

"No!" she cried. "Are you beasts and barbarians! What do you think I am? Do you think I am an animal! Do you think I am a slave!"

The iron was leveled. It approached the circular aperture in the vise, through which, deeply into her fair thigh, it would be thrust, and held, burning and hissing, until its work was done, until the girl was marked, and well, as slave meat.

"You are bluffing!" she cried. "You cannot be serious!"

She then learned that the intention of the iron with respect to her body was quite real.

The vises were spun loose. Her hands were freed of the restraining slave bracelets, only then to be tied with a cord behind her. Dismayed and sobbing she was freed of the rack and put on her knees, head down, at the auctioneer's feet. The rack and the brazier, the iron returned to it, were removed from the central block. The girl then, naked and kneeling, her hands bound behind her, at the auctioneer's feet, lifted her head and looked wildly out at the crowd. She had been branded.

"She does not know what has happened to her," said Ginger.

"She knows," said Evelyn.

"But she does not yet fully understand it," said Ginger.

"No," said Evelyn.

"But she will soon understand it, and fully," said Ginger, "even so stupid a slave."

"Yes," said Evelyn.

The auctioneer then removed the long, supple kaiila quirt from his belt. Twice he struck the girl across the back. She cried out in pain. Her education had now commenced. No time, now, would be lost in teaching her her condition. He dragged her to her feet by the hair and bent her backwards, displaying the bow of her beauty to the crowd.

"I have a bid of five tarsks on this slut," he called. "Do I hear more? Do I hear more?"

"Is she trained?" called a man.

"Train her yourself," called the auctioneer, "to your own pleasures." It was understood, of course, that these barbarians were not trained. They had not yet been taught, as far as I could tell, even the proper modes of kneeling before a master.

"Five five!" called a man.

"Good! Good!" called the auctioneer, displaying the slave. "Do I hear more?"

"Can she speak Gorean?" called a man. I smiled. It was clearly understood that these barbarian slaves could not speak Gorean.

"Train her like a sleen or a kaiila, on her hands and knees," said the auctioneer. "She will soon learn what is required of her."

"Pose her!" called a man.

"In what way, Noble Sir?" inquired the auctioneer, obligingly. He then, following the instructions of the fellow, sat the girl down, near the front of the central block, her left leg under her, her right leg extended and flexed, her right side facing the fellow, her shoulders back, her head turned sharply to look at him. In this way the curves of her right leg, and the lines of her figure, are pleasantly displayed.

"Imagine her in your collar!" challenged the auctioneer.

"Kneel her!" called a man.

The auctioneer then knelt the girl near the front of the central block. She knelt back on her heels. Her knees were widely spread. Her back was straight, her head high.

"Five seven!" called a man.

"Five seven!" repeated the auctioneer.

"Get her on her feet, so we can see her legs!" called a man.

"Belly her!" called another.

"Make her walk!" called a man.

"Kneel her, with her head to the ground!" called another.

"Put her through slave paces!" called another.

I looked to the side. One of the fellows there was the short,

muscular fellow who wore the low, broad-brimmed hat. I recalled he had purchased at least four or five of the girls from
the side blocks. They had been excellent females, in my opinion, but they had not seemed to be, at least on the whole, the
choicest merchandise available to him, and for similar costs.
It was almost as though he were purchasing them for some
purpose other than that for which slave girls are commonly
purchased. I did not, now, understand his apparent interest in
the red-haired slave now being vended. She, surely, was the
sort of woman that would be purchased, at least usually, to
fulfill one of the more common purposes of slave girls.

"Men are beasts," said Ginger.

"Yes," said Evelyn.

There was the sound of a quirt lashing flesh. The red-
haired girl cried out in pain.

"She does not even know what they want her to do," said
Ginger.

"She is a stupid slave," said Evelyn.

"She will learn," said Ginger.

"We all learn," said Evelyn.

I had noted, during the course of the evening, that more
than one of the attendants about, and the auctioneer, too, had
noted the presence of the two tavern girls in the crowd. They
had not taken any action, however, to eject them. I found
this of interest. Perhaps they thought them to be with me and
that I, so to speak, was answerable for them. Again I was
puzzled as to why they would be clinging about me. As I had
not volunteered to accompany one or the other of them back
to her master's tavern they should have attempted, after a bit,
to apply their beauty and enslaved wiles to the enticement of
a more likely prospect. It was surely not their business to be
standing about observing slave sales. Even now, perhaps, their
masters had taken slave whips down from the walls, curious
as to their absence.

I gave my attention again to the central block. By now the
red-haired beauty had been put through several slave paces,
such as were feasible for her, her hands bound with the cord
behind her back. She now, trembling, lay on her belly, licking
and kissing at the auctioneer's kaiila boots.

"Is she vital?" called a man.

The auctioneer pulled her to her feet by the hair and
turned her about, facing the crowd.

I heard some men shouting outside in the street. The two girls inched more closely to me.

The auctioneer, his quirt now hooked on his belt, stood behind the red-haired girl. He put his left hand in her hair, and pulled her head back, and placed his right hand on her right hip. She suddenly screamed and writhed, squirming. But she could not free herself from his grip. "No, please!" she screamed. "No!" she sobbed. Then she cried out, "No! Oh, no!" Then she sobbed, "No! No! No! Yes! Yes! No. No. No!" Then he released her, and she fell to her knees on the block, sobbing, crimson with shame.

"Good," said the fellow near me, he in the broad-brimmed hat.

I smiled. The lovely new slave, even freshly branded, had, in the hands of the auctioneer, betrayed herself.

"She will make a hot slut," said Ginger.

"She will not be able to help herself, no more than we," said Evelyn.

I was inclined to agree with the tavern girls. Clearly the red-haired girl had strong slave latencies.

"Six!" called a man.

"Six five!" called another.

"Six seven!" called another.

"Six eight!" called another.

"Six nine!" called another.

There was now a commotion at the door. We heard shouting behind us. The auctioneer looked to the back of the room, angrily. Seven or eight men, in the boots and garb of drovers, thrust in the door. Two or three of them carried half-emptied bottles of paga. Two of them had drawn swords in their hands. The tavern girls seized my arms, trying to make themselves small, behind me. The men, I gathered, were drovers, members probably of the same crew that I had seen arrive earlier, those who had driven their kaiila, crying out and shouting, through the streets.

"Gentlemen!" cried the auctioneer. "Do not break the peace! Sheathe your steel! There is a sale in progress."

"There they are!" cried a fellow, one of the drovers, pointing towards us. He was a young, dark-haired, rough-looking fellow. The tavern girls cried out with misery. I shook them loose from my arms. The fellow slammed his steel into his sheath and strode towards us. Another fellow, one who looked much like him, was but a foot behind him. They were, I assumed, brothers.

"The Hobarts," said a man, "from the Bar Ina."

The fellow in advance seized Evelyn by the arms and shook her viciously. I was afraid he might break her little, collared neck. "I sought you at the tavern," he said to her, angrily. "You knew we would bring stock to town this night."

"And you, little slut," snarled the other, "what of you?" He seized Ginger by the hair with both hands and threw her cruelly to his feet. I was pleased to see that he knew how to handle a slave. She looked up at him, her head held up to face him, her small hands futilely on his wrists, tears in her eyes. "Why were you not in the tavern of Randolph, awaiting me?" he demanded.

I deemed now that I better understood why the two girls had not been at their respective taverns, why they, it seemed, in effect, under the pretense of soliciting business for the establishments of their masters, had been hiding in the sales barn of Ram Seibar. What I did not understand was why the personnel of the sales barn had not driven them away. The presence of two such luscious tavern girls at the sale might surely distract the attention of at least some of the buyers. This was the more puzzling as, in the past, I had gathered, they had been, in similar situations, driven from the premises, being lashed across the calves. This, then, was apparently not their first offense in such matters.

The first young fellow then spun Evelyn about and hurled her a few feet from him, toward the door. "Precede me to the tavern, Slave," he said.

"Yes, Master," she wept.

"And you," said the other, throwing Ginger to her belly, toward the door, "get your ass to the tavern of Randolph."

"Yes, Master," she said.

I saw two attendants, at the door, look at one another, tensely, uneasily. I did not understand this reaction. What was it to them if these two women were to be conducted back to their respective taverns, there to be returned to their intimate labors?

The first of the young fellows turned about, and glared at me. I observed the sheath. It was at his left hip. He was apparently right-handed. I observed the right hand. It did not tense to move toward the blade's hilt.

He was obviously angry. I met his gaze, dispassionately.

The girls had now sought me out, I realized, hoping that I might provide them with some sort of shelter, or protection. I presumably seemed large, and strong. I carried a blade. Too, I was a stranger in town and would know nothing of the Hobarts, or the crew of the Bar Ina, or whoever it might be, that might be interested in them. In their way, given my lack of knowledge in these matters, they had been trying to take advantage of me. I found this irritating. They had, of course, seriously miscalculated in this matter. As I was not intending to take them to an alcove myself I would not have afforded them, no more than any other Gorean male, the least protection. They belonged totally to their masters and, more generally, to men. They were slave girls. Still, it would not have pleased me if this fellow, or fellows, these drovers, thought they were taking them away from me.

The fellow lashed out. What occurred then was done rapidly. I am not certain that all present clearly understood what was done. I caught his wrist and, twisting it, jerked him forward and off balance, at the same time kicking forcibly upwards. I then, bending his wrist back, thrust him to the side. The other fellow was caught with a backwards kick, his steel no more then halfway from its sheath. As I had not been facing him he had apparently been taken by surprise by this blow, by its direction, its nature and force. Untrained men often expect assaults to occur frontally. Various options in the martial arts, of course, are available to the practiced combatant. My blade was free from my sheath before his knees began to sag. I faced the drovers then, my blade drawn. He crumpled to the floor. Men quickly cleared space about us.

"Well done!" said the fellow in the broad-brimmed hat.

I faced five drovers, their steel drawn. Bottles were cast aside.

"The first man who attacks," said the auctioneer, from the height of the central platform, "is a dead man."

The drovers looked about. Attendants in the sales barn held leveled crossbows trained on them. The short, heavy quarrels lay in their guides. The cables were taut. Fingers rested on the triggers.

Angrily the drovers sheathed their steel. They gathered up their two fallen comrades and, supporting them, with dark looks, withdrew from the sales barn.

"The two leading fellows there," said the man with the

broad-brimmed hat, "were Max and Kyle Hobart, from the Bar Ina. They will not make pleasant enemies."

I shrugged. I resheathed my steel.

The two tavern girls, auburn-haired Ginger and dark-haired Evelyn, frightened, began to move unobtrusively toward the door.

"One moment, young ladies," called the auctioneer, pleasantly.

"We are going, Masters," said Ginger, plaintively.

"Perhaps not," said the auctioneer.

"Masters?" asked Ginger, frightened. Behind her there was the heavy ropish sound of heavy cordage being dropped. She spun about. The exit was blocked by the reticulated structure of a stout, hempen slave net. She caught with her fingers at the net, and then, frightened, looked back over her shoulder. "Masters?" she asked.

Evelyn immediately knelt. "Please forgive us, Masters," she said. "Please do not whip us!"

Ginger then knelt, and swiftly, beside Evelyn. "No, Masters," she said. "Please do not whip us."

"Who is your master?" asked the auctioneer.

"Randolph, of Kailiauk," said Ginger.

"Russell, of Kailiauk," said Evelyn.

"No, pretty little slaves," said the auctioneer. "Your master is the house of Ram Seibar."

"Master?" asked Ginger.

"You have been nuisances long enough," said the auctioneer.

"Master?" asked Ginger, frightened.

"Two days ago you were purchased from your respective masters," said the auctioneer. "You have now, as we anticipated, effected your self-delivery."

The girls looked at one another in terror.

"Your time of being bothers to the house of Ram Seibar is now at an end," said the auctioneer.

There was much laughter among the men at the rich joke played on the two slaves.

"Remove their collars," said the auctioneer to an attendant. He removed the collars. The keys were correct. Doubtless they had been supplied by their former masters, probably at the time of the transactions effecting their purchase.

"Get your clothes off," said the auctioneer.

Swiftly the girls complied. Ginger removed even the

beaded cuff on her left ankle. Evelyn removed even the black-ribbon choker on her throat. They were then stark naked. Both, I saw, had been well branded.

They looked about themselves, frightened.

Their clothing, with the collars, was collected by an attendant. Such articles, doubtless, would be returned to their former masters.

"We have here, for sale," laughed the auctioneer, "two of the prettiest tavern girls in Kailiauk. Should you doubt this, scrutinize them closely."

The girls shrank back. Men laughed.

"We are willing to consider any bid over a silver tarsk for them," said the auctioneer. "However, we encourage their buyers to see that their pretty, curved asses are removed from Kailiauk."

There was more laughter.

"Can you communicate with these other slaves?" asked the fellow in the broad-brimmed hat of the two stripped tavern girls. He indicated some of the girls on the side blocks.

Ginger approached one of the girls. Evelyn, too, approached her.

"Do you speak English?" asked Ginger in English.

"Yes, yes!" said the girl, startled.

"What of the others who were with you?" asked Ginger. "Can they speak English?"

"Most," said the girl, "as a second, if not a first language."

Ginger then turned to the fellow in the broad-brimmed hat. "I can communicate with most of them, I think," she said, in Gorean. "If there is a particular girl you are interested in I can interrogate her specifically."

The man pointed to the naked red-haired girl, her hands bound behind her, on the central platform.

"Do you speak English?" asked Ginger.

"Yes," said the girl, pulling at her bonds, "yes!"

"Yes," said Ginger to the man in the broad-brimmed hat, in Gorean.

He nodded. I could see that he was pleased by this. That seemed to be the woman he was interested in having understand him, and clearly. I did not think he was particularly concerned, truly, about communicating with the others. The uses to which he intended to put them, I gathered, did not require subtleties of communication. His desires with respect to their performances, I gathered, could be adequately conveyed by such means as the boot and whip.

"What is the language in which you have been speaking to these women?" he asked of Ginger.

"English, Master," she said.

He indicated Evelyn. "Does this slave, too, know this English?" he asked.

"Yes, Master," said Ginger.

Evelyn nodded. "Yes, Master," she said.

I smiled. Two girls, doubtless, could train the red-haired barbarian more quickly than one. For example, they could work her in shifts.

"You speak English," cried the girl on the side block, the collar and chain on her throat, "what is this place and how did I come here!"

"This is the world called Gor," said Ginger, "and you were brought here by spacecraft."

"What manner of place is this," begged the girl, lifting the chain on her collar, "and is this how they treat all women?"

"I shall not expatiate on what manner of place this is," said Ginger, "for you, yourself, shall soon learn, and well. And this is not how they treat all women. Women on this world, most of them, enjoy a status and freedom of which you, from Earth, cannot even conceive. Their raiment is splendid, their station is lofty, their mien is noble, their prestige is boundless. Dread them, and fear them—"

The girl looked at her, frightened.

"For you are not such a woman," said Ginger.

The girl clutched the chain, kneeling on the block.

"No," said Ginger, "you are not such a woman. You are less than the dust beneath their feet."

"I—I do not understand," said the girl, stammering.

"You are the sort of woman who will wear rags," said Ginger, "who will rejoice if a crust of bread is thrust in your mouth."

"I—I do not understand," said the girl.

"You will learn the weight of bonds, the lash of the whip," said Ginger. "You will learn to crawl, and bend, and obey."

The girl looked at her with horror.

"You will learn that you are an animal," said Ginger.

"An animal?" said the girl, frightened.

"Yes," said Ginger, "and worth less than most animals."

"What sort of woman am I, then?" asked the girl.

"Can you not guess?" asked Ginger.

The girl looked at her, terrified.

"A female slave," said Ginger.

"Let us now have a bid on the two tavern girls," called the auctioneer. "We must have at least a tarsk apiece for them!"

The girl shook her head numbly, disbelievingly. "No," she whispered. "No."

Ginger regarded her.

"It cannot be," said the girl.

"It is," said Ginger.

"Not a female slave," said the girl. She lifted the chain, disbelievingly, on her neck.

"Yes," said Ginger.

"No!" said the girl. "No!" She clutched the chain on her neck in terror.

"Yes," said Ginger.

The girl leaped suddenly to her feet and, crouching over, with the fullness of her small strength, began to tear wildly at the chain. "No," she cried, "not a female slave! No!"

The men watched, with interest.

Then the girl, sobbing, her small hands raw, and cut, ceased her struggles.

"I am chained," she said, numbly, to Ginger.

"Yes, you are," said Ginger, adding, "—Slave."

There was the sudden lash of the five-stranded Gorean slave whip and the girl cried out and sank down on the block, kneeling, with her head down, making herself as small as possible. Five times did the attendant lash her beauty. Then she lay on her stomach on the block, sobbing, the collar and chain on her neck, her fingernails tight in the wood. "I will be good, Masters," she wept. "I will be good."

"Do I hear a bid on the tavern girls?" asked the auctioneer.

"Five copper tarsks apiece!" laughed a man.

Ginger bit her lip, in anger. There was laughter.

"Stand straighter, Slave," said a man.

Ginger straightened her body, and lifted her head.

"Miss, oh, please, Miss!" called the red-haired girl, plaintively, on her knees, stripped, her hands tied behind her with the cord, from the central block.

Ginger was startled. The red-haired slave had spoken without permission. She turned to face her.

"Am I, too, a slave?" called the red-haired girl.

Ginger looked about, and sensed that she might respond, without being beaten. The experienced slave girl is very sensitive to such things.

We saw the auctioneer remove the kaiila quirt from his belt.

"Yes," said Ginger, "you are all slaves!"

"And you?" inquired the red-haired girl.

"We, too, are slaves," said Ginger, indicating herself and Evelyn. "Do you think free women would be so rudely stripped and brazenly displayed? We, and these others, are on sale! Do you doubt that we are slaves? See our brands!" She turned her left thigh to the central platform. Evelyn, too, turned so that the red-haired girl might, as she could, observe her brand.

"You are branded!" said the red-haired girl. "You are only branded slaves!"

"Consider the mark burned into your own lovely hide," said Ginger.

The girl regarded her own thigh, fearfully.

"It is no different from that which we wear," said Ginger.

The girl regarded her with horror.

"It marks you well, does it not?" asked Ginger.

"Yes," said the girl, in misery.

"As ours do us," said Ginger.

"Then I, too, am nothing but a branded slave?" said the red-haired girl.

"Precisely," said Ginger.

"Then I, too, at least in theory, could be put up for sale," she said, aghast.

"Bids have already been taken on you," said Ginger. "You are up for sale."

"No!" cried the girl. "I am Millicent Aubrey-Welles, of Pennsylvania. I cannot be for sale!"

"You are a nameless slave animal, being vended for the pleasure of Masters," said Ginger.

"I am not for sale!" cried the girl.

"You are," said Ginger. "And I, for one, would not pay much for you."

Wildly the red-haired girl tried to attain her feet but the auctioneer, his hand in her hair, twisted her and threw her on her belly before him. Twice he lashed her with the quirt. "Oh!" she cried. "Oh!" He then stepped away from her. He laughed. She had squirmed well. Her body was obviously highly sensitive. This portended well for her quality as a slave. She lifted her head, wildly, to Ginger. "I am truly to be sold?" she begged.

"Yes," said Ginger.

"Oh!" cried the girl, in pain, again quirted by the auctioneer. "Oh! Oh!" She had again spoken without permission. Then she lay quietly, scarcely moving, beaten, frightened, on the block. She did not care to feel the quirt again. I think, lying there, she now began, more fully and explicitly than she had dared before, to comprehend the actuality of her condition, that she might be, in fact, what she seemed to be, a lashed, soon-to-be vended slave.

"What were these women inquiring of you?" inquired a man, of Ginger.

"They desired a clarification of their condition, Master," responded Ginger.

"Are they dim-witted?" asked the fellow.

"I do not think so, Master," said Ginger. "It is only that they come from a world which has not prepared them to easily grasp the nature of certain realities, let alone that they might find themselves implicated in them."

"I see," said the man.

"But do not fear, Master," said Ginger, "we learn swiftly."

"That is known to me," he grinned.

Ginger looked down, swallowing hard. It was true. On Gor, girls learned swiftly.

I saw the fellow in the broad-brimmed hat, behind Ginger and Evelyn, make a sign to the auctioneer.

"If there is no one here now who wishes further to examine the tavern girls, prior to their sale, I will have them removed to a holding area," said the auctioneer.

Ginger and Evelyn, startled, exchanged glances. As no one spoke, the auctioneer nodded to two of the attendants. In a moment the girls, the upper left arm of each in the grasp of an attendant, were conducted, bewildered, through a side door from the hall.

The fellow in the broad-brimmed hat, I gathered, had influence in Kailiauk. He was, obviously, at any rate, taken seriously in the house of Ram Seibar.

When the heavy door had closed behind the tavern girls, he said to the auctioneer, "One five apiece."

"Are there any other bids?" inquired the auctioneer.

There was silence in the room. It interested me that there were no other bids.

"One five," agreed the auctioneer. "One five, for each."

The fellow in the broad-brimmed hat then pointed to the girl on the central block. This did not surprise me. I had gathered that he might be interested in her. The purchase of the two tavern girls, further, I had surmised, was intimately connected with this interest. He wanted them, doubtless, to be used in her training, in particular, I supposed, with her training in Gorean. Other aspects of her training he might see fit to attend to himself. Needless to say, it is pleasant to train a beautiful woman uncompromisingly to one's most intimate pleasures. Further, there was no doubt that the girl on the block was a beauty. Yet, in some way, I still found his interest in her somewhat puzzling. She was, obviously, in complexion, coloration, refinement, figure and beauty, quite different from the other girls he had purchased. Perhaps he was a fellow with wide divergence in his tastes.

"We have a bid on the slave of six nine," said the auctioneer. With his foot he moved her bound hands a bit upward on her back. He then stood with his right boot on the small of her back. "Six nine," he said, looking at the fellow in the broad-brimmed hat.

"Seven five," said the fellow.

The auctioneer then removed his boot from the prone body of the slave and, by the hair, pulled her up to her knees.

"Seven five," said the fellow.

The auctioneer then, by the hair, pulled the girl to her feet. He then, with his quirt, indicated that the girl should suck in her gut and lift her head. She did so.

"Very well," said the fellow in the broad-brimmed hat. "Seven eight."

The auctioneer seemed hesitant.

"Seven nine, then," said the fellow.

This, I took it, was the bid the auctioneer had been waiting for. It was an even silver tarsk, or an even hundred copper tarsks, of the sort common in Kailiauk, figured in multiples of ten, over the earlier standing bid of six nine.

"Are there any other bids?" called the auctioneer. I sensed there would not be any. Too, I did not think the auctioneer expected any. To be sure, it was doubtless his business to inquire explicitly into the matter.

The girl trembled, her chin obediently high.

No more bids were forthcoming. No one, it seemed, cared to bid against the fellow in the broad-brimmed hat. I found this of interest. I had not found this sort of thing before in a Gorean market.

"Deliver her to the holding area," said the auctioneer, addressing himself to an attendant near the foot of the block. The fellow, then, climbed to the height of the block. "She is yours," said the auctioneer to the man in the broad-brimmed hat. The attendant seized the girl by the arms. It was only then, I think, that the former Millicent Aubrey-Welles, from Pennsylvania, realized that she had been sold. She was conducted from the surface of the block.

"That," said the auctioneer, "concludes the final auction of the evening. Permit me to remind you all that the market is not yet closed. It remains open for another Ahn. Peruse now, if you would, in the time remaining before we close, the lovely morsels, dainties for your delectation, fastened on the slave plates to the sides. In a lesser house any one of them would doubtless be worthy the central block. Yet, here, in the house of Ram Seibar, in this house of prizes and bargains, no one of them is likely to cost you more than a silver tarsk!"

I glanced about, at the girls on the side blocks. A few pretended to brazen indifference. Most, however, only too obviously, were terrified. I think there was not one among them who did not, now, understand that she was a slave. I think there was not one among them who did not now realize that she might soon, and totally, belong to a man.

"To the side blocks, please, Noble Sirs," invited the auctioneer, with an expansive gesture of his open hand, "to the side blocks!"

The men began to drift to the side blocks. Several went toward the block of the girl with whom Ginger had spoken. She had looked well under the attendant's whip. Several of the girls whimpered. A woman's first sale, I suspected, is often the hardest.

"Come with me," said the fellow in the broad-brimmed hat. He then turned about, and went through a side door.

Puzzled, I followed him.

On the other side of the door we found ourselves in a holding area, a long, shedlike structure ancillary to the main hall. It was wooden-floored and the narrow floor boards were laid lengthwise. About every five feet a linear set of these boards was painted yellow, thus, in effect, making long, yellow lines, parallel to the sides of the structure, on the floor. At the head and foot of these lines, also in yellow, were painted numbers.

On one of these lines, number six, there knelt, one behind the other, in tandem fashion, seven girls. They were barbarians, but they had been knelt in the position of pleasure slaves, back on their heels, knees wide, hands on their thighs, backs straight, heads up.

"You handled yourself well in the hall," said the fellow to me. "It is my suspicion that you are no stranger to war."

"I have fought," I admitted.

"Are you a mercenary?" he asked.

"Of sorts," I said.

"Why are you in Kailiauk?" he asked.

"I am here on business," I said, warily.

"Are your pursuers numerous?" he asked.

"Pursuers?" I asked.

"You are doubtless in flight," he said. "Would you give me a hand with these chains?" He then bent down and, from some things, his, I gathered, near one wall, he had picked up several loops of light chain, with spaced, attached collars. He slung these loops over his left shoulder and joined me, near the last girl kneeling on the line.

He handed me a collar, at the chain's termination. I clasped it about the neck of the last girl on the line. It closed, locking, with a heavy metallic click.

"I am not in flight," I said.

The girl whimpered, collared and on the chain.

"I see," grinned the fellow.

"Why should you think I am in flight?" I asked.

"Skills such as yours," he said, "do not bring their highest prices in the vicinity of the perimeter." He handed me another length of chain, with its collar.

"Oh," I said. I added the next girl to the chain. The collars had front and back rings, were hinged on the right and locked on the left. This is a familiar form of coffle collar. The lengths of chain between the collars were about three to four feet long. Some were attached to the collar rings by the links themselves, opened and then reclosed about the rings, and some of them were fastened to the collar rings by snap rings. Another common form of coffle collar has its hinge in the front and closes behind the back of the neck, like the common slave collar. It has a single collar ring, usually on

the right, through which, usually, a single chain is strung.
Girls are spaced on such a chain, usually, by snap rings. An
advantage of the first sort of coffle arrangement is that the
chain may, as girls are added or subtracted, be shortened or
lengthened. A chain which has been borne by fifty girls
would, of course, be impracticably heavy for five or six. An
advantage of the second arrangement is that girls can be easily spaced on the chain, more or less closely together, and
can be conveniently removed from, and added to, the chain.
Which chaining arrangement is best for a given set of girls
depends, of course, on the particular intentions and purposes
of their master. The fellow in the broad-brimmed hat had
opted, of course, for the first arrangement. This suggested to
me that he expected girls, for one reason or another, to be
subtracted from the chain.

"If you are not now in flight," he said, "I suggest that you
consider its advisability."

I looked at him. He handed me another length of chain
and a collar.

"You should leave town, and soon," he said.

I put another girl on the chain.

"Why?" I asked.

"The vanity of the Hobarts, a proud folk," he said, "was
much stung this night, and before female slaves. They will
come with their men, with crossbows and swords. They will
want their revenge."

"I do not fear them," I said.

"When do you intend to leave Kailiauk?" he asked.

"In the morning," I said.

"Good," said he. "I would not alter my plans."

"I have no intention of doing so," I said. Martial dalliance
was not germane to my mission.

"Put her on the chain," said the fellow, handing me another collar and length of chain.

I added a blonde to the chain. He then handed me another
chain segment and collar, unlooping it from his shoulder.

"What are you going to do?" he asked.

"I have purchased some trade goods," I said. "It is my intention to enter the Barrens."

"That is dangerous," said he.

"That is what I have heard," I said.

"Do you know any of the languages? Do you know even
ion?" he asked.

"No," I said.

"Avoid them, then," he said.

I then added another girl to the coffle, a short-haired, sturdy-legged brunet.

"I am determined," I said.

The fellow lifted the girl's short, dark hair. "It will be difficult to braid this hair," he said, "but it will grow."

I then, taking a collar and a length of chain from him, added the next girl to the coffle. She was also a brunet.

"I am curious," I said, "as to the nature of the girls you have purchased. These seven, though surely outstandingly attractive, seem to me to have been rather exceeded in beauty by several of the others, whom you did not choose to buy."

"Perhaps," he grinned. He handed me another collar, and length of chain, unlooping it from his shoulder.

"Please don't put me in a collar," said the seventh girl, looking up, tears in her eyes. She had spoken in English. She had light-brown hair. I put the collar on her throat, and locked it. She was then naught but another lovely component in the coffle. She put back her head, and choked back a sob.

"Are you truly determined to enter the Barrens?" asked the fellow.

"Yes," I said.

"How many kaiila do you have?" he asked.

"Two," I said, "one to ride, another for the trade goods."

"That is fortunate," said the fellow. "No more than two kaiila are to be brought by any single white man into the Barrens. Too, no party of white men in the Barrens is permitted to bring in more than ten kaiila."

"These are rules in Kailiauk?" I asked.

"They are the rules of the red savages," he said.

"Then," said I, "only small groups of white men could enter the Barrens, or else they would be on foot, at the mercy of the inhabitants of the area."

"Precisely," said the fellow.

Two slave girls, blindfolded, their hands tied behind them, were then thrust into the room. An attendant, holding them by the arms, brought them forward, and then, at the indication of the fellow in the broad-brimmed hat, knelt them down over the yellow line, in front of the hitherto first girl in the coffle. Both were frightened. They were Ginger and Evelyn. "To whom have we been sold?" begged Ginger. "Where are we being taken?" begged Evelyn. The attendant then, with his booted foot, kicked Ginger to her side on the floor. Then he took Evelyn's hair in his left hand and with his right hand lashed her face twice, with the palm and then the back of his hand, snapping it from side to side. He then knelt them again, on the line. "Forgive us, Masters," begged Ginger. "Forgive us, Masters," begged Evelyn, blood at the side of her mouth.

I then, with materials supplied by the fellow in the broad-brimmed hat, added Ginger and Evelyn to the coffle.

"The three of them, together," said the attendant, "come to ten nine. The other will be brought forward in a moment."

I saw the coins change hands.

The small wrists of Ginger and Evelyn pulled futilely at their bonds.

In a moment, as the attendant had suggested, the red-haired girl was introduced into the room.

"She is a beauty," I said to the fellow in the broad-brimmed hat.

"That she is," he said, "and, beyond that, it is the sort of girl she is. She will make a superb slave."

The girl, then, half stumbling, was brought forward. Rudely she was thrust down to her knees, where the fellow in the broad-brimmed hat indicated, at the head of the coffle. To her horror her knees were kicked apart. Her chin was then pushed up. In a moment she was fastened with the others.

I looked down at the red-haired girl. The man in the broad-brimmed hat lifted her hair, displaying it to me. "It is long enough to braid," he said.

"If one wished it," I said. I myself tended to prefer, on the whole, long, loose hair on a slave, tied back, if at all, with a headband or, behind the head, with a cloth or string.

He let her hair fall back, down her back.

"She would bring a high price," I said, "in almost any market with which I am familiar."

"I will be able to get five hides of the yellow kailiauk for her," said the man.

"Oh, no, Master!" cried Ginger, suddenly, dismally. "No, Master!" protested Evelyn. "Please, no! Please, no!"

The man in the broad-brimmed hat bent down and, one after the other, untied the wrists of Evelyn, Ginger and the red-haired girl. Ginger and Evelyn were trembling, half in ʜysteria. Yet they had presence of mind enough to place their hands, palms down, on their thighs. The palms of the red-haired girl, forcibly, her wrists in his grasp, were placed on her thighs. When her left hand wished to stray to her brand he took it and placed it again, firmly, palm down, on her thigh.

"Yes, Master," whispered the girl, in English. I was pleased to see that she was intelligent. A fresh brand is not to be disturbed, of course.

The fellow in the broad-brimmed hat then removed the blindfolds from Ginger and Evelyn. "Oh, no!" wept Ginger. "No, no!" wept Evelyn. "Not you, please!" They regarded who it was who owned them, in dismay, and with horror. Yet, I think, but moments before, surely they had sensed, and surely feared, who he might be. Their worst fears had now seemed confirmed. I did not understand their terror. He seemed to me a genial enough fellow. "Sell us, beloved Master!" begged Ginger. "Please, Master," begged Evelyn, "we are only poor slaves. Take pity on us! Sell us to another!" "Make us pot girls!" begged Ginger. "Shackle us! Send us to the farms!" "We are only poor slaves," wept Evelyn. "Please, please, Master, sell us to another! We beg you, Beloved Master. Sell us to another!"

"The house of Ram Seibar," said the fellow, amused, "wishes you both taken from Kailiauk."

Several of the other girls now, I noted, were frightened and apprehensive. The red-haired girl, too, seemed frightened. They could not understand Gorean but the terror of the other slaves was patent to them. None of them, I noted, to my satisfaction, had dared to break position. Already, I conjectured, they had begun to suspect what might be the nature of Gorean discipline.

"Master!" wept Ginger.

"Please, Master!" wept Evelyn.

"Position," snapped the man in the broad-brimmed hat.

Immediately the girls knelt back in the coffle, back on their heels, their knees wide, their hands on their thighs, their backs straight and heads lifted. Seeing this, the other girls, too, behind them, hurriedly sought to improve their posture. The red-haired girl, who could not see behind her, from the sound of the command, and the movements in the chain, reaching her through the back collar ring, fearfully sensing what was going on, straightened herself as well.

"These two girls, the second and third," I said, indicating

Ginger and Evelyn, "seem quite disturbed to discover that you are their master."

"It surely seems so," granted the fellow in the broad-brimmed hat.

"Why should they regard you with such terror," I asked, "more than seems necessary on the part of a slave girl with respect to her master?" It is natural for a slave girl, of course, to regard her master with a certain trepidation. She is, after all, an animal, who is owned by him, over whom he has total power. The rational slave girl will almost never intentionally displease her master. First, it is just too costly to do so. Secondly, for reasons that are sometimes obscure to men, these having to do with her being a female, she seldom desires to do so.

"I do not think that it is I, personally, whom they regard with such terror," he grinned.

"What then could be the source of such terror?" I asked.

"Who knows what goes on in the heads of pretty little slaves," he said.

"You seem evasive," I observed.

"Perhaps," he admitted.

"Your coffle," I said, "is striking, an assemblage of chained beauties. Yet I think there seems a rather clear distinction between the first three girls and the last seven, and, if I may say so, between the first and the second two."

"Yes," he said, "that is true. Observe the last seven girls. Do you know their nature? Do you know what they are?"

"What?" I asked.

"Pack animals," he said. "They are pack animals."

"I thought they might be," I said. The fellow's itinerary now seemed clear to me. No more than two kaiila, I remembered he had said, may be brought in by any given white man.

"And the first girl," I asked, "is she, too, to be a pack animal?"

"She, too, will serve as a pack animal," he said, "as will they all, but, ultimately, I have a different disposition in mind for her."

"I see," I said.

"She will be worth five hides of the yellow kailiauk to me," ̣said.

᠁n you will make a splendid profit on her," I said.

"Yes," said he. A robe of yellow kailiauk, even in average condition, can bring as much as five silver tarsks.

I looked at the red-haired girl in the coffle, the former Millicent Aubrey-Welles. She did not even know she was the subject of our conversation.

"And what of these other two?" I asked, indicating Ginger and Evelyn.

"By means of them I can communicate with the red-haired girl," he said. "In their barbarous tongue they can make clear to her, and quickly, the nature of her condition, and the efficiency, intimacy and totality of the services that will be required of her. Too, they can teach her some Gorean, which will keep them all busy, and help me train her."

"I see," I said.

He adjusted the remainder of the chains and collars on his shoulder. He had not come to the sales barn, apparently, knowing exactly how many girls he would purchase. It is difficult to anticipate such things accurately, of course, particularly when buying in lots. Much depends on what is available and what turns out to be the going prices on a given night. "The treks can be long," he said.

"Treks?" I asked.

"Yes," he said.

"I note," I said, "that all of these girls are barbarians, even the second and third girl. Why have you not purchased some Gorean girls for your pack train?"

"For pack animals it is surely more appropriate to use meaningless barbarians than Gorean girls," he said.

"Of course," I granted him.

"But there is, of course," he grinned, "another reason, as well."

"What is that?" I asked.

"These barbarian girls will march along in their coffle as ignorant and innocent as kaiila," he said.

"Whereas?" I asked.

"Whereas," he grinned, "Gorean girls might die of fear."

Ginger and Evelyn moaned.

"These slaves," I said, indicating the two former tavern girls, "seem not totally ignorant."

"Even these slaves," he said, indicating Ginger and Evelyn, "who seem so transfixed with terror, do not even begin, I assure you, to have any idea as to what might lie before them."

The two girls shuddered. Their will, of course, was nothing. They, like the animals they were, must go where their masters pleased.

"I take it that you, with your pack train, intend to enter the Barrens," I said.

"Yes," said he.

"Tomorrow morning?" I asked.

"Yes," said he.

"You are, then, a trader?" I asked.

"Yes," he said.

"I have sought along the perimeter for one named 'Grunt'," I said.

"That is known to me," he said.

"None seemed to know of his whereabouts, or clearly," I said.

"Oh?" he said.

"I found that unusual," I said.

"Why?" he asked.

"This fellow, Grunt," I said, "is presumably a well-known trader. Does it not seem strange, then, that no one would have a clear idea as to his location?"

"That does seem a bit strange," agreed the fellow.

"It is my thought," I said, "that this fellow, Grunt, has many friends, that he inspires loyalty, that these friends desire to protect him."

"If that is so," he said, "then this Grunt, in at least some respects, must be a lucky man."

"Do you know him?" I asked.

"Yes," he said.

"Do you know where he is?" I asked.

"Yes," he said.

"Do you think you could direct me to his whereabouts?" I asked.

"I am he," he said.

"I thought so," I said.

9

WE CROSS THE IHANKE

"It is here," said Grunt, turning about on his kaiila. "See the wands?"

"Yes," I said. We were now some two pasangs east of Kailiauk.

"Here is one," said Grunt, "and there is another, and another."

"I see," I said, shading my eyes.

The grass was to the knees of the kaiila. It came to the thighs of the slave girls, in brief one-piece slave tunics, of brown rep-cloth, with deep cleavages, in throat coffle, bearing burdens on their heads.

The wand before us was some seven or eight feet high. It is of this height, apparently, that it may be seen above the snow, during the winter moons, such as Waniyetuwi and Wanicokanwi. It was of peeled Ka-la-na wood and, from its top, there dangled two long, narrow, yellow, black-tipped feathers, from the tail of the taloned Herlit, a large, broad-winged, carnivorous bird, sometimes in Gorean called the Sun Striker, or, more literally, though in clumsier English, Out-of-the-sun-it-strikes, presumably from its habit of making its descent and strike on prey, like the tarn, with the sun above and behind it. Similar wands I could see some two hundred yards away, on either side, to the left and right. According to Grunt such wands line the perimeter, though usually not in such proximity to one another. They are spaced more closely together, naturally, nearer areas of white habitation.

Grunt now turned back on his kaiila to look out, eastward, over the broad grasses and low, rolling hills. The terrain beyond the wands did not appear much different from the terrain leading up to them. The hills, the grass, the arching blue sky, the white clouds, seemed much the same on both sides of the wands. The wands seemed an oddity, a geographical irrelevance. Surely, thrust in the earth, supple in the wind, with the rustling feathers, they could betoken nothing of significance. The wind was fresh. I shivered on the kaiila.

For those who might be interested in such things, we came to the wands in the early spring, early in Magaksicaagliwi, which is the Moon of the Returning Gants. The preceding moon was the Sore-Eye Moon, or Istawicayazanwi. Because of its uncertain weather, the possible freezes and storms, and its harsh winds, this month had been avoided by Grunt. The next moon was Wozupiwi, the Planting Moon, which term, in the context, I find extremely interesting. It seems to make clear that the folk of the area, at one time, were settled, agricultural peoples. That, of course, would have been before the acquisition of the kaiila, which seems to have wrought a local cultural transformation of the first magnitude. One often thinks of a hunting economy representing a lower, in some sense, stage of cultural development than an agricultural economy. Perhaps this is because, commonly, agriculture provides a stabler cultural milieu and can, normally, support larger populations on less territory. A single human being can be agriculturally supported by less than an acre of land. The same human being, if surviving by hunting, would require a territory of several square miles. Here, however, we seem to have a case where peoples deliberately chose the widely ranging, nomadic hunting economy over an agricultural economy. The mobility afforded by the kaiila and the abundance of the kailiauk doubtless made this choice possible, the choice of the widely ranging hunter, the proud and free warrior, over the farmer, denied distant horizons, he who must live at the mercy of the elements and in bondage to his own soil.

Grunt sat astride his kaiila, a lofty, yellow animal, looking eastward, out beyond the wands. Behind him there was a pack kaiila, laden with goods. A thong ran from the pierced nose of the beast to a ring at the back of his saddle. I, too, was astride my kaiila, a black, silken, high-necked, long-fanged beast. To my saddle, too, was tethered a pack kaiila. Various goods were borne by our pack animals, both of the four-legged and two-legged varieties. My goods were all laden on my pack kaiila. Grunt's goods, on the other hand, of course, were distributed over his eleven beasts of burden, the kaiila and the ten other pack animals. My goods, substantially, consisted of blankets, colored cloths, ribbons, mirrors and beads, kettles and pans, popular in the grasslands, hard candies, cake sugar and chemical dyes. Grunt carried similar articles but he, as well, as I had not, carried such items as long nails, rivets, hatchets, metal arrowheads, metal lance points, knife blades and butcher knives. The knife blades and long nails are sometimes mounted in clubs. The blades, of course, may also be fitted into carved handles, of wood and bone. The rivets are useful in fastening blades in handles and lance shafts. The metal arrowhead is a convenience. It is ready-made and easy to mount. It is not likely to fracture as a stone point might. Similarly it makes dangerous trips to flint-rich areas unnecessary. The butcher knives are usually ground down into a narrow, concave shape. They do not have the sturdiness for combat. They are used, generally, for the swift acquisition of bloody trophies.

I saw Grunt straighten himself in the high-pommeled saddle. He lifted the reins. He kicked back with his heels, suddenly, smiting the animal in the flanks. It started, and then, in its smooth, loping stride, crossed the line of the wands. Grunt rode some twenty yards ahead, and then pulled back the kaiila, twisting its head back with the reins, wheeling it about to face us. He loosened the long, coiled whip fastened with a snap strap at the right of his saddle, and rode back towards us, along the right side of the coffle of barefoot, scantily clad, neck-chained beauties. "Hei! Hei!" he called. He cracked the whip in the air, twice. He then rode about the rear of the coffle, and advanced, on his kaiila, along its left side. He was right-handed.

"We are women, and only helpless slaves!" cried out Ginger. "Please, Master, do not take us across the line of the wands!"

"Reconsider, Master, we beg of you!" cried out Evelyn.

"Hei! Hei!" cried Grunt.

"Please, no, Master!" cried out Ginger.

"Please, no, no, Master!" cried out Evelyn.

Then the whip lashed down. More than one girl cried out with pain. Then the whip fell, too, on Ginger and Evelyn. They screamed, struck.

"Hei! Hei!" called Grunt.

"Yes, Master!" wept Ginger.

"Yes, Master!" wept Evelyn.

"Hei! Hei!" urged Grunt.

The coffle, then, to the snapping of the whip, led by the terrified red-haired girl, the former Millicent Aubrey-Welles, from Pennsylvania, began to move ahead. Ginger and Evelyn, in their places, stumbled forward, red-eyed and almost numb with terror. Other girls, smarting from the pain and feeling the jerking of the chain on their collars, weeping, followed, they, too, in their appropriate places, precisely where their master wished them, places made clear by their collars and chains. Only Ginger and Evelyn, I surmised, had any inkling as to the nature of the place into which they were being taken, and they, too, in the final analysis, were only barbarians. They, too, at least as yet, would not be able to understand where they were being taken, what was being done to them, not fully, not yet in its full meaning. I thought it just as well that the girls, even Ginger and Evelyn, were substantially ignorant. This made it easier to march them across the line of the wands. I watched the girls, the burdens on their heads, their necks chained, moving through the tall grass. They were now crossing the line of the wands. I wondered if they could even begin to suspect the terrors into which they were entering. Yes, I thought to myself, it is better this way. Let them, for the time, remain ignorant. They would learn soon enough what it might mean, in such a place, in the place of the kailiauk and the high grasses, to be a white female.

Grunt, on his kaiila, had now taken his place at the head of the line, the pack kaiila behind him.

I looked at the red-haired girl, first in the coffle, the burden balanced with her small hands on her head. Grunt, I knew, had some special disposition in mind for her. Yet, now, she, like the others, served as a mere pack animal, one of the beasts of his coffle, bearing his goods.

No white man, I recalled, was to bring more than two kaiila across the line of the wands. No group of white men was to bring more than ten kaiila across that seemingly placid boundary.

The red-haired girl looked well in the coffle, moving in the grass, the chain on her neck, in the brief slave tunic. So, too, did the others. Slave girls are beautiful, even those who must serve as mere beasts of burden. Grunt, I recalled, in urging his coffle forward, had not struck the lead girl, his lovely red-haired beast, with the lash, as he had several of the others. He had chosen, for some reason, to spare her its stroke. This was, I suspected, because he had something more in mind for her than a burden and a place in the coffle. He had, clearly, something else in mind for her. He was apparently willing to take his time with her, and to bring her along easily and gently, at least for a time. This was, perhaps, because she seemed already to understand that it would be her business to please men, and that she was a slave. She would have to understand later, of course, what it was to be a slave, fully. That would be time enough for her to feel the boot and the whip.

"It is here," Grunt had said.

I looked again ahead, out beyond that seemingly placid boundary, out beyond the wands.

I checked my weapons. Then I, too, urged my kaiila forward. In a few moments I and my pack kaiila, too, had crossed the line of the wands.

"It is here," Grunt had said.

I pulled up the kaiila and looked behind me. Now I, too, had crossed that boundary marked by the supple feathered wands. I saw the feathers moving in the wind. Now I, too, had crossed the Ihanke. Now I, too, was within the Barrens.

I urged my kaiila forward again, after Grunt and the coffle. I did not wish to fall behind.

10

I SEE DUST BEHIND US

"You are aware, are you not," I asked Grunt, "that we are being followed?"

"Yes," he said.

It was toward the noon of our second day in the Barrens.

"I trust that their intentions are peaceful," I said.

"That is unlikely," he smiled.

"Are we not yet in the country of the Dust Legs?" I inquired. This was a perimeter tribe which, on the whole, was favorably disposed towards whites. Most trading was done with Dust Legs. Indeed, it was through the Dust Legs that most of the goods of the interior might reach civilization, the Dust Legs, in effect, acting as agents and intermediaries. Many tribes, apparently, would not deal on a face-to-face basis with whites. This had to do with the hatred and suspicion fostered by that tradition called the Memory. Too, it was often difficult to control their young men. Although small trading groups were welcomed in the country of the Dust Legs, such groups seldom penetrated the more interior territories. Too many of them had failed to return. Grunt was unusual in having traded as far east as the country of the Fleer and the Yellow Knives. Too, he had entered, at least once, the country of the Sleen and the Kaiila. Some of these territories, apparently, had scarcely been penetrated since the days of the first white explorers of the Barrens, men such as Boswell, Diaz, Bento, Hastings and Hogarthe.

"Yes," said Grunt.

"Why, then, do you conjecture that their intentions may be hostile?" I asked.

"They are not Dust Legs," he said.

We wheeled our kaiila about, and the coffle stopped. The girls put down their burdens, gratefully. We observed the dust in the distance, some pasangs across the prairie.

"They are, then," I speculated, "Fleer or Yellow Knives."

"No," he said.

"I do not understand," I said.

"Observe the dust," he said. "Its front is narrow, and it does not behave as though raised by the wind."

"The wind direction, too," I said, "would be incorrect."

"Accordingly," said Grunt, "you conjecture that the dust is raised by the paws of running kaiila."

"Yes," I said.

"In that you are correct," he said. "What else do you note?" he asked.

"I do not understand," I said. I was growing apprehensive. It was early in the day. I had little doubt but what the distant riders could overtake us, and easily, before nightfall.

"It is so obvious," said Grunt, "that you have noted it, but have not considered its significance."

"What?" I asked.

"You can detect that dust," he said.

"Yes," I said, "of course."

"Does that not seem to you of interest?" he asked.

"I do not understand," I said.

"To raise dust like that, in this terrain," said Grunt, "you must ride across draws, rather than avoid them, and you must ride in a cluster, where the dust will rise, cloudlike, rather than rise and fall, in a narrow line, swiftly dissipated by the wind."

"What are you telling me?" I asked.

Grunt grinned. "If we were being followed by red savages," he said, "I do not think that you, with your present level of skills, would be aware of it."

"I do not understand," I said.

"That dust," he said, "does not rise from the paws of the kaiila of Dust Legs, nor of Yellow Knives nor Fleer. It is not raised, at all, by the kaiila of red savages. They would not ride so openly, so carelessly, so stupidly. They would avoid, where possible, grassless, dry areas, and they would ride at intervals, in single file. This arrangement not only obscures their numbers but lowers and narrows the dust line."

"White men, then, follow us," I said.

"I thought they would," said Grunt.

"They cannot be white men," I said. "Observe the front of dust. That must be raised by fifteen or twenty kaiila."

"True," smiled Grunt. "They are fools."

I swallowed, hard. A law, imposed on white men entering their lands by red savages, had been violated.

"Who are they?" I asked.

"I have had trouble with them before," smiled Grunt. "I have been waiting for them."

"Who are they?" I asked.

"They want you," he said. "I thought they would follow this time. You are the bait."

"I?" I asked.

"You came with me of your own free will, did you not?" he asked.

"Yes," I said, irritably.

"Accordingly," he grinned, "you cannot blame me."

"I am not interested in blaming anyone," I said. "I would just like to know what is going on."

"They will also be interested in the second and third girls," he said.

I looked to Ginger and Evelyn, lying in the grass, exhausted, their burdens beside them.

"They are the Hobarts," I said, "and the men from the Bar Ina."

"Yes," said Grunt.

"You said they would not make pleasant enemies," I said.

"They will not," he said.

"We cannot outrun them with the girls," I said. "We must make a stand." I looked about, swiftly, for high ground or shelter.

"No," said Grunt.

"What, then, are we to do?" I asked.

"We shall continue on, as we were," said Grunt. "We shall not even suggest, by our behavior, that we are aware of their approach."

"I do not understand," I said.

"To be sure," said Grunt, "we should waste little time." He then rode his kaiila about the coffle of girls, cracking his whip, viciously. Several cried out in fear. They had already felt that whip, through the thin brown cloth of their slave tunics or across the backs of their legs. "Hei! Hei!" called Grunt. "On your feet, you stupid sluts, you luscious beasts! Up! Up! Burdens up! Burdens up! Have we all day to dally? No, my luscious beasts, no! Burdens up! Burdens up!" The girls scrambled to their feet, struggling to lift their burdens. The whip cracked again and a girl cried out with pain, one more tardy than the rest. Then she, too, gasping, tears in her eyes, stood ready in the coffle, the burden balanced on her head. "On!" said Grunt, with a gesture of his whip, wheeling about on his kaiila. "On!" With the sound of chains and collars, and some frightened sobbing, the neck-shackled beauties again took up the march.

I drew my kaiila alongside that of Grunt. "I think we must either run," I said, "abandoning the girls and the goods, or stop, and make a stand."

"I do not think we should make a stand," said Grunt. "We could kill the kaiila and use them, in effect, as a fort and shelter, but, even so, we would be severely outnumbered."

I said nothing. I feared his assessment of the situation was only too sound.

"If we were red savages," said Grunt, "we would run. Then, hopefully, when the pursuers were strung out, over pasangs, we would turn back on them and, two to one, one engaging, the other striking, finish them off. If this did not seem practical we might separate, dividing our pursuers, and meet later at a prearranged rendezvous, thence to return under the cover of darkness to recover, if possible, what we had lost."

"That is interesting," I said. "Indeed, that seems a sensible plan. Let us put it immediately into effect."

"No," said Grunt.

"Why not?" I asked.

"It is pointless," he said.

"Why is it pointless?" I asked.

"It is pointless," he said, "because we are in no danger."

I looked back at the approaching dust. "We are not in danger?" I asked.

"No," said Grunt, not looking back. "It is they, rather, who are in danger, grave danger."

"I think," I said, angrily, "that we are fools."

"No," said Grunt, quietly. "It is they who are the fools."

11

SLAVE INSTRUCTION;

IT SEEMS WE ARE NO LONGER BEING FOLLOWED

"You seem apprehensive," said Grunt.

"They should have caught up to us by now," I said.

I stood at the edge of our small camp, in a few trees, nestled beside a small stream. It was the late afternoon.

"No," said Grunt. "Put it from your mind."

I turned back to the camp.

Ginger and Evelyn had been freed from the coffle, to gather wood and cook, and attend to the chores of the camp. The collars and chains had been rearranged on the other girls, in such a way that, by an alternation of the position of snap locks and chain segments, a free collar was now at each end of the coffle. These collars had then been fastened about two small trees, thus confining the girls, other than Ginger and Evelyn, to the line between the two trees. Last night the coffle had been taken four times about a small, sturdy tree and then the collar of the first girl had been fastened to the collar of the last girl. That, too, would be, I supposed, the procedure tonight. There are many ways to keep a line of girls in place overnight, of course. A common way is to bind their wrists behind their backs and then place them on the ground, supine, the head of one to the feet of the other. A given girl, then, by thongs on her collar, is tied to the left ankle of the girl on her left, and to the right ankle of the girl on her right; similarly, the girl on her left is thonged, by thongs passing about her collar, to the given girl's left ankle, and the girl on the given girl's right is thonged, by thongs passing about her collar, to the right ankle of the given girl.

"I am first girl," said Ginger, walking back and forth before the line of girls, kneeling before her, a switch in her small hand, "and Evelyn is second girl." She indicated Evelyn. She spoke in English, a language held in common by the new barbarian slaves. Five spoke English natively; three were American, including the red-haired girl, and two were British; two of the other girls were Swedish, and the last girl, with the short, dark hair, was French. "You will address myself, and Evelyn, as Mistress," she said. "You will learn your lessons well, both those of the language and of service."

The girls looked at one another.

"This is a switch," said Ginger, lifting the supple switch. She then struck one of the girls, one of the Swedish girls, with a stinging, slashing blow at the side of the neck.

"This is a switch," repeated Ginger.

"Yes, Mistress," said the red-haired girl, swiftly. I was pleased to see that she was quite intelligent. "Yes, Mistress," said the other girls. "Yes, Mistress!" said the Swedish girl, tears in her eyes.

"Evelyn and I," said Ginger, "do not intend to do all the work of the camp alone. In time, some of you, at least, will be freed to assist in our labors."

The girls, quickly, glanced at one another.

"Little fools!" laughed Ginger. "You are all little fools! Kneel straighter, little fools!"

Quickly the girls complied.

"Do not think of escape," she said. "There is no escape for you."

Several of the girls reddened.

"Consider your garb," said Ginger. "It is distinctive. It is that of a slave."

Several of the girls looked down at the scanty, revealing cloth in which they had been placed.

"Similarly, you are barbarians," said Ginger. "Even as you learn the language of masters, your accent will continue to betray you. Similarly, even should you learn to speak flawlessly such things as the fillings in your teeth and the vaccination marks on your arms will continue to mark you as barbarian. So, too, will such things as the fact that you have no Home Stone and no caste, and will be ignorant of a thousand things known to any Gorean. No, do not think that you can easily shed your barbarian origin."

Some of the girls looked at her, angrily.

"Too," said Ginger, "thrust up your tunics. Examine your left thighs!"

The girls did so.

"You are marked," said Ginger. "You are branded."

The girls smoothed down their tunics, some of them with tears in their eyes.

"So," said Ginger, "put all hopes of escape from your mind. It is a meaningless, foolish dream, inappropriate in a Gorean slave girl. There is no one here to save you. There is no place to go, nowhere to run. If you should seem to escape, you will be picked up by the first man who finds you, who will then return you to your master, for punishment, or keep you for his own slave. You, there! On your belly!"

The Swedish girl, frightened, she who had been struck previously, twisted in the coffle chain and put herself on her belly. The girls on her left and right knelt, frightened, heads low, collar chains taut, looking at her.

Ginger went to the girl and thrust up the tunic. "See these tendons," she asked, "at the back of each knee?"

"Yes, Mistress," said more than one girl.

She laid the switch, cool and green, across the tendons. The Swedish girl shuddered. "It is a common punishment for a runaway girl," said Ginger, "that these tendons are severed. The girl, then, can never stand again, but must, if she is permitted to live, drag herself about by her hands. Sometimes such girls are gathered up by masters and used as beggars, on street corners."

Several of the girls cried out with fear.

Ginger then rose to her feet and stepped away from the Swedish girl, who then, frightened, smoothing down her tunic, together with the girls on her left and right, resumed her original kneeling position.

"You are barbarians," said Ginger. "You have been brought to Gor to be slaves, and that is what you are, and it is all that you are. Do not forget it!"

"No, Mistress," said more than one girl.

"In most cities and towns," said Ginger, "you would even find your pretty necks fastened in locked, steel collars."

"Like animals!" protested a girl.

"You are animals," said Ginger, "and the sooner you understand that, the easier it will be for you. You are beautiful, owned animals."

Several of the girls shuddered.

"And he who owns you," said Ginger, "he to whom you belong, is your master."

"Would he be our total master?" asked the red-haired girl, looking at me.

"Yes, your absolute and total master," said Ginger.

I gave no sign that I had understood the red-haired girl's question.

"But how can we be slaves?" asked a girl.

"Your question is stupid and foolish," said Ginger. "You are slaves. It is as simple as that. Do not be misled by the myths and rhetorics of your former world. Indeed, even on that world slavery exists. Slavery, as you will learn, is a very real institution, and, further, it is one in which you are profoundly implicated. You are totally and legally, as well as in practical fact, the property of your master."

The girl shrank back, in horror.

"My lessons for you today," said Ginger, "are basically quite simple. I think they may be grasped even by intellects such as yours, those of slave girls. First, you are slaves, and that is all you are, nothing more, only slaves. Second, do not even think of escape. There is no escape for you. Slaves you are, my dears, and slaves you will remain."

More than one of the girls, her head in her hands, shrank back, weeping.

It seemed to me that Ginger had certainly spoken bluntly to the new barbarian slaves, but, still, I felt, on the whole, it had been appropriate for her to do so. It is kindest, I think, in the long run, to proceed rather along the lines that she had. The sooner a new slave's delusions are dispelled the better it is, normally, for all concerned.

"Come now, my pretty slaves," said Ginger, "kneel straight. Back straight, heads up. Back on your heels there! Spread those pretty knees. Yes, that is the way men like it. Put your hands, palms down, on your thighs. Good. Good. Excellent!"

The girls now knelt in the coffle as pleasure slaves.

"Mistress," said a girl.

"Yes, pretty slave," said Ginger.

"You speak of men," said the girl.

"Yes," said Ginger. "You are female slaves. You now, in a general sense, belong to men."

Several of the girls looked at her, frightened.

"Doubtless you were taught many idiotic things about both yourselves and men on your old world. Doubtless, in your hearts, perhaps late at night, in bed, or in the morning, or at odd, lonely moments, in spite of your educations and conditionings, your trainings, you recognized the falseness of these teachings."

I saw that several of the girls looked very frightened. I saw that they understood, only too well, what Ginger was saying.

"You would understand, or sense, at such times," said Ginger, "the meaning of your slightness, your beauty and your needs. You would have understood that you were yearning women, in effect without men. You would have understood then something of the grand themes of nature, of dominance and submission, and your own obvious, natural place in such an organic scheme. At such times, perhaps, if you dared, you might have longed for the hands of a master on you, a magnificent, ruthless male who could fulfill you, who would put you to his feet and own you, who would answer your deepest needs, who would command you, who would dominate you, absolutely, and ravish you for his merest pleasure, and at his least whim, who would force from you, to your joy, the totality of love and service you were born to bestow."

The girls looked at her, terrified.

"On this world," said Ginger, "there is no dearth of such men and you, my dears, are female slaves."

"Are we not permitted resistance?" asked a girl.

"No resistance is permitted," said Ginger, "unless it be the master's will. That is a subtle point. You will have to learn to tell when the master desires resistance, that he may crush it mercilessly, and when he does not."

Several of the girls swallowed, hard.

"As female slaves," said Ginger, "you will be, as a general rule, a rule on which your very life may depend, absolutely docile, totally obedient, and fully pleasing."

"We would have to be anything, and do anything, then, fully," said a girl, "that we are commanded."

"Yes," said Ginger, "and with the utmost talent, skill and perfection that you can muster."

"Mistress," said the red-haired girl.

"Yes, Red-haired Slave," said Ginger.

"Is the slave girl also," asked the red-haired girl, "at the sexual mercy of her master?"

"Absolutely, and fully, and in every way," said Ginger.

Several of the girls gasped, shrinking back in their chains.

"You will learn," said Ginger.

"Yes, Mistress. Thank you, Mistress," said the red-haired girl. She looked at me, and then, quickly, shyly, put her head down. In the brown slave tunic, with the chain on her neck, she looked almost demure.

"Feed them," said Ginger.

Evelyn then threw each of the girls a piece of meat, throwing it to the grass before them. She removed these pieces of meat from the slender greenwood spit on which they had been roasted.

"Do not use your hands," warned Ginger, slapping the switch in her left palm.

"Yes, Mistress," said more than one of the girls.

I watched them, kneeling, leaning forward, palms down on the grass, heads down, eating at the meat.

"A pretty lot," said Grunt, behind me.

"Yes," I said.

The red-haired girl, eating at the meat, looked up at me, and then, shyly, again lowered her head.

"See that girl," asked Grunt, "the one with red hair?"

"Yes," I said.

"She is a virgin," he said.

"Oh?" I said.

"Yes," he said, "I tested her body this morning."

"I see," I said. I recalled that the girl, in the sales barn, had proclaimed her virginity. It had been done in the throes of the misery of her sale, when she had pleaded not to be brazenly exposed to the buyers. Her pleas, of course, had not been heeded.

"It is unfortunate," I said, "that she is a virgin."

"Why?" asked Grunt.

"Because she is quite pretty," I said.

"I do not understand," he said.

"Her virginity will doubtless improve her price," I said.

"Not in the Barrens," he said.

"No?" I asked.

"No," said Grunt. "They take virginity seriously only in their own women."

"I see," I said.

158   *John Norman*

"If you were going to buy a she-tarsk," asked Grunt, "would its virginity matter to you?"

"No," I said, "of course not."

"If she pleases you," he said, "you may have her, or any of the others, if you wish."

"Thank you," I said.

"What are slaves for?" he asked.

"True," I grinned.

"If you take her, however," he said, "take her, the first time, with gentleness."

"Very well," I said.

"It will be time enough later for her to learn what it is to be a true slave," he said.

"I understand," I said.

Grunt then turned away.

"Grunt," I said. He turned about. He still wore the broad-brimmed hat. I had never seen him without it.

"Yes," he said.

"The Hobarts," I said, "the men who were following, what of them?"

"If they were still following us," he said, "they would have arrived by now."

"Yes," I said.

"So they are no longer following," he said.

"I am prepared to believe that," I said.

"So put the matter from your mind," he said.

"What became of them?" I asked.

"It is time to sleep now," he said.

"What became of them?" I asked.

"We shall make a determination on that matter in the morning," he said. "In the meantime, let us sleep."

"Very well," I said.

12

I LEARN WHY WE ARE NO LONGER BEING FOLLOWED;

WE ADD TWO MEMBERS TO OUR PARTY

We saw a small gray sleen, some seven or eight feet in length, lift up its head.

We urged our kaiila down the slope, into the shallow declivity between two low hills.

My stomach twisted. We had smelled this before we had come upon it.

The sleen permitted us to approach rather closely. It was reluctant to leave its location. There were insects on its brown snout, and about its eyes. Its lower jaw was wet.

"Hei!" cried Grunt, slapping the side of his thigh.

The beast seized another bite and, whipping about, on its six legs, with its almost serpentine motion, withdrew.

"It is clean work," said Grunt, "the work of Dust Legs." This tribe I knew, in its various bands, was regarded as the most civilized of the tribes of the Barrens. In the eyes of some of the other tribes they were regarded as little better than white men.

"This is clean work?" I asked.

"Relatively," said Grunt.

I sat astride the kaiila, surveying the scene. I counted some twenty-one bodies. They were stripped. There were no kaiila. Insects swam in the air above several of the bodies. One could hear their humming. Two jards, fluttering, fought in an opened abdominal cavity. Several yellow fleer stalked about, and some perched on motionless limbs. Saddles and clothing, cut to pieces, lay strewn about.

I moved the kaiila slowly among some of the bodies, threading a path between them. It stepped daintily. It hissed and whined, uneasily. I did not think it was at ease in this place.

"I see no kaiila," I said to Grunt, "no weapons. I see little of value."

"It was taken," said Grunt.

I looked down at the slashed bodies. Arrows had apparently been pried loose from the flesh, that they might be used again.

"Are things usually done in this fashion?" I asked Grunt.

"This is not bad," said Grunt. "This is the work of Dust Legs."

"They are the friendly fellows," I said, "the congenial, pleasant ones."

"Yes," said Grunt.

The tops of the skulls, and parts of the tops of the skulls, in the back, of several of the bodies were exposed. It was here that the scalp and hair, in such places, had been cut away. These things could be mounted on hoops, attached to poles, and used in dances. They could be hung, too, from lodge poles, and parts of them, in twisted or dangling fringes, could decorate numerous articles, such as shields and war shirts.

"I do not understand all the cutting," I said, "the slashing, the mutilation."

"That sort of thing," said Grunt, "is cultural, with almost all of the tribes. The tradition is an ancient one, and is largely unquestioned. Its origins are doubtless lost in antiquity."

"Why do you think it is done?" I asked.

"There are various theories," said Grunt. "One is that it serves as a warning to possible enemies, an attestation of the terribleness of the victors as foes. Another is that the practice is connected with beliefs about the medicine world, that this is a way of precluding such individuals from seeking vengeance later, either because of inflicted impairments or because of terrorizing them against a second meeting."

"Surely leaving a litter behind like this," I said, "might serve as a warning."

"True," said Grunt, "but, too, I think it is generally understood that this sort of thing produces fear not so much as a desire for revenge, at least among the savages themselves."

"Your second theory you take most seriously, then?" I asked.

"Not really," said he. "If one's objective was really to terrorize or to inflict vengeance-precluding injuries, then it seems that the corpses, regularly, would be blinded, or have the hands and feet cut off. On the other hand, those particular injuries are very seldom inflicted."

"Why, then, do you think it is done?" I asked.

"I think," said Grunt, "that it is done in the joy and lust of victory, that it ventilates powerful emotion, that it expresses vengeance and hatred, and, indeed, pleasure and life, and that it is done, too, to show contempt for the enemy and to humiliate him, thereby demonstrating one's own superiority."

I regarded Grunt.

"In short," said Grunt, "it is done because it elates them, and fills them with power and joy."

"I see," I said.

"Surely you are familiar, as I suspect you are, with such carnage, with such practices?" he smiled.

"Yes," I said, "I am." I was a warrior.

"I thought so," said he.

I turned my kaiila to face Grunt.

"Let us not, then, feel so superior to these gentle and kindly folk," he said.

"Very well," I said.

Grunt laughed.

I looked about. "It is a good thing we did not bring the girls," I said.

"It was for this reason," said Grunt, "that I left them in the camp."

I nodded. They, beautiful, frightened, half-naked slaves, shackled by the neck in the Barrens, did not need to see this. Let them not be concerned, at least as yet, with what might be the fate of an enslaved white female in such a world.

"There is not enough wood about to burn these bodies," I said. "We shall have to bury them."

"They are to be left as they are," said Grunt. "It is the usual way of the Barrens."

We turned our kaiila about, to leave this place.

"Help," we heard. "Please, help."

Grunt and I looked at one another.

"Over here," said Grunt. He moved his kaiila to our left, and turned it.

He looked down, from the lofty saddle. He smote his thigh, and laughed. I urged my kaiila to his side.

Below us, half concealed in the tall grass, on their backs, lay the two fellows I recognized as the brothers, Max and Kyle Hobart. They were stripped and their hands were thonged behind their backs. They could not rise to their feet. Each wore a crude, single-position, greenwood leg-spreader.

"It is a present to me, from my friends, the Dust Legs," laughed Grunt, "the leaders of those who followed us."

"A thoughtful present," I said. "Now they are yours."

"And a rich joke it is, too," laughed Grunt. "See?"

"Yes," I said. Max and Kyle Hobart wore leg-spreaders. These are commonly reserved by the red savages for their white female slaves. They wore single-position leg-spreaders. One ankle, by thongs threaded through a pierced end, is fastened tightly to one end of the sturdy spreader. The other ankle is then pulled to a corresponding position at the other end of the pole where, by means of another thong passed through another hole, drilled at that point in the spreader, it is fastened securely in place. More sophisticated spreaders have several positions. In the simplest case a series of holes is drilled in the pole and the girl's ankles are merely fastened on the pole at whatever separation the master desires. In more sophisticated devices, two, or even three, poles or boards are used, which can slide apart, and are fastened at given points by pegs or thongs. In this latter sort of device the girl's ankles, fastened at the far ends of the pole or board, need not be untied and retied. One may then, in accordance with one's moods, and at one's convenience, regulate the distance between them.

These spreaders may be used in a variety of ways, of course. Sometimes they are used for the wrists, the pole or board then usually behind the girl's back. Too, they may be used in concert with other devices. In the lodges of Warrior Societies, for example, as a portion of the amusements accompanying a feast, a girl may be richly used in one, her hands tied behind the back of her neck, in the draw cords, looped once or twice about her neck, of the sack drawn over her head. In this way she fears all the men of the society for she does not know who it was who was the most cruel to her. Too, she regards all the men of the society with mixed feelings of sensual uneasiness, for she does not know which one among them it was who made her yield most ecstatically, most abjectly, as a slave. This is thought good by the men for the camaraderie of the society. To be sure, eventually she is usually awarded to one or another of the society members. This will usually be either to he who was most cruel to her or to he who made her yield most abjectly, most rapturously. She will learn which it is when she, in the privacy of his own lodge, after her labors, is ordered to his furs. Not unoften, in-cidentally, it turns out that these two fellows are the same, that he who most cruelly and effectively dominated her as a master is also he to whom she yielded most abjectly as a slave.

"Please," said the fellow called Max Hobart.

"Please," said he called Kyle Hobart.

"You are stripped," said Grunt.

"They took our clothing," said Max Hobart.

"You wear leg-spreaders," laughed Grunt.

"They put us in them!" said Kyle Hobart.

"As though you might be women," said Grunt.

"Yes," said Max Hobart, squirming. He tried to rise. He could not, of course, do so.

"Thus do the Dust Legs demean you," said Grunt, "treating you as no more than women."

"Please," moaned Max Hobart.

"Please," begged Kyle Hobart. "We are helpless!"

Grunt, moving the reins of the kaiila, pulled the beast's head away. I followed him. The kaiila in the area of the pe-rimeter, those ridden by white men, are generally controlled by a headstall, bit and reins, in short, by a bridle, not by a nose rope, as is cultural in the Tahari. Different areas on Gor give witness to the heritage of differing traditions. The bridle used by the red savages, incidentally, usually differs from that used by the white men. The most common form is a strap, or braided leather tie, placed below the tongue and behind the teeth, tied about the lower jaw, from which two reins, or a single double rein, a single loop, comes back over the beast's neck. The jaw tie, serving as both bit and headstall, is usually formed of the same material as the reins, one long length of material being used for the entire bridle.

"Wait!" begged Max Hobart. "Wait!"

"Do not go!" begged Kyle Hobart.

"We will die, if left here!" cried out Max Hobart. "We have been tied by red savages! We cannot free ourselves!"

Grunt stopped his kaiila. "Exposure on the prairie, to die of thirst, or hunger, or of the predations of animals, is what they deserve," he said.

I shrugged. The decision in this matter seemed to me his.

"Please!" cried out Max Hobart, plaintively.

"Yet, perhaps I could spare them this horror," mused Grunt. "It would inconvenience me little to do so."

"I do not suppose the Dust Legs would object," I said.

"They left them in my keeping," said Grunt.

"That is true," I said. "What are you going to do?"

"Cut their throats," said Grunt.

"I see," I said.

He brought his kaiila back to where the two men lay bound in the grass. I followed him. He tossed me the reins of his beast and, drawing his knife from a beaded sheath, slipped from the saddle to the ground. In an instant he crouched beside Max Hobart and, holding the fellow's hair in his left hand, had his blade across his throat.

"No!" whispered Max Hobart, hoarsely. "No! Don't kill me! Please, do not kill me!"

"Have mercy on us!" begged Kyle Hobart.

Grunt looked up at me.

"In this way, of course," said Grunt, "I get nothing from them."

"A poor bargain from the point of view of a merchant," I observed.

"Do you think they might have some worth?" asked Grunt.

"Perhaps to someone," I said.

"They seem two stalwart, handsome lads," said Grunt. "I might, from someone, be able to get something for them."

"That seems to be possible," I said.

Max Hobart lay back in the grass, gasping, the knife removed from his throat.

Grunt, from his saddlebags, removed two collars. He joined them, by means of snap locks, with a length of chain. He then put them on the necks of Max and Kyle Hobart.

"Slave collars!" gasped Max Hobart.

"Yes," said Grunt. Grunt looked up at me. "Their wrists

are adequately thonged for now," he said. "Later, in the camp, we shall provide them with proper manacles."

I nodded.

"Are you going to make us slaves?" asked Max Hobart.

"For the time you may account yourselves mere prisoners," said Grunt. "It is when you are purchased that you will be truly slaves."

"Do not put us in your coffle," begged Max.

"You will be put at the end of the coffle," said Grunt.

"You would chain us behind slave girls?" asked Max.

"You will surely admit that you are the least desirable of the elements in the coffle. Accordingly, you will be chained in the position of 'last girls.'"

Max moaned, lying in the grass.

"I assure you," said Grunt, "our friends, the red savages, both men and women, will find that quite amusing."

"Please," begged Max.

"But do not fear," said Grunt, "you will not be expected to bear burdens."

Max regarded him, miserably.

"It is the women who are the pack beasts, who will bear the burdens," said Grunt.

Max nodded, numbly.

"You will discover that there are some advantages to bringing up the rear of the coffle," said Grunt. "You may then, for example, observe the women before you, bearing their burdens. You are not, however, to so much as touch them, even though they are slaves. Do you understand?"

"We understand," said Max, miserably.

"Yes," said Kyle.

Grunt looked about and found some shreds of shirts which, cut to pieces, lay about in the grass. He tied some of these pieces together and bound them about the hips of the Hobarts. They regarded their new garments, decided for them by Grunt, with dismay.

"We are not slave girls," protested Max.

"The red savages, as you may not know," said Grunt to me, though doubtless he was speaking primarily for the benefit of the Hobarts, "are rather strict about the privilege of wearing the breechclout."

"Oh?" I said.

"Yes," said Grunt. "It is not permitted to women, even to their own women, nor, of course, is it permitted to slaves."

"I understand," I said. The breechclout of the Barrens, incidentally, consists of a single piece of narrow material. This may be of tanned skin but, not unoften, is of soft cloth. It is held in place by a belt or cord. It commonly goes over the belt or cord in the back, and down and between the legs, and then comes up, drawn snugly tight, over the belt or cord in the front. In cooler weather it is often worn with leggings and a shirt. In warmer weather, in camp, it is usually the only thing that a male will wear.

"For a slave, or a prisoner, to wear a breechclout might be regarded as pretentious or offensive," said Grunt, "an oversight or indiscretion calling for torture or, say, for being set upon by boys on kaiila, with war clubs."

"I understand," I said.

The Hobarts looked at one another. Their garments, like those of female slaves, would not be permitted a nether closure.

Grunt cut the thongs binding the ankles of the Hobarts to the leg-spreaders. "On your feet," he said.

They struggled to their feet, chained together by the neck.

Grunt mounted to the high saddle of his kaiila. He looked down on them. "You are my prisoners," he said, "totally, and when sold will be slaves. You will be perfectly docile and totally obedient. At the least sign of refractoriness or insubordination on the part of either one of you, both will be slain. Is that clear?"

"Yes," said Max, miserably.

"Yes," said Kyle.

"That way lies our camp," said Grunt, pointing. "Move!"

The two Hobarts, stumbling, the chain on their necks, proceeded in the direction indicated.

I turned about in the saddle to view once more the torn, bloodied grass, the motionless figures, the insects and birds, the place where, yesterday, in brief compass, carnage had touched the prairie.

"Come along," said Grunt.

"I am coming," I said.

He rode after the Hobarts.

In a moment I had urged my kaiila after him.

When he reached the Hobarts he unhooked his whip from its saddle ring and, throwing it out behind him, and then bringing it forward, he lashed them. "Hurry!" he called. "Har-ta! Faster! Faster! Har-ta! Har-ta!"

They hurried on before him, stumbling and gasping, helplessly herded, driven, responding to his will and the imperious strokes of his whip, neck-chained and bound, his enemies. I smiled. It is pleasant to have one's enemies in one's power.

I did not look back.

13

BLANKETS AND BONDS;

I DO A FAVOR FOR GRUNT

I lay on one elbow.

When she reached my vicinity she knelt down, in the brief brown slave tunic.

She trembled. She did not speak.

I regarded her for a time. Her head was down.

I then lay back on my blankets, on the grass. I put my hands under the back of my head, on the folded saddle blanket beneath my head. The kaiila saddle and the kaiila quirt lay to one side. I looked up at the stars, and the three moons of Gor. It is difficult to convey the majesty of a Gorean night in the Barrens, because of the vastness of the sky and the depth of the blackness, and the contrasting brightness of the stars. The large extents of wilderness on the surface of Gor and the absence of large-scale artificial illuminations, of course, permit starlit nights, almost anywhere, to manifest themselves with a splendor that would be almost breath-taking to one accustomed to the drab, half-gray, polluted, semi-illuminated, dim, nocturnal atmospheres of Earth. In the Barrens, however, and in places such as the Tahari, probably because of the relative levelness of the terrain, horizon to horizon, these effects seem even more accentuated, even more stupendous, more spectacular, more unbelievable and astounding.

I did not speak to the girl. I did not wish to hurry her. I let her continue to kneel there in the grass, a few feet from me.

I heard one of the kaiila moving about on its tether, biting at the grass, pawing the turf.

I continued to regard the stars.

"Master," she said.

"Yes," I said. She had spoken in Gorean.

"I have been sent to your blankets," she said.

I rose on one elbow, to regard her. Her lower lip trembled. She looked very lovely, in the brief brown slave tunic. Her throat was bare, having been released from the collar in the coffle.

"I have been sent to your blankets," she whispered.

"I understand," I said.

She tried, with her small fists, to pull together the sides of the tunic, to protect, as she could, the rounded, interior contours of her softness from the garment's apparently thoughtless disclosure. I smiled. Did she not know it was a slave's garment? Did she not understand the statement that was made by that deep, V-shaped, plunging division in the tunic, terminating only at her belly, that the woman who wore it was owned by men, that she was a slave?

At a gesture from me she removed her hands from the sides of the garment and placed them on her thighs.

She then knelt there in the grass, and I looked at her.

She put her head down, not meeting my eyes. She, a new slave, was not yet used to being looked at, truly looked at, as a woman, by a Gorean master.

I continued to regard her.

I found her reserve charming.

She lifted her head, frightened.

At as little as a snapping of my fingers, she must strip herself and hurry naked, licking and kissing, to my arms.

It is pleasant to own women.

"I do not know what to do, or what to say," she moaned, to herself, in English.

We had now been five nights in the Barrens. This woman, and the others, tutored by Ginger and Evelyn, had now picked up a smattering of Gorean. I was pleased with her progress in the language, and it seemed to me the best of her chained peers. Yet it was still, of course, piteously limited. The phrase which she had repeated more than once, "I have been sent to your blanket," for example, had not been spoken as a slave girl in full cognizance of its meaning, humbly making it clear that her nearness to the male was not illicit, and begging him to consider her for his pleasure-use, but rather as though it might have been spoken by rote, merely a set of words committed to memory, and as though she was desperate not to forget it or mispronounce it. She had doubtless learned the phrase by repetition, from Ginger or Evelyn. Still, doubtless, they would also have taught her its meaning, or at least as much of its meaning as could be absorbed by a raw Earth slave in her present stage of training. She doubtless thus understood its meaning, but did not, presumably, understand it in its full meaning, as what it might mean, fully, to present herself as a Gorean slave girl for the pleasure of a master.

"I cannot even speak your language," she said, miserably, in English. "I am stupid. I cannot remember anything. It is all gone from me!"

I saw that in her terror the little Gorean that she knew had eluded her.

"Forgive me, Master," she then said, suddenly, in Gorean. "Forgive me, Master. Forgive me, Master."

I was pleased to see that she could remember at least that much Gorean.

She put her head down, trembling.

I saw that I would not be able, at least for the time, to communicate with her in Gorean. Obviously the Gorean she knew was largely unavailable to her now and it was, moreover, extremely limited anyway in her current stage of linguistic development.

"Forgive me, Master," she wept, in Gorean.

I smiled. That simple phrase had doubtless on many occasions, though not always, saved many stripped, collared slaves from fearful punishments.

Her shoulders shook. Her head was down.

It is not necessary, of course, to be able to communicate verbally with a woman to teach her that she is a slave. Women are highly intelligent. They quickly understand such objects as the chain and the whip. Indeed, much may be done with means so simple even as the stroke of a hand, the twisting of an arm, the manner in which her body is penetrated. Yes, she can learn much, even before she has learned to speak your language.

I considered the girl kneeling in the grass, trembling. I glanced to the nearby kaiila saddle, and the quirt. I could always strip her and throw her on her belly or back over the polished leather of the saddle. I might then, with the aid of the quirt, and caressing her, begin to induce in her some modicum of understanding concerning her condition.

"I have been sent to your blankets, Master," whispered the girl, in Gorean, lifting her head.

She was not yet ready for the saddle and the quirt, I saw. Yet, if I assessed her correctly, I thought, it would not be long. She was good slave stuff.

I beckoned to her, gently.

Timidly the girl, on her hands and knees, crawled to me through the grass. I then took her in my arms and, gently, put her to her back beside me. She was tense. She made as though to lift her lips to me, timidly, but I put my hand over her mouth. She looked up at me, frightened. My hand was tight over her mouth. She was held motionless. She could not begin to speak.

"I speak your language," I said to her, very quietly. Her eyes widened. I had spoken in English. I did not let her speak. "This is not particularly important," I said, "but you are not, without my permission, to speak of it to anyone. Do you understand?"

She nodded her head, as she could, my hand tight over her mouth. I then removed my hand from her mouth.

"You speak English," she said, wonderingly.

"Yes," I said.

"Is it your intention to rescue me, and the other girls?" she whispered. "Oh!" she said. Her head was forced back, my hand under her chin, my fingers tight at the sides of her jaw.

"Where is your collar?" I asked.

"In the coffle," she said.

"In the coffle, what?" I asked.

"In the coffle—Master!" she said.

"What are you?" I asked.

"I am informed I am a slave," she said, my hand tight under her chin. "Oh!" she said, her head forced farther back, my grip tightened.

"What are you?" I asked.

"A slave!" she said, tensely. "I am a slave, Master!"

"Do you think, now," I asked, "that you are to be rescued?"

"No, Master," she said. "No, Master!"

"There is no rescue for you," I said, "nor for the other slaves on your chain."

"No, Master," she said. "We are slaves."

"Does it disturb you to speak of your slavery in your native language?" I asked.

"No, Master," she said.

I looked down into her eyes. She averted her gaze. "Why did you think I might consider rescuing you?" I asked.

"Were you not once of Earth?" she asked.

"Once," I said.

"Surely then," she said, "you must be sensitive to our plight, imbonded women of Earth."

"Women of Earth have often been imbonded," I said. "Bondage is no novelty for the Earth female. Her fittingness for the collar has long been recognized. On Earth at this very moment many women are held in public bondage, and many others, it is difficult to conjecture their number, serve in secret bondages. Too, throughout the course of human history, in the past, as well as today, many women have found themselves enslaved. Your predicament, or plight, if you please, is thus far from unique. You, and those with you, are merely another handful of slaves, imbonded females, merely new and fresh instances of a historically familiar commodity."

"Yes, Master," she said.

I removed my hand from her throat and face. She gasped, fearfully, but did not stir from my side. Her breasts heaved, under the thin rep-cloth of the slave tunic.

"You may now begin again," I said. "Return to your original position. You may speak in English."

"Yes, Master," she whispered. Fearfully she then crept from my side. In a moment she knelt as she had before, a few feet from me, in the grass.

"Master," she said.

"Yes?" I said.

"I am a slave girl," she said. "I have been sent to your blankets."

"Excellent," I said. "You are a pretty slave."

"Thank you, Master," she said.

"Approach, Slave," I said.

"Yes, Master," she said, and, on her hands and knees, crawled to my side.

I then took her in my arms and, as I had before, put her to her back, beside me.

"I am a virgin," she said.

"I know," I said. "The results of your body's testing, shortly after your purchase, were made known to me by Grunt, your master."

"Yes, Master," she said.

"Such information is public among Masters," I said.

"Yes, Master," she said.

I held the cloth of the slave tunic, moving it between my fingers. "This is thin, flimsy cloth," I said.

"Yes, Master," she said.

"It reveals you well," I said.

"Yes, Master," she said.

"And you have pretty legs," I said.

"Thank you, Master," she said.

"You are tense," I said.

"Forgive me, Master," she said.

"Do you know what is to be done to you tonight?" I asked.

"I am to be deflowered," she said.

"That is a ridiculous expression," I said. "It is absurd. Rather, you are to be opened, an act which, in the case of a slave, is in the interest of all men."

"Yes, Master," she said.

"This is unlikely to be painful," I said, "but, if it is, the pain will be brief, and the soreness will be temporary."

"I understand," she said.

"If you should prove unusual in some respect, although this is extremely rare," I said, "we can, tomorrow, grind one of Grunt's trading knives into a lancet."

"I understand," she shuddered. This seemed to me better than leaving the matter to the red savages. They tend to be impatient in such respects, even with their own women. A homemade lancet, sterilized in boiling water, seemed to me preferable to a sharpened kailiauk bone or a whittled lodge peg.

"But your penetration is, obviously," I said, "only a mere technicality."

"Obviously," she said, I thought a bit ironically.

"But," I said, "beyond that incidental triviality, do you understand why you have been sent to my blanekts, what the purpose is from your point of view, what is the purpose on which you are to be intent?"

"Yes, Master," she said.

"What?" I asked.

"I am to please you with my body," she said.

"You do not understand," I said.

"Master?" she asked.

"That is far too limited," I said. "You are to please me with the wholeness of your womanhood, in the fullness of your slavery."

"The Gorean master, then," she said, "would desire, and own, all of me."

"Yes," I said.

"I had hoped it might be so," she whispered.

"What?" I asked.

"Nothing, Master," she whispered.

"It is only on your former world, if anywhere," I said, "that a man is interested only in a woman's body."

"Yes, Master," she said.

"And I doubt that," I said, "even on that muchly perverted dismal orb."

"Yes, Master," she said.

"To be sure," I said, "the bodies of women are not without interest, and they look well in slave chains."

"Yes, Master," she said.

"But you must understand that what wears the chains, so curvacious, beautiful and helpless, is the whole woman."

"I understand, Master," she said.

"You do not have a name yet, do you?" I asked.

"No," she said. "My master has not yet named me."

"What was your former name?" I asked.

"Millicent Aubrey-Welles," she said. "Oh!" she said. "Your hand!"

"Do you object?" I asked.

"No," she said. "I am only a slave. I may not object."

"That is an unusual name," I said. My hand rested, softly, on her left thigh.

"Such names are not unusual in the social stratum which once was mine," she said.

"I see," I said.

"My family is from the upper classes, the very upper classes, of my world."

"I see," I said.

"I now lie beside you in a slave tunic," she said. "But I am an upper-class girl, a very upper-class girl. You must understand that."

"Once you were," I said.

"Yes, Master," she said.

"You are now only a nameless slave," I said.

"Yes, Master," she said.

I smiled.

"I was a debutante," she said.

"I understand," I said.

"We are used to consolidate family alliances," she said, "and are given as awards, in matings, to energetic young men, often rising in our fathers' companies."

"A form of slavery," I said, "but without the honesty of the collar."

"Yes," she said, bitterly.

"Women have often been used for such purposes," I said.

"My aunt told me that it was all that I was good for," she said.

"Your aunt was mistaken," I said.

She gasped. My hand moved higher on her thigh.

She controlled her breath. My hand, now, was again still.

"We, of course," she said, "would be permitted our clubs, our activities, our parties, our affairs."

"Yes," I said.

"But it would be a meaningless existence," she said, "meaningless." "Oh!" she said.

My fingers now rested on her brand. "What is this?" I asked.

"My brand," she said.

"You must be a slave," I said.

"Yes, Master," she said.

"Your existence on Gor," I said, "you will find far from meaningless. You will find it quite meaningful, I assure you."

She shuddered.

"It is rather something else which you will find is meaningless on Gor," I said.

"What, Master?" she asked.

"You, yourself," I said.

"Me?" she asked.

"Yes," I said, "for you will be only an article of property, a meaningless, purchasable trinket, a worthless bauble, an owned woman, a slave."

She looked at me with horror.

"Surely you are aware that you may be purchased or sold, or bartered, or given away, or commanded, as men please, that you are naught but an imbonded woman, a totally meaningless slave?"

"Yes, Master," she moaned.

"Did you wear a white gown, of ankle length, when you were presented as a debutante?" I asked.

"Yes, Master," she said.

My hand was now tight upon her brand. "Say," I said, " 'I am now naught but a branded slave on Gor.' "

"I am now naught but a branded slave on Gor," said the girl.

I moved my hand upward, to her hip, and to the sweetness of her waist at the hip.

"Your hand is high beneath my tunic, Master," said the girl.

"Do you object?" I asked.

"No, Master," she said. "I am a slave. I may not object."

"The clothing in which you were exhibited to the buyers," I said, "which was removed for their interest, in your sale, did not seem to me the clothing of a debutante. It seemed to me rather the clothing of a girl, and a certain sort of girl, who works in an office."

"I wished to avoid the imminent and obvious fate of the debutante," she said, "to be bartered for position and power on the marriage market."

"This was the occasion, doubtless, in which your aunt expressed her view that such, in effect, was all you were good for."

"Yes!" she said. "Oh!" she said.

"You have lovely curves," I said.

"Are you warming me for my taking?" she asked.

"They would bring a high price," I said.

She moaned.

"Your aunt," I said, "surely had a very limited conception of your utilities. It probably never even entered her ken, for example, that you might one day be a scantily clad, branded slave."

"Master?" asked the girl.

"On the other hand," I said, "she knew you very well, and, in some way, may have been touching on something of importance."

"I do not understand," said the girl.

"I do not mean to insult you, a girl from Earth," I said, "but you are obviously extremely feminine. You have, doubtless, a large number of female hormones in your body."

"Master?" she asked.

"Your aunt was then, perhaps, trying to convey to you that your most congenial and appropriate destiny, what might be best for you, what might be most natural for you, would be for you to find yourself naked in the arms of a man."

"As little more than a slave?" she asked.

"As perhaps no more than a slave," I said.

"I cannot help it that I have a feminine face, that I have a feminine body," she said. "I cannot help it that I am feminine!"

"Why would you want to help it?" I asked.

"It is wrong to be feminine!" she said.

"That is obviously false," I said. "What is your next point?"

"I know that I am feminine," she wept. "I have known it for years, from my desires and feelings, even from before the interior truths of my reality manifested themselves so unmistakably, so unrepudiably, in my body, shaping and curving me for the destiny of the female, and for the lustful, appraising eyes of men."

I regarded her, not speaking.

"I am afraid to be feminine!" she said.

"Why?" I asked.

"Because," she wept, "I sense that it is, ultimately, to be the slave of men."

"You desired to prove your aunt wrong," I said.

"Yes," she said. "I would prove that I was independent, that I was capable, that I could achieve success on my own. My talents would be obvious. I would be hired promptly. I would be rapidly advanced. I would become a female executive. That would show my aunt! That would show myself! That would show men!"

"What happened?" I asked.

"I took money and left home," she said. "I scarcely informed my family as to my decision or whereabouts. I went to a great city. It is called New York. I rented expensive quarters. Confidently, I sought a significant position in business."

"And then?" I asked.

"Alas," she said, ruefully, "I found my credentials sorrily lacking. I could find no work of the sort in which I was interested."

"I see," I said.

"After weeks of misery and frustration," she said, "I contacted my family. A position was immediately arranged for me."

"I see," I said.

"It was not, however, at all, what I had hoped for," she said. "I became, in effect, the secretary to a female executive, her 'girl' in the office. She took charge of me and, in effect, prescribed my mode of dress and behavior."

"It was largely due to her, then," I said, "that you wore the attractive garments you did, when you were stripped for the buyers at the house of Ram Seibar?"

"Yes," she said, "and she even prescribed that the pearls I wore must be synthetic, as being more befitting than real pearls a girl in my position."

"I see," I said. "Did you protest this?"

"I did not wish to lose my job," she said.

"I see," I said. I was pleased to learn that she had not worn the false pearls of her own volition. That would surely mitigate her culpability in the matter, at least to some extent, in Gorean eyes. She had, of course, agreed to wear them. That they might regard as important. That agreement, of course, had been formed, in a sense, under duress. The Goreans, on the whole a fair folk, would doubtless take that into consideration. The degree of duress might be regarded as significant. The matter was surely subtle. Grunt, in any case, as I knew him, would not be interested in punishing her for that action, as it had taken place when she was free. That life was behind her now. Her whippings, now, doubtless, would be functions of such things as whether or not she was sufficiently pleasing as a female slave. Still, I would inform Grunt of this development. He would find it of interest. Masters find almost everything about their slaves of interest. Too, it would please him.

"And so," she said, "I continued to run her errands, to answer her telephone in a pretty voice, to do her filing, to bring her her coffee, to address her deferentially, to smile at her clients and walk in a certain way past them."

"I understand," I said.

"Doubtless she enjoyed having me do this," she said, bitterly, "my station in society having been so superior to hers."

"Perhaps," I said. "I do not know."

"It was to be made clear to all her colleagues," she said, angrily, "that I was only a girl, fit for lowly labors and being pleasing to her superiors. Clearly I was a different sort of woman from her!"

"Perhaps you were," I said.

"Dressed as I was, forced to behave as I was," she said, "how could men see me as executive material?"

"Doubtless it would be difficult," I said.

"Yes," she said.

"You are very feminine," I said, "perhaps you are not executive material."

She squirmed, angrily.

"She well used my femininity, my meaninglessness, my prettiness," she said, "to highlight, to point up and accentuate, by contrast, her own quite different image, that of strength and competence, of decisiveness, of command, of authority and power."

"I have seen such women naked," I said, "in a collar, kissing the feet of men."

"Oh?" she said.

"But they are not so beautiful as you," I said.

She was silent.

"Do you feel that your treatment by her was motivated by some insecurity on her part, by fear for her position or status, that she may have seen you as a threat?"

The girl was silent for a moment. Then she said, "No, I do not think so."

"That is interesting," I said.

"I could not have begun to compete with her," she said.

"You were not that sort of woman," I said.

"No," she said.

"Do you think she disliked you, or hated you?" I asked.

"I don't think so, really," she said, slowly.

"Can you conceive it possible that she may have seen you rather more as you were, than as you saw yourself?"

"Master?" she asked.

"She may have dressed you as she did," I said, "and treated you as she did, and made you do the things you did, for a very good reason."

"Why?" she asked.

"Because you are feminine," I said.

She was angrily silent.

"Did you enjoy doing the things you were told?" I asked. "Did you enjoy obeying?"

"Sometimes," she whispered.

"Did you object, truly, to the clothing you were expected to wear?" I asked.

"No," she said, "not truly. I like pretty clothes, and the eyes of men on me."

"As a Gorean slave girl," I said, "you will often find the eyes of men on you, though whether or not you will be permitted clothing will be a function of the decision of your master."

"Yes, Master," she said.

"How were you taken?" I asked.

"After work," she said. "It was dark. I was driving back to my building. I stopped at a red light. Suddenly, to my horror, a narrow chain was looped about my throat. 'Drive as I direct,' said a male voice, from behind me. I could not scream. The chain was tight. I was terrified. He had been hidden in the car, behind the back seat. He tightened the chain a quarter of an inch. I could not breathe. I realized he could, if he wished, strangle me in an instant. A car honked behind us. 'The light has changed,' he said. He relaxed the chain, slightly. 'Continue on this street,' he said, 'in the outside lane, at a speed not exceeding twenty-five miles an hour.' I pulled away from the intersection. 'You will obey all my directions,' he said, 'immediately and to the letter, and you will address me as "Sir." ' 'Yes,' I whispered. The chain tightened. 'Yes, Sir,' I whispered, fighting for breath. The chain then relaxed, slightly."

"You were already being taught to obey, and to treat men with respect," I said.

"Yes, Master," she said. " 'Do not try anything foolish,' he said, 'such as stalling or damaging the vehicle, for I can slay you in an instant, before I make my departure.' 'Yes, Sir,' I said. 'You may look in the rear-view mirror, if you wish,' he said. 'You have my permission.' I looked in the rear-view mirror, terrified. About my throat, closely looped, was a narrow golden chain. It was controlled by two narrow wooden handles, in his hands."

"It was a girl-capture chain," I said. "It is to be distinguished sharply from the standard garrote, which is armed with wire and can cut a throat easily. The standard garrote, of course, is impractical for captures, for the victim, in even a reflexive movement, might cut her own throat."

"Whatever it was," she said, "it was very effective. It controlled me perfectly."

"Of course," I said. "That is why it is used."

"In a few moments, the man made an adjustment in the chain, spinning one of the wooden handles. He could then control it with one hand. He tightened it, half choking me, and then released it, slightly. He had well displayed his power over me. He then released it a bit more. 'That's better, isn't it, Baby?' he asked. 'Yes, Sir,' I said. 'Good,' he said, 'we have a long drive ahead of us.' We then drove on, I terrified, he giving me directions. From other cars it would have seemed merely that a man, leaning forward, perhaps smiling, perhaps conversing with me, was in the back of my vehicle. If any saw the slender golden chain about my throat they did not, doubtless, conjecture its significance."

"He was not masked?" I asked.

"No," she said.

"A mask would have aroused suspicion," I said.

"Yes," she said. " 'Do not fear to look upon my face, if you wish,' he said, 'for you will not see it again, after you have been delivered.' 'Delivered!' I exclaimed. 'Yes,' he laughed, 'delivered, my pretty goods.' We then drove on. He let me engage in what, I suppose, are the standard threats and pleas of the captured girl, but, then, when he grew weary of this amusement, he stopped me. A slight pressure on the chain sufficed. We then continued to drive on. The terrain became more remote, more desolate. Soon we were driving on graveled roads. Then we were driving on dirt roads, dark and lonely, lined with trees. I grasped very little of what was going on. I was terrified. The chain was on my throat. The beams from the headlights seemed wild on the road ahead of me. 'Slow down here,' he said, 'and pull into those trees, and stop.' I obeyed his commands. I switched off the car lights and turned off the car engine. I had delivered myself, though to whom, or what, or for what I had no idea. He took me from the car by the chain and soon I was in the hands of other men. He left, dropping the chain, with its handles, in the pocket of his jacket. I was thrown to my stomach in the grass. My hands were fastened behind me in some sort of metal restraining device. It was snug, and inflexible. My ankles were crossed and tied together with a short piece of rope. A metal anklet of some sort was fastened on my left ankle."

"A girls identificatory anklet," I said. "It is removed after her delivery to Gor."

"A boxlike device was then placed near my head," she said. "It was hinged at one end and, on the other side, where it opened, there were matched, semicircular openings. My head then, by the hair, was placed in this box, and it was closed, enclosing my head, and shutting snugly about my neck. This opening was then further closed by wrapping a thick cloth about my neck and thrusting it up, so that it filled the space between my neck and the edges of the now-closed semicircular openings."

"Interesting," I said.

"My head enclosed in the box," she said, "I heard a car being driven away. It was doubtless my own, driven by the fellow with the chain."

"That is quite likely," I said. "He would wish to have a means to return to the city and, of course, it would be important to abandon or dispose of the car far from the scene of the abductors' rendezvous."

"And I must remain behind," she said, bitterly.

"Of course," I said. "You were then only a delivered capture."

"A gas was then entered into the box," she said. "I tried to struggle. A man's foot held me in place. I lost consciousness. I awakened, I do not know how much later, in a grassy field on this world, chained by the neck with other girls."

"Interesting," I said. "I do not know, but you may have been stored for a few days, perhaps even a few weeks."

"Stored?" she asked.

"Yes," I said, "perhaps hibernated. Then, when the order was complete, it could have been shipped in its entirety."

"You speak of me as though I might be an object," she said, "a mere commodity."

"You are," I said.

"Yes, Master," she said.

I thrust the slave tunic up and then, pulling her to a sitting position, I pulled it off, her arms rising, over her head.

"Do you object?" I inquired.

"No, Master," she said. "I may not object. I am a slave."

I cast the scanty garment to the side, on the grass.

"Lie down," I told her, "on your back, with your arms at your sides, the palms of your hands up, facing the moons of Gor."

"Yes, Master," she said.

"Lift your left knee, slightly," I told her.

"Yes, Master," she said.

I stood and looked down at her.

"I now lie exposed before you, as a slave, Master," she said.

"Is that fitting and proper?" I inquired.

"Yes, Master," she said.

"Why?" I asked.

"Because I am a slave," she said.

"The answer is correct, and suitable," I said.

"Yes, Master," she said.

"Are you a new slave?" I asked.

"Yes, Master," she said.

"That is incorrect," I said.

"Master?" she asked.

"The only sense in which you are a new slave," I said, "is that it has not been long since your legal imbondment."

"Master?" she asked.

"For years, you have been a slave," I said, "only one who was not yet properly owned, a technicality recently remedied on Gor."

She looked up at me.

"This is what, implicitly, in effect, your aunt was recognizing," I said, "though perhaps not fully consciously. It seems to have been recognized even more clearly by your former superior, the female executive. She dressed you, and treated you, did she not, as, in effect, a slave?"

"Yes," said the girl, angrily.

"I think," I said, "in spite of other possible considerations and advantages which might have been involved in her behavior and attitudes, she was trying to be kind to you, trying to make it clear to you what you were, trying to encourage you to be true to your own nature."

"Perhaps!" said the girl, angrily.

"You like pretty clothes, do you not," I asked, "and like to be attractive to men?"

"Yes!" she said.

"On Gor," I said, "as opposed to your world, it is customary to enslave slaves."

She looked up at me, angrily.

"On Gor," I asked, "have you been branded, and enslaved?"

"Yes, Master," she said.

"Why?" I asked.

"Because I am a slave?" she asked.

"Yes," I said.

She turned her head, angrily, to the side.

I looked down at her. She was exquisitely beautiful. I did not doubt but that Grunt could get five hides of the yellow kailiauk for her.

"Look at me, Slave," I said.

She regarded me, quickly. "Yes, Master," she said.

"Slaves such as you, on Earth," I said, "not legally imbonded, often use their beauty to their own advantage. It opens doors. It smoothes ways. It makes things easy for them. They use it to further careers, to buy wealth, and to belittle other women."

"Yes, Master?" she whispered.

"But here, on Gor," I said, "things are quite different."

"Yes, Master," she said.

"Here, on Gor," I said, "your beauty is owned, and fully, as are you."

"Yes, Master," she said.

"To whom does your beauty belong, on Gor?" I asked.

"To the master," she said.

"Yes," I said, "and it is he, not you, my dear, who will decide what is to be done with it, fully, and how it is to be used."

"Yes, Master," she said.

"Your palms," I said, "have them facing upward, to the moons of Gor."

"Yes, Master," she said.

"Have you had your slave wine?" I asked.

"Ginger, one of my Mistresses," she said, "forced me to drink a bitter beverage by that name."

"Why has your Master, Grunt, sent you to my blankets?" I asked. "Why has he himself not seen fit to open your slave's body to the pleasures of men?"

"I do not know, Master," she said.

I crouched down beside the naked body of the former Miss Millicent Aubrey-Welles, who had been a debutante, now that of a mere slave, supine on my blankets.

"What are the duties of a slave?" I asked.

"They are complex, and manifold, Master," she said.

"Speak generally," I said.

"We are to be absolutely docile," she said, "totally obedient and fully pleasing."

"Are there any qualifications to that?" I asked.

"No, Master," she said, "there are no qualifications. We are slaves."

"And are you prepared to fulfill the duties of a slave?" I asked.

"Yes, Master," she said, "and I must, Master, for I am a slave."

"The answers are correct, and suitable, Slave," I said.

"Thank you, Master," she said.

"I am to take your virginity," I said. "You understand that?"

"Yes, Master," she said.

"Would you prefer that your virginity would have been taken from you while you were a free woman?" I asked.

"No," she said, "rather as a will-less slave, as I am now, subject to the decision and imperious will of a strong master."

I held my hand, opened, a bit above her left breast. She arched her back, pressing that marvelous, lush contour of her enslaved softness against my hand. I did not move my hand. She lay back, tears in her eyes. "You well know how to humiliate a slave, Master," she said. I smiled. The test had been an interesting one.

"Do you think, in time, you will prove to be a hot slave?" I asked.

"Hot?" she asked.

"Yes," I said, "responsive, sexually vital, owned, helplessly and uncontrollably passionate."

"I do not know, Master," she said. "What if I do not?"

"Then you will presumably be slain," I said.

She shuddered with terror.

"But do not fear," I said. "Most masters are patient. You will, most likely, have a month or more in which to develop the appropriate secretions and spasms."

She looked at me, with misery.

"I do not think it is anything to worry about, really," I said. "Most girls, under the circumstances, find very little difficulty in becoming passionate female slaves. Too, the entire Gorean milieu contributes to the development of passion in the female slave. She is dressed in a certain way, for example; she is commonly collared; she is subject to discipline; her performances are commanded, and subject to scrutiny and improvement, and so on. The main thing is to attempt to be fully pleasing to the Master, in every way. Too, you will commonly have a gauge of your progress; if your master is not pleased you will be beaten or whipped."

"I see," whispered the girl.

"I have seen girls such as you before," I said. "They commonly develop into the hottest of slaves."

She trembled, frightened.

"Remember," I said, "it will be to your advantage to be a hot slave, and, indeed, the hottest slave you can be. This will make you more pleasing to your master, and to those to whom he, at his caprice, consigns you."

"Yes, Master," she said.

"The true wonder in these matters," I said, "and what seems most delightful to me, is the way, gradually, the girl's heat begins to develop from within, until she is transformed, in effect, into a needful slave. She is then, of course, not only legally and physically at the mercy of men, but needfully, as well."

"How much a slave she would be then!" exclaimed the girl.

"No one claims that the Gorean slave girl has an easy lot," I said.

"How piteous to be such a girl!" she said. "Surely men would have mercy on her!"

"Perhaps," I said, "if she is sufficiently beautiful, and sufficiently pleasing."

"Do you think I will develop such passion?" she asked, frightened.

"Yes," I said.

"Do you think, then," she asked, "that men might be moved to show me mercy?"

"You already begin to sense what you might become, don't you?" I asked.

"Yes," she whimpered.

"It is a good sign," I said.

"Do you think that if I became such a girl, Master, men might show me mercy?" she asked.

"Perhaps," I said, "—if you were sufficiently beautiful, and sufficiently pleasing."

"I would try to be both," she said.

"You are a slave, aren't you?" I asked.

"Yes, Master," she said.

"I think it likely that you would be shown mercy, at least

upon occasion," I said. "But you, yourself, in a few weeks, will better know the answer to your question."

"In a few weeks?" she asked.

"Yes," I said, "when you find yourself on your knees at the feet of a man, or on your belly, crawling to him, to lick his feet, to beg his least touch."

I then, gently, began to caress her. In a few moments, interestingly, she began to moan.

"I am a slave," she whimpered, looking up at the stars, the Gorean moons.

"You may now request your fulfillment," I informed her.

"I request my fulfillment, Master," she said.

"I will be gentle with you this time," I said, "but sometimes, you must understand, you will be used quite differently, for example, with contempt or scorn, or brutality, or cruel indifference, or, perhaps, with ruthless power."

"Yes, Master," she said.

"Similarly," I said, "you will learn to serve in whatever position your master dictates and in whatever garb, or lack of garb, he pleases."

"Yes, Master," she said.

"And sometimes, too," I said, "you may have to serve in bonds, even cruel bonds, such things as thongs, and cords and chains."

"Yes, Master," she said.

"And sometimes, too," I said, "will-lessly, even though your back and legs may still sting from his lash."

"Yes, Master," she said.

"You will learn to serve him whenever, wherever and however he wishes," I said.

"Yes, Master," she said.

"And perfectly," I said.

"Yes, Master," she said.

"For he is the Master, and you are the Slave," I said.

"Yes, Master," she said.

"For you are nothing, and he is all," I said.

"I understand, Master," she whispered.

"Are you now prepared to be opened?" I asked.

"Yes, Master," she said.

I looked down into her eyes.

"Open me, Master," she said. "Open me, I beg you, as a slave, for the pleasures of men!"

"Very well," I said, and then, as she cried out softly, I

opened her, a nameless slave, who had once been Miss Millicent Aubrey-Welles, from Pennsylvania, a debutante, for the pleasures of men.

"Please, do not put me back so soon with the others, Master," she begged.

"It is nearly morning," I said.

"Please, Master," she said. She clutched me beneath the blankets, pressing her warm, vulnerable softness against me. "Please," she begged. The blood on the interior of her left thigh had now dried. When it was fresh I had taken some on my finger and forced it into her mouth, and onto her tongue, forcing her to taste it. "Yes, Master," she had whimpered. I had also traced the common Kajira mark, the common slave-girl mark, that which was the same as her brand, on her thigh in the blood, and had then smeared its residue down and onto her left calf. In the morning I wanted to make sure that the other girls in the coffle were perfectly clear on how she had spent the night and what had been done to her.

"Perhaps," I said.

"Thank you, Master," she whispered, happily.

I put out my hand, to the side. The grass was cold with dew. It was still dark.

She kissed me, softly. "How incredible do I find my current reality," she marveled. "Suddenly, it seems, I find myself a slave, and naked in the blankets of a master, on a world far from my own."

I said nothing.

"And only, it seems, a common slave," she said.

"Your reality is precisely what it seems," I assured her. "You are a slave, and only a common one."

"Yes, Master," she said.

"Your brand should tell you that," I said.

"I am not familiar with Gorean brands," she said.

"Yours is a common slave brand," I said. "It marks most property girls. You share it with thousands."

"I was of high station on my own world," she said, petulently.

"Here, on Gor," I told her, "your station, your status, your class, your prestige, are gone, taken with your name and freedom. Here you are only another slave, another domestic animal."

"I behaved as one, didn't I?" she asked, rolling onto her back, looking up at the dark sky.

"It was fitting and proper," I told her.

"How shamed I am," she said.

"Of your responsiveness?" I asked.

"Yes," she said.

I smiled. The third and fourth time I had used her she had yielded almost as a slave.

"I cannot help it," she said, "that I am responsive in the arms of a master."

"You are not supposed to help it," I said.

"I suppose if I had not been responsive," she said, "you would have beaten me."

"Yes," I said.

"Truly?" she asked.

"Yes," I said.

"I betrayed myself," she said.

"Let us think clearly about this matter," I suggested.

"Your assertion might be construed as meaning that you had committed some treason against yourself, or, perhaps, as meaning merely that you had revealed, or manifested, yourself. Let us consider, first, the matter of treason. A free woman might, possibly, feel that she had betrayed herself, in this sense, if she had so yielded to a man as to supply him with some perhaps subtle hint as to the latency of her slave reflexes. A slave girl, on the other hand, cannot commit treason against herself in this sense, for she is a slave. To commit this type of treason one must have a right, say, to deceive others as to one's sensuality, to conceal one's sexuality, and so on. The slave girl, an owned animal, under the command of her master, does not have this sort of right. Indeed, she has no rights. Accordingly, she cannot commit this sort of treason. Her legal status precludes its possibility. She may, of course, rationally, fear the consequences of her responsiveness being discovered, thus increasing, perhaps to her terror, in a slave culture, her desirability. Similarly she may lie, or attempt to lie, about her responsiveness, but she is then, of course, merely a lying slave and, when found out, will be treated accordingly."

"Such treason, then," she said, "can be committed only by a free woman."

"Yes," I said. "It is a luxury not permitted to the slave."

"It is a function only of the free woman's right to lie, and defraud, others?" she asked.

"Yes," I said. "It is possible, of course, for the slave, subjectively, psychologically, to feel that she has committed this treason, for she may, mistakenly, be still regarding herself, implicitly, as a free woman."

"But she cannot, in fact, have committed it, because she is a slave?" asked the girl.

"Yes," I said.

"I understand, Master," she said, bitterly.

"You see," I said, "you were still regarding yourself, implicitly, at least at the moment, as a free woman, or, perhaps better, more narrowly, as retaining at least one of the rights of a free woman."

"I am not to be beaten, am I, Master?" she asked.

"Not at the moment, at least," I informed her.

"Thank you, Master," she said.

"The second sense in which you might have intended your remark about betraying yourself, though I think it was not the sense in which you did intend it, would be the innocent sense, quite appropriate for a slave girl, of revealing or manifesting significant aspects of your nature. In this sense, of course, a slave girl has no alternative other than to betray herself. She is under an obligation, and a quite harsh and strict one, to release, manifest and reveal, fully, and in all its depths and facets, the profundities of her nature, the profundities of her femaleness."

"Yes, Master," she said.

"I think now," I said, "it is time to chain you with the others."

"You can just take me and chain me with them, can't you?" she said, angrily.

"Yes," I said.

"You took my virginity," she said. "Does that not mean anything to you?"

"No," I told her.

"It was, after all," she said, "only the virginity of a slave!"

"Precisely," I said.

She squirmed angrily.

"Are you angry?" I asked.

"Am I permitted anger?" she asked, warily.

"I will permit it, for now," I said.

"Yes," she said, "I am angry."

"Your concern is not well-warranted," I said. "Your first having was merely the ungating of a slave, her breaching, her opening, an unimportant prefatory technicality in the history of her bondage."

"Of course!" she said.

"Would you be so concerned about a boar's opening of a she-tarsk?" I asked. She had seen animals of this sort in the streets of Kailiauk, in the dawn of the day following her sale, when she and the others had been marched out towards the Ihanke. They are used, not unoften, in small Gorean towns, to scavenge garbage. Ginger and Evelyn had identified the animals for them. They had also informed them that, in many towns, such an animal might, in a market, bring a higher price than they themselves.

"I am the she-tarsk!" she said. "I am the slave!"

"Do you think that you are important?" I inquired.

"No, Master," she said.

"There, you see," I said.

"Yes," she said, "I see." She lay back, angrily.

There was a narrow rim of light in the east now. The air was still damp, and chilly.

"Do you respect me?" she asked.

"No," I told her.

She gasped, in misery.

"Kiss me," I told her, "fifty times, and well."

"Yes, Master," she said, and began to kiss me about the face and neck. I counted the kisses. There were fifty of them. Then she lay down beside me.

"You used me well, earlier," she said.

"You are a mere slave," I said. "It is simple to use a mere slave well."

"Doubtless girls such as myself are often well used," she said.

"Yes," I said.

"And we must submit, unquestioningly, to even our most contemptuous and brutal usage," she said.

"Of course," I said. "Are you distressed?"

"No, Master," she said. "Not really. It is only that I am not used to being an animal, a slave."

"I understand," I said.

"In your use of me," she said, "you did not give me a name, not even for your use of me."

"No," I said.

"Was that deliberate?" she asked.

"Yes," I said.

"A clever way to make clear to me that I was only a fondled animal, helpless in your arms."

I did not speak.

"I can scarcely begin to cope with my feelings," she said. "They are so troubled, so tumultuous."

"Speak," I said.

"I must lie there," she said. "I could not escape. I must submit!"

"Yes," I said.

"I was controlled. I was owned!"

"Yes," I said.

"I was powerless," she said. "How you dominated me!"

"You were used with great gentleness," I said, "though also, to be sure, with firmness and authority, as befits a slave. As for domination, you cannot yet even begin to suspect what it is for a woman to be dominated by a master."

"She would be so owned," she whispered.

"Yes," I said.

"Can you understand my feelings of utter helplessness, and humiliation?" she asked.

"I think so," I said.

"I have other feelings, as well," she whispered.

"What?" I asked.

"I cannot believe how I yielded in your arms," she whispered.

"You are merely a slave who yielded," I said. "You have not yet begun to learn, as a slave, what is the nature of true slave yieldings."

"Doubtless I will be taught," she said.

"You are beautiful," I said. "It is not unlikely."

"I had never dreamed that sensations such as you induced in me could exist," she whispered.

"They were largely the result of your own initial responsiveness," I said, "plus the fact that you realized you were a slave. They cannot even form a sound basis, I would suppose, on which you could begin to even remotely conjecture the nature of the feelings and sensations which lie before you. Beyond the sensations which you have hitherto experienced lie infinite horizons."

"I am afraid," she said.

"To your feelings of humiliation and helplessness, then," I said, "we may also add the emotion of fear."

"But I have other emotions, other feelings, too, Master," she said.

"Oh?" I asked.

"Yes, Master," she said.

"What?" I asked.

"Eagerness," she said, "pleasure, curiosity, excitement, sensual arousal, a desire to please, a desire to serve, a desire to be owned and mastered, a desire to be true to my basic and radical femaleness."

"I see," I said.

"Never before tonight," she said, "have I, now only a nameless slave, felt so much in contact with my femininity. I have learned tonight that being a woman is a real thing to be. It is not a biological triviality. It is not an insignificant, regrettable concomitant of a genetic lottery. It is something real and important in itself, something precious and wonderful."

"I agree," I said.

"And it is not to be a man," she said.

"No," I said. "I do not think so."

"Strange," she said, "that I should have learned this only stripped, and in the arms of a master, and on a world far from my own."

"It is not strange that you should learn this on a world far from your own," I said, "for your world is like a distorting lens, perverting even the most conspicuous lineaments of biological reality, nor is it strange that you should learn it as a stripped slave. Your stripping, particularly as it was done by a man, or at the command of a man, should put you in touch with certain female realities, such as your beauty, and its softness, and its subjectability to male domination; it should also, through exposure, and through various, subtle skin stimulations, heighten your vulnerability and sensitivity; this will enable you to feel more keenly and enable you to understand, more clearly, certain basic truths, such as the differences between men and women, and that you, whatever you are, are not a man."

"Yes, Master," she said.

"Lastly, and most importantly," I said, "you find yourself a slave. Female slavery is the institutionalized expression, in a civilization congenial to nature, of the fundamental biological relationship between the sexes. In the institution of female slavery we find this basic relationship recognized, accepted, clarified, fixed and celebrated. A civilization, you see, need not inevitably be a conflict with nature. A rational, informed civilization can even, in a sense, refine and improve upon nature; it can, so to speak, bring nature to fruition. Indeed, a natural civilization might be the natural flowering of nature itself, not an antithesis to nature, not a contradiction to nature, not a poison nor a trammel to it, but a stage or aspect of it, a form which nature itself can take."

"I fear even to understand such thoughts," she said, "let alone consider whether or not they might be true."

"Consider the case of the female slave," I said. "She was once a primitive, brutish female, innocent of legalities but, in effect, owned. She is now, commonly, a collared, imbonded beauty, properly marked as merchandise, effectively displayed and marketed, and owned in the full right of law."

"Yes, Master," said the girl.

"Who can doubt but what here civilization, as nature's refinement or expression, has wrought an improvement?"

"Surely, no one, Master," whispered the girl.

"Too, you will note that civilization has increased the control of the girls and the effectiveness of bondage, the marking, the identification of masters, the papers of sale, and so on. Escape, then, for all practical purposes, becomes impossible."

"Yes, Master," she said.

"And you are such a girl," I said.

"Yes, Master," she said.

"I am now going to put you with the others," I said. I stood up, thrusting the blankets to one side. She drew her legs up, feeling the coldness of the air. I looked down at her, she looking up at me. She was very beautiful.

"I am at your feet," she said.

"How do you feel?" I asked.

"Very feminine, very female," she said.

"How do you explain these feelings?" I asked.

"That I am a woman, at the feet of a strong man," she said, "one who dominates me, one who masters me, one whom I must obey."

"You do not speak like a woman of Earth," I said.

"I have learned much on Gor," she said, "and I have learned much this night."

I looked down at her, arms folded.

She put out her fingers, touching the dark blankets. Then, again, she looked up at me. "It is where we belong, isn't it, Master?" she asked.

"Yes," I said.

"I have always known it in my heart," she said, "but I never thought it would come true."

I went to pick up her tunic. I felt the blades of wet, cool grass cut at my ankles. I tossed her the tunic. She knelt, holding it. It was tiny, in her hands. On it, dark and wet, moist in its fibers, were the marks of dew.

She clutched the tunic, looking at me. She did not draw it on.

"I am no longer a virgin, Master," she said.

"That is known to me, I assure you," I said.

"I am now only a full and opened slave," she said, "no different from other girls, one, like them, readily available at the master's least desire."

"Yes," I said.

"I am not sore, Master," she said.

I nodded.

"But that does not make any difference, does it?" she asked.

"No," I said.

"Master," she whispered.

"Perhaps now you should garb yourself," I said.

"This is garb?" she asked, smiling, holding out the tunic. "It is scarcely a scanty rag."

"It leaves little doubt as to your charms," I admitted.

"It does not even have a nether closure," she said.

"It is not supposed to," I said. "Do you know why?"

"That I may be reminded that I am a slave," she smiled, "that my vulnerability may be heightened, that I may be immediately available to masters."

"Ginger and Evelyn have taught you that," I said.

"They have taught us many things," she said.

"What about intimate secrets of slave love-making?" I asked.

"No, Master," she said.

"The little she-sleen are doubtless guarding such secrets from you," I said. "I shall speak to Grunt in the morning. It will not prove to be in their interest to persist in this particular reticence."

"Yes, Master," she said, frightened.

"They will teach you, and the other jewels on the coffle, all they can, and quickly," I said. "Failure will be cause for severe discipline."

"Yes, Master," she whispered.

"An ignorant free woman is a commonplace," I said. "An ignorant slave is an absurdity."

"You mean I am actually to be taught how to please a man, trained?" she asked.

"Yes," I said, "trained, as the lovely animal you are."

She looked at me, frightened.

"And I advise you to learn your lessons well," I said.

"Yes, Master," she said.

"You are doubtless familiar, from your former world, with arts such as sewing and cooking, commonly thought appropriate for women," I said.

"Of course, Master," she said.

"Can you cook and sew?" I asked.

"No, Master," she said. "Such arts, I thought, were for lower women."

"You will learn them," I said.

"Yes, Master," she said.

"But beyond such arts as cooking and sewing, arts commonly thought appropriate for women, arts with which you are familiar, there are, obviously, many other arts. It should thus come as no surprise to you that among these other arts should be certain delicate, delicious and intimate arts, arts particularly appropriate to the female slave."

"I suppose not, Master," she said.

"You are not a wastrel free woman," I said. "You are a slave. You must earn your keep."

She trembled.

"Why do you think you were purchased?" I asked.

She put her small hand before her mouth, fearfully.

"Take your hand away from your mouth," I said. "I would see the lips of the slave."

Swiftly she lowered her hand.

"Straighten your back," I said.

She did so.

"The free woman," I said, "lies down, and waits to see what will happen. The female slave kneels beside her master, and begs to please him. The free woman deems it sufficient that she should exist, the slave girl, on the other hand, is expected not only to exist, but to excel; indeed, she fears only, commonly, that she may not be sufficiently marvelous for her master. It is little wonder that most men find the free woman, in her inertness, her ignorance and arrogance, boring. It is little wonder that most men prefer to order her rival to their furs, the helpless, collared, curvacious, lascivious, feminine slave."

"I was once a free woman," said the girl.

"There is hope for the free woman," I said. "She may be put in a collar, and stripped, and made subject to the whip. She may then, enslaved, be trained, too, for the pleasure of men."

"Yes, Master," whispered the girl.

"Training, then, should not come as a surprise to you," I said. "It is quite natural for female slaves to be given training."

"Yes, Master," she said.

"Expect, then, to be trained," I said.

"I shall, Master," she said.

I regarded her.

Suddenly she flung herself on her belly across the dark blankets. She reached to my left ankle and holding it with her small hands, began to kiss at my foot. "Slaves may beg to please their masters, may they not?" she asked.

"Yes," I said.

"I beg to please my Master," she said. Her lips were warm and soft on my foot.

"I am not your master," I said.

"All free men are my masters," she said, "as all free women are my mistresses."

"That is true," I granted her.

"I beg to please you, as my Master," she said, "and, indeed, tonight, in these blankets, you are my master, for it is you who have opened me and to whom I have been consigned in these hours for your pleasure."

It was true. I was her current use-master. In these hours, in my blankets, she must be to me as my own slave. In these hours, in my blankets, for all practical purposes, I owned her.

I felt her tongue.

"Consider me," she whispered, "for your renewed pleasure."

It is pleasant, as you might well imagine, receiving such attentions from a woman. It is particularly pleasant, I assure you, when she is a slave, for then she is owned, and you may do with her what you wish.

"Please, Master," she begged.

"Perhaps," I said.

"Slaves such as I are not trained only by women, are we, Master?" she asked.

"No," I said. "Many Goreans believe that the finest of slave trainers are men, and that only a man with a whip, and total power over a woman, can properly teach her to be a slave."

"Do you have a whip, Master?" she asked.

"My belt will do," I told her.

"Yes, Master," she said.

"But, in my opinion," I said, "this is oversimple. I believe that other women, particularly if they are slaves themselves, can be superb slave trainers. Many slave houses, of course, maintain both male and female trainers. My own theory is that if a girl is to have but one trainer, it is doubtless best for that trainer to be a man, for the girl, in her bondage, is almost certain to have to relate primarily to men, to please, placate and serve them, and so on. On the other hand, I think it is also undeniable that a girl can learn much from another girl, one who has survived, and is surviving, as a slave."

"Surviving?" she asked.

"Yes," I said, "for the slave girls who are not pleasing are commonly killed."

She put the side of her head fearfully down on my foot.

"Be pleasing," I told her.

"Yes, Master," she said.

"But most girls," I said, "not only survive as slaves, but thrive as slaves."

"Master?" she asked.

"Yes," I said. "You may find this hard to grasp now, but most girls, as you will learn, once they discover its authenticity and inescapability, blossom joyously, submitted, in their bondage; in it they occupy their place in nature; in it, subject to the authority and power of strong men, owned and mastered uncompromisingly as mere slaves, they obtain their deepest biological self-realization, their ultimate fulfillment. In it, in their place in nature, they become women, as outside of it, they cannot. As the true woman is the true slave, no woman can become a true woman who is not a true slave."

"Men and women, then," she said, "are not the same."

"No," I said. "Men are the masters. Women are the slaves. Your world has taught both sexes to strive for what are, in effect, masculine, or neuteristic, values. This produces unhappiness and frustration for both sexes. Hormonally normal women find it difficult or impossible to achieve happiness through the adoption of, in effect, transvestite values. Similarly this perversion of values complicates or precludes, for the glandularly normal male, the achievement of a natural biological fulfillment. Both sexes, then, frequently fail to obtain happiness, or fall far short of the happiness of which they are both capable, that happiness which is a consequence of maintaining a biological fidelity to their separate natures."

"The lies, the hypocrisies, the pretentions of pseudo-masculinity will not be permitted to me on Gor, will they, Master?" she asked.

"Not in the least," I told her, "for you are a slave."

"Yes, Master," she said.

"Does this displease you?" I asked.

"No, Master," she said.

"Does it please you?" I asked.

"Yes, Master," she said.

"Even the girl who does not have a female trainer," I said, "will often seek out more experienced girls, to beg them for their intimate counsels and their secrets of love and beauty. Sometimes she purchases these by such tiny gifts, of food and such, as may be within her province, or by performing portions of the other's labors, and so on. Indeed, much of the chitchat of slave girls, in their gatherings, has to do, in one way or another, with the pleasing of masters."

"It is in our best interest to fulfill our duties well," she said.

"But the best trainers you will have," I said, "will be your particular masters, and yourself. There is a specific magic, so to speak, and chemistry, between each master and each slave. Each master is different, and, so, too, deliciously, is each slave. Each master will train his own girl according to his own interests and tastes, and each girl, in the private and intimate context of the particular master/slave relation, by means of her intelligence and imagination, owned, will train herself to be his special slave, specifically and personally."

"I understand, Master," she said.

"But, even given the uniqueness of each bondage relation," I said, "there are still certain common denominators in all such relations, which must not be lost sight of, such as the legal status of the slave, that she is, ultimately, only an article of property, that she is liable to discipline and punishment, and that she is totally subject to the will of the master."

"Yes, Master," she said.

"But beyond this," I said, "beyond the concern with an individual master, you will learn, more generally, how to be pleasing to men. You may be sold to a stranger, or given to one, or fall into the hands of a stranger, or group of strangers. You may know little or nothing of your master, or masters, other than the fact that he holds total power over you, and he may know little or nothing of you, other than the fact that your lovely hide is marked with the brand of the female slave. You thus begin again, anew, your struggle to convince a master that there may be some point in keeping you about, that there may be some point in putting a bit of gruel in a bowl, or hollowed stone, for you, or thrusting a crust of bread in your mouth. You attempt to convince him of this, of course, even though he is unknown to you, even though he is a total stranger to you, by serving him, and superbly, as a female slave. Do you understand what I am saying?"

"Yes, Master," she said, "that I must learn, in general, how to be pleasing to men."

"Yes," I said, "this any slave girl must learn, such things as the kisses, the touches, the squirmings, the thousand submissions."

"Yes, Master," she whispered.

"But, do not fear," I said, "such modalities are not learned in vain. They will be required of you even by a love master, and, indeed, he will doubtless require them from you with a harshness, an amplitude and exactness far beyond that of a more casual owner."

"But, why, Master?" she asked.

"Because you are," I said, "in the final analysis, as he will wish you to remember, only his slave. Too, do you think he would require less from you, a love slave, than from some more common girl chained at his feet?"

"No, Master," she said.

"Are you silent?" I asked.

"It seems strange to think of serving a love master with the same proficiencies with which I must serve any other man, as a mere slave," she said.

"Your skills and talents are surely as much, or more, at his disposal, as they are at the disposal of any other male," I said.

"True," she said.

"Do you object?" I asked.

"No, Master," she said. "I would want to serve my love master, to the best of my ability, with whatever skills or talents I might have."

"And he would see that you do so," I said.

"Yes, Master," she said. Suddenly she sobbed.

"What is wrong?" I asked.

"I am so frightened," she said. "This world terrifies me, and on it I am only a naked slave. I do not know what to do. I am afraid. I am so ignorant. I know nothing. I am so frightened. I am only a slave."

"You speak truly, ignorant slave," I said. Did she expect me to comfort her?

She turned her head to the side, and laid her left cheek on the blankets at my feet. "Please put your foot on my neck, Master," she said.

I did so, with just enough pressure that she could feel its weight, and that of my body.

"You could now," she said, "with one motion of your foot, kill me."

"Yes," I said.

"Please do not kill me, Master," she said. "Instead, take pity on me, I beg of you, and find me pleasing."

I took my foot from her neck. "I shall inspect you," I told her. "You may kneel before me."

Swiftly she rose from her stomach to kneel before me.

"Knees wide," I told her, "back on heels, stomach in, head high, hands on thighs, shoulders back, breasts thrust out."

I moved her hair back, behind her shoulders, and smoothed it out. It would not, thus, interfere with my view. I appraised her, slowly, carefully. "It is not impossible," I told her, at length, "that a man might find you pleasing."

"Make me please you," she begged.

"Rather," I said, "I shall permit you to beg to please me, and as a slave."

"I beg to please you, Master," she said.

"As a slave?" I asked.

"Yes, Master," she said, "I beg to please you—and as a slave."

"But you are untrained," I said, scornfully.

"Train me," she begged, tears in her eyes.

I regarded her, dispassionately.

"Train me, Master," she begged. "Train me, please, Master!"

"Take your hair from behind your left shoulder," I said, "and hold it before, and against, your lips. Part of the hair keep before your lips and against them. Another part of the hair, the center strands, take back between your lips, so that you can feel it on the soft interior surfaces of your lips. A portion of this same hair take then back against your teeth, and a portion of that back, between the teeth. Now purse your lips and, while remaining kneeling, rise from your heels, and lean forward, gently and submissively."

And thus began the training of a nameless slave on the plains of Gor.

In a few moments I thrust her back to the blankets.

"Do I train well, Master?" she asked.

"Yes," I said, "pretty slave. You are an apt pupil, and you train well."

She snuggled against me.

"It is a tribute to your intelligence," I said.

"Thank you, Master," she said.

"And to your genetic predisposition to slavery," I said.

"Yes, Master," she said.

A woman's acquisition of slave arts follows a steep learning curve, far beyond what would be expected was the template, or readiness, for these arts not intrinsic to her nature. She learns them far too swiftly and well not to be, in effect, a born slave.

"Oh!" she said, and then I again took her.

This time the slave squirmings of her, though inchoate and rudimentary, were unmistakable.

"How long has it been since you were a virgin?" I asked.

"A thousand years," she smiled. "I think perhaps ten thousand years."

"Do you feel now less than you were before," I asked, "less important, somehow less significant?"

"No," she said, "I feel ten thousand times more important, more significant, than I was before."

"Virginity, as I understand it, in English," I said, "is sometimes spoken of as though it might be something which could be lost. In Gorean, on the other hand, it is usually conceived of as something which is to be outgrown, or superseded."

"Interesting," she said.

"What, in English," I asked, "is a woman who is not a virgin?"

She thought for a moment. "A nonvirgin, I suppose," she said.

"This type of distinction is drawn in various ways in Gorean," I said. "The closest to the English is the distinction between 'glana' and 'metaglana.' 'Glana' denotes the state or virginity and 'metaglana' denotes the state succeeding virginity. Do you see the difference?"

"Yes," she said, "in Gorean virginity is regarded as a state to be succeeded."

"Another way of drawing the distinction is in terms of 'falarina' and 'profalarina.' 'Profalarina' designates the state preceding falarina, which is the state of the woman who has been penetrated at least once by a male."

"Here," she said, "the state of virginity is regarded as one which looks toward, or has not yet attained, the state of falarina."

"Yes," I said. "In the first case, virginity is seen as something to be succeeded, and, in the second, it is seen as something which is conceived of as merely antedating the state of falarina. It takes its very meaning from the fact that it is not yet falarina."

"Both of these situations are quite different from the English," she said. "In English, as I see now, interestingly, virginity is spoken of as a positive property, and nonvirginity, in spite of its obvious and momentous importance, and even its necessity, presumably, for the continuation of the species, seems to be regarded as being merely the absence of a property, or the privation of a property."

"Yes," I said. "It is as though the whole spectrum were divided into the blue and the nonblue. Properly understood the nonblue is every bit as real, and is even more extensive and variegated than the blue."

"Yes," she said.

"It is thus that pathological conceptions, ingrained in common speech, can produce distorted notions of reality," I said.

"I understand, Master," she said.

"In Gorean, as not in English," I said, "the usual way,

however, of drawing the distinction is in terms of 'glana' and 'falarina.' Separate words, these, are used for the separate properties or conditions. Both conditions, so to speak, are accorded a similar status. Both are regarded as being equally real, equally positive, so to speak."

"Yes, Master," she said.

"Sometimes, metaphorically, in English, however," I said, "a distinction is drawn between the virgin and the woman, a distinction which is almost Gorean in tone. Strictly, of course, in English, one might be both a woman and a virgin."

"Do Goreans speak freely of these things?" she asked.

"Free persons do not commonly speak freely of them," I said. "For example, whether a free woman is glana or falarina is obviously her business, and no one else's. Such intimate matters are well within the prerogatives of her privacy."

"Such matters, however, I suspect," she said, "are not within the prerogatives of a slave's privacy."

"No," I said. "Such matters are public knowledge about slaves, as much as the color of their hair and eyes, and their collar size."

"And my most intimate measurements?" she asked.

"Public knowledge," I assured her, "if anyone should be interested."

"What privacy am I permitted, then?" she asked.

"None," I told her.

"And what secrets?" she asked.

"None," I told her.

"I see," she said.

"You perhaps now understand, a little better than before," I said, "what it will be to be a slave."

"Yes, Master," she said.

"Your opening, for example, is not to be kept a secret," I said.

"The blood you smeared on my leg will see to that," she smiled.

"Do you fear the criticism, the derision, or ridicule, of the other girls?" I asked.

"I fear only," she said, "that I may not have sufficiently pleased my master."

"Excellent," I said.

"As they, too, soon shall fear," she said.

"Yes," I said. I wondered if she knew how truly she spoke. The girls on a chain, once opened and made to serve, usually begin to compete among themselves, and soon, to see who can serve the masters best, and those who do not enter earnestly into this competition, it might be mentioned, are usually the first to be fed to sleen.

"I was glana," she smiled. "Now I am falarina."

I put my hand, forcibly, over her mouth. Then I removed it from her mouth. "Such expressions," I said, "are commonly to be spoken of, and by, free persons. They are not to be applied to slaves, any more than to tarsk sows."

"Yes, Master," she said.

"You were white silk," I said. "Now you are red silk."

"We are not even entitled to the same words as free persons in such matters?" she asked.

"No," I told her.

"I understand, Master," she said, tears in her eyes.

"Even here, however," I said, "you will note that both words suggest a similar status. Both notions are equally positive, both properties are conceived of as being equally real."

"That is true," she said.

"To be sure," I said, "'white' in the context of 'white-silk girl' tends less to suggest purity and innocence to the Gorean than ignorance and naivety, and a lack of experience. 'Red,' in the context of 'red-silk girl,' on the other hand, connotes rather clearly, I think, experience. One expects a red-silk girl, for example, not only to be able to find her way about the furs, but, subject to the whip, owned and dominated, perhaps chained, to prove herself a sensuous treasure within them."

"I am red-silk," she said. "Have me."

"Perhaps," I said. I began to touch her, gently.

"Ohhh," she said, "yes."

"Do you like that?" I asked.

"Must I respond to such a question?" she asked.

"Yes," I said.

"Yes, Master," she said. "I like it." She closed her eyes. "Oh, yes," she said, "I like it."

"Master," she said, looking up at me.

"Yes," I said.

"More than once tonight," she said, "you have mentioned binding, or chaining."

"Yes," I said.

"I would fear to be bound or chained," she said.

"All the more reason to bind or chain you," I said.

She shuddered.

"Master," she said.

"Yes," I said.

"Why would you bind a woman who is a slave?" she asked. "She knows that there is no escape for her. She is not going to run away. She knows that you may do with her as you please."

"It holds her in a given position," I said, "for your leisured work upon her body."

"That is true," she said.

"But the primary reasons," I said, "are, as you might suspect, psychological, both from the point of view of the master and the slave. She, chained, or bound, is helpless. She knows that she might, at the master's whim, be slit like a larma. This increases her terror, her vulnerability, her desire to be found pleasing. This makes her feel more slavelike and, accordingly, more ready to respond to the touch of the master. From the master's point of view, of course, this is also stimulating. It is pleasant for a man to have absolute power over a woman, to have her bound or chained in a position of his choosing, and to know that she must submit to whatever he chooses to do to her. In this situation the equations of nature, those of dominance and submission, are intensified. This is felt by both the master and the slave. Too, to be sure, there is, for physiological reasons also, commonly, some boosting of the female's responses, as the result of the binding, the restraint. The orgasmic spasms, somewhat restricted, or, perhaps better, channeled, regulated and controlled, confined within the parameters set by the master, must then seem more intense, more concentrated."

"I see," she whispered.

"But the main thing, in my opinion," I said, "is the psychological effect on the woman, the bringing home to her, in clear, forcible and undeniable terms, the reality of her situation, that she is helpless, that she is at his mercy, that she, regardless of her will, is now his to do with as he pleases, that she is owned, that she is his slave, and that he is her master."

"I would be terrified to be bound," she said.

I saw that she wished to be bound.

I continued to caress her.

"Master," she whispered.

"Yes," I said.

"Bind me," she whispered.

"Do you beg it?" I asked.

"Yes," she whispered. "I beg to be bound."

"Kneel," I told her, "quickly."

Swiftly then did she kneel, and looked at me, frightened.

"I have changed my mind," she said.

"Do not break position," I told her.

"Yes, Master," she said.

I went to my saddlebags, with the kaiila saddle, and withdrew two fairly short lengths of soft, pliant, braided black leather, each about twenty-five inches in length.

I pulled back her right wrist a bit and tied it to her right ankle. I left her about six or seven inches of slack between wrist and ankle. "This is a common open-legged tie," I said. "It is not good for general security, but it is a good, and familiar, slave tie." I then fastened her left wrist to her left ankle, as I had done with her right wrist and ankle. "When finished with you," I said, "I might simply bind your wrists behind you and tie your ankles together. That is a familiar and effective security tie. If you had not been sufficiently pleasing I might pull up your bound ankles and tie them to your wrists. Your neck, of course, might always be tied to a stake, or bound to a tree."

I then stood up and stepped back, to observe my handiwork. "An advantage of this tie," I said, "is that a girl may kneel in it comfortably for hours, perhaps beside a master's chair, while he works, and is not yet ready for her."

She pulled a little, almost surreptitiously, at the leather on her wrists, leading back to her ankles.

"Is this all?" she asked, timidly.

"I see that there are potentialities of this tie which, as yet, you have not discerned," I said.

I then took her by the hair and threw her forward on the blankets, on her belly.

"Struggle," I told her.

She did so, helplessly. Then she ceased her struggles.

"An interesting perspective on a woman," I said. "Too, bound in this position she is seldom in doubt as to the fact that she is a slave. Too, in time, it can be quite painful." She groaned, and I, mercifully, thrust her to her side. She looked up at me, frightened. "Whereas this tie," I said, "is not good for general security, it is quite adequate for specific security, namely, security in a specific situation, in this case, in the presence of the master or a keeper. For example, under observation, you cannot very well employ your right hand in the attempt to undo the knot on your left ankle. If the tie, of course, is accomplished with chains, then it is also adequate for a general security, an aesthetic and delicious general security, a chain neck leash being added, naturally, to restrict movement." I then put her on her back. Her knees were drawn up and her hands held helplessly at her sides. "Now," I said, "I think you can see one of the main virtues of this tie. The woman is quite helpless, absolutely, and there is not the least impedence to the master's approach."

She seemed to shrink back in the bonds.

"Please, untie me," she said.

I thrust apart her knees.

"Oh!" she said.

I held her knees apart, not permitting her to close them.

"I do not want to be tied like this!" she cried. "I did not know it would be like this. I am too helpless! Please, untie me! Free me! Loosen my bonds! Do not keep me tied like this! No! Please!"

I regarded her.

She looked at me in fear. She squirmed, helplessly.

"What do you know of me?" I asked her.

"Nothing," she said, "only that you are my master."

"What might I do to you?" I asked.

"Anything," she said.

I withdrew my hands, permitting her to close her knees, which she did, immediately, clenching them fearfully together.

"You have tied me like a pig," she said.

"The pig," I said, "is not a Gorean animal. To be sure, you are trussed rather like a she-tarsk."

"You have tied me, then," she said, "like a she-tarsk!"

"Do not flatter yourself," I said, "that you enjoy a status as high as either that of the pig or she-tarsk. Your status is lower than that of either. It is that of the female slave."

"You have bound me, then," she said, "as a slave!"

"Now you speak the truth," I informed her.

"What are you going to do with me?" she asked.

"Whatever I wish," I said.

She moaned. She pulled weakly at her wrist tethers, fastening her wrists to her ankles.

"Do you begin to sense now," I asked, "what it might be for a woman to be bound by a man?"

"Yes, Master," she whispered.

"Can you escape?" I asked.

"No, Master," she said.

"Are you powerless?" I asked.

"Yes, Master," she said. "I am powerless, totally."

"What will be done to you?" I asked.

"I do not know!" she wept. "I am helpless. I am a slave. I am at your mercy. It is you who will decide what is to be done with me."

"Perhaps I will whip you, lashing you with my belt," I said. "Perhaps I will kick you, again and again, convincing you of your worthlessness. Perhaps I shall kneel across your body, slapping you, methodically, again and again, until you beg for mercy. Perhaps I shall merely, for my amusement, beat you senseless."

"Please, Master, no," she said.

"Perhaps it shall be the quirt," I said. "Perhaps I shall use the quirt on you, lengthily, as on a recalcitrant she-kaiila."

"No, Master," she said. "Please, no, Master!"

"Are you recalcitrant?" I asked.

"I am not recalcitrant," she said. "I am docile, and obedient. I am ready to please you, and I desire to please you."

"Perhaps I will butcher you," I said. "Perhaps I will take you."

She looked at me, in horror.

"Would you prefer to be butchered or taken?" I asked.

"Taken, Master," she said. "I beg to be taken."

"The taking of a free woman," I asked, "in which, to some extent, her dignity, pride and status are respected, or the taking of a slave?"

"I am a slave, Master," she said. "I beg that of a slave."

I looked at her knees, clenched closely together. "Spread your knees apart, widely," I told her.

"Yes, Master," she said.

"Now beg," I told her.

"I beg," she said.

In moments it was necessary to thrust her hair, balled and wadded, into her mouth, and I put my hand, too, over her mouth. Her eyes were wild. She kicked wildly at the pliant, braided black leather, again and again. Then, mercifully, I unbound her limbs and I let her straighten her trembling body in the blankets. With one finger I pulled the wet hair from her mouth. She was gasping, and shuddering. I held her closely for a few minutes, that she might, while thus warmed and sheltered, make some adjustment to this new dimension which she had discovered in her being.

"What was it?" she whispered.

"It was a small one," I reassured her.

"What was it?" she whispered.

"It was the first, I think, of your slave orgasms," I said. I then rose from her side and threw her the tiny slave tunic. "Put it on," I said. She did so, and I then lifted her gently in my arms and carried her to the chain. I put her down there, on her side, softly, in the grass. When I lifted the opened collar to place it about her throat, she put her hands on my wrists, and softly kissed my hands. She looked at me, her eyes wondrous, and soft.

"I did not know it could be like that," she said.

"It was only a small thing," I said.

"There could be more?" she asked.

"You have not yet begun to learn what it can be, to be a slave," I said.

She looked at me, frightened.

I then snapped the collar about her throat.

"Do you know, ultimately," I asked, "who will prove to be your one best trainer?"

"No, Master," she said.

"You, yourself," I said, "the girl, herself, eager to please, imaginative and intelligent, monitoring her own performances and feelings, striving lovingly to improve and refine them. You yourself will be largely responsible for making yourself the superb slave you will become."

"Master?" she asked.

"The collar," I said, touching it, "is put on from without, but what it encircles, the slave, comes from within."

"Master?" she asked.

"Slavery," I told her, "true slavery, comes from within, and you, my lovely little red-haired beast, I assure you, as was evidenced by your behavior and performances this night, are a true slave. Do not fight your slavery. Allow it freely and spontaneously, candidly, sweetly and untrammeled, to manifest itself. It is what you are."

"Yes, Master," she said.

"That, too," I said, "will save you many bouts with the lash."

"Yes, Master," she said.

I then turned about and left her, on the chain. "Master!"

she called, but I did not turn back. She would stay there, on the coffle, where I had put her. She was only a slave.

I returned to my blankets and lay down again, to sleep for a few Ehn before the camp began to stir.

Nothing of importance had transpired. I had merely done a favor for Grunt, my friend, opening a slimly bodied, red-haired girl for him, one of his slaves.

To be sure, she was pretty, and first on the coffle.

14

IT IS A GOOD TRADING;
PIMPLES;
I LEARN SOMETHING OF THE
WANIYANPI;
CORN STALKS;
SIGN;

GRUNT AND I WILL
PROCEED EAST

The red-haired girl cried out in pain and fear, struck from her knees back in the grass by the plump, scornful woman of the red savages, a sturdy-legged matron of the Dust Legs. She looked up at her in terror. Slave girls know that they have most to fear from free women.

"Wowiyutanye!" hissed the Dust-Leg woman at the frightened girl lying on her side in the grass before her.

"Yes, Mistress," said the girl in Gorean, uncomprehendingly.

The men at the trading point scarcely paid them any attention.

I sat nearby, a blanket spread out before me, on which I had spread out various of the trade goods, mostly mirrors, dyes and beads this afternoon, which I had brought into the Barrens.

The Dust-Leg woman threw the girl to her right side in the grass and pulled up the tunic on her left thigh. The girl, terrified, did not resist. "Inahan!" called the Dust-Leg woman to the others about, pointing to the brand on the girl's thigh. "Guyapi!"

"Ho," said one of the men, agreeably. "Inahan," agreed another.

"Winyela!" announced the woman.

"Inahan," said more than one man.

"Cesli!" said the woman scornfully to the girl.

"Please do not hurt me, Mistress," said the girl, in Gorean.

"Ahtudan!" cried the woman at her, angrily, and then she spat upon her.

"Yes, Mistress," said the red-haired girl. "Yes, Mistress!" She then pulled up her legs and looked down, into the grass.

The Dust-Leg woman turned away from her and came over to where I sat behind the blanket. She beamed at me. The Dust Legs, on the whole, are an affable, open-hearted and generous people. They tend to be friendly and outgoing.

"Hou," said the woman to me, kneeling before the blanket.

"Hou," said I to her.

It is difficult not to like them. Most trading is done with them. They tend to be the intermediaries and diplomats of the western Barrens.

The woman opened a rectangular hide envelope, a parleche, slung on a strap over her shoulder. In it were various samples of beadwork and some small skins. She put some of these things on her edge of the blanket.

"Hopa," I said, admiringly. "Hopa."

She beamed, her teeth strong and white in her broad, reddish-brown face.

She pointed to a small mirror, with a red-metal rim. I handed it to her.

I glanced back. Behind us and to the side the red-haired girl, timidly, frightened, had resumed a kneeling position. I do not think that she had personally offended the Dust-Leg woman. I think it was rather that the Dust-Leg woman simply did not entertain any great affection for white female slaves. Many women of the red savages, in spite of the wishes of their men, do not approve of such soft, curvacious, desirable trade goods being brought into the Barrens.

The Dust-Leg woman carefully examined the small mirror.

I looked beyond her, to a few yards away, where several

kaiila, of the visiting Dust Legs, were tethered. There, with
the animals, there knelt a white female slave of the Dust
Legs, another of their animals, a two-legged one, and lovely
legs they were indeed, doubtless by the paws of her master's
beast. She wore a brief garment of fringed, tanned skin, rent
and stained, doubtless a castoff from some free woman's
shirtdress, shortened to slave length. She was wet with sweat
and dark with dust. Her hair, which was dark, was wet, and
tangled and matted. Her legs, bloodied and muchly scratched,
were black with dust and sweat. Here and there one could see
where the trickle of perspiration had run through the dust.
On her thighs where she had rubbed her hands the dust was
streaked in wet smears. She had been run beside her master's
kaiila, and apparently not slowly.

Grunt was engaged in conversation with four or five of the
Dust-Leg men. Then he rose to his feet, and went to his
stores, to bring forth a fine hatchet.

The female slave of the Dust Legs, kneeling by the kaiila,
wore a beaded collar, about an inch and a half in height. It
was an attractive collar. It was laced closed, and tied snugly
shut, in front of her throat. The patterns in the beading were
interesting. They indicated her owner. Similar patterns are
used by given individuals to identify their arrows or other
personal belongings. It is particularly important to identify
the arrows, for this can make a difference in the division of
meat. It is death to a slave, incidentally, to remove such a
collar without permission. Furthermore the collar is fastened
by what is, in effect, a signature knot, a complex knot, within
a given tribal style, whose tying is known only to the individual who has invented it. It is thus, for most practical
purposes, impossible to remove and replace such a collar
without the master, in his checking of the knot, by untying
and retying it, being able to tell. Suffice it to say, the slaves of
the red savages do not remove their collars. The girl kept her
head down. She apparently was not being permitted to raise
her eyes at the trading point. She might, thus, if the master
wished, have come and gone from the trading point without
having seen anything or recognized anything, unless perhaps
the grass between her knees and the paws of her master's
kaiila. Gorean slaves, incidentally, wherever they may be
found, say, in the cities or in the Barrens, are generally kept
under an iron discipline. It is the Gorean way.

"Two," said the Dust-Leg woman, in Gorean, holding up two fingers. She indicated the mirror, now lying before her, and two beaded rectangles, drawn from her parfleche. This type of beadwork is popular in curio shops in certain Gorean cities, far from the perimeter; it may also be fashioned by leather workers into various crafted articles, such as purses, pouches, wallets, belt decorations, envelopes and sheaths. Interestingly this type of article is more popular away from the perimeter than near it. It is not merely that it is more common nearer the perimeter but, I think, that it serves as a reminder, near the perimeter, of the reality and proximity of the red nations, whereas these same nations, or tribes, far from the perimeter tend to be regarded not only as remote but as almost mythical peoples. The ear-splitting cry of a Kaiila warrior, for example, has seldom awakened a good burgher of Ar from his slumbers.

"Five," I suggested to the Dust-Leg woman. I recalled that Grunt had, two days ago, at another trading point, received five such rectangles for a similar mirror. I smiled when I made this suggestion to the Dust-Leg woman. In such trading, it is a good idea, on both sides, to smile a great deal. This makes the entire exchange, if one takes place, a good deal more pleasant for both parties. Not only are tensions eased but vanities are less likely to become involved in the trading. It is easier, if one is smiling, to get a little less than one would like, or to give a bit more than one might otherwise choose to. Concessions, thus, for both sides, are less like defeats and more like favors bestowed on friends. In the long run, this increases the percentage of mutually satisfactory bargains, and the individual who has found dealing with you satisfactory, of course, is more likely to deal with you again. He becomes, in effect, a customer. It is better to make less profit on a customer and have him come back than make a higher profit and not see him again. These, at any rate, were the sentiments of Grunt, who seemed popular with the Dust Legs, and, as far as I can tell, they are substantially sound.

I glanced again to the white female slave of the Dust Legs, kneeling, eyes down, in her beaded collar, by the kaiila. I thought if she were washed and combed she might not be unattractive. It was easy to see why Dust-Leg men might find such goods of interest. It might be pleasant to have such a lovely animal about, to cook one's meat, to keep one's lodge

and please one, humbly and obediently, in the furs. I could
also see why Dust-Leg women could view such a commodity
with distaste and contempt. How could they, free, begin to
compete with a slave? How could they even begin to do so,
unless they, themselves, also became slaves?

"Two," said the Dust-Leg woman.

"Five," I said. My interest in the Barrens, of course, was
not in trading. As far as I was concerned I might have given
the woman the mirror. On the other hand, I realized, and
Grunt had made it clear to me, too, that one must not insult
the red savages nor deal with them unrealistically, particularly in the light of other traders and merchants who might
follow me. If I gave away goods, or traded them too cheaply
this would suggest that I was delivering cheap or inferior
merchandise, an inference it would not be in our interest for
the red savages to draw. Too, if they thought the goods
sound, they might think they had been paying too highly for
them in the past, or expect that future dealers would deal
with them similarly, which, of course, they would not be
likely to do, nor be able, realistically, to afford to do.

One of the Dust-Leg men was examining, with great care
the hatchet which Grunt had shown him. Grunt excused himself and rose to his feet. One does not hurry red savages in
their perusals of products.

Grunt went again to his stores and brought forth some
packages, wrapped in waxed paper. "Canhanpisasa," said
Grunt. "Canhanpitasaka. Canhanpitiktica." He then began to
pass out, to the Dust-Leg men and women about, pieces of
candy, lumps of cake sugar and flakes of dried molasses. The
woman with whom I was dealing, too, received a palmful of
molasses flakes. She smacked her lips. Grunt and she then exchanged what I took to be appropriate civilities and
compliments.

She pointed to Grunt. "Wopeton," she said. "Akihoka
Zontaheca."

I looked at Grunt. I knew one of his names among the
red savages was Wopeton, which means Trader, or Merchant

"She says I am a skillful and honest fellow," he said.

"Hopa! Wihopawin!" he said to her.

The plump woman doubled over, laughing. 'Hopa', I knew
meant 'pretty' or 'attractive'.

"Wawihaka! Wayaiha!" she laughed.

"I told her she was a pretty woman," said Grunt, "and

now she is teasing me. She says I am a joker, one who makes others laugh."

"Two," said the Dust-Leg woman to me.

"Five," I said to her.

Grunt looked about, the sweets in his hand. He saw a red youth near the men, sitting together. He motioned him to come closer. The lad wore a shirt, leggings and a breechclout, so much perhaps because he was visiting at a trading point. Grunt offered him some of the sweets. The young man shook his head, negatively. He was eyeing the red-haired girl.

"Ah!" said Grunt. Then he turned to the red-haired girl. "Strip," he told her. Swiftly, unhesitantly, a slave, frightened, she did so. "Be flattered," said Grunt to her. "Our young visitor finds you of greater interest than some bits of molasses." He then put his boot squarely in her back and thrust her forward, on her belly, before the young man. "Please him," he said.

"Master?" she asked.

"Rise to your knees before him," he said. "Remove his breechclout with your teeth. Attempt to interest him in you."

"Yes, Master," she wept. But it would not be the first time she had pleased one of Grunt's visitors.

Grunt watched the girl struggle to her knees. He replaced the sweets, wrapping them, carefully in his pouch.

The girl looked up, frightened, at the red youth.

"Four," I said to the Dust-Leg woman. I supposed I should have actually set my original price higher. Already I would obtain less for the small mirror than Grunt had for a comparable item the day before yesterday.

"Winyela," said the Dust-Leg woman, in disgust, glancing behind me to the red-haired girl.

I glanced back. Frightened, and humbly, and delicately, she was pleasing the youth. I had little doubt but what he would find her of interest.

"Winyela," said the Dust-Leg woman, and spat into the grass.

A few yards away, near the kaiila, the white slave girl of the Dust Legs kept her head down, not daring to raise it.

Grunt had now gone back to the coffle, where most of his girls huddled together, the chain on their necks, and removed Ginger, and Ulla and Lenna, the two Swedish girls, from the chain. All of the girls in the camp, with the exception of the red-haired girl, had now been named. In each case their former Earth name had been put on them, but now, like a brand, by their master's decision, as a slave name. The two Americans, beside the red-haired girl, were Lois and Inez; the French girl was Corinne; the two English girls were Priscilla and Margaret. That the red-haired girl had not been named as yet was not a function of the fact that either Grunt or myself saw any difficulty with Millicent as a slave name. The former debutante's name seemed to us quite suitable for a slave's name. It was rather that he did not yet wish her to be named. She was to continue, for the time, as a nameless slave. The object of this was to lower her standing in the camp, and to assist in her training. Granting her in hospitality to various of his guests had a similar object. Grunt now came forward, Ulla and Lenna bent over, one on each side of him, their hair in his hands. Ginger followed, a pace or two behind. Five of his girls were, now, not in the coffle, four of these being the red-haired girl, and Ginger, and Ulla and Lenna. The other was the English girl, Margaret, whom he had put naked, her legs pulled up, under a kailiauk hide, on the grass.

Grunt threw both of the girls to their knees near the sitting men. He then jerked their tunics from them. "Bring your hair forward, over your breasts," he said. "Cover yourselves, as best you can." His commands were translated, rapidly and expertly, by Ginger. The two girls complied immediately. They covered themselves, as they could, with their hair. They crossed their hands and covered their breasts. They clenched their knees together. They put their heads down.

The seated men laughed. It amused them to see slaves in such postures. Did they think they were free women, before captors? Yet, too, I think there were few there who were not aroused seeing the women in this position. Such a position, in its pathetic pretense to modesty, begs to be rudely terminated; it taunts the master, in effect, to the ensuing and uncompromising exposure of the slave. Such a position, if prolonged more than a few moments, can become a nuisance or inconvenience to the master. It is, thus, seldom lengthily tolerated. Its primary value, and there is little other reason for permitting the slave to assume it, is to lead her to believe, and hope, that she may be accorded some tiny particle of dignity or respect, an illusion which then, to her shame and humiliation, may be totally shattered by the master.

Grunt then drew in the grass, with the heel of his boot, a circle, some ten feet or so in width.

He then looked to the Dust Legs. One of the men stood up and pointed to Ulla. Grunt then ordered her to stand in the circle, orders conveyed by Ginger, which, frightened, half crouched over, she did.

I saw that the red youth now had the red-haired girl on her back in the grass.

"Resist, to the best of your ability," said Grunt to Ulla. She nodded her head, frightened, hearing the translation from Ginger.

The Dust Leg then, with a rawhide thong, stepped into the ring in the grass. Ulla tried to resist him, as best she could, but, in a moment, bruised and vomiting, he not having been gentle with her, she was on her belly in the grass, her hands being jerked behind her and tied. He then put her on her back on the grass, pulling her up so that she rested on her elbows. He kicked her legs apart.

"Eca! Eca!" said the other men.

"Eca!" agreed Grunt, heartily.

"You, Lenna, my dear, now," said Grunt. "Into the circle! Fight! Fight!"

Ginger translated this, but I think Lenna needed little in the way of translation.

Clearly Lenna did not wish to be abused, as had been Ulla. On the other hand she knew she must obey, and to the best of her ability.

Another red warrior leaped into the circle, a bit of rawhide thong loosely in his mouth. Lenna struck wildly out at him and he seized her wrist turning her about and thrusting her wrist high and painfully behind her back. She screamed. I feared he would break her arm. Then he kicked her feet out from under her and she was on her belly. He then seized her by the hair with both hands and yanked her up on her knees and bent her backwards, until her head was at the grass, exhibiting the bow of her captured beauty for his fellows. Then he threw her forward, again, on her belly, and, in a moment, kneeling across her body, had lashed her wrists tightly behind her body. He then, like his fellow, turned her to her back, pulled her up, so that she rested on her elbows, and, standing up, over her, kicked her legs apart, too. Ulla and Lenna, together, then, lay in the circle, up on their elbows, their legs kicked apart. The second fellow had handled Lenna even more rapidly, I thought, than had the first fellow handled Ulla. Both girls had been speedily vanquished, and both now, helpless, lay trussed, their legs symbolically spread, at the feet of their conquerors.

"Eca!" said the men. "Eca!" commended Grunt. "Eca!"

"Remember," said Grunt to the helpless Ulla and Lenna, "you are to be totally pleasing to masters. You are never, unless commanded to do so, to resist or oppose them in any way. Your hands could be cut off or you could be tortured and killed."

"Yes, Master," said the girls, fearfully, in Gorean, following Ginger's translation.

Ulla looked at the man who had vanquished and bound her. Lenna regarded the man who had served her similarly, and with such dispatch. Neither of them, I think, had expected to be made so helpless so quickly, and with such strength. Lenna and Ulla exchanged glances and then looked away from one another, reddening, shamed. They had been well bound, as women, and as slaves. Doubtless they were wondering what it would be like to be owned by such men.

Grunt then sat down and began to talk with the other men, not the two still standing, as though nothing had happened, as though it had been only a bit of sport with two imbonded sluts, only an amusement for the entertainment of his guests.

One of the standing men pointed to Ulla, and said something. The other pointed to Lenna, and, too, said something.

"Oh?" asked Grunt, innocently.

I smiled to myself. It is hard for a man to subdue and bind a naked woman without wanting her. I thought Grunt would get an excellent price for the two beauties.

The red-haired girl, whimpering, was still lying beneath the red youth, clutched in his arms. She looked at me, frightened. He was again, eagerly, at her body. She had well succeeded, it seemed, as her master had desired, in arousing his interest. He had turned her about, roughly, curiously, this way and that, from time to time, caressing her and examining her, and making her please him. There was some blood at her mouth, where, once or twice, he had cuffed her. I saw her hands, half wanting to grasp him, half wanting to thrust him back. He was speaking to her in Dust Leg, slowly and clearly. "Yes, Master," she whimpered, in Gorean. "Yes, Master." It amused me that the youth, like so many individuals to whom only one language is familiar, so familiar that it seems that all humans must, in one way or another, be conversant with it, seemed to think that the girl must surely understand him if only he would speak slowly enough and with sufficient distinctness. Grunt, of course, might have helped her, but he was engaged in business. I, myself, though I had acquired a few words of Dust Leg, had little more idea, specifically, of what the youth was saying than the girl did. His tone of voice suggested that he was not commending her on her beauty, a pastime on which red masters are inclined to waste little time with their white slaves, but ordering her to do something. "Relax," I told the girl. "Let loose of yourself. Feel. Yield."

She looked at me, frightened.

"You are a slave," I told her. "Yield, and yield fully—and as a slave."

She then, gratefully, clutched the youth, and put her head back, rapturously sobbing and shuddering.

I then saw that my presence, interestingly, had had an inhibiting influence on her. She had been on the brink of yielding, a nerve's width away, but had been fighting her feelings and herself, apparently shamed to yield as a slave to another man in my presence.

She cried out with pleasure, clutching the red youth.

"Winyela," said the Dust-Leg woman, scornfully.

Slave girls must yield, and fully, to any man. Their entire mental set, so to speak, in the furs, is oriented toward providing the master with marvelous pleasures, and, in their own case, to feel as richly and deeply as possible, and, in the end, in an uncompromised and delicious capitulation, submitting fully to their master, to obtain the surrender spasms of one who is merely a vanquished woman, naught but an owned and degraded slave. This is quite different from the mental set taken by the free woman to the furs, of course, with attendant deleterious consequences for the free woman, in so far as any woman could be called free who is not surrendered and owned. The free woman is expected to pervert her nature in the furs, behaving as a cultural identical rather than as what she is by nature, the servant and slave of her master. It is little wonder that the free woman, concerned with her putative identicality, her status, her image, her dignity and pride, is often inhibited and sexually inert in the furs. The Goreans say that if one has never had a slave one has never had a woman. Similarly there is a secret saying, among Gorean men, that no female is a woman, who has not been made a slave. The free woman, often, fears to feel. The slave, on the other hand, fears not to feel, for she may then, in all likelihood, be punished. The same frigidity which may be accounted a virtue among free women, figuring in their vanity competitions, how well they can resist men, is commonly among slaves an occasion for the imposition of severe discipline; it can even constitute a capital offense. The degraded slave has little choice but to yield, and yield well. An interesting question arises as to whether a woman, permitted her own will in the matter, as a slave is not, can be forced to yield. There are two answers to this question, and the division between the answers is primarily a function of the time involved. Within a given amount of time, say, half of an Ahn, some women can resist some men. On the other hand, there will be some men whom they cannot resist and to whom, despite their will in the matter, they will find themselves uncontrollably yielding. Given a longer amount of time, however, any woman may be made to yield, whether she wishes to or not, by any man. Sometimes, after such a yielding, she is then collared. "Resistance is now no longer permitted," he tells her. "Yes, Master," she says. She now knows that she, as a slave, must open herself to feeling, and even seek it avidly, even knowing whence it leads, to the acknowledgement of the male as her master, and of her as his slave.

Behind me the red-haired girl was whimpering with pleasure in the arms of the red youth.

"Winyela," snorted the Dust-Leg woman, contemptuously.

"Four," I said, recalling her attention to our bargaining.

"Two," she said, eyeing the mirror.

"Four," I said.

"Three," she said, suddenly, beaming, the fine, strong teeth bright in her broad, reddish-brown face.

"Three," I agreed. I saw she wanted the mirror.

I gave her the mirror and she gave me the three beaded rectangles. She then rose up, well pleased, and took her leave. I folded up the blanket with the goods, and the beaded rectangles, within it. I had certainly not driven a difficult bargain. Grunt, two days ago, had received five such articles for a similar mirror. I should, I supposed, have set my original price higher.

I looked to my right and I saw the two red warriors tying

beaded collars on the necks of Ulla and Lenna. Kailiauk robes lay on the grass. Earlier today Grunt had fashioned a travois for his pack kaiila. Such a device, the poles crossing over the withers of the kaiila, reduces the animal's speed but makes it possible for it to transport a heavier weight. Travois are common, particularly in the movements of camps, among the red savages. The travois, I suspected, would be heavily laden by the time Grunt was ready to return to Kailiauk.

I glanced to where the kaiila of the Dust Legs were located. The girl there, the dark-haired girl in the beaded collar, still knelt as she had been placed, at the paws of her master's kaiila. Her head was still down. She did not look up. She was under excellent discipline.

Between where the men sat and the coffle, a bit to the right, was the spread-out kailiauk robe under which Grunt had put Margaret, naked, her legs drawn up. She had been under the robe for hours. It would be hot under the robe, in the sun, and there would be insects in the grass. I grinned. I think she was learning her slavery. It was a clever trick on Grunt's part. Certainly the Dust Legs who, like most red savages, are an inquisitive, observant folk, would be curious as to the precise nature of the goods which lay beneath that robe. Clearly it was a woman. Was Grunt trying to hide her?

I saw leather thongs put on the necks of Ulla and Lenna, the beaded collars thrust up to admit them. These thongs were then tied to the high pommels of the kaiila saddles. Such saddles are not uncommon among the red savages, though they are commonly used for visiting, trading and ceremonial journeys. In hunting and war the red savage commonly rides bareback. The thongs were some seven or eight feet in length and the red savages knelt Ulla and Lenna down, their hands still tied behind them, by the forepaws of their kaiila.

One of the red savages was now walking over to the kailiauk robe beneath which lay Margaret.

The red youth now rose from the side of the red-haired girl, adjusting his breechclout. He then indicated that she should roll onto her stomach, which she did. He then slapped her twice, commending her. Her hands clutched at the grass. He then sauntered away.

I walked over to her. "It seems I have served my purpose," she whispered, angrily, in English.

"One of your purposes," I said, "for the time being." I spoke to her in English.

She rose to her hands and knees, and looked up at me. She put down her head, reddening. I laughed at her. She looked up again, angrily, and then, again, put down her head, blushing. "Why did you make me yield?" she asked.

"You wanted to," I said. "And, besides, as a slave, you must yield."

She did not speak.

"Are you angry?" I asked.

"Yes," she said.

"I heard you cry out, and whimper with pleasure," I said.

"It is true," she said. "I did want to yield. How terrible I must be."

"Such feelings," I said, "such desires to yield, are not only permitted of the slave, but required of her."

"Required?" she said.

"Yes," I said. "Do not confuse yourself with a free woman. You are quite different from her."

"And as a slave," she said, "I had to yield. I had no choice, did I?"

"No," I said. "The slave must yield, and fully."

"How can you respect me?" she asked.

"Assume the belly position, and kiss my feet, Slave," I said.

She did so.

"What now was your question?" I asked.

"How—how can you respect me?" she asked, half choking.

"I do not," I told her. "Do you know why?"

"Yes, Master," she said.

"Why?" I asked.

"Because I am a slave," she said.

"True," I said.

"How strong are the men of this world," she said, wonderingly. "How they own, and dominate us. How, before them, can we be anything but women?"

"Your question about respect was stupid," I said. "Perhaps you should be lashed."

"Please do not lash me, Master," she said.

I turned to leave. "Master," she said.

"Yes," I said.

"Tonight," she said, "I beg to be taken from the coffle for your pleasure."

"Tonight," I said, "I think I may be more in the mood for Lois or Inez, or perhaps Priscilla. We shall see. And tonight, in the coffle, you will be bound, hand and foot. Perhaps that will teach you to ask stupid questions."

"Yes, Master," she said.

I then went over to the kailiauk hide where one of the Dust Legs was standing. Grunt had joined him there. Grunt seemed reluctant to lift the hide.

"Hou," I said to the Dust Leg.

"Hou," said he to me.

"Ieska!" called one of the Dust Legs, rising to his feet, from where the men had been sitting. This was another of the names by which Grunt was known in the Barrens. It literally means one who speaks well. Less literally, it is used as a general expression for an interpreter.

Grunt excused himself and went to see what the man wanted. He was the fellow who had been looking at the hatchet. The fellow was holding up three fingers, and then he pointed to the dark-haired girl kneeling by the kaiila.

In an instant she had been summoned, and she hurried to him, as she could, with her head down, following the sound of his voice. When she reached her master and Grunt her master put his hand under her chin and thrust up her head. She looked about, startled, wildly, now permitted to regard her surroundings. She saw the other kaiila, the men, Grunt, myself, the girls in the coffle. Then she was stripped and knelt naked, before Grunt. He had her rise and turn slowly, her back arched, her hands behind the back of her head, before him. Then he again knelt her.

"Tarl," called Grunt to me. I went to him, and he tossed me his whip. "See if she whips well," he said.

The girl looked up at me, frightened.

"On your hands and knees," I told her.

She assumed this posture.

Much can be told of the responsiveness of a girl by how she moves beneath the whip.

I would give her three lashes. After all I was not whipping her, but testing her.

I would not strike her with my full strength, but, on the other hand, she must know clearly that she had been struck.

How else could the test prove significant?

She cried out, thrown to her belly by the first stroke. I then administered the second stroke. She cried out in misery and turned to her side, pulling up her legs. I then struck her a third time and she cried out again, sobbing, and pulled up her legs even more.

I thought she moved well beneath the whip. She obviously felt it, keenly.

"On your hands and knees," said Grunt. He then, as she shuddered, felt her, she recently impressed with the might of men over her, she freshly lashed.

"Good," said Grunt.

She became Grunt's for three hatchets. She was, after all, only a white female slave and they were fine hatchets.

"Ieska! Wopeton!" called the fellow by the kailiauk hide.

We left the dark-haired girl on the grass, where she had been lashed, and then purchased.

The Dust Leg requested that the kailiauk hide be thrown aside. Grunt, a shrewd fellow, appeared to demur, and, indeed, even invited the fellow to examine the other girls on the coffle. The fellow, however, scarcely cast a glance at them, but they shrank back, under even so cursory an examination, fearing to belong to a red master. He did look for a longer moment at the red-haired girl but Grunt said something to him, and he turned from her again to speculate on what might lie concealed beneath the kailiauk hide. Grunt apparently did not wish to release the red-haired girl in a common sale. He had, it seemed, another disposition in mind for her. I remembered he had speculated that he would get five hides of the yellow kailiauk for her. No, she had not been brought along, marched into the Barrens, as a mere beast of burden. He had something else in mind for her.

One or two of the other Dust Legs now came over to where lay the kailiauk hide, concealing Margaret, the stripped English girl. The first Dust Leg was now showing signs of impatience. He was no fool. It was clear to him that Grunt, if he truly, seriously, wished to hide a girl, would presumably cache her, bound and gagged, out of sight, perhaps in a slit trench a pasang or so away. As it was, the kailiauk hide was presumably a device to arouse the interest of a possible buyer. The Dust Leg doubtless realized this. Further, he doubtless realized that his interest, in spite of the obviousness of this stratagem, was piqued. I could not blame him, accordingly, for feeling some irritation or resentment. I hoped Grunt knew what he was doing. He had already, in his trick with Ulla and Lenna, in my opinion, been treading on dangerous ground. Suddenly the Dust Leg, Grunt speaking to him, broke out in laughter. It took me a moment or so to understand what was happening, but, in an Ehn, it became quite clear. The Dust Leg, if interested, was to bid, sight unseen, on what lay beneath the kailiauk hide. The whole thing was, in effect, a joke and a gamble. The matter now put in a clearer light, the Dust Leg, and his fellows, were delighted. He tried to walk about and peep beneath the hide and Grunt, with great apparent earnestness and seriousness, hurried about, tugging down the hide at the edges. Red savages, on the whole, are fond of jokes and gambles. Their jokes, to be sure, might sometimes seem a bit eccentric or rude to more civilized folk. A favorite joke, for example, is to tell a young man that his kaiila offer to the parents of his prospective woman has been refused, thus plunging him into despair, until, with roars of laughter, he is informed that it has been accepted. This type of thing, incidentally, does not count, culturally, as a violation of truth telling, a practice which the red savages take with great seriousness. Gambling, too, is of great interest to the savages. Common games are lots, dice and stone guessing. Betting, too, may take place in connection with such things as the fall of arrows, and the appearance and movements of animals, particularly birds. Kaiila races, perhaps needless to say, are very popular. An entire village is likely to turn out to watch such a race. What was going on, further, could not be clearly understood unless it is understood that the Dust Legs knew and respected, and liked, Grunt. Such a game they would not have played with a stranger. Theoretically, one supposes, a high bid might be made on what lay concealed beneath the hide and then the hide, the bid accepted, might be withdrawn to reveal a wench as ugly as a tharlarion, but the Dust Legs knew, in the practical context, that Grunt would not do this to them. They understood, in the context, that he would be sure to put something not only good, but very good, beneath that hide. Similarly, since bids are almost always lower on an unseen commodity, he would be, in effect, making them a gift. The Dust Leg refused, with great drama, to go higher than two hides for what lay beneath the hide. Grunt, he made it clear, must now either accept or reject that offer. It was, of course, accepted, and Grunt, with some flair, threw off the hide.

Margaret, suddenly exposed, cried out with fear. She blinked against the light and made herself, lying on her side, as small as possible. Curled naked on the grass, revealed, terrified, owned, she was exquisite. The two friends of the Dust Leg shouted out with pleasure and, striking him about the shoulders and back, congratulated him on his good fortune. Margaret cringed at their feet. The Dust Leg, more than pleased, tried to get Grunt to accept at least one extra hide for the girl, but this, of course, Grunt magnanimously refused to do. A bargain struck was, after all, a bargain to be adhered to. He was, after all, was he not, a merchant? Margaret was jerked to her knees and the Dust Leg tied his beaded collar on her throat. He then bound her small wrists tightly before her body with a long thong and, pulling her to her feet, led her away, by the free end of the thong, followed by his friends, to his kaiila.

"They are very pleased," I said to Grunt.

"I think so," he said.

We watched the Dust Legs mounting up now, most of them, both men and women, preparing to take their leave. Ulla and Lenna were now on their feet, their hands still tied behind their backs, their neck thongs tied to the high, decorative pommels of their masters' saddles. Their masters regarded them. They then slapped the girls' naked flanks with possessive pleasure, as though they might have been kaiila. They then climbed to their saddles, leaving the girls afoot, naked, neck-thonged, near their stirrups. The girls looked up at their masters with fear and then, as the kaiila moved, hurried along beside the lofty animals, the grass to their thighs. I had little doubt but what they would soon be taught their duties, both those outside the lodge and those within it. I then saw Margaret, looking wildly over her shoulder, being drawn along, by the thong on her wrists, at the side of her own master's beast. She, too, would doubtless soon receive instruction on the modalities of pleasure and service to be exacted by a red master of a female slave, and one who was merely white.

We watched the Dust Legs moving away, across the grasses.

"It was a good trading," I said.

"I think so," said Grunt. "We were all, I think, well satisfied."

"Do you think the two fellows with Ulla and Lenna are

sufficiently pleased?" I asked. "You did, it seems, maneuver them to some extent."

"I do not think they minded being maneuvered," he said. "Did you not see how they struck the girls on their flanks, so possessively, so pridefully, so good-naturedly? They are more than enough pleased to have such girls on their tethers, to lead them home, to add them in with their kaiila and other stock."

"You are right," I said.

"Take this one to the stream," he said, indicating the dark-haired girl we had acquired for the three hatchets, she lying on the grass near us, "and see that she has a bath."

"I will," I said. "What are you going to do?"

"We will make camp here," he said.

"Here?" I asked.

"There is water nearby," he said, "and wood."

"You are going to stay for a time at the trading point?" I asked. This puzzled me. This was the last trading point in the territory of the Dust Legs. It did not seem to me likely that more Dust Legs were to be expected, certainly not for some time. I myself was anxious to move eastward.

"For tonight," he said.

"We could make five pasangs before dark," I said.

"We will camp here tonight," he said.

"Very well," I said.

He went over to the girl lying in the grass. "Womnaka, Amomona," he said. "Womnaka, Wicincala."

"Ho, Itancanka. Ho, Wicayuhe," she said.

"She speaks Dust Leg," he said. "She then will also be conversant with Kaiila. These are two closely related languages, or, better, two dialects of a single language. Fleer is also related to them, but more remotely."

"She responded to your commands earlier," I said. "She must know Gorean, too."

"Do you speak Gorean?" he asked. She might, after all, know only certain commands, much as might a sleen.

"Yes, Master," she said.

"I shall attend to the camp," said Grunt, looking about. "See that she has a bath at the stream."

"All right," I said.

"Do not hurry with her," he said. "There is no hurry in returning."

"All right," I said. Grunt was looking about, scanning the surrounding grasslands. Then he went to the coffle, where Ginger was waiting. He would free certain of the girls and set them about their duties. We would make camp, it seemed, early this day.

I looked down at the girl at my feet. She looked up at me. I kicked her. She winced. "On your hands and knees," I said.

"Yes, Master," she said.

I indicated to her the direction of the stream.

"Yes, Master," she said.

She would crawl to it. She was a slave.

"You whipped me well," she smiled, kneeling in the shallow stream, pouring water on her body.

"You whip well," I commended her.

"Thank you, Master," she said.

The sexually responsive woman whips well. This is probably a function of the high degree of her skin sensitivity and the depth and vulnerability of her feelings. Her sensitivity and responsiveness make her peculiarly helpless under the lash. She who writhes best under the lash, so say the Goreans, writhes best in the furs.

"The water," I said, "has wrought quite a transformation in you." She was now, substantially, cleaned. Most of the dust and blood, the grime, the dirt and sweat, had been washed away. Her dark hair, wet now, seemed very dark, very shiny. She knelt in the water, removing tangles and snarls from her hair.

"No longer, at least," she said, "am I womnaka."

"What is that?" I asked.

"Master does not speak Dust Leg or Kaiila?" she asked.

"No," I said.

"It is something which exudes much odor," she laughed.

"What did Grunt, who is your master, the fellow in the broad-brimmed hat, call you?" I asked.

"'Wicincala'," she said, "which means 'Girl', and 'Amomona', which means 'Baby' or 'Doll'."

"I see," I said. I myself prefer the application of such expressions not to slaves, but to pretentious free women, to remind them that they, in spite of their freedom, are only women. They are useful, by the way, in making a free woman uneasy, their use suggesting to her that perhaps the male is considering shortly enslaving her. In speaking to a slave I prefer expressions such as 'Slave' or 'Slave Girl', or the girl's name itself, she understanding clearly, of course, that it is only a slave name. "And what did you call him?" I asked.

" 'Wicayuhe', 'Itancanka'," she said, "words which mean 'Master'."

"I thought so," I said.

I sat on the bank, watching her work with her hair. She was now combing it out, with her fingers. She would not yet be entitled, of course, to use the common brush and comb alotted for the use of the coffle. The other girls, unless the masters intervened, would vote on whether or not she was to be granted its use. This is a way of encouraging a new girl to be congenial and to participate equitably in the work. One negative vote will keep the brush and comb from a new girl. The suspension of brush-and-comb privileges is also used, upon occasion, by the first girls as a disciplinary measure, within the coffle. Other disciplinary measures practiced among girls themselves involve such things as bonds, the control of rations and switchings. Girls, thus, under the control of first girls, reporting to the masters, commonly keep a good order among themselves. All, of course, including the first girls, are in all things subject, ultimately, to the total authority of the master.

"Ginger!" I called.

Ginger, in a moment, came running to the stream.

"Bring the comb and brush," I told her.

"Yes, Master," she said. Her authority, as that of any slave, could be overruled by any free person.

In a few moments Ginger returned with the comb and brush. "Give her the comb," I said. I, myself, took the brush, which I placed beside me. Ginger waded into the stream and gave the comb to the new girl. "You do not yet have general comb-and-brush privileges," she informed her. "Unless, of course, the masters order it," she added.

"Yes, Mistress," said the new girl, bowing her head to her.

Ginger returned to the bank and, somewhat mollified, turned to regard the new girl, who was now combing her hair with the comb of kailiauk horn.

"She is rather pretty," said Ginger.

"I think so," I said. She was slim, and beautifully shaped.

"She might be worth four hides," said Ginger.

"Perhaps," I said. Ginger then took her leave.

I regarded the girl. She was looking at me, slowly combing her hair.

"Thank you for permitting me the use of the comb and, perhaps later, the brush," she said.

"It is my pleasure," I informed her, truthfully.

I regarded her. She was quite beautiful, and her beauty was a thousand times more exciting than that of a free woman, for she was a slave.

"Master examines me with candor," she said, shyly.

"You are a slave," I said.

"Yes, Master," she said. One might, in the case of a free woman, in deference to her modesty or dignity, avert one's gaze from her beauty. This consideration, of course, is seldom, if ever, accorded to a slave. One may examine her slowly and with care, and with attention to detail, and, if one feels she deserves it, with open and unconcealed admiration. It is not unusual for a Gorean male, who tends to be uninhibited in such matters, to clap his hands, or strike his thigh, or shout with pleasure, upon seeing a bared slave. These responses, which might be thought embarrassing or inappropriate in the case of a free woman, may fittingly be accorded, of course, to slaves, who are only lovely animals. Even in the case of free women, the Gorean male, incidentally, disdains to feign disinterest in female beauty. He, for better or for worse, has not been made a victim of the glandular suppression and life-shortening psychosexual reductionism inflicted, in varying degrees, on so many males in more pathological cultures. His civilization has not been purchased at the price of his manhood. His culture has not been designed to deny nature, but, startlingly perhaps, to some minds, to fulfill it.

She continued to comb her hair. She turned her head to the side, slowly drawing the comb through it. "Do I detect," she asked, "that Master may not find a slave fully displeasing?"

"No," I said. "I do not find you fully displeasing."

"A slave is pleased," she said.

I smiled.

"Do you think I might be worth four hides?" she asked.

"Whether you are or not might easily be determined," I said.

"Of course, Master," she laughed. "I am a slave."

"You now look quite different from what you did when you were purchased," I told her.

"It is difficult to remain fresh and presentable," she said, "when run through brush at the side of a kaiila, a thong on one's throat."

I nodded.

"I trust," she said, "that I shall not be so served in this camp."

"You, and the others," I said, "will be treated precisely as we please, in all things."

"Yes, Master," she said, quickly. She stopped combing her hair.

"Continue to groom yourself, Slave," I said.

"Yes, Master," she said.

"What was your name among the Dust Legs?" I asked.

"Wasnapohdi," she said.

"What does that mean?" I asked.

"Pimples," she said.

"You do not have any pimples," I said.

"Master may have noticed that my thighs are not marked," she said.

"Yes," I said.

"I am not one of those girls from the towns, who has been branded," she said. "Oh, do not fear," she laughed, "that we are not well understood as slaves. In the camps, and among the tribes, our red masters keep women such as I in our collars, to remove one of which without permission is death."

I nodded.

"And, too," she said, "what could a white woman in the Barrens be but a slave?"

"True," I said.

"We are thus, in our way, well marked," she said.

"Yes," I said.

"I was born Waniyanpi, in one of the Waniyanpi enclosures of the Kailiauk," she said, "the product of a forced mating, between parents unknown even to themselves, parents selected and matched by the red masters, parents who, even though they were Sames, were forced to perform the Ugly Act, hooded and under whips, on the day of Waniyanpi breeding."

"There is much here I do not understand," I said. "What are Waniyanpi? Who are the Kailiauk?"

"Many of the tribes permit small agricultural communities to exist within their domains," she said. "The individuals in these communities are bound to the soil and owned collectively by the tribes within whose lands they are permitted to live. They grow produce for their masters, such as wagmeza and wagmu, maize, or corn, and such things as pumpkins and squash. They are also to furnish labor when required and may be drawn upon, at the whim of their masters, for individual slaves. When one is taken from the enclosure one ceases to be Waniyanpi and becomes a common slave, an ordinary slave, one owned by an individual master. Usually daughters are taken, for the red masters find them pleasing as slaves, but sometimes, too, young men are taken. The word 'Waniyanpi' itself means literally 'tame cattle'. It is an expression applied to the collectively owned slaves in these tiny agricultural communities. The Kailiauk is a tribe federated with the Kaiila. They speak closely related dialects."

"Do the parents come from within the same community?" I asked.

"No," she said. "For the day of breeding the men, hooded and in coffle, are marched between the small communities. On the day of breeding they are led to the selected women, already hooded, tied and awaiting them. The breeding takes place in the wagmeza fields, under the eyes of the masters."

"You spoke of an Ugly Act?" I said. I did not like the sound of that. It reminded me of a distant and sick world, the world of tittering, of embarrassment and dirty jokes. How much more honest are the whips and collars of Gor.

"The Sames," she said, "disapprove of all sexual relations between human beings, and particularly between those of different sexes, as being demeaning and dangerous."

"I can see where some might regard sexual relations between partners of opposite sexes as being demeaning for the woman," I said, "for in such relations she is often handled, owned and put in her place, but, on the other hand, if she belongs in her place, and it is her natural destiny to be owned and handled, it is not clear, ultimately, how this sort of thing can be demeaning for her. Rather, it seems it would be fully appropriate. Indeed, treating her in any other way, ultimately, would seem to be far more demeaning. But how can such relations be regarded as dangerous?"

"They are not regarded as being dangerous to health," she said, "but as being dangerous to the Teaching."

"What is the Teaching?" I asked.

"That men and women are the same," she said. "That is the central tenet of the Waniyanpi."

"Do they believe it?" I asked.

"They pretend to," she said. "I do not know if they really believe it or not."

"They believe men and women are the same," I marveled.

"Except," she smiled, "that women are regarded as somewhat superior."

"Their beliefs then," I said, "seem not only to be obviously false but actually inconsistent."

"Before the Teaching one must surrender one's reason," she said. "To scrutinize it is a crime. To question it is blasphemy."

"It lies, I suppose," I said, "at the roots of Waniyanpi society."

"Yes," she said. "Without it Waniyanpi society would collapse."

"So?" I said.

"They do not take the disintegration of their society as lightly as you do," she smiled. "Too, you must understand the utility of such a view. It constitutes an excellent philosophy for slaves."

"I am not even sure of that," I said.

"It, at least," she said, "gives men an excuse not to be men."

"That seems true," I granted her.

"It helps them to remain Waniyanpi," she said. "They are thus less likely to attract the attention, or excite the anger, of their red masters."

"I understand," I said. "I think I also understand why, in such a society, the women are regarded as somewhat superior, as you put it."

"It is only that they are implicitly regarded as superior," she said. "Explicitly, of course, all subscribe to the thesis of sameness."

"But why are the women regarded, implicitly, as superior?" I asked.

"Because of the contempt felt for the men," she said, "who will not assert their natural rights. Also, if men refuse the mastery, someone must assume it."

"Yes," I said.

"There are always masters," she said, "whether one pretends it is not so, or not."

"In the hands of women," I said, "the mastery becomes an empty mockery."

"Mockery has no choice but to assert itself," she said, "when reality is foresworn."

I was silent.

"The Waniyanpi communities are sources of great amusement to the red masters," she said.

I thought of what is sometimes spoken of by the red savages as the Memory.

"I understand," I said.

The red savages doubtless found their vengeance a sweet and fitting one. How almost incomprehensibly cruel it was, how horrifying, how brilliant and insidious.

"The Teachings of the Waniyanpi," I said, "were doubtless originally imposed on them by their red masters."

"Perhaps," she said. "I do not know. They may have been invented by the Waniyanpi themselves, to excuse to themselves their cowardice, their weakness and impotence."

"Perhaps," I admitted.

"If one is not strong it is natural to make a virtue of weakness."

"I suppose so," I said. I then speculated that I had perhaps judged the red savages too harshly. The Waniyanpi, it then seemed likely, may have betrayed themselves, and their children. In time, of course, such teachings, absurd though they might be, would come to be taken for granted. In time they would come to be sanctioned by tradition, one of humanity's most prized substitutes for thought.

"You, yourself," I said, "do not seem much infected by the lunacy of the Waniyanpi."

"No," she said. "I am not. I have had red masters. From them I have learned new truths. Too, I was taken from the community at an early age."

"How old were you?" I asked.

"I was taken from the enclosure when I was eight years old," she said, "taken home by a Kaiila warrior as a pretty little white slave for his ten-year-old son. I learned early to please and placate men."

"What happened?" I asked.

"There is little more to tell," she said. "For seven years I was the slave of my young master. He was kind to me, and protected me, muchly, from the other children. Although I was only his slave, I think he liked me. He did not put me in a leg stretcher until I was fifteen." She was then silent. "I have combed my hair," she said.

"Come here," I said, "and kneel here." She rose from the water, it dripping from her body, and came and knelt on the grass, on the bank of the small stream, where I had indicated. I took the comb from her and laid it to the side. I then took the brush and, kneeling behind her, began to brush out her hair. It is not unusual for Gorean masters to comb and groom slaves, or ornament them personally, much as they might any animal that they owned.

"We were gathering berries," she said. "Then I saw him, suddenly, almost angrily, cutting a stick, and notching it with his knife. Too, he had thongs. I was afraid, for I had seen other white slaves put in such devices. He turned to face me. His voice seemed loud, and full, and husky. "Take off your dress," he said, "and lie down, and throw your legs widely apart." I began to cry, but I obeyed him, and quickly, for I was his slave. I felt my ankles lashed tightly to the stick, the stick behind them. I had not realized that he had grown so strong. Then he rose to his feet and looked down at me. I was helpless. He laughed with pleasure, a man's laugh, who sees a woman tied before him. I was crying. He crouched down beside me. Then, suddenly, scarcely before I understood what I was doing, I opened my arms to him, overcome suddenly by the stirrings of my womanhood. He embraced me. I began to sob again, but this time with joy. The first time it was finished almost before we realized it. But he did not leave me. For hours we remained among the tiny fruit, talking and kissing, and caressing. Later, near dusk, he freed me, that I might gather berries for him, and feed them to him. Later I lay on my belly before him and kissed his feet. That night we returned to the village. That others in the village might understand what had happened, he did not permit me to ride behind him, on his kaiila. He tied my hands behind my back and marched me at his stirrup, a thong on my neck tied to the pommel of his saddle. Two children had left the camp that morning. What returned to it that night were a master and his claimed white slave. I was very proud. I was very happy."

"What then happened?" I asked. I stopped brushing her hair.

"I loved my master," she said, "and I think that he, too, cared for me."

"Yes?" I said.

"That it seemed he had grown fond of me brought ridicule on him from his comrades," she said. "To this sort of thing, as you might not know, red savages, in their tribal groups, are extremely sensitive. To allay these charges he, in his anger, would berate me publicly, and even beat me in the presence of others. At last, to put an end to the matter, and perhaps fearing these charges might be true, he sold me to an older man, one from another village. After that I had many masters, and now I have yet another."

I then began again to brush her hair. "Was it the lad who gave you the name Pimples?" I asked.

"Yes," she said. "I was given the name at puberty and, for some reason, it was never changed. Red masters commonly give such names to their white slaves, trivial names that seem fitting for slaves. My first year as the slave of my young master I was not even given a name. I was referred to only as Wicincala, or 'Girl.' I was later called 'Wihinpaspa', which means lodge-pin or tent-pin, probably because I was little and thin. Then later, as I have mentioned, I was called 'Pimples', 'Wasnapohdi', which name, partly because of habit, and partly because it amused my masters, was kept on me."

"You are neither little nor thin," I said, "and, as I have earlier remarked, you do not have pimples."

"Perhaps I might bring four hides," she laughed.

"It is not impossible," I said. "Do you think your first master would recognize you now?" I asked.

"I do not know," she said. "I would suppose so."

"Do you remember him?" I asked.

"Yes," she said. "It is difficult to forget the first man who tied you."

"Do you love him?" I asked. I laid the brush aside.

"I do not know," she said. "It was long ago. He sold me."

"Oh," she said, her hands now thonged behind her back. She tensed.

"Did your red masters teach you well what it is to be a slave?" I asked.

"Yes, Master," she said.

I tightened the knots on her wrists.

"Do you think your lot will be easier with us?" I asked.

"I do not know, Master," she winced.

"It will not be," I assured her.

"Yes, Master," she said.

I bent down and kissed her on the side, on one of the long welts raised by the whip stroke, one of the blows in virtue of which she was assessed.

"You struck me with great force," she said.

"No, I did not," I said.

She shuddered. "You are then very strong," she whispered.

I turned her about, and put her on her back, before me. I knelt beside her and sniffed her belly. "Again," I said, "you are womnaka."

"I am only a slave," she said. "Does it please you, or displease you, that I am unable to resist you?"

"It does not displease me," I said. I then touched her.

"Oh," she cried, eyes closed, squirming helplessly, rearing half upward, trussed, then falling back. She looked at me, wildly.

"You are indeed a slave," I told her.

"Yes, Master," she said.

"Do you beg to be had?" I asked.

"Yes, Master," she said. "Yes, Master!"

"First," I said, "you will earn your keep. You will be put to work."

"Yes, Master," she said.

I then pulled her to her knees and lay then on one elbow, indolently, watching her. She then, on her knees, her hands bound behind her, with her hair, her mouth and body, needfully and desperately, began to please me. In a short while I took her and threw her beneath me.

"Aiii!" she sobbed. "I yield me your slave, my Master!" She was superb. I wondered if the lad who had been her former master, and who now must be a man, and had sold her, had any idea as to the wonder, the surrendered, curvacious, obedient, orgasmic triumph, which his little Lodge-Pin or Pimples, now a ravishing, helpless beauty, had become. Had he any notion of this it was difficult to imagine that he would be able to rest until he had once again fastened his beaded collar on her throat. Clearly she was now the sort of woman for whom men might kill.

"Am I worth four hides, Master?" she asked, gasping.

"Five," I assured her.

She laughed, and kissed me happily.

"This is Wagmezahu, Corn Stalks," said Grunt. "He is Fleer."

"Hou," said Corn Stalks.

"Hou," said I to him.

"Is the new slave satisfactory?" asked Grunt.

"Quite," I said.

"Good," he said.

I sat back, cross-legged, away from the fire. I now understood why Grunt had been scanning the plains. I now understood why he had wished to remain at the trading point. He had, doubtless, been waiting for this Fleer. This was also, doubtless, the reason he had encouraged me to take my time with the new girl, which I had, that they not be disturbed. Although the Fleer speak a language clearly akin to Kaiila and Dust Leg there had often been strife among them. Thusly the Fleer had waited before coming to the camp. If the Dust Legs knew of his presence in their country they had not chosen to do anything about it, perhaps in deference to Grunt.

Grunt and the Fleer spoke largely in sign, this being easier for them than the attempt to communicate verbally.

I sat back from the fire, watching them closely. It was now late at night. Grunt had shortened the coffle by two collars and chain lengths. I had put the new girl in Margaret's place, after Priscilla and before the Hobarts. This was the position of "Last Girl," which, fittingly, not counting the Hobarts, she would occupy, being the newest girl on the coffle. Coffle arrangements, incidentally, are seldom arbitrary. One common principle of arrangements is in order of height, with the tallest girls coming first; this makes a lovely coffle. Sometimes, too, coffles are arranged in order of beauty or preference, the most beautiful or the most preferred girls coming first. Coloring and body type can also be important. It is for such reasons, perhaps, that the coffle is sometimes spoken of as the slaver's necklace. Sales strategies, too, can enter into the formation of a coffle, as, for example, when a girl is put between two plainer girls to accentuate her beauty, or a superb girl is saved for last, and many other considerations, as well, can enter into the formation of a coffle. When one sees a chain of beauties, fastened together, say, by the neck, or the left wrist or left ankle, it is well to remember that their locations on that sturdy, metallic bond, keeping them precisely where the master wishes, are seldom likely to be merely fortuitous. After I had carried the new girl to the chain and put her on the grass, locking the collar on her, I went to the redhaired girl and, as I had earlier promised her, bound her hand and foot. She had asked a stupid question, one pertaining to respect. She would spend the night tied.

"Is the new girl pleasing?" she had asked me, reproachfully.

"Yes," I said.

"More pleasing than I?" she asked, lying at my feet, her hands tied behind her, her ankles crossed and bound, her neck in the coffle collar.

"Yes," I said. "She is an experienced slave. You are only a new slave. You have much to learn."

"Yes, Master," she said.

I then, for good measure, gagged her. She must learn that she was a slave.

Corn Stalks, after a time, took his leave. Before he left Grunt gave him some hard candy and a fine steel knife.

"You seem moody," I said to Grunt. He had returned to the fire, and sat before it, not speaking.

"It is nothing," he said.

"I should like to learn some Dust Leg," I said.

"I will teach you some, as we ride," he said.

"If I learn some Dust Leg, I should be able, to some extent, to communicate with Kaiila," I said.

"Very easily," said Grunt, "for they are much the same, and, too, you would be able to make yourself understood to the Kailiauk, and, to some extent, to the Fleer."

"I have heard little of the Kailiauk," I said.

"They are not well known west of the perimeter," he said. "Their country lies to the south and east of that of the Kaiila."

"Mostly," I said, "you spoke to Corn Stalks in sign."

"Yes," he said. "It is easier for us." He looked at me. "To learn sign," he said, "would probably be more useful to you, all things considered, than learning a smattering of Dust Leg."

"Teach me sign," I asked.

"To be sure," he said, "it would be wise for you to learn some Dust Leg or Kaiila. There is no substitute for being able to converse with these people in their own language. Sign, as far as I know, is common to all the tribes of the Barrens."

"Why are they called Dust Legs?" I asked.

"I do not know," said Grunt, "but I think it is because they were the last of the major tribes to master the kaiila. Afoot, they were much at the mercy of the others. Their heritage as traders and diplomats may stem from that period."

"It is an interesting hypothesis," I said.

"I can teach you hundreds of signs in a short time," said Grunt. "It is a very limited language, but in most situations it is quite adequate, and, because many of the signs seem so appropriate and natural, it can be easily learned. In four or five days you can learn most of what you would need of sign."

"I would like to learn something of Dust Leg and Kaiila, and also sign," I said.

"I will be pleased to help you," said Grunt.

"Grunt?" I asked.

"Yes," he said.

"After I came to join you," I said, "Corn Stalks did not stay long."

"He does not know you," said Grunt.

I nodded. Goreans, in general, not merely red savages, tend to be wary of strangers, in particular those who speak other languages or come from other territories or cities. There is only one word in Gorean, incidentally, for stranger and enemy. To be sure, the specific meaning intended is usually clear in the context. Goreans are not unaware that there may exist such things as familiar enemies and friendly strangers.

"He did not do trading, as far as I know," I said.

"No," said Grunt. "We talked. He is a friend."

"What is the sign for a red savage?" I asked.

Grunt rubbed the back of his left hand from the wrist to the knuckle with his right index finger. "The general sign for a man is this," he said. He held his right hand in front of his chest, the index finger pointing up, and raised it in front of his face. He then repeated the sign for the red savage. "I am not clear on the specific rationale for the sign for the savage," he said. "You will note, however, that the same finger, the index finger, is used in the sign, as in the sign for man. The origins of some of these signs are obscure. Some think the sign for the red savage has a relation to the spreading of war paint. Others think that it means a man who goes straight or a man who is close to the earth, to nature. Doubtless there

are other explanations, as well. This is the sign for friend."
He then put his first two fingers together and raised them upward, beside his face. "It probably means two men growing
up together."

"Interesting," I said. "What does this mean?" I put the
middle fingers of my right hand on my right thumb, extending
the index and little finger. This suggests a pointed snout and
ears.

"You have seen Dust Legs make that sign," he said. "It
means a wild sleen. It is also used for the Sleen tribe. Do you
know what this means?" He then spread the index finger and
the second finger of his right hand and drew them from the
left to the right, in front of his body.

"No," I said.

"That is the sign for a domestic sleen," he said. "You see?
It is like the spread poles of a travois, which might be drawn
by such an animal."

"Yes!" I said.

"What is this?" he asked, drawing his right index finger
across his forehead, from left to right.

"A white man?" I asked.

"Yes," he said. "Good."

"It is like the line of the brim of a hat, across the forehead," I said.

"Good," he said. "And this?" With the fingers of both
hands slightly curved, he made downward motions from the
top of his head to the shoulders. It was as though he were
combing hair.

"A woman?" I asked.

"Good," he said. "Good. And this?"

"A white woman?" I asked.

"Yes," he said. He had traced a line with his right index
finger across his forehead, from left to right, and had then
opened his hand and moved it downward, toward his shoulder, in the combing motion. "What do you think this means?"
he asked. He then made the combing motions with his hand,
and then lowered his head and looked at his left wrist, which
he grasped firmly in his right hand, the left wrist, the weaker
wrist, helpless in the grip of the stronger.

"I am not sure," I said.

"The second sign indicates bondage," he said.

"A female slave?" I asked.

"Yes," said Grunt, "but, more generally, it is another sign

which may stand for any white woman, and is often used in this way."

"The same sign then," I said, "that sign, stands for both white woman and female slave?"

"Yes," he said. "It is the most common way of referring to a white woman. You see, in the Barrens, all white women are regarded as being female slaves. Our friends of the plains divide white women into those who have already, properly, been imbonded, and those who, improperly, have not yet been imbonded."

I considered the nature of women, and their desirability. "That distinction makes sense to me," I said. "But are there no women of the red savages themselves who are slaves?"

"Of course, there are," said Grunt. "They are fond of carrying off women of the enemy to make their own slaves. Surely you can imagine how pleasant it is for these fellows to be served, and as a slave, by one of the enemy's women."

"Of course," I said.

"Such a woman may be designated as follows," he said, "by use of the sign woman, followed by the sign for the red savages, followed by a bondage sign."

"I see," I said. He had illustrated his words with the sign.

"If the context is clear," he said, "the signs simply for a female slave may be used."

"I understand," I said.

"Here is another way of designating a white woman or a female slave," he said. He then made the sign for woman, followed by a downward striking motion, as though holding a switch. "Sometimes, too," he said, "when the context is clear, this sign alone may be used." He then spread the first and second fingers of his right hand and laid them over the index finger of his left hand. "You see?" he asked. "It is ankles bound on a leg stretcher."

"I see," I said.

"The meanings in these signs are clear," he said, "the weaker who is held by the stronger, she who is subject to the whip, and she whose ankles may be spread at her master's pleasure."

"Yes," I said.

"What is this?" asked Grunt. He held his left hand with the palm in, before his chest, and placed the index and second finger of his right hand astride the edge of his left hand.

"A rider?" I asked.

"Kaiila," he said. Then, holding his hands as he had, he rotated his hands in tiny circles, as though the kaiila were in motion. "That is to ride," he said.

"I see," I said.

"What is this?" he asked. He placed his left fist in front of his mouth and sliced between it and his face with the edge of his opened right hand.

"I do not know," I said.

"Knife," he said. "See? One holds the meat in one's hand and clenches it between the teeth, too. Then one cuts a bite from the meat, to eat it, thus the sign for knife."

"Good," I said. "And what does this mean?" I drew an imaginary line across my throat with my right index finger. I had seen Corn Stalks make this sign in his talk with Grunt.

Grunt's eyes clouded. "It is the sign for the Kaiila," he said, "the Cutthroat Tribe."

"Oh," I said.

"You may have seen this sign," said Grunt. "It is an interesting one." He then held his fists in front of his chest, his thumbs almost touching, and then spread his fingers out, horizontally.

"I have no idea what it means," I said.

"Does it remind you of nothing?" he asked. He repeated the sign.

Suddenly the hair on the back of my neck rose. "It is like men breaking out of columns," I said, "fanning out, to take up positions for battle."

"Yes," said Grunt. "It is the sign for soldiers." He then added to it the sign for riding, that of the kaiila in motion.

"Kaiila soldiers," I said. "Cavalry."

"Yes," said Grunt, soberly. He then held both fists close to his chest, with the backs of his hands down and the index fingers curved. He then made a forward, circular motion.

"Wheels?" I said. "Wagons."

"Yes," said Grunt.

These last signs had been used by Corn Stalks. Grunt knew that I had seen them.

"I do not mean to pry," I said.

"It is all right," said Grunt.

"We need not continue," I said.

"It is all right," said Grunt.

I held my hands near the ground, with my fingers curved upward and slightly apart. I then swung my hands out in a small, upward curve.

"Grass," said Grunt.

I held my right hand, palm down, even with my shoulder, and lowered it, until it was about eighteen inches from the ground.

"Height," said Grunt. "High. High grass. Summer."

The Summer solstice had taken place a few days ago.

I folded my arms, the right arm resting on top of the left. I then raised both hands until my fingers pointed skyward.

"The spreading of light," said Grunt. "Day. Light."

I repeated the gesture twice more.

"Three days," said Grunt. "Three days ago, we may suppose."

I raised my hands in front of my body, my fingers slightly curved. I then swept my hands together in a looping curve.

"Many," said Grunt. "Much. Plenty."

I rubbed the back of my left hand from the wrist to the knuckle with my right index finger.

"Red savages," smiled Grunt. "Fleer," he then said. "Kaiila, Sleen, Yellow Knives, Kailiauk."

I had smote my hands slowly together three times. It was like the beating of wings. It now stood, I saw, for the Fleer tribe. The fleer is a large, yellow, long-billed, gregarious, voracious bird of the Barrens. It is sometimes also called the Corn Bird or the Maize Bird. I had then drawn my finger across my throat. That stood for the Kaiila, the Cutthroat tribes. The sign for the Sleen tribe had been the same as that for the sleen, the resting of the middle fingers of the right hand on the right thumb, extending the index and little finger, this suggesting the animal's pointed snout and ears. The sign for the Yellow Knives had been the sign for knife, followed by the sign for fleer. I later learned the sign for knife alone would suffice for this tribe. In the compound sign fleer presumably occurs as a modifier in virtue of the bird's coloration. Adjectives in sign commonly, though not always, follow the noun, so to speak. This arrangement is doubtless to be expected, for it reflects a common grammatical feature of the spoken languages of the red savages. The word 'mazasapa', for example, literally means 'black metal'. 'Maza' is the word for 'metal' and 'sapa' is the word for 'black'. We would translate the expression, of course, as 'iron'. The sign for

Kailiauk, as I had expected, was to hold up three fingers, suggesting the trident of horns adorning the shaggy head of this large, short-tempered, small-eyed, lumbering ruminant.

"You have an excellent memory," said Grunt. I had been, of course, as best I could, reconstructing portions of the conversation which I had earlier seen take place between Corn Stalks and Grunt.

I held my hands in front of my body, with the palms facing one another, with the left hand a bit ahead of the right. I quickly brushed the right palm past the left palm.

"Fast," said Grunt. "Quick. Hurry."

I held my left hand before my body, palm out, with my index and second fingers spread, forming a "V." I held my right hand at my right shoulder, the index finger pointing up. I then, quickly, brought my right index finger down, striking into the space between the index finger and second finger of my left hand.

"Kill," said Grunt, soberly. "Hit. Strike."

I followed this with the sign for many, and then the signs for white man and white woman, and for soldiers, and kaiila soldiers, or cavalry.

"Yes," said Grunt.

"What is this sign?" I asked. I cupped my right hand close to the ground, my fingers partly closed. I then raised it a few inches from the ground, with a short, wavy motion.

"It is the sign for fire," said Grunt. "Flames."

"It preceded this sign," I said. I then held my fists close to my chest, with the backs of my own hands down, my index fingers curved. I then made the forward, circular motion, indicative of turning wheels. "This latter sign, as I recall," I said, "signifies wagons."

"It does," said Grunt. "Yes."

I was then silent. I did not feel much like speaking. I listened to the crackle of the fire.

"A wagon, or wagons, of course," said Grunt. "The specific meaning depends on the context. It is the same with many signs."

"I understand," I said.

"Three days ago, or some three days ago," said Grunt, "a large party of red savages, consisting of Kaiila, Yellow Knives, Sleen, Fleer and Kailiauk fell suddenly upon a wagon train and a column of soldiers, both infantry and cavalry. Wagons were burned. There was a massacre."

"I think I know the parties," I said. "The first left Kailiauk sometime before I reached it. They were settlers. The second must have been the mercenaries of Alfred, a captain, from Port Olni. He left Kailiauk shortly before we did."

Alfred, not stopping to trade, and moving swiftly, not slowed by a coffle of slaves, had, it seemed, made contact with the settlers. Doubtless they would have welcomed his presence. I wondered as to the fate of the settlers and soldiers, and if any survived. Alfred had seemed to me as though he might be a good commander. He would not have been familiar, however, I speculated, with the warfare of the Barrens. He had perhaps rated his red foes too lightly. He had perhaps discounted their possible numbers or skills.

I thought of the squarish wagons which had been with the soldiers, doubtless concealing the beasts of Sardak and Kog. There had been seventeen such wagons. If these beasts had been destroyed I might, perhaps, consider leaving the Barrens. Zarendargar, then, would be safe, at least until another such force might be sent against him. Perhaps Priest-Kings, through their agents, might monitor towns such as Fort Haskins and Kailiauk.

I thought, too, briefly, of the red-savage youth, Urt, the red slave, supposedly a Dust Leg, who had been with the soldiers. If the red savages had found him in his chains, fastened to a white man's wagon, they might have chosen, with amusement, to leave him there, to die. I thought, too, of the lofty, veiled Lady Mira, of Venna. No doubt now, she no longer wore her veils. I did not think the red savages would have killed her. There are better things to do with such women. Doubtless she would have been stripped, a thong perhaps on her neck, and assessed as casually as a tethered kaiila. If her captors found her of interest, perhaps they would give her a chance, albeit perhaps only a slim one, to strive to save her life, by absolute and total submission, and pleasingness, as a slave.

I did not fail to note, incidentally, that several, often mutually hostile tribes, had cooperated in the attack, with its attendant destruction and killing. The Memory, as it is called, and their hatred for the white man, had taken priority, as it commonly did, over their bloody and almost continuous intertribal differences. The red savages, I speculated, if they wished, with their numbers, and their unity, conjoined with an approximate technological parity in weapons, should be able to hold the Barrens indefinitely against white intrusion.

"It is a horrifying thing," said Grunt, almost numbly.

"Yes," I said. "What does this mean?" I asked. I placed my right hand against my heart, with the thumb and fingers pointing down and slightly cupped.

"Heart," said Grunt.

I then lowered my hand toward the ground. I had seen Corn Stalks do this, after his account of the battle, if battle it had been.

"The heart is on the ground," said Grunt. "My heart is on the ground. I am sad."

I nodded.

"My heart, too," said Grunt, "is on the ground. I, too, am sad."

I nodded. "Do you think there were survivors?" I asked.

"In actions of this sort," said Grunt, "our friends of the plains are seldom inclined to leave survivors, but perhaps they did, perhaps, say, some children, to be herded to Waniyanpi camps, to be raised with Waniyanpi values, suitable for slaves, or, say, perhaps, some females whose exposed curvatures at their feet they might have found acceptable. Who knows? They are the victors. It would depend on their whim."

"What of a red slave of white men?" I asked.

"Male or female?" asked Grunt.

"Male," I said.

"I do not think I would give much for his chances," said Grunt.

"I thought not," I said.

"We should perhaps turn back," mused Grunt.

I did not speak.

"It will be dangerous to move eastward now," he said. "The blood of the young men will be high. The killing lust may yet be with them."

"They have done, surely," I said, "what they purposed. They have enforced their laws, against both the innocent and the guilty. They will now be returning to their tribal areas."

"Smaller parties can be more dangerous than larger parties, at such a time," said Grunt. "The larger party has done its work and is returning to its home, presumably under the command of a *blotanhunka*, a war-party leader, usually a fellow of mature and experienced judgment. He exerts control;

he commands restraint. The smaller party may consist of young men, insufficiently disciplined, urging one another on to yet another hazard or feat, fellows who are unwilling for the fun to be over, fellows who are eager to try for yet one more killing, fellows who wish to obtain yet one more trophy."

"Such, you fear, might linger in the area?" I asked.

"Sometimes they are even left behind," said Grunt, "to track survivors who might have hidden in the grass."

"But we were not of the attacked parties," I said.

"One might hope, of course," said Grunt, "that they would be sensitive to such distinctions."

"We have not broken the laws," I said.

"We are white," said Grunt.

"I must move eastward," I said. It was important for me to determine the fate of the Kurii who had been with the mercenaries.

"Grunt," I said.

"Yes," he said.

"It is my understanding, gathered along the perimeter, that you are unusual among traders, that you, of all of them, have penetrated most far into the Barrens, and know them best of white men."

"Perhaps," said Grunt. "It is hard to tell about such things."

"It was for this reason that I sought you out," I said.

He regarded me, not speaking.

"I have something among my stores, which I would show you," I said. "I suspect that it is something which you have seen, or that you have seen similar things and are familiar with their origins."

"I shall be pleased to look at it," he said.

I returned to the fire in a few moments, and, on the dirt, in the light of the flames, spread the hide which Samos and I had obtained in the ruined tarn complex some four pasang from the northeast delta gate of Port Kar.

"It is a story hide," said Grunt.

"Can you read it?" I asked.

"Yes," he said.

"But you are not reading it," I said. I noted that he did not, with his eye or finger, trace the spiraling account painted on that almost-white, softly tanned surface.

"I have read it," he said. "Where did you get it?"

"Near Port Kar," I said.

"Interesting," he said.

"Why?" I asked.

"It is so far away," he said. "It is in the delta of the Vosk."

"This hide, I gather," I said, "has passed through your hands."

"Last fall," he said, "I obtained it from Dust Legs. They, in turn, had it from Kaiila."

"Do you know from what band of Kaiila?" I asked.

"No," he said.

"To whom did you sell the hide?" I asked.

"To Ram Seibar, in Kailiauk," he said.

"It all fits!" I said.

"You are not a trader," said Grunt. "What is your true business in the Barrens?"

I pointed to the painting of the two feathers near the beginning of the narrative. "The painter's name," I said, "seems to have been Two Feathers." I recalled that Kog had surmised this, in his interpretation of the hide.

Grunt shrugged. "That is not necessarily the case," he said, "at all. The two feathers may be a talisman, or a luck sign. They may indicate a place. They could even indicate that the hide's painter has two coups, each coup being marked by one feather."

"I see," I said. This was indeed unwelcome news. Suddenly my task, and the Barrens, seemed far more formidable.

"It is easier to interpret sign, which can occasionally be difficult, than to interpret a story hide. The conventions on the hide, and its meanings, are often more idiosyncratic, more personal."

"Do you often deal in story hides?" I asked.

"No," said Grunt. "To encounter one among trade goods is quite uncommon."

"Ram Seibar paid well for this, did he not?" I asked.

"He paid a double tarn, of gold," said Grunt.

"He seemed anxious to obtain it?" I asked.

"He did not even bargain," said Grunt. "Yes."

I nodded. For such a coin one might easily buy five girls.

"What is your business in the Barrens?" asked Grunt.

"Do you see this beast?" I asked. I pointed to the image on the representation of a shield, that painted at the conclusion of the hide's account. It was the image of a Kur, the left ear half torn away.

"Yes?" said Grunt.

"I seek it," I said.

He regarded me.

"No," I said. "I am not mad."

"That is a beast of a medicine vision," said Grunt. "It is not a real beast."

"It is real," I said. "I do not know, beyond that, whether or not it occurred in a medicine vision."

"I have never seen such a beast," said Grunt.

"They are not indigenous to the Barrens," I said.

"You think it is now in the Barrens," said Grunt.

"I am sure of it," I said. "And I think, too, that there may be several others, as well." I did not know what had been the fate of the Kurii who had been with the mercenary captain, Alfred, of Port Olni. It was possible, of course, that they had been destroyed in the attack on his column and the wagon train.

"Are you a hunter?" asked Grunt.

"In my way," I said.

"The Barrens are large," said Grunt.

"Do you think the hide is Kaiila?" I asked.

"I obtained it from Dust Legs, who obtained it from Kaiila," he said. "Whether or not it is originally Kaiila, I do not know."

"I must venture to the country of the Kaiila," I said.

"To do so, you will have to pass through Fleer country, and the lands of Sleen and Yellow Knives," he said.

"As far as I know, I have not broken their laws," I said.

"You are white," said Grunt. "You may be attacked at their pleasure, whether or not you have broken their laws."

"I understand," I said.

"You are leaving in the morning?" he asked.

"Yes," I said.

"You understand the dangers?" he asked.

"I think so," I said.

"I will accompany you," he said.

"You need not do so," I said.

"It is already summer," said Grunt. "I did not come this far to turn back."

"You, too, would go eastward, then?" I asked.

"Yes," he said.

"Is it your intention to go to the land of the Kaiila?" I asked.

"Yes," said he. "I have business there. I was there last summer."

"Have you a bargain to keep?" I asked.

"Yes," he said, "and it is important that I keep it. It is important that I maintain my integrity with these people, that I speak, as it is said, with a straight tongue."

"When are you to be there?" I asked.

"In Kantasawi," he said, "the moon when the plums are red." This was the moon following the next moon, which is known variously as Takiyuhawi, the moon in which the tabuk rut, or Canpasapawi, the moon when the chokecherries are ripe.

"Will this give you time to return to Kailiauk?" I asked. Otherwise he would have to winter in the Barrens. The red savages themselves sometimes found it difficult to survive the long and severe winters, particularly if the hunting was poor.

"Two moons will be sufficient to return to Kailiauk," said Grunt, "if one does not stop for trading." The two moons he had in mind, as I later learned, were Canwapegiwi, the moon in which the leaves become brown, and the moon known variously as Wayuksapiwi, the Corn-Harvest Moon, or Canwapekasnawi, the moon when the wind shakes off the leaves. The autumnal equinox occurs in Canwapegiwi.

"What is important about Kantasawi?" I asked.

"It is the moon during which the Bento herd enters the country of the Kaiila. It is a time of the gathering of the Kaiila, of great hunts and dances."

"I would welcome your company," I said. I did not question him further on the nature of his business with the Kaiila.

"It is then decided," said Grunt. "We shall leave, and together, in the morning."

"Good," I said.

The girls, in their neck shackles, of course, did not know of our decision, nor of what might be involved in it. This was appropriate, for they were merely slaves.

"On the way to the country of the Kaiila, I would like to examine the field of the killings, the massacres," I said.

Grunt looked at me, puzzled.

"I have determinations to make there," I said.

"It is not far from here," he said.

"I thought not," I said.

"It will not be pleasant," he said.

I nodded. Yet I must determine if Kurii were among the fallen, and, if possible, their number.

"Tonight," said Grunt, getting up, "you may use Priscilla, if you wish."

"No," I said, "not tonight."

"I understand," said Grunt.

I remained for a time sitting by the fire. Then, after a time, I, too, retired.

15

THE FLEER

"Here," said Grunt, pointing down from the saddle of the lofty kaiila, "you see the wagon tracks, the ruts?"

"Yes," I said. We found them where they had emerged from a small stream. The tracks were several days old.

"It will not be far now," he said.

"You have seen the smoke?" I asked. I referred to the slow liftings of smoke, rising from low buttes, behind us and to our left, and before us, and to the right. The distance between the two fires was probably some ten to fifteen pasangs.

"Yes," said Grunt, "but its intent is not hostile, as I read it. It is, rather, informational. It is doing little more than marking our passage."

Such signals are common on the plains, but perhaps not so common as mirror signals. The code in mirror signals, conveyed by the pacing and number of flashes, is very similar to that of the smoke signals. The signals, incidentally, are not a substitution cipher, for the languages of the red savages, not being written languages, in any conventional sense, do not have a standardized alphabet or syllabary. The signals, of which there are some fifty or sixty, have conventionalized meanings, such as 'We are Kaiila', 'Who are you?', 'Go back', 'We have counted coup' and 'We are returning to camp'. The common smoke signal is produced by placing greenery, such as branches, leaves or grass, on a fire. The smoke produced is then regulated in its ascent by the action of a robe or blanket, the manner of its releasing being a function of the conventions involved. At night such signals can be conveyed by the number and placement of fires, or by a single fire, alternately revealed and concealed by the action, again, of a robe or blanket. Other common signaling methods, incidentally, involve such things as the use of dust cast into the air, the movement of robes and the motions imparted to a kaiila.

"I do not care to be under surveillance in this fashion," I said.

"In a way it is heartening," said Grunt. "You see, they are letting you see that you are under surveillance. If their intentions were hostile, or immediately hostile, they would not be likely to be so open about the matter."

"That is true," I admitted.

"As I read the smoke," he said, "it is saying that a small party of white men is moving eastward. The smoke on the right is merely acknowledging the receipt of this message."

"I hope you are right," I said.

"That would be the customary reading," said Grunt. "To be sure, the customary meanings are sometimes rearranged to conceal the true meaning. For example, a message which commonly means that kailiauk have been sighted may, by prearrangement, be understood to communicate an intention of attack to a collaborative force."

"Marvelous," I said, bitterly.

Grunt shrugged. "These people," he said, "must survive with one another."

"Hold!" said Grunt, suddenly, tensing.

The rider had appeared very suddenly, over a small rise in front of us, some twenty yards away. He reined in his kaiila. Dust swept about the paws and legs of the beast.

"Do not reach for your weapons," said Grunt. "He is Fleer," he added.

"How do you know?" I asked.

"The hair," said Grunt, "is worn in the high pompadour, combed back."

"Like Corn Stalks," I said. The fellow's hair came down his back, flowing even over the spine of the kaiila. He was riding bareback. He carried a long, feathered lance, and a small, round shield, a war shield, on which were inscribed medicine signs.

The fellow moved his kaiila down the slope towards us.

"Be careful," said Grunt. "He has made two killings and has counted several coup. The scarlet circles on the feather indicate killings, the red marks on his legs, and on the nose of the kaiila, show coups."

The Fleer reined in his kaiila a few feet from us. Grunt relaxed in his saddle and smiled, broadly. He raised his right hand to the side of his face, the index and middle fingers extended upwards and held together, the other fingers closed.

"He has no saddle," said Grunt. "His body, and that of his kaiila, are still painted with coup marks. Undoubtedly he took part in the action of a few days ago."

Grunt then, still smiling, clasped his left hand with his right, and shook it. This, too, is used by some tribes as a sign for friend.

"Kodakiciyapi," said Grunt. "Hou, Koda. Hou, Mitakoda." 'Peace, friendship,' had said Grunt, 'Greetings, Friend. Greetings, my friend,' in Dust Leg. He then added, in Kaiila, for good measure, substantially the same message. "Hou, Kola. Hou, Mitakola. Olakota. Wolakota." 'Greetings, Friend. Greetings, my friend. Peace, Peace, Friendship.'

The fellow regarded us, not speaking, either verbally or in sign.

I was not certain that Grunt was wise in addressing him in the dialect of the Kaiila, for the Fleer and Kaiila are hereditary enemies. On the other hand, interestingly, the many affinities between their languages suggest a common ancestor. The distinction between dialects and languages, as the dialectical divergencies increase, can become, at times, almost arbitrary. Most people, for what it is worth, regard Fleer and Kaiila as different languages. Certainly the Fleer and Kaiila do, and few see much profit in arguing the point with them.

"Wopeton," said Grunt, pointing to me. "Wopeton," he said, pointing to himself. This is the word in both Dust Leg and Kaiila for a trader, or merchant.

The fellow did not drop his lance into the attack position, grasping it firmly, anchoring it under his right arm.

"Do not move," said Grunt.

The fellow then, kicking back with his heels into the flanks of his kaiila, moved his beast about us, and our party.

"Stand straight," called Grunt to the coffle, which now, in our pause, had put down its burdens. "Keep your heads up, but do not meet his eyes. It is you who are the merchandise, the beauties, the slaves, not he. It is not yours to examine, but to be examined, not yours to consider, but to be considered."

I thought Grunt was wise not to have the girls look into the eyes of the Fleer warrior. Such an exchange of glances, or looks, can be like an electric shock, an encounter almost fearfully significant. Who knows what each might recognize in the eyes of the other? Does she see in his eyes that he is one such as might be her master? Does he see in her eyes that she is one who could not help but acknowledge herself, and soon, despite what she might now take to be her desires, his helpless and natural slave? Sometimes, at as little as a meeting of eyes, masters and slaves know one another. "I must have her. She is mine," he tells himself. "I belong to him. I am his slave," her heart whispers to her.

This matter of eye contact is interesting and has many facets. One of the most initially frightening and disturbing things to Earth women brought to Gor as slaves is the way Gorean men look at them. They are not used to being looked at as women, truly, with appraisal, desire and ownership. This tends, in the beginning, when they are still new to their collars, to confuse and frighten them, but also, of course, as it will continue to do, and even more powerfully, to stimulate them. It is the first time that they have found themselves in the order of nature, and as what they are, and it is the first time that they have found themselves being looked at, frankly, and honestly, within the order of nature, and as what they are, females, appropriate objects of male predation and desire. This recognition of her femaleness, and this joy in release and self-discovery, often comes as a stunning revelation to the Earth female. Never again, once having discovered this, does she retreat to the conditioned ideals of neuterism and pseudomasculinity, nor, indeed, even if she desired to do so, would her masters permit it. Sometimes in training, incidentally, or as a discipline or punishment, the slave is not permitted to look into the eyes of the master. Indeed, sometimes, in training, she is not permitted to raise her eyes above the belt of the trainer. Also, it must be recognized that many slaves often, and perhaps all slaves sometimes, find it difficult to look into the eyes of the master. He, after all, holds total power over them and they fear to displease him. What if he should interpret her gaze as suggesting the least insubordination or insolence? Are they truly prepared to have the soles of their feet lashed or to live on bread crusts for the next five days? But, on the other hand, there is, on Gor, in circles of the mastery, no discouragement, commonly, of eye contact between masters and slaves.

Indeed, in the deep and profound relationships of love and bondage, such eye contact is usually welcomed and encouraged. What can be understood of the glances of masters and slaves by those who have been united only in lesser relationships? Too, to be sure, from the practical point of view, it is useful for a girl to be able to look into the eyes of the master. In this way she may be able to better read his moods, and desires, and, accordingly, be able the better to serve him, in the process perhaps saving herself a few cuffings and beatings, such as might be garnered by a less alert, more slothful, laxer girl. To be sure, all girls, upon occasion, are cuffed or beaten. This is good for them, and helps to remind them that they are slaves. Beauty in a slave girl, incidentally, and most slaves are beautiful, for this is the sort of woman that tends to be enslaved, does not excuse poor service. The most beautiful girl must serve with the same perfection as the lesser girl. Gorean masters are uncompromising on this point.

From the point of view of the master, too, not only is it pleasant to look into the eyes of a slave, but there are certain practical advantages attached to doing so. For example, one might, in her eyes, read desire, and thus order her to perform an act which she, even though a slave, might not have dared to beg to perform, or, say, by looking into her eyes, one might determine if she has been up to something or has neglected something to which she should have attended. Has she been into the sweets? Has she, perhaps gossiping and dawdling with the other girls, been amiss in the discharge of her duties? Perhaps the shopping has not yet been done? Perhaps the laundry has not yet been finished? Such infractions call for discipline. But perhaps, in lieu of discipline, the master will accept the performance of desperate placatory services on the part of the offending slave. The decision is his. I would, incidentally, advise the slave to be superb.

The Fleer warrior stopped his kaiila by Priscilla, the second to the last girl on the coffle, and lifted up her chin with the iron point of his lance. It was a trade point, some nine inches long, socketed, with two rivets.

He then backed his kaiila away from her.

Priscilla had not met his eyes, as Grunt had advised them.

Grunt did not want to do business with the Fleer. He wished only to traverse the area in peace.

The kaiila snorted and threw up its head, and squealed, its mouth wrenched by the jerking back of the jaw rope.

On its nose were red lines, coup marks, matching those on the warrior's legs. Its eyes were outlined with wide circles of black paint. On its left forequarter was drawn a zig-zag line, indicating lightning. On its right forequarter there were five inverted "U's." Its right ear bore a V-shaped notch. On its left flank there was an opaque red circle with a waving red line descending from it. Also on the left flank, and on the right flank, too, there was a black, horizontal line, with a semi-circular, curved blue line above it. The coup marks and the inverted "U's" were exploit markings. The inverted "U's" indicated kaiila stolen from the enemy, the mark itself being a stylized convention whose heritage, I did not doubt, might be traced back to another animal, and another world and time. The circles painted about the eyes and the line of lightning on the left forequarter were signs in the medicine of war. The medicine use of the circles was to enable the beast to see clearly and far and that of the line to impart to its motion something of the same suddenness, the same swiftness and power, as attends the movement of lightning, that dread natural phenomenon, itself. The opaque circle with the wavy line descending from it was a wound mark, the location of the mark indicating a former wound site, the redness standing for blood, of course, and the descending line for bleeding. I did not know the meaning of the notched ear, if it had a meaning, or of the other marks on the animal's flanks.

The Fleer moved his kaiila about, on the other side of the coffle, so that he might look at the girls, one by one. None of them, as Grunt had advised, met his eyes. They kept their heads high, and looked ahead, knowing themselves scrutinized as the pretty, meaningless beasts they were.

"Our friend," said Grunt to me, "is a member of the Blue-Sky Riders, a warrior society of the Fleer."

"One should be careful of such fellows?" I asked.

"I would think so," smiled Grunt.

"You are gathering this membership from the marks on the kaiila's flanks?" I asked.

"Yes," said Grunt, "the dark line of the earth, the over-arching dome of the blue sky."

"I see," I said. Most tribes had several warrior societies. These societies had much influence within the tribes and, on an alternating basis, to preclude any one society from becoming predominant, a good deal of power. Their members were expected to set an example in the war and the hunt.

"I do not think he means us harm," said Grunt. "He is merely curious."

Warrior Societies in the tribes have many functions. They are a significant component of tribal existence. Such societies, on an alternating basis, do such things as keep order in the camps and on the treks. They function, too, as guards and police. It is part of their function, too, to keep the tribes apprised as to the movements of kailiauk and to organize and police tribal hunts. Such societies, too, it might be noted, are useful in various social ways. They provide institutions through which merit can be recognized and rewarded, and tribal traditions freshened, maintained and renewed. They preserve medicine bundles, keep ceremonies and teach histories. It is common for them to give feasts and hold dances. Their rivalries provide an outlet for intratribal aggression, and the attendant competitions supply an encouragement for effort and a stimulus to excellence. Within the society itself, of course, the members profit from the values of alliance, camaraderie and friendship. Needless to say, each society will have, too, its own medicines and mysteries.

I watched the Fleer, carefully. How intricate, actually, is the structure and governance of a tribe.

"The ear of his kaiila is notched," I said to Grunt. "Is that an eccentric mutilation or is it deliberate, perhaps meaningful?"

"It is meaningful," said Grunt. "It marks the kaiila as a prize animal, one especially trained for the hunt and war."

The girls continued to look ahead. They wisely avoided direct eye contact with the appraising warrior, thus perhaps precipitating an encounter crisis, in which, perhaps because of misconstrual or misinterpretation, he might feel prompted to action. There are various ways in which a woman may look into the eyes of a man. One way, of course, is with a direct and self-assured gaze, as though she might be the equal of the brute who regards her, the way of the free woman. This is not to be recommended, of course, for a woman who is scantily clad and has a chain on her neck. Such an insolence, at the least, would be likely to win her beauty a bout with the five-stranded Gorean slave lash. Why do some women look into the eyes of a man in this fashion? It is an interesting question. Some think that it is their way, perhaps even half consciously, of challenging him to their subduing, of challenging him to make them a woman, a slave. It is not unusual for a woman, at any rate, who has looked into the eyes of a man in that fashion to discover, later, that she is looking into his eyes in quite a different fashion, that whereas she once may have regarded him directly, and insolently, she now, perhaps kneeling stripped at his feet, in a locked collar, bearing his identificatory device, lifts her eyes to his rather differently, doing so now as a mere slave girl to her master.

The Fleer backed his kaiila from Ginger, the animal almost crouching back on its haunches.

There was blood about the jaws, and lips, of the kaiila, from where, earlier, he had jerked back on the jaw rope. I saw the muscles within the kaiila's flanks move beneath the paint.

"Oh!" said the red-haired girl, first in the coffle, startled as the point of his lance had scraped the back of the black-iron collar on her neck. Then she was quiet. He was lifting her sheen of red hair on the point of his lance, moving it in the sun, to see it glisten and reflect the light. He was curious as to such hair. It is extremely rare in the Barrens. Grunt had not permitted her to cut it, or even to trim and shape it. That could be done later. Now he wanted it to grow, and to be, apparently, as long as possible. The Fleer let the hair fall from the lance, and then he laid the side of the metal point of the lance on the edge of the girl's collar, the metal touching the right side of her neck. She shuddered, but she did not otherwise move. She, a slave, was under good discipline. I thought that was fortunate for her. Her movement, of course, the shuddering, this responsiveness, was revealing, and would have been to any man familiar with female slaves. It did not escape the detection of the Fleer.

Curious he now returned his kaiila to the position of the last girl on the coffle, whom we were calling Pimples, the Gorean translation of her former name, originally given to her by a Kaiila master, 'Wasnapohdi'. In Dust Leg, incidentally, the expression has the same meaning. I could detect, subtly, now, that Grunt was tense. He wanted the Fleer to be gone by now. I found myself, too, probably because of Grunt, growing more tense. I hoped that our reactions would not be evident to the Fleer, who was several yards away. One by one, with the side of the lance, the Fleer, moving along the line, touched the girls. Pimples cried out, softly, touched on the right thigh. Then, at various places, on the calf, or the thigh, or ankle or neck, unexpectedly, not knowing where they would be touched, the other girls, too, were touched, Priscilla, Inez, Lois, Corinne, Evelyn, Ginger and the red-haired girl. Each of the girls could not help but respond in her own way to the Fleer's test, that of the unexpected touch of a man's weapon to her body.

"I trust he will not want any of them," said Grunt.

"I hope not," I said. We did not object to the assessment of the girls, of course, for they were slaves. Their assessment was no different from the assessment of kaiila, except, of course, that somewhat different properties, on the whole, would be under assessment. What we did not want was trouble.

The Fleer backed his kaiila from the red-haired girl. With the side of his lance he had touched her left thigh, and then, with the point of the lance, he had raised the hem of her skimpy tunic to her waist. Then, riding before her, he had, with the point of the lance, thrust aside the sides of her tunic. She had then been well revealed to him. The exposed slave, the former Miss Millicent Aubrey-Welles, the debutante from Pennsylvania, I saw, was quite beautiful. In the Barrens she might well be worth five hides of the yellow kailiauk.

We regarded the Fleer, who had now ridden his kaiila again before us.

He did not come so close to us that he could not, easily, drop his lance into the attack position.

"Do not move," said Grunt to me, smiling at the Fleer.

The Fleer suddenly smiled broadly. He shifted his lance to his left hand, which pleased me. He held his right hand near his body, with the palm down and the thumb close to his left breast. Then, with his right arm horizontal, he swept his hand outward and a bit to the right. This meant "good," that which is level with the heart. He then pointed to the girls. He moved his flat right hand in a horizontal circle, clockwise, as Earth clocks move, not Gorean clocks, in front of his chest. This meant "all;" the circle being complete. He then grinned again.

Grunt then lifted his right hand, the back of it near his right shoulder. His index finger pointed forward and the other fingers were closed, with his thumb resting on his middle finger. He then moved his hand a bit to the left and, at the same time, touching the thumb with the index finger, made a closed circle. "Yes," had said Grunt. He then made the sign for "all" and the sign for "good," in that order. "All is good," or "all right," he had said. He then extended his hands in a forward direction, the palms down, and lowered them. "Thank you," was the meaning of this sign. He then held his hands at the level of his chest, with his index fingers pointing forward and the other fingers closed. He drew back his right hand, to the right, some inches, and then he brought it forward again, the index finger still extended, and moved it over his left hand. The first portion of this sign means "time," and the second portion indicates, presumably, the forward movement of time. Literally this sign, in both its portions, indicates "future," but it is used also for "good-bye," the rationale being perhaps similar to that in locutions such as 'I'll be seeing you' or 'Until we meet again'. The sign for past, incidentally, is also the sign for "before." The sign for "time," predictably, enters into the sign for "before," but, in this case, it is followed by the thrusting forth and drawing back of the right hand. This is perhaps to suggest moving backward in time.

The Fleer grinned, and shifted his lance again to his right hand. Then, suddenly, with a wild whoop, and kicking his heels back into the flanks of his kaiila, he raced away.

"I have always had good relations with the Fleer," said Grunt.

I watched the rider racing away. He was a member of the Blue-Sky Riders. One does not come easily into membership in such a society. I was sweating.

"I thought he might want one or more of the girls," I said.

"He probably has, on the whole, as good or better in his own camp," said Grunt.

"Perhaps," I said.

We looked at the girls. Several were still trembling, from the Fleer's assessment. The red-haired girl smoothed down the skirt of the tunic and, with her small hands, drew together, as she could, the sides of the tunic. She, of all, it seemed, was the most shaken. To be sure, it was she, of all of them, who had been the most objectively assessed.

"The Fleer was impressed," said Grunt. "Did you see?"

"Yes," I said.

"I am proud of all of them," said Grunt. "Did you see how they responded to the touch of his lance?"

"Yes," I said.

"They are good stuff," said Grunt.

"I think so," I said.

"And I am grateful to you, for your help, in beating them, and helping to teach them their bondage," he said.

I shrugged. I had, it must be admitted, derived much pleasure from the coffle, picking out one or another of them, when the whim or urge might strike me, for my slave use. I regarded them. Their necks were lovely in their iron collars and chains. Last night I had had Priscilla, the English girl, weeping in my arms. Before that I had had Lois, the short, blond American girl. She looked particularly well in chains.

"Your tutelage of them in submission and servitude, the instructional abuse to which you have subjected them," said Grunt, "may prove to be instrumental in saving their lives."

"They are eager pupils," I said, "having now come to understand that they are truly slaves."

"Good," said Grunt.

I wondered why Grunt had administered so little, if any, of this form of instruction to his coffled properties. Surely he could see, as well as any other, their desirability and beauty.

"Up with your burdens, my pretty beasts!" called Grunt. "Do you think you are fed for nothing? Do you think we can dawdle here all day! No! We must march!"

"What do you think the Fleer was doing here?" I asked.

"He was probably left behind to kill survivors," said Grunt.

"We are, of course, in Fleer country," I said.

"He was in the paint of war," said Grunt.

"He did not show hostility towards us," I said.

"We were not involved in the action," said Grunt.

"The site of the action, I gather," I said, "is quite close."

"I fear so," said Grunt.

"Perhaps we should ride well ahead of the coffle," I said.

"I think that is probably true," said Grunt.

16

THE KUR;
I MEET WANIYANPI;

I HEAR OF THE LADY MIRA

"It occurred here," said Grunt, "obviously."

We looked down from the rise, onto the valley below.

"I had thought it would be worse," I said. I remembered the grisly aftermath of the attack on the Hobarts' men.

Below us there lay little more, seemingly, than overturned and scattered wagons, some burned. Harness was cut. The carcass of a draft tharlarion, here and there, loomed in the grass. Most of the animals, however, had apparently been cut free and driven away.

"It could be worse than you think," said Grunt. "Much death might lie about in the grass."

"Perhaps," I said.

"Yet there seem few scavengers," he said.

I looked behind us. The red-haired girl, first in the coffle, stood near us. The other girls, then, and the Hobarts, in their place, came up with her.

We had forgotten them, in coming over the rise, in seeing the wagons. Now there seemed little purpose in warning them back. Too, it did not seem as sickening as we had feared, what lay before us.

"The attack presumably did not take place at dawn," said Grunt, "and, presumably, it would not have occurred late in the day."

"Your surmise is based on the scattering of the wagons," I said, "that they are not defensively circled, but are aligned, as for the march."

"Yes," said Grunt.

"And the attack would not take place late in the day," I said, "because of the possibility of survivors escaping under the cover of darkness."

"That is it," said Grunt. "It is my speculation that the wagons were being opened and aligned for the march."

"If that is true," I said, "we should find the remains of evening fires, large cooking fires, with circled stones, near the wagons, not the absence of fires, nor the smaller remains of midday fires."

"Yes," said Grunt.

We then began to move our kaiila down the rise, toward the wagons. There were several of them. Some were turned awry, some were overturned, and some stood mute and stark in their tracks, unattended, as though waiting to be utilized, the grass about their axles, the heavy beams of their tongues sloping to the earth. Most of the wagons were charred to one extent or another. In none was the canvas covering intact. It had either been torn away or burned. The curved supports for the canvas, which were metal, in most cases remained. Against the sky they had a macabre, skeletal appearance, not unlike exposed ribs. The irregular line of the wagons extended for something like a pasang. As we came closer we could see, here and there, and sometimes within the wagons, discarded and shattered objects. Chests had been overturned and broken open. I saw a doll in the grass and a man's boot. Flour from rent sacks had been scattered on the grass.

"There are the remains here of evening fires," I said, moving the kaiila past some circles of stones.

"Yes," said Grunt. These fires presumably would have been within the wagon circle. The attack, then, it seemed clear, would have occurred in the morning, probably during, or shortly after, the hitching up of the draft tharlarion. The number of cut harnesses suggested the second alternative. Here and there I saw an arrow in the grass. The comparative fixity of these objects, almost upright, leaning, slim and firm, contrasted with the movement of the grass which, in the wind, bent and rustled about them.

The kaiila suddenly, with a snort, shifted to the right. I kept the saddle. I restrained the beast, forcibly. I jerked the reins to the left and kicked back, into the silken flanks of the animal.

"What is it?" asked Grunt.

I was looking down, into the grass.

"What is it that you see in the grass?" asked Grunt.

"Death," I said. "But no common death."

I threw the reins to Grunt, and dismounted. "Stay back," I warned the girls.

I examined what was left of the body.

"No Fleer or Yellow Knife did that," said Grunt.

"No," I said.

The head was lacerated, but the wounds were superficial. The throat, however, had been bitten through. The left leg was gone.

"It must have been a survivor," said Grunt. "The body is clothed. He must have been returning to the wagons, perhaps to search for food."

"I think so," I said.

"Then a wild sleen must have caught him," said Grunt.

"The sleen is primarily nocturnal," I said. I had seen such things before. I did not think the body bore the marks of a sleen.

"So?" said Grunt.

"Look," I said. Between my thumb and forefinger there was a dark, viscous stain. I wiped my fingers on the grass.

"I see," said Grunt. "Too," said he, "note the torn earth. It is still black. Grass uprooted near the body, there, has not dried yet. It is still green."

"Put a quarrel in your guide," I advised him. It seemed reasonably clear this attack had occurred within the Ahn.

Grunt looped the reins of my kaiila over the pommel of his saddle.

I stood up, and looked about me.

I heard Grunt arm his bow, drawing back the stout cable, his foot in the bow stirrup, then slotting the quarrel into the guide.

I shuddered, and quickly mounted the kaiila, taking back the reins from Grunt. I was pleased to be again in the saddle. Mobility is important in the Barrens. Too, the height considerably increases one's scanning range.

"It is still here, somewhere," I said. I glanced to Grunt's bow. He would have, presumably, but one shot with it.

"What is it?" asked Grunt. "A beast, one of the sort which you seek?"

"I think so," I said. "Too, I think that it, like the other fellow, is a survivor. That it has lingered in the vicinity of the wagons suggests to me that it, too, was wounded."

"It will be, then, extremely dangerous," said Grunt.

"Yes," I said. Certainly pain, hunger and desperation would not render any such beast the less dangerous.

A few feet to the left of the kaiila there was a keg of sugar, which had been split open. A trail of sugar, some four inches wide, some three or four yards long, drained through the split lid, had been run out behind it. It had probably been carried under someone's arm. This trove was the object of the patient industry of ants, thousands of them, from perhaps a hundred hills about. It would be the prize, doubtless, in small and unrecorded wars.

Grunt and I moved our kaiila forward. Behind us I heard the red-haired girl vomit in the grass. She had passed too closely to the body.

"Look!" cried Grunt. "There, ahead!"

"I see it," I cried.

"Do they not care to defend themselves?" he inquired.

"Hurry!" I said, urging the kaiila forward.

We raced ahead. We were some half pasang beyond the line of strewn, charred wagons behind us. We now approached other wagons, but scattered about. These were the wagons for which I had earlier sought in vain, the smaller, squarish wagons, which had been with the mercenary column. They, too, seemed broken. Two were overturned. Some had been burned to the wagon bed, others missed a roof or a roof and wall. To none of them were harnessed tharlarion. Given their distance from the other wagons and their distribution in the grass I took it that they had broken their column and sped away, as best they might. They had not had the time, or the presence of mind, perhaps, to form a defensive barrier.

Near some three of these wagons there was a small group of figures, perhaps some fifteen or twenty men. One stood out a bit from the others. It was he who was most obviously threatened by the brown, looming shape which had apparently emerged from the grass near them. I did not know if they had disturbed the beast, or if it had been moving towards them, until then, at its choice, unseen. The man held a shovel, but he had not raised it to defend himself. His posture did not seem brave, but rather phlegmatic. Could it be he did not understand his danger?

"Hurry!" I cried to the kaiila.

The paws of Grunt's beast thundered beside my own. "He is insane!" cried Grunt.

The beast itself seemed puzzled, uncertain, regarding the man.

Never before, perhaps, had it found itself viewed with such incomprehension.

The men wore gray garments, open at the bottom, which fell between the knee and ankle.

The beast turned its head suddenly to face us. In less than a handful of Ehn I pulled up the kaiila, rearing and squealing, between the beast and the man.

The beast snarled and took a step backward. I saw that it was neither Kog nor Sardak.

"Get back!" I warned the men.

Obediently they all, including the fellow who had been most forward, drew back.

I did not take my eyes from the beast. It raised one darkly stained paw. The hair between the digits was matted and stuck together. I supposed this was from the kill a pasang or so back.

I backed the kaiila a step or two from the beast. "Back away," I told the men. They obeyed.

The fur of the beast was rent and thick, here and there, with clotted blood. I think, more than once, it might have been struck with lances. It had perhaps lost consciousness in the grass, from the loss of blood, and had been left for dead. It was not the sort of thing the red savages would mutilate. They were unfamiliar with it. They would presumably classify it with sleen or urts, not men.

The beast, snarling, took a step forward.

"It is going to attack," said Grunt. "I can kill it," he said. He raised the crossbow.

"Do not fire," I said.

Grunt did not discharge the weapon.

"Look at it," I said.

The beast regarded Grunt, and then myself. Its lips curled back over the double ring of white fangs.

"It is showing contempt for us," I said.

"Contempt?" said Grunt, puzzled.

"Yes," I said. "You see, he is not similarly armed."

"It is a beast," said Grunt. But he lowered the weapon.

"It is a Kur," I said.

The beast then backed away from us, snarling. After a few feet it turned and dropped to all fours, moving through the grass. It did not look back.

I moved the kaiila a few feet forward, to where it had originally stood in the grass. I wished to study the pattern of grasses there. Then I returned to where Grunt, and the others, were waiting.

"You should have let me kill it," said Grunt.

"Perhaps," I said.

"Why did you not have me fire?" asked Grunt.

"It has to do with codes," I said.

"Who are you, truly?" asked Grunt.

"One to whom codes were once familiar," I said, "one by whom they have never been completely forgotten."

I brought my kaiila about, and before the fellow who had been most obviously threatened by the beast.

"I feared there might be violence," he said.

"I have examined the grass, whence the beast arose," I said. "It had been approaching you, unseen. It was stalking you."

"I am Pumpkin," he said. "Peace and light, and tranquillity, and contentment and goodness be unto you."

"It was stalking you," I said, the kaiila moving uneasily beneath me.

"Sweetness be unto you," said the fellow.

"Did you not realize the danger in which you stood?" I asked. "You could have been killed."

"It is fortunate, then, that you intervened," he said.

"Are you so brave," I asked, "that you faced the beast so calmly?"

"What is life? What is death?" he asked. "Both are unimportant."

I looked at the fellow, puzzled. Then I looked, too, to the others, standing about. I saw now they wore gray dresses, probably their only garments. The hems of these dresses fell between their knees and their ankles. Men, they appeared ungainly and foolish in these garments. Their shoulders were slumped. Their eyes were spiritless and empty. Rags were bound about their feet. I saw, however, to my interest, that two of them now held feathered lances.

I looked again to the fellow who had been most threatened by the beast.

"Sweetness be unto you," he said, smiling.

I saw then that he had not been brave. It had been only that he had little to live for. Indeed, I wondered if he had been courting destruction. He had not even raised his shovel to defend himself.

"Who are you?" I asked these fellows.

"We are joyful dung," said one of the fellows, "enriching and beautifying the earth."

"We are sparkles on the water, making the streams pretty," said another.

"We are flowers growing in the fields," said another.

"We are nice," said another.

"We are good," said another.

I then again regarded he who seemed to be foremost among them, he who had called himself Pumpkin.

"You are leader here?" I asked.

"No, no!" he said. "We are all the same. We are sames! We are not not-the-sames!" In this moment he had showed emotion, fear. He moved back, putting himself with the others.

I regarded them.

"We are all equal," he said. "We are all the same."

"How do you know?" I asked.

"We must be equal," he said. "It is the teaching."

"Is the teaching true?" I asked.

"Yes," said the man.

"How do you know?" I asked.

"It is the test of truth," he said.

"How do you know?" I asked.

"It is in the teaching," he said.

"Your teaching, then," I said, "is a circle, unsupported, floating in the air."

"The teaching does not need support," said the fellow. "It is in and of itself. It is a golden circle, self-sustained and eternal."

"How do you know?" I asked.

"It is in the teaching itself," said a fellow.

"What of your reason?" I asked. "Do you have any use for it?"

"Reason is very precious," said a fellow.

"Properly understood and employed it is fully compatible

with the teaching, and, in its highest office, exists to serve the teaching."

"What, then, of the evidence of your senses?" I asked.

"The senses are notoriously untrustworthy," said one of the fellows.

"What in the senses might seem to confirm the teaching may be kept," said one of them. "What might, mistakenly, seem incompatible with the teaching is to be disregarded."

"What arguments, or what sorts of evidence, if it could be produced," I asked, "might you take as indicating the falsity of the teaching?"

"Nothing is to be permitted to indicate the falsity of the teaching," said the fellow who had been foremost among them.

"That is in the teaching," explained another one of them.

"A teaching which cannot be disconfirmed cannot be confirmed, either," I said. "A teaching which cannot, even in theory, be disconfirmed is not true, but empty. If the world cannot speak to it, it does not speak of the world. It speaks of nothing. It is babble, twaddle as vacant as it is vain and inane."

"These are deep matters," said the fellow I had taken to be their leader. "As they are not in the teaching, we need not concern ourselves with them."

"Are you happy?" I asked. Verbal formulas, even vacuous ones, like music or medicine, I knew, might have empirical effects. So, too, of course, might have truncheons and green fruit.

"Oh, yes," said the first fellow quickly. "We are wondrously happy."

"Yes," said several of the others.

"Sweetness be unto you," said another.

"You do not seem happy," I said. I had seldom seen a more tedious, bedraggled, limp set of organisms.

"We are happy," insisted one of them.

"True happiness," said another, "is keeping the Teaching."

I drew forth my blade, suddenly, and drew it back, as though to slash at the foremost fellow. He lifted his head and turned his neck toward me. "Peace, and light, and tranquillity, and contentment and goodness, be unto you," he said.

"Interesting," I said, thrusting the blade back in my scabbard.

"Death holds few terrors for those who have never known life," said Grunt.

"What is life? What is death?" asked the fellow. "Both are unimportant."

"If you do not know what they are," I said, "perhaps you should not prejudge the issue of their importance."

I looked over to the two fellows who held the feathered lances. "Where did you find those lances?" I asked.

"In the grass," said one of them. "They were lost in the battle."

"Was it your intention to use them, to defend yourselves from the beast?" I asked.

"No," said the fellow. "Of course not!"

"You would prefer to be eaten?" I asked.

"Resistance is not permitted," said the fellow.

"Fighting is against the teaching," said the other fellow, he with the second lance.

"We abhor violence," added another.

"You lifted the lances," I said. "What were you going to do with them?"

"We thought you might wish to fight the beast," said one. "Thusly, in that instance, we would have tendered you a lance."

"And for whom," I asked, "was the second lance?"

"For the beast," said the fellow with the first lance.

"We would not have wanted to anger it," said the fellow with the second lance.

"You would let others do your fighting for you," I asked, "and you would have abided the outcome?"

"Yes," said the fellow with the first lance. "Not all of us are as noble and brave as Pumpkin."

"Who are these people?" I asked Grunt.

"They are Waniyanpi," said Grunt. "They have the values of cowards, and of idiots and vegetables."

The coffle, by now, had approached. I noted that none of the Waniyanpi lifted their eyes to assess the scantily clad loveliness of Grunt's chained properties.

I again regarded Pumpkin who seemed, despite his denial, first among them.

"To whom do you belong?" I asked.

"We belong to Kaiila," said Pumpkin.

"You are far from home," I said.

"Yes," said Pumpkin.

"What are you doing here?" I asked.

"We have been brought here to cleanse the field," he said. "We are to bury the dead and dismantle and burn the wagons, disposing likewise of similar debris."

"You must have been marched here long before the battle," I said.

"Yes," said Pumpkin.

"Did you see the battle?" I asked.

"No," said Pumpkin. "We were forced to lie on our stomachs, with our eyes closed, our limbs held as though bound, watched over by a boy."

"To guard you?" I asked.

"No, to protect us from animals," said Pumpkin.

"To the west," I said, "among the other wagons, there is a part of a body."

"We will find it," said Pumpkin.

"The field is mostly cleared," said Grunt. "There must have been other groups of Waniyanpi here, as well."

"That is true," said Pumpkin.

"Are they still about?" asked Grunt, nervously.

"I do not know," said Pumpkin. The object of Grunt's concern, potent as it was, did not occur to me at the time.

"How many of the large wagons, such as those to the west, were there?" I asked.

"Something over one hundred of them," said Pumpkin.

"How many of these smaller, squarish wagons, such as this one, were there?" I asked, indicating the remains of the nearest wagon, one of those which had been with the mercenary column.

"Seventeen," said Pumpkin.

This information pleased me. There had been seventeen such wagons with the original column. They were, thus, all accounted for. The beasts which had inhabited them, presumably one to a wagon, given the territoriality and irritability of the Kur, presumably would then have been afoot. Most then, presumably, might have been slain.

"How many graves have you, and the other Waniyanpi, dug?" I asked.

"Over one thousand," he said.

I whistled. The losses had been high, indeed.

"And you must understand," said Grunt, "the savages clear the field of their own dead."

For a moment I was stunned.

"It was a rout, and a massacre," said Grunt. "That much we learned from Corn Stalks."

"How many of the graves," I asked Pumpkin, "were those of settlers, those from the large wagons?"

"Something over four hundred," said Pumpkin. He looked back to the others for corroboration.

"Yes," said more than one.

"The settlers must have been wiped out, almost to a man," said Grunt.

I nodded. The first attack had presumably taken place there, on that part of the column. Too, they would have been less able, presumably, to defend themselves than the soldiers.

"Something in the neighborhood of six hundred soldiers then fell," said Grunt.

"Yes," said Pumpkin.

"Yes," said another of the fellows behind him.

"That is extremely interesting," I said to Grunt. "It would seem to follow that some four hundred of the soldiers escaped."

"That they did not fall on the field does not mean that they did not fall," said Grunt. "They may have been pursued and slain for pasangs across the prairie."

"The wagons seem to have been muchly looted," I said. "Our friends may have paused for plunder. Too, I do not know if their style of warfare is well fitted to attack a defensive column, orderly and rallied, on its guard."

Grunt shrugged. "I do not know," he said.

"Beasts," I said to Pumpkin, "such as that which threatened you, how many of them, if any, did you bury or find dead?"

"Nine," said Pumpkin. "We did not bury them, as they are not human."

I struck my thigh in frustration.

"Where are these bodies?" I asked. I wished to determine if Kog and Sardak were among the fallen.

"We do not know," said Pumpkin. "The Fleer put ropes on them and dragged them away, into the fields."

"I do not think they knew what else to do with them," said one of the fellows.

I was angry. I knew of one Kur who had survived, and now it seemed clear that as many as eight might have escaped from the savages. Indeed, many savages, for medicine reasons, might have been reluctant to attack them, as they did not appear to be beings of a sort with which they were familiar. What if they were from the medicine world? In such a case, surely, they were not to be attacked but, rather, venerated or propitiated. If Sardak had survived, I had little doubt he would continue, relentlessly, to prosecute his mission.

"Do you wish to know of survivors?" asked Pumpkin. "You seem interested."

"Yes," I said.

"Other than soldiers, and beasts, and such, who might have escaped?"

"Yes," I said.

"Some children were spared, young children," said Pumpkin. "They were tied together by the neck in small groups. There were four such groups. The Fleer took one group, consisting of six children. The other three groups, consisting of five children apiece, were taken by the Sleen, the Yellow Knives and Kailiauk."

"What of the Kaiila?" I asked.

"They did not take any of the children," said Pumpkin.

"The children were very fortunate," said one of the fellows before me.

"Yes," said another. "They will be taken to Waniyanpi camps, and raised as Waniyanpi."

"What a blessing for them!" said another.

"It is always best when the teaching can be given to the young," said another.

"Yes," said another. "It is the surest way to guarantee that they will always be Waniyanpi."

I wondered if the horrors and crimes perpetrated on one another by adults could ever match the cruelties inflicted on children. It seemed unlikely.

"There were some other survivors?" I asked.

"Some nubile young women," said Pumpkin, "but we did not look much at them. They were naked. Rawhide ropes were put on their necks. Their hands were tied behind them. They must accompany the masters, on their tethers, walking beside the flanks of their kaiila."

"And what, do you conjecture," I asked, "will be their fate?"

"We do not dare speculate," said Pumpkin, looking down, confused and dismayed, hotly reddening.

"They will be made slaves," I said, "crawling and kneeling

to men, and serving them abjectly, and totally, in all ways."

Pumpkin shuddered.

"It is true, is it not?" I asked.

"Perhaps," mumbled Pumpkin. He did not raise his eyes. I saw that he feared manhood, and sex.

"Would you not like one so serving you?" I asked.

"No, no!" he cried, not raising his eyes. "No, no, no!"

The vehemence of his answer interested me. I looked about, at the other Waniyanpi. They did not meet my eyes, but looked down.

"Were there other survivors?" I asked Pumpkin.

He looked up at me, gratefully. "Two," he said, "but, it seems, one of them only for a time."

"I do not understand," I said.

"A boy, a Dust Leg, I think," said Pumpkin. "He was a slave of the soldiers. He was left staked out, over there, on that hill. We are to keep him alive until we leave the field, and then leave him here, to die."

"That would be the lad, the young man, who was with the column, the slave, one called Urt," I said to Grunt.

Grunt shrugged. He did not know this. I had, to be sure, spoken more to myself than to him.

"Who is the other?" I asked.

"An adult woman," said Pumpkin, "one whom, I think, was also with the soldiers."

"Excellent!" I said. "Is she blond, and fair of body?"

"She is blond," said Pumpkin, "but we are not permitted to observe whether or not she be fair of body."

"It would be the Lady Mira, of Venna!" I said to Grunt. "Excellent! Excellent!"

"Do you know her?" asked Grunt.

"We met once, on the road," I said. "But our meeting, now, will be of a different sort." I laughed.

"What is wrong?" asked Grunt.

"Nothing," I said. I was pleased, first, that the Lady Mira lived. It is pleasant that such women live, particularly when they are put in collars and chains. Secondly it amused me that the fair agent's utility to Kurii had been, in this unexpected and charming fashion, so abruptly and conclusively terminated. Thirdly she could doubtless be persuaded, in one way or another, to give me a first-hand account of the battle, at least in so far as it had swept in its courses about her.

"Where is she?" I asked Pumpkin.

"Over there, behind that wagon," said Pumpkin. "We put her there so that we would not have to look at her."

I regarded the Waniyanpi. I wondered why they were as they were.

"Lift your skirts," I told them, "to your waists, quickly."

They obeyed, shamed.

"No," said Grunt. "They are not castrated. It is done through the mind, through the training, through the Teaching."

"Insidious," I said.

"Yes," said Grunt.

"You may lower your dresses," I told the Waniyanpi.

Quickly they did so, smoothing them, blushing.

I urged my kaiila toward the wagon which Pumpkin had indicated.

17

THE SLAVE

"You!" she cried, struggling to her feet.

I dismounted swiftly and easily, approaching her, from the kaiila.

"Why is your kaiila quirt drawn?" she asked.

I lashed her once, savagely, with the quirt, between the neck and shoulder, on the left side. I did not see any point in wasting time with her. "Kneel," I said.

Swiftly she knelt, clumsily in the apparatus in which she had been confined. She looked up at me. There were tears, and wonder, in her eyes. It was the first time, perhaps, she had been thusly struck.

"You do not avert your eyes from me," she said.

"It would be difficult to do so," I admitted. I could no longer, then, pursue my business in haste, as I had intended. Her loveliness, simply, did not permit it. She was stunning. I stood before her, savoring her beauty.

"Please," she protested, tears in her eyes.

I walked slowly about her.

She tossed her head, to throw her hair forward, over her breasts.

I took her hair on, and lifted it, with the quirt, and threw it again behind her shoulders. She shuddered as the leather touched her body.

Again I regarded her.

"How dare you look at me in that fashion?" she asked.

"You are beautiful," I explained.

"You struck me," she chided.

"Indeed," I said, "your beauty might be adequate even for that of a slave."

"Oh?" she said.

"Yes," I said. This was a high compliment which I had paid to her.

"You struck me," she said.

I slapped the kaiila quirt in my palm. "Yes," I said.

"You struck me as though I might have been a kaiila, or an animal," she said.

"Yes," I said.

"I am free!" she said.

"You do not appear to be free," I said. She knelt before me, stark naked. She wore an improvised girl-yoke. This consisted of a stout branch, about two inches thick, and some five feet in length, drilled at the center and near the extremities. It fits behind the back of the girl's neck. A long, single thong of rawhide fastens the girl in place. Her left wrist is thonged and then the thong is passed through the drilled aperture in the left end of the yoke. Her wrist is pulled tight to the yoke. The same thong is then taken behind the yoke and passed through the center hole, whence, after having been knotted, to prevent slippage to the left, and having been looped about the girl's neck, usually some five times, and having been knotted again, to prevent slippage to the right, it is returned through the same hole, whence it is taken behind the yoke to the hole drilled at the right-hand extremity of the apparatus. It is passed through that hole and then, of course, is used to fasten the girl's right wrist in place, tightly against the yoke. When this action is completed then, as you can see, the whole package is neatly tied. The knots near the throat bands, in preventing slippage, serve two functions; they hold the girl's wrists against the yoke and, at the same time, prevent any undue stress from being placed on the throat bands. The function of the throat bands is to hold the girl's throat in the yoke, securely and perfectly, not to cause her discomfort, nor to strangle her. Gorean men are not fools in tying women. Longer yokes, such as this, incidentally, are commonly used for marches.

Confined as she is, with her arms extended, a girl can exert almost no leverage to free herself. Smaller yokes, some two to two and a half feet in length, similarly constructed, can be used for other purposes, such as enjoying a girl in the furs. Afterwards she can always be kenneled or chained. A soft, braided leather rope, a trade rope, cored with wire, some fifteen or twenty feet in length, was looped some five times about the girl's left ankle, and tied, thence being run to the axle of the nearby wagon to which she was tethered. This is a useful sanitary provision as the girl, then, need not sit or lie too near to her own wastes. The wire coring in the rope, of course, tends to discourage the attempt to chew through the bond. Light chains, sheathed in silk, or satin or velvet, incidentally, have this utility as well, as well as their intrinsic strength, more than adequate for the securing of a female.

Three separate thongs, incidentally, two short and one long, are sometimes used for this type of securing of the female. In this way of doing things each wrist is tied in the center of one of the short thongs. The two free ends of the short thong are then taken back through the hole and, once through the hole, are simply knotted, heavily. This knot cannot, of course, be drawn back through the small drilled hole by the girl. Her wrists are thus held in place. One end of the longer thong is taken through the center aperture and that thong is then looped about the girl's throat, usually, again, some five times, and then returned through the center aperture. Once through the aperture it is knotted together, heavily, with the other end of the thong. Again, of course, this knot, a heavy one, prevents the thongs from slipping back through the narrow aperture. The girl's neck is thus held closely to the yoke. This, too, of course, is an effective way of securing a girl. Indeed, there is, in my opinion, normally little to choose from between these two yoke ties. Which is preferred may well depend on matters so trivial as the nature and lengths of the binding material available, for example, ropes, cordage, binding fiber, twisted silk, thongs or straps. If there is a preference, perhaps it would be for the single-bond tie. It is stout, and, in its unity, aesthetically attractive. Second only to the absolute helplessness of the female in her ties, in the Gorean mind, is the attractiveness of her bonds. They should be used to enhance her beauty as well as to imprison it with absolute perfection.

These yoke ties, incidentally, are not to be confused with a stock tie, or a stock yoke. This is normally a pair of hinged planks, with matched, semicircular openings in the planks. The girl's wrists and neck are placed appropriately between the planks, aligned with the semicircular openings. The planks are then closed and tied or locked shut. Her neck and wrists, then, of course, helplessly, are fixed in place. They find themselves enclosed in effective and perfect constraints. This yoke is sometimes placed on a girl while she is on her back. If the planks are sufficiently wide the girl cannot see what the man is doing to her. She can only feel it. Similar sensations may be induced in a woman by putting her in a slave hood. She may then either be bound or not, as the master pleases.

"Nonetheless," she said, "I am free!"

"How do you know?" I asked.

"I am not branded," she said uncertainly.

"You do not need to be branded to be a slave," I said. "Surely you know that."

"Rescue me," she said. "Free me! I will pay you much!"

I smiled. Did this lovely agent of Kurii really think that I might even consider freeing her?

"Free me!" she said. "I will pay you much!"

"Did you enjoy being struck?" I asked.

"No!" she said.

"You will then answer my questions truthfully, directly and clearly," I told her.

"What do you wish to know?" she asked.

"You are beautiful in the yoke," I said.

"Thank you," she said, uncertainly.

"It becomes you," I said.

"Thank you," she whispered.

"You might have been born a slave," I said.

She looked at me. "Thank you," she said.

"Describe to me, in brief compass, the course of the battle," I said.

I turned about, for I had heard a small noise behind me. Several of the Waniyanpi had now come to the vicinity of the wagon.

"I see you have found her," said Pumpkin.

"Yes," I said. I noted that neither he, nor the other Waniyanpi, looked obviously and directly on the woman, though she was beautiful and bound. "Was it you," I asked, "who stripped this beauty?"

"No, no," said Pumpkin, hastily. "That was done by the red masters."

"It must have been you, then," I said, "who yoked her, and so prettily and well."

"No, no!" said Pumpkin, hastily. "That, too, was done by the red masters."

"I see," I said. I had surmised, of course, that it would not have been the Waniyanpi who had removed the woman's clothing, or who had secured her, so simply, yet so efficiently and brilliantly.

"We did, however," said Pumpkin, "tether her behind the wagon, looking away from her as much as possible, that we would not have to look at her."

"The red masters permitted this?" I asked.

"Yes," said Pumpkin. "In amusement, they acceded to our pleas."

"That was kind of them," I said.

"Yes," said Pumpkin.

"Describe to me the course of the battle, as you understand it," I said to the stripped, blond captive, giving her once again my attention.

"Please," she said, "who are these people? They do not even look at me. Am I so ugly or repulsive?"

"You are neither ugly nor repulsive," I said. "In a common Gorean market you would bring a good price for a medium-grade slave girl. Accordingly, you are quite beautiful."

"Who are they?" she whispered. "Are they men?"

"They are called Waniyanpi," I said, "which in Dust Leg and Kaiila means 'tame cattle.' "

"Are they men?" she asked.

"That is an interesting question," I said. "I do not know."

The girl shuddered. Of Gorean birth, she was unfamiliar, in numbers, at least, with such organisms. Had she been of Earth origin, of course, she would have been far less startled, for then such creatures would have been much more familiar to her. In the polluted meadows of Earth graze numerous Waniyanpi.

"Begin," I told her.

"We feared nothing," she said. "Our forces, we believed, were invincible. We did not anticipate trouble. Surely it would be insanity to attack us. Insufficient pickets were put out. Watches were not well kept."

"Go on," I said.

"Ten days ago, today, as I have counted this," she said, "the attack took place. It began near the eighth Ahn. The wagons had been aligned. The tharlarion were harnessed. A small group of red savages, mounted, was seen to the southeast. Alfred, captain of Port Olni, commanding two hundred riders, for sport as much as anything, rode forth to frighten them away. We climbed on the wagons to watch."

Alfred, of course, should not have personally commanded the excursion. That expedition, if it had been mounted at all, should have been led by a junior officer.

"In a moment, then, behind us, suddenly, rising from the grass, on foot, screaming, brandishing weapons, there arose, it seemed, hundreds of savages. They had crawled to these positions through the grass. The grass seemed alive with them. They swept through the wagons. The most fearful things, I think, happened with the larger wagons, those with the families, to the west. They were almost defenseless. My own wagon was with the soldiers. In the southeast, then, rising from the gullies and draws, there suddenly seemed hundreds of riders. Alfred had been lured into a trap. He, suddenly finding himself disastrously outnumbered, wheeled about and, pursued, fled back to the wagons. I think he lost many men. When he reached our camp the wagons to the west were already aflame. He would not rush to their relief. He rallied his men and ordered a retreat to the north. It had been from this direction that the savages had attacked on foot."

"What of the infantry?" I asked.

"It must fend for itself," she said.

I nodded. It was not difficult to follow Alfred's thinking. The savages on foot would not be able to stop the cavalry, and the pursuers from the south or southeast might be detained at the wagons. It was there, of course, that they would encounter the unsupported infantry.

"Drivers leaped from the wagon boxes, fleeing for their lives," she said. "I cried out. My own driver was nowhere to be seen. The tharlarion, frightened in the turmoil, hitched up, moved this way and that with the wagons, mostly toward the east, away from the smoke and noise. I lost my footing. I regained it, in the wagon. I could not stop the tharlarion. The reins were not in my grasp. I was dragged a quarter of a pasang before the wagon stopped, through soldiers, through wagons and other men. I saw one of the infantrymen kill a cavalryman, striking him from behind with his pike, and take his kaiila. Alfred turned his mounted forces to the north, but, to his dismay, he saw that his plan had been anticipated. From the north, now, and the west, came new swarms of mounted red savages."

I nodded. Certainly the savages would have anticipated an attempted escape in the sector where they had appeared to position what, in effect, was their temporary infantry. The planning that had gone into the attack revealed intelligent and careful thought. In particular the placement and timing of the attacks showed a fine sense for what might be the likely directions and phases of a battle's development. Tactical instructions in a melee, incidentally, are normally administered to the red savages, in their units, commonly warrior societies, or divisions of such societies, by blasts on a whistle, formed from the wing bone of the taloned Herlit, or movements of a long, feathered battle staff.

"Confused men swept about my wagon. I saw Alfred, turning about, wheeling this way and that, on his kaiila. I put out my hand to him. I cried out to him. He looked at me, but then paid me no attention. Infantrymen, here and there, were fighting cavalrymen for their mounts. The cavalrymen, cursing, slashed down at them. The savages from the south and southeast had struck against the lines of infantrymen with their lances. The lines had held."

I nodded, encouraging her to speak. Gorean infantry, with staggered lines and fixed pikes, their butts anchored in the earth, could usually turn an attack of light cavalry.

"I cried out again to Alfred, but he paid me no attention," she said.

The red savages, I speculated, would have been surprised that they had been unable to force their way through the infantry lines. Such lines, of course, can usually be outflanked.

"Men seemed everywhere," she said. "There was the clash of arms, the squealing of kaiila. The savages now from the north and west swept through the wagons. Some passed within feet of me. Some were naked, none seemed to wear more than the breechclout. They screamed hideously. They were covered with paint, and their mounts, too. Feathers were in their hair, and tied, too, in the silken hair of their beasts. I saw a man's brains struck out not more than a few feet from me."

"What of the beasts from your own wagons," I asked, "those who can bear arms, who can go on two feet when they choose?"

She looked up at me.

"I know of them," I said. "Speak." I slapped the quirt solidly into my palm. I would not have had the least compunction in laying it liberally to the beauty of my fair interlocutress.

She seemed frightened.

"How many of them were there?" I asked.

"Seventeen," she said.

"What became of them?" I asked.

"When the battle began they emerged from their wagons," she said. "Some killed some of the men about, even our own soldiers, who did not know what they were. Some fought savages. Some were slain by savages. Some, in a small group, together, made their way northward, through the fighting. The savages seemed, on the whole, reluctant to attack them."

"How many escaped?" I asked.

"I do not know," she said. "Perhaps seven, perhaps eight."

This report seemed congruent with what I had learned from Pumpkin and the Waniyanpi, and with my own conjectures.

"Continue," I said to the girl.

"Taking advantage of the confusion, momentary, among the red savages, following their failure to break the line of the infantry, Alfred ordered his men through his own infantry lines, and led them again to the southeast. His action disrupted the infantry, trampling soldiers, buffeting them aside. The red savages then poured through the breached line. Some perhaps pursued the escaping column but most, I think, remained to finish their battle with the infantry, with which they were then, following the escape of Alfred, much embroiled."

"Too," I said, "they would presumably not wish to give the infantry a chance to reform, to close its lines again and set up a solid perimeter."

She shrugged. "Perhaps not," she whispered. "Then it seemed, again, that all about me were hurtling kaiila and screaming savages, and paint and feathers."

"These were doubtless the concerted forces of the red savages," I said, "being applied to the destruction of the infantry."

"I think so," she said.

"Were there any survivors?" I asked.

"I do not think so," she said.

"Alfred made good his escape?" I asked.

"I think so," she said.

"How many men did he have with him?" I asked.

"I do not know," she said. "Perhaps three hundred, perhaps four hundred."

"What did you do?" I asked.

"I lay down in the wagon, and hid," she said. "They found me later, in the afternoon, after the battle. Two men pulled me forth from the wagon bed. They thrust back my veils and hood. I was thrown to my knees on the grass and one of the men held my wrists, crossed, before my body. The other drew back a heavy club, the termination of which contained a heavy, wooden, ball-like knob. They were preparing, apparently, to dash out my brains. A word was spoken. The men stepped back. I looked up to see a tall savage, mounted astride a kaiila. It was he who had spoken. He motioned for me to rise and, unsteadily, terrified, I did so. These men were all hideous, and fearful, in their paint and feathers. He said another word and, in a moment, I had been stripped before him, absolutely naked. He then leaned down from the back of the beast and pointed to its forepaws. I shrank back, frightened. He said another word and again, suddenly, I was much as I had been before, only now stripped, kneeling on the grass, my hands crossed and held before me by one man, the other readying his club to strike out my brains. 'No, no,' I cried, 'please, no!' The man on the kaiila again spoke, and again I was released. Once more he pointed to the forepaws of his kaiila." She shuddered. She stopped speaking. There were tears in her eyes. I saw that it would be difficult for her to continue.

"Yes?" I said.

"Must I continue?" she asked.

"Yes," I said. I did not see fit to show mercy to her. She was a slave.

"This time," she said, "I crawled to them on my belly. I put down my head. I kissed the beast's paws. I licked and sucked them. I cleaned them of dirt and dust with my teeth, even the nails."

"Excellent," I said.

She looked at me, dismayed.

"Yes," I said, "excellent."

She put down her head.

The woman, of course, had been being assessed for slavery. First, she had been stripped. In this, once the garments, and the tiresome robes of concealment, had been removed from her, once she had been exposed to the view of masters, fully, it had been determined that her face and figure, in themselves, did not militate against the plausibility of her being imbonded; they were desirable enough, other things being equal, to be of interest to men. They were good enough, other things being equal, to own. There are many beautiful women, of course. Beauty, strictly, is not even a necessary condition for bondage, let alone a sufficient condition for it. Many women, in fact, do not even become beautiful, truly beautiful, until after they have been collared.

In the second portion of her test, she had been commanded. On her knees, stripped, held, the club being lifted, she had become aware of the consequences of failing this second portion of her test. She had then, in effect, petitioned that this second portion of her test be readministered to her. She had begged then, in effect, to be given a second chance to prove her suitability for slavery. This chance, in the mercy of her captors, had been given to her. She had crawled to the paws of the savage's kaiila and there, on her belly, cleaned them with her tongue and mouth. This was a behavior suitable for a slave, even one who was not, at the moment, desperately striving to save her own life. Her performance at the paws of the kaiila had apparently been adjudged adequate by the savages. She knelt now before me, alive.

The significance of the test is clear. In performing such intimate acts, and on the mere beast of the master, the humbled suppliant, the captured girl, acknowledges to both herself and others, nonrepudiably and publicly, that she is proposing herself as a serious candidate for bondage, that she is begging to be enslaved. Too, of course, such performances give the master an opportunity to observe the touch, the sensitivity, the techniques and skill of the girl. If she cannot even function at the paws of a kaiila what should one expect in one's own furs? If she cannot even do well with an animal, what reason is there to expect that she could do better with a man? The most significant aspect of this test, of course, is that it gives masters a means for determining not only whether or not the girl is truly begging to be enslaved but, more importantly, whether or not she is, truly, a slave. No girl is regarded as having passed this test who has not, in her performances, made it clear to all, save perhaps herself, that it is truly a slave who lies at the paws of the kaiila. This revelation becomes manifest through subtle behavioral cues, usually physical, but sometimes verbal, as well.

I regarded the woman kneeling before me. That her brains had not been dashed out by the club of the savage indicated to me not only that she had, intimately and lengthily, in her performances, petitioned to be enslaved, but that she had, in these same performances, proved herself a slave. I wondered if she knew that she was a slave. I surmised that she still thought herself free. This delusion could always be dispelled at the convenience of a master. In the beginning, incidentally, the cues which reveal slavery in a woman can sometimes be subtle. Later, of course, as she grows in her slavery, as she realizes that her deepest and most profound nature may not only be revealed, but must be revealed, that it is not only permissible to reveal her womanhood, but that it must be revealed, and fully, she, in accord with this liberation, undergoes a marvelous transformation; she tends to become vital and sensuous, and loving, and happy. This is a beautiful transformation to see in a woman. Happy is he who has a slave.

"After your performances," I said, "doubtless you expected to be well and lengthily ravished."

"Yes," she said, "almost from the first moment I felt the warm grass under my belly, almost from the first moment I put my mouth to the paws of that beast."

"And were you?" I asked.

"No," she said, angrily. "I was bound, and given to these people."

"I see," I said. I had thought that it would be so.

"Do not fear," said Pumpkin to the stripped beauty, kneeling in the primitive yoke, well fastened in it, "your trials and tribulations, your embarrassments, your hardships, your miseries, will soon be over."

"Do not slay me," she begged.

"That may be done to you, if Masters wish," I told her.

She turned white. I saw that, on some level, she understood that she was a slave.

"But you are very fortunate," said one of the Waniyanpi.

"The masters have seen fit to show you mercy," said another.

"At least for the time," said another.

"Masters?" she asked.

"Your masters, and ours," said Pumpkin, "Bondwoman."

"Bondwoman!" she cried, struggling in the yoke. But she

did not try to rise to her feet. I think this was because I was present.

"Yes," said Pumpkin.

"We are going to call her Turnip," said one of the Waniyanpi.

"I am a free woman," she cried. "I am the Lady Mira, of the City of Venna!"

I smiled to myself. How naive seemed the kneeling slave, Turnip.

"By the instructions of our masters," said Pumpkin, "you are to be taken as you are, yoked and unclothed, to the compound."

"Compound?" she asked.

"Yes, Garden Eleven, our home," said Pumpkin.

"You will be happy there," said one of the Waniyanpi.

"We all are," insisted another.

"Unfortunately," said Pumpkin, "you are to be taken there on a tether, marched across the grasslands, without clothing and in your yoke, much as might be any common Gorean slave, whose slavery is being impressed upon her."

"And, doubtlessly," she said, acidly, "I will give you much pleasure on the trek."

"We will look forward to the pleasure of your company," said one of them.

"I see," she said.

"I do not think you do," I said, "at least as yet."

"Do not fear," said Pumpkin. "You will be treated, at all times, with total dignity and respect."

"We will not even look at you, at least not directly," said another.

"That is," said another, "until your shame has been covered."

"Shame?" asked the girl.

"Your beauty, your prettiness," explained another.

"Not all the Sames, those who have the unimportant and negligible property of femaleness, are as—as healthy appearing as you," said another.

"Thus you might make them feel that they were not the same as you, or that you were not the same as they," said another.

"They would not like that," said another.

"It is shameful not to make people feel they are the same," said another.

"Because everyone is the same, really," said another, "of course."

"Of course," said another.

"Too," said Pumpkin, "it can trouble the Sames who have the unimportant and negligible property of maleness. It may make them have certain kinds of feelings."

"Not me," said one of the Waniyanpi.

"Nor I," said another. "I never have such feelings."

"But not all of us," said Pumpkin, "are as strong and good as Carrot and Cabbage."

"I myself," said another, "can look on such things and not have the least feeling."

A chorus of admiration thrilled the Waniyanpi.

"Nor as Beans," said Pumpkin. "But for some of us your healthy appearance can be extremely disturbing."

"It makes me sick," said another.

"It makes me ill, too, to look upon it," said another. "I threw up when first I saw it."

"Good," said another fellow.

"It disturbs me," said another fellow. "I admit that it is true."

"An honest confession," said Pumpkin. "You are to be congratulated on your candor and veracity. The next task is to seek improvement."

"Yes," said the fellow who had spoken, contritely. "Perhaps if I were permitted to look upon it more often I might manage to steel myself against it."

"Plunge rather into arduous, time-consuming, mind-occupying labors," said Pumpkin.

"And bathe often in cold streams," advised another.

The fellow looked down. I did not blame him. I myself did not relish bathing in cold streams. I preferred warm baths, being attended by a beautiful female slave. After all, should a free man be expected to apply his own oils, scrape the dirt from his own skin with the strigil and towel himself?

"You see," said Pumpkin to the captured girl, "your appearance, even if it were not so healthy looking, perhaps, can cause some of us to think certain thoughts and have certain feelings. It can even bring about movements in our bodies. This makes it harder to be Sames. And it is shameful not to be Sames."

"For we are Sames," said another. "Everyone knows that."

"And thus it is," said Pumpkin, "that your appearance can cause shame, and as it causes shame, it must be shameful."

"Too," said another, "it can distract from truly important things."

"Such as being Sames," said another.

"Yes," said Pumpkin.

The girl shuddered, convinced perhaps that she was in the presence of lunatics. Madness is an interesting concept. As some define it, it is a function of the social conventions obtaining at a given time. In the country of the mad, thusly, only the sane will be accounted insane. Acquiescence to contemporary axiological conventions, of course, is not the only possible conceptual approach to such matters. Another approach might be to envision a world compatible with reality and congenial to human nature, a world in which science, even social science, might be free, a world in which truth would not be against the law, a world designed not for the crippling, distortion and torture of humanity but for its fulfillment.

"But do not fear," said Pumpkin to the girl, "for, soon, when we reach the compound, you will be decently clothed."

"Like you?" she asked. She regarded the long, gray, coarse, clumsy dresses on the Waniyanpi with distaste.

"These garments help us to suppress our desires and keep us humble," said one of the Waniyanpi.

"We are reminded by them that we are all Sames," said another.

"That we all, when all is said and done," said another, "are naught but Waniyanpi."

This seemed to make sense to me. The human being has a tendency to be consistent, no matter from what eccentric premises he may begin. He will normally behave in a way, accordingly, that befits his clothing. This is perhaps the deeper sense of the English expression that clothing makes the man.

"Better to be stripped and have a string of hide tied on one's neck!" said the girl, angrily.

"What is done to those in your compound who are not the same?" I asked.

"We attempt to convert them," said one of the men.

"We plead with them. We reason with them," said another.

"And what if you cannot convince them of the glories of sameness?" I asked.

"We then drive them out, into the Barrens, to die," said another.

"It grieves us to do so," said another.

"But it must be done," said another.

"The contagion of their heresy must not be permitted to infect others," said another.

"The good of the whole must take precedence over the good of the parts," said another.

"You kill them?" I asked.

"No!" cried one.

"We cannot kill!" said another.

"It is against the Teaching," said another.

"But you banish them, on the supposition that they will perish in the Barrens," I said.

"Thusly, it is the Barrens which kills them, not us," said another.

"We are thus innocent," said another.

"Such banishment is acceptable to the Teaching?" I asked.

"Of course," said another. "How else is the compound to be ridded of them?"

"You must understand," said another, "it does not please us to do that sort of thing."

"It is done only after every other alternative has been exhausted," said another.

"Difference strikes at the root of sameness," said another. "Sameness is essential to civilization itself. Difference, thus, threatens society and civilization itself."

"It must thus be eradicated," said another.

"There is, thus, only one value, one virtue?" I asked.

"Yes," said another.

"One is one," said another, profoundly, "self-identical and the same."

"Sixteen is sixteen, too," I said.

"But sixteen is only sixteen times one, and thus all reduces to one, which is one," said another.

"What about one-half and one-half?" I asked.

"They add up to one," said another.

"What about one-third and one-third, then?" I asked.

"Each of those is but one number," said another, "and, thus, each is one, and one is one."

"What of the diversity you see about you," I asked, "say, of kaiila and sleen?"

"One kaiila and one sleen are both one, which is one," said another fellow.

"What about zero and one?" I asked.

"Zero is one number and one is one number, and thus each is one, and one is one," said another.

"What about nothing and one?" I asked.

"One is one, and nothing is nothing," said another, "so one is left with one, which is one."

"But you would have at least one nothing, wouldn't you?" I asked.

"Nothing is either nothing or one," said another. "If it is nothing, then it is nothing. If it is one, then it is one, and one is one," said another.

"Thus, all is the same," said another.

"You are spouting total gibberish," I said. "Are you aware of that?"

"To the unenlightened profundity often appears gibberish," said another.

"Indeed," said another, "and to some who have lost their enlightenment it can also appear gibberish."

"The more absurd something seems, the more likely it is to be true," said another.

"That seems absurd," I said.

"And, thus," said the fellow, "it, in itself, by the same proof, is shown most likely to be true."

"Is that supposed to be self-evident?" I asked.

"Yes," said another.

"It is not self-evident to me," I said.

"That is not the fault of its self-evidence," said another. "You cannot blame its self-evidence for that."

"Something which is self-evident to one person may not be self-evident to another," said another fellow.

"How can it be self-evident to one and not to another?" I asked.

"One may be more talented in the detecting of self-evidence than another," said another.

"How do you distinguish between what merely seems self-evident and that which is truly self-evident?" I asked.

"The Priest-Kings would not deceive us," said another.

"How do you know?" I asked.

"That is self-evident," said another.

"Have you ever been mistaken about what is self-evident?" I asked.

"Yes, frequently," said Pumpkin.

"How do you explain that?" I asked.

"We are weak, and frail," he said.

"We are only Waniyanpi," said another.

I regarded Pumpkin.

"To be sure," he said, "there is a place for faith in all of this."

"A rather large place, I conjecture," I said.

"Large enough," he said.

"How large is that?" I asked.

"Large enough to protect the Teaching," he said.

"I thought so," I said.

"One must believe something," said Pumpkin.

"Why not experiment with the truth?" I said.

"We already believe the truth," said one of the fellows about.

"How do you know?" I asked.

"The Teaching tells us," said another.

"You must understand," said another, "that we do not like putting people out to die. It makes us very sorry to do this. On the occasions of an expulsion we often eat a meal in silence, and weep bitter tears into our gruel."

"I am sure it is a touching sight," I said.

Pumpkin looked down toward the girl. He did not look directly at her, but she knew herself to be the object of his attention, indirect though that attention might have been.

"Teach me your Teaching," she said. "I want to be a Same."

"Wonderful," said Pumpkin. He almost reached out to touch her, so pleased he was, but suddenly, fearfully, he drew back his hand. He blushed. There was sweat on his forehead.

"Excellent," said more than one of the Waniyanpi.

"You will not regret it," said another.

"You will love being a Same," said another.

"It is the only thing to be," said another.

"When we reach the vicinity of the compound," said Pumpkin, "and you are unbound and properly clothed, in suitable Waniyanpi garb, you will lead us all through the gate, preceding us, this thus attesting to your honor amongst us and the respect in which you are held."

"I shall look forward eagerly to my reception into the compound," said the girl.

"And so, too, shall we, welcome citizen," said Pumpkin.

He then turned to the others. "We must now return to our work," he said. "There is refuse to be gathered and debris to be burned."

When the Waniyanpi had filed away, taking their leave, I turned to regard the girl.

"They are mad," she said, "mad," squirming in the yoke.

"Perhaps," I said. "I suppose it is a matter of definition."

"Definition?" she said.

"If the norms of sanity are social norms," I said, "by definition, the norm is sane."

"Even if the society is totally misrelated to reality?" she asked.

"Yes," I said.

"Even if they think they are all urts, or lizards or clouds?"

"I gather so," I said, "and in such a society the one who does not think that he is an urt, or, say, a lizard or a cloud, would be accounted insane."

"And would be insane?" she asked.

"On that definition," I said.

"That is a preposterous definition," she said.

"Yes," I admitted.

"I do not accept it," she said.

"Nor do I," I admitted.

"Surely there can be a better," she said.

"I would hope so," I said, "one that was framed with a closer regard for empirical reality, the actual nature of human beings, and such."

"Someone is insane," she said, "who believes false things."

"But we all, doubtless, believe many false things," I said. "Theoretically a society could believe numerous false propositions and still, in normal senses of the word, be regarded as a sane, if, in many respects, a mistaken society."

"What if a society is mistaken, and takes pains to avoid rectifying its errors, what if it refuses, in the light of evidence, to correct its mistakes?"

"Evidence can usually be explained away or reinterpreted to accord with treasured beliefs," I said. "I think it is usually a matter of degree. Perhaps when the belief simply becomes too archaic, obsolete and unwieldy to defend, when it becomes simply preposterous and blatantly irrational to seriously continue to defend it, then, perhaps, if one still continues, compulsively, to defend it, one might speak of insanity."

"I should think so," she said.

"But even then," I said, "other concepts might be more fruitful, such as radical obstinacy or institutionalized irrationality."

"Why?" she asked.

"Because of the vagueness of the concept of insanity," I said, "and its often implicit reference to statistical norms. For example, an individual who believed in, say, magic, assuming that sense could be made of that concept, in a society which believed in magic, would not normally be accounted insane. Similarly, such a society, though it might be regarded as being deluded, would not, in all likelihood, be regarded as insane."

"What if there were such a thing as magic?" she asked.

"That society, then, would simply be correct," I said.

"What of these people who were just here?" she asked. "Are they not insane?"

"By carefully chosen definitions, I suppose we could define them into sanity or into insanity, depending on whether we approved of them or not, but it is difficult to derive satisfaction from victories which are achieved by the cheap device of surreptitiously altering a conceptual structure."

"I think they are mad, insane," she said.

"They are at least mistaken," I said, "and, in many respects, are different from us."

She shuddered.

"The most pernicious beliefs," I said, "are not actually beliefs at all, but, better put, pseudobeliefs. The pseudobelief is not assailable by evidence or reason, even theoretically. Its security from refutation is the result of its cognitive vacuity. It cannot be refuted for, saying nothing, nothing can be produced, even in theory, which could count against it. Such a belief is not strong, but empty. Ultimately it is little more, if anything, than a concatenation of words, a verbal formula. Men often fear to inquire into their nature. They tuck them away, and then content themselves with other concerns. Their anchors, they fear, are straw; their props, they fear, are reeds. Truth is praised, and judiciously avoided. Is this not human cleverness at its most remarkable? Who knows in what way the sword of truth will cut? Some men, it seems, would rather die for their beliefs than analyze them. I guess that it must be a very frightening thing to inquire into one's beliefs. So few people do it. Sometimes one grows weary of blood-stained twaddle. Battles of formulas, you see, as nothing can count against them, are too often decided by wounds and iron. Some men, we have noted, are willing to die for their beliefs. Even larger numbers, it seems, are willing to kill for them."

"It is not unknown for men to fight for false treasures," she said.

"That is true," I said.

"But, in the end," she said, "I do not think that the battles are fought for the formulas."

I regarded her.

"They are only standards and flags, carried into battle," she said, "stimulatory to the rabble, useful to the elite."

"Perhaps you are right," I said. I did not know. Human motivation is commonly complex. That she had responded as she had, however, whether she was right or wrong, reminded me that she was an agent of Kurii. Such folk commonly see things in terms of women, gold and power. I grinned down at her. This agent, stripped and in her yoke, was well neutralized before me. She was no longer a player in the game; she was now only a prize in it.

"Do not look at me like that," she said.

"I am not of the Waniyanpi," I said, "Female."

"Female!" she said.

"You had best begin to think of yourself in such terms," I said.

She twisted, angrily, in the yoke. Then she looked up at me. "Free me," she demanded.

"No," I said.

"I will pay you much," she said.

"No," I said.

"You could take me from these fools," she said.

"I suspect so," I said.

"Then carry me off with you," she said.

"Do you beg to be carried off?" I asked.

"Yes," she said.

"If I did so," I said, "it would be as a slave."

"Oh," she said.

"Do you still beg to be carried off?" I inquired.

"Yes," she said.

"As a surrendered slave," I asked, "a total and abject slave?"

"Yes!" she said.

"No," I said.

"No?" she said.

"No," I said.

"Take me with you," she begged.

"I am going to leave you precisely where you are," I said, "my lovely mercenary."

"Mercenary?" she said. "I am not a mercenary! I am the Lady Mira of Venna, of the Merchants!"

I smiled.

She shrank back on her heels. "What do you know of me?" she asked. "What are you doing in the Barrens? Who are you?"

"You look well in the yoke," I said.

"Who are you?" she said.

"A traveler," I said.

"You are going to leave me here, like this?" she asked.

"Yes," I said.

"I do not want to go to a compound of these people," she said. "They are insane, all of them."

"But you begged to be taken to their compound," I said, "to be taught their Teaching."

"I did not want to die," she said. "I did not want to be put out to die."

"You had best pretend well to believe their teaching," I said. "They would not, most likely, look lightly on being deceived in this respect."

"I do not want to live a life of hypocrisy," she said.

"Doubtless many live such a life in the compound of the Waniyanpi," I said.

"Should I try to believe their absurdities?" she asked.

"It might be easier on you, if you could," I said.

"But I am not a fool," she said.

"To be sure," I said, "it is easiest to subscribe to odd beliefs when they have been inculcated in childhood. The entrenchment of eccentric beliefs is commonly perpetrated most successfully on the innocent and defenseless, even more successfully than on the ignorant and desperate."

"I am afraid of them," she said.

"They will treat you with dignity and respect," I said, "as a Same."

"Better a collar in the cities," she said, "better to be abused and sold from a public platform, better to be a slave girl fearful and obedient at the feet of her master."

"Perhaps," I said.

"I am afraid of them," she whispered.

"Why?" I asked.

"Did you not see how they would not look at me? I am fraid they will make me ashamed of my own body."

"In all things," I said, "remember that you are beautiful."

"Thank you," she whispered.

To be sure, the danger of which she spoke was quite real. t was difficult for one's values not to be affected by the alues of those about them. Even the marvelous beauties and rofundities of human sexuality, I knew, incredibly enough, n some environments tended to trigger bizarre reactions of nxiety, embarrassment and shame. To the average Gorean uch reactions would seem incomprehensible. Perhaps such nvironments, apart from semantic niceties, might simply be egarded, if any, as insane. How tragic, in particular, it is, to ee such reactions being absorbed by children.

"Do you truly think I am beautiful?" she asked.

"Yes," I said.

"Then take me with you," she begged.

"No," I said.

"You would leave me with them?" she asked.

"Yes," I said.

"Why?" she asked.

"It amuses me," I said.

"Tarsk!" she cried.

I held the quirt before her face. "You may kiss it," I told er, "or be beaten with it."

She kissed the quirt, the supple, slim leather.

"Again," I told her, "lingeringly."

She complied. Then she looked up at me. "You called me mercenary," she said.

"I was wrong," I said. "You are only a former mercenary."

"And what am I now?" she asked.

"Surely you can guess," I said.

"No!" she said.

"Yes," I assured her.

She struggled in the yoke, unavailingly. "I am helpless," e said.

"Yes," I said.

She straightened her body. She tossed her head. "If you ok me with you," she said, "I would doubtless be your ave."

"Totally," I told her.

"It is fortunate for me, then," she said, "that I will accompany the Waniyanpi to their camp. There I will be free."

"The Waniyanpi are all slaves," I told her, "slaves of the red savages."

"Do the savages live in the compounds?" she asked.

"Not normally," I said. "They normally leave the Waniyanpi much alone. They do not much care, I think, to be around them."

"Then, for most practical purposes," she said, "they are slaves without masters."

"Perhaps," I said.

"Then I, too, would be a slave without a master," she said.

"For most practical purposes, for most of the time, I suppose," I said. The Waniyanpi, incidentally, are owned by tribes, not individuals. Their slavery, thus, is somewhat remote and impersonal. That one is owned by a collectivity, of course, may obscure one's slavery but, in the final analysis, it does not alter it. Some slaves believe they are not slaves, because their masters tell them so.

"That is the best sort of slave to be," she said, "one without a master."

"Is it?" I asked. Lonely and unfulfilled is the slave without a master.

"When I was taken prisoner," she said, "I feared I would be made a slave, a true slave. I feared a tether would be put on my neck and I would be run to the camp of a master, sweating at the lathered flank of his kaiila, that there I would be his, to be dressed, and worked and used as he pleased. I feared that hard labors and degradation would be mine. I feared that a beaded collar would be tied on my neck. I feared that I would be subject to ropes and whips, unsparingly applied if I were in the least bit unpleasing. Mostly I feared being alone with him in his lodge, where I must, at his smallest indication, serve him intimately, and abjectly and lengthily, as his least whim might dictate, with the full attentiveness and services of the female slave. You can imagine my terrors at the mere thought of finding myself so helplessly belonging to a man, so helplessly in his power, so helplessly subject to his mastery and domination."

"Of course," I said.

"And so it is," she said, "that I rejoice that I am to be spared all that. I am astonished at my good fortune. How foolish were the red savages to be so lenient with me!"

"They are not fools," I said.

"They took other girls," she said, "I heard, to their camps."

"Yes," I said.

"That was not done with me," she said.

"No," I said.

"They spared me," she said.

"Did they?" I asked.

"I do not understand," she said.

"You were found with the soldiers," I said. I then turned rom her and mounted the kaiila.

"Yes?" she asked.

"The other girls were simply made slaves," I said. "They vill now have the honor of serving worthy masters."

"And I?" she asked.

"You, being found with the soldiers," I said, "and obvi-usly a personage of some importance, were singled out for unishment."

"Punishment?" she asked.

"Yes," I said. Indeed, I thought to myself, how much the ed savages must hate the soldiers, and those with them, and ow subtle and insidious they had been.

"But I am to be respected and accorded dignity," she said, neeling below me in the grass, in her yoke. "I am to be sent • live with Waniyanpi!"

"That is your punishment," I said. I then turned the kaiila bout, and left her behind me, in the grass, in her yoke.

18

CUWIGNAKA;

SLEEN, YELLOW KNIVES AND KAIILA

"This is the lad of whom the Waniyanpi spoke," said Grunt. I joined my party on the crest of a small rise, at the eastern edge of the field of battle. He was some twenty years of age, naked, and staked out in the grass. Near him, on a lance thrust butt down in the turf, there was wound a white cloth. This marked the place in the grass where he had been secured. I did not understand, at that time, the significance of this form of marker, nor of the cloth.

"Is this the fellow you thought it might be?" asked Grunt.

"Yes," I said, looking down at the young man. "He is the one who was with the column." He was not now chained. His chains had been removed. He was now secured in a fashion more familiar to the Barrens.

"He is Dust Leg," said Grunt.

"I do not think so," I said. "Do you speak Gorean?" I asked him.

The young man opened his eyes, and then closed them.

"I have spoken Dust Leg to him, and Kaiila, and some Fleer," said Grunt. "He does not respond."

"Why?" I asked.

"We are white," said Grunt.

"He is not in good condition," I said.

"I do not think he will last much longer," said Grunt. "The Waniyanpi, doubtless by instruction, have given him little in the way of water or sustenance."

I nodded. They were to keep him alive until they left the field, as I recalled. Then he was to be left to die. I glanced from the rise back down into the shallow declivity between the low, grassy hills. I could see the Waniyanpi there, gathering and piling debris. I could see the remains of some wagons, too, and that behind which I had left the girl in the yoke.

"Do not consider interfering," said Grunt.

I went to my pack kaiila and fetched a verrskin water bag. It was half full.

"He is in the care of the Waniyanpi," said Grunt.

I bent down beside the lad, and put one hand gently behind his head. He opened his eyes, looking at me. I think it took him some moments to focus.

"He is in the care of the Waniyanpi," said Grunt.

"He does not seem to me well cared for," I said.

"Do not interfere," said Grunt.

"His body shows signs of dehydration," I said. I had seen this sort of thing in the Tahari. I had, from my own experience, some inkling of the suffering which could accompany this sort of deprivation.

"Do not," said Grunt.

Gently, cradling it partly in my arm, I lifted the water bag. The liquid moved inside the leather.

The lad took some of the water into his mouth and I withdrew the bag. He looked at me. Then, suddenly, with hatred, he turned his head to the side and spat out the water into the grass. He then lay back again, as he had before, his eyes closed. I stood up.

"Leave him," said Grunt.

"He is proud," I said, "proud, like a warrior."

"It would have done nothing anyway," said Grunt, "but prolong his agony."

"What is the significance of this lance," I asked, "with the cloth wound about it?"

"It is a warrior's lance," said Grunt. "Do you not see what the cloth is?"

"It is part of the loot from the wagon train, it seems," I said. The cloth was white. It did not seem to be trade cloth.

"You are probably right," said Grunt. "But do you not see what it is?"

I looked more closely. "It is a woman's dress," I said.

"Yes," said Grunt.

I returned to the pack kaiila, and restored the water bag to its place.

"We must be on our way," said Grunt, nervously. "There have been Waniyanpi about, from various compounds," he said.

I recalled that we had obtained this information earlier from the Waniyanpi with whom we had conversed. Then, too, this had seemed to disturb Grunt. Its significance, as I now recognize, was clear. Interestingly, at the time, I did not fully appreciate its import.

"What are you doing!" said Grunt.

"We cannot leave him here like this," I said. I crouched beside the lad, my knife drawn.

"Do not kill him," said Grunt. "That is the business of the prairie, of thirst, of hunger, or roving sleen."

"Stop!" said Grunt.

My knife was at the leather thongs binding the lad's left ankle to its stake.

"You understand nothing of the Barrens," said Grunt. "Leave him alone. Do not interfere!"

"We cannot leave him here like this," I said.

"The Waniyanpi would have done so," said Grunt.

"I am not of the Waniyanpi," I said.

"See the lance, the dress," said Grunt.

"What are their significance?" I asked.

"He did not support his comrades in arms," said Grunt. "He did not join them on the warpath."

"I see," I said. He who refuses to fight, of course, permits others to do his fighting for him. He lets others take the risks, sometimes grievous and perilous, which it is his duty to accept and share. Why are others less special and precious than he? The moral stature of such an individual I leave to the conjecture of others. The heinous exploitation of others implicit in such a behavior, incidentally, seems seldom to have been noticed. All things considered, it does not really take much courage to be a coward. Such a behavior, generalized, of course, means the destruction of the community. Thus, paradoxically, only in a community of the brave can the coward thrive. His very prosperity he owes to the community he betrays.

"But the lance is not broken," I said.

"No," said Grunt.

"Of what tribe is the lance?" I asked.

"Kaiila," he said. "This may be told by the binding, and by the lateral red marks near the head of the shaft."

"I see," I said.

My knife then finished cutting the thongs at the lad's left ankle.

I then went to the thongs at his right ankle.

"Stop," said Grunt.

"No," I said.

I heard the cable of a crossbow being drawn above and behind me. It was then fixed in place. The quarrel was then laid in the guide.

"Will you truly loose your shaft at me?" I asked Grunt, not turning about.

"Do not force me to fire," he said.

"We cannot leave him here like this," I said.

"I do not wish to fire," said Grunt.

"Do not fear," I told him. "You will not do so."

I heard the quarrel removed from the guide, and the cable's surcease of tension.

"We cannot leave him here like this," I said.

I then went to the thongs on the boy's left wrist.

"Your friend must care for you deeply," he said, in Gorean. "He did not kill you."

"You speak Gorean," I smiled.

"You are fortunate to have such a friend," said the lad.

"Yes," I said.

"Do you know what you are doing?" asked the lad.

"Probably not," I said.

"I did not take the warpath," he said.

"Why not?" I asked.

"I had no quarrel with the Fleer," he said.

"That is between you and your people," I said.

"Do not free me," he said.

My knife paused.

"Why not?" I asked.

"I have not been staked out in order to be freed," he said.

I did not respond to this. Then my knife finished cutting

through the thongs on his left wrist. In a moment I had cut through the thongs, too, at his right wrist.

"I am a slave," he said. "Now I am your slave."

"No," I said. "You are free."

"Free?" he asked.

"Yes," I said. "I free you. You are free."

"Free?" he asked, numbly.

"Yes," I said.

He rolled to his side, scarcely able to move.

I stood up, and sheathed my knife.

"Now you have done it," said Grunt, glumly.

"You knew we could not simply leave him here like that," I said.

"I?" asked Grunt.

"Yes," I said. "Why else would you have come to this hill?"

"Do you think I am weak?" he asked.

"No," I said. "I think you are strong."

"We are fools," he said.

"Why?" I asked.

"Look," he said.

Approaching from three directions were groups of mounted warriors, some fifteen or twenty in each group, lofty on their kaiila, barbarous in their paint and feathers.

"Sleen, and Yellow Knives," said Grunt, "and Kaiila, too."

"You are Kaiila, aren't you?" I asked the lad.

"Yes," said he. I had thought he would be. I did not think that Dust Legs, from whom he had been purchased by whites, near the Ihanke, would have sold one of their own tribe into slavery. The lance near him, too, that about which was wound the white dress, was, according to Grunt, a lance from that tribe. It was Kaiila, thus, presumably, who had fastened him down.

"I feared this," said Grunt. "There were several groups of Waniyanpi about. We heard that. Naturally, then, keepers for them would be in the vicinity, in force. We saw smoke coming to this place. Too, to the southeast, now, there is smoke."

"Yes," I said, now noticing it.

"That is camp smoke," said Grunt, "cooking for the evening meal."

I nodded. I now, for the first time, fully, understood Grunt's earlier noticed lack of ease.

"Surely we have broken no law," I said.

"They have superior advantages in numbers and arms," said Grunt. "I do not think they need more law than that."

"And you have freed me," said the lad, sitting on the grass, rubbing his wrists and ankles. I was surprised that he could sit up.

"You are strong," I observed.

"I am Kaiila," he said.

"Surely there is no law to the effect that you should not be freed," I said.

"There is no law specifically to that effect," he said, "but I would not count on their being much pleased about it."

"I can understand that," I said. Scanning, I noted the approaching groups of riders. I counted fifty-one riders, in all.

"If there were such a law," asked the youth, "would you have broken it?"

"Yes," I said.

"The nearest are Sleen," said Grunt. "Those to the south are Yellow Knives. From the east approach Kaiila."

The lad tried to climb to his feet, but fell. Then, again, he struggled upwards. He then stood. I supported him. He seemed to be very strong for one so young.

"You are Kaiila," said Grunt.

"Yes," said the youth.

"We will expect you, then," said Grunt, "to intercede for us with the Kaiila."

"It was they who staked me out," he said.

"Oh," said Grunt.

I smiled to myself. I had feared as much.

"They may want only gifts," said Grunt.

I watched the unhurried advance of the groups of riders. They were giving us time to consider their approach. There seemed a subtle menace in this leisured advance, in this time and in this place.

"Only generous gifts, hopefully," said Grunt.

"It will be my people who will be the most dangerous," said the youth, with pride.

I was not at all sure that that was the case.

"What is your name?" asked Grunt.

"Your people called me 'Utt'," he said. "The Dust Legs called me 'Nitoske'."

"Woman's Dress," said Grunt. "Quick, Lad, what do the Kaiila call you? We cannot call you 'Woman's Dress.'"

"Cuwignaka," said the lad.

Grunt spit disgustedly into the grass.

"What is wrong?" I asked.

"It means the same, only in Kaiila," said Grunt. "Moreover, in both dialects, it is actually the word for a white woman's dress."

"Wonderful," I said. "What shall we call you?" I asked the lad.

"Cuwignaka," he said. "Woman's Dress."

"Very well," I said.

"It is my name," he said.

"Very well," I said.

Then the savages were about us. With a rattle of chain the girls in the coffle, whimpering, huddled together. I was prodded in the shoulder with the butt of a lance. I stood my ground as well as I could. I knew they were looking for the least sign of anger or resistance.

"Smile," said Grunt. "Smile."

I could not smile, but, too, I did not offer resistance.

19

IN THE DISTANCE;

THERE IS THE SMOKE OF COOKING FIRES

Evelyn cried out with misery as the tether was knotted about her neck. Her small wrists pulled futilely at the bonds which held her hands confined behind her back. Then, stumbling, she was thrust beside Ginger, and Max and Kyle Hobart. All had been stripped.

"Hi," cried the Sleen warrior, a high warrior in their war party, and kicked back into the flanks of his kaiila. The animal squealed and snorted, moving to the side and then forward. In a moment it was following the line of withdrawing warriors, led by their war-party leader, he followed by the banner-bearer, carrying the crooklike, feathered staff, used in giving directions in battle, and then the others.

It was he, it seemed, who would lead them in triumph into their camp. He held the tethers of the Hobarts, and Ginger and Evelyn. Two other Sleen, too, then followed, who would bring up the rear, riding behind the column, some yards behind the captives.

Grunt stood behind, his fists clenched.

Near Grunt, on their stomachs, stripped, lying in a standard binding position, their ankles crossed and their wrists held crossed behind them, placed in a tandem line, head to feet, one after the other, were Corinne, Lois, Inez and Priscilla. Priscilla made a tiny noise and winced as a Yellow-Knife

warrior, kneeling across her body, tied her wrists behind her
back. One ties the last girl in such a tandem line first. That
way the other girls are less likely to bolt. A girl, thus, does
not see the girl before her bound until she herself has been
bound.

I watched the withdrawal of the Sleen war party. They
were well pleased with their share of the loot. Ginger and Evelyn were lovely prizes and the Hobarts would doubtless
prove useful in heavy work and, as boys, minding the kaiila
herds.

The Yellow-Knife warrior now tied Inez's hands behind
her back.

The coffle chains and the manacles which had bound the
Hobarts lay discarded in the grass.

The red-haired girl was on her hands and knees in the
grass, naked, warriors, some on foot, some astride kaiila, Yellow Knives and Kaiila, gathered about her.

Lois's hands were tied behind her back.

"Hopa," said one of the Kaiila warriors, one mounted, a
tall, broad-shouldered fellow, with long braids, tied with red
cloth, looking down on the red-haired girl. He touched her on
the left arm with his long-bladed lance, the blade of tapering,
bluish, chipped flint. She looked up at him, frightened, and
then, unable to meet his eyes, quickly lowered her head.
"Wihopawin," commented the warrior.

A Yellow Knife crouched near the girl.

The mounted Kaiila warrior said something to Pimples,
whom, it had been quickly established, in the interchanges,
was conversant in Kaiila. "Ho, Itancanka," said Pimples. She
then quickly went to the red-haired girl and knelt her, with
her hands behind the back of her head and her head back.
"Breasts out," she told her in Gorean. The red-haired girl
then knelt in this fashion, with her elbows back and her
breasts thrust forward. Tears came to her eyes. It is a common position for slave assessment.

Corinne's hands were tied behind her back.

"Hopa," said more than one Kaiila, looking at the red-
haired girl.

I wondered if the former debutante from Pennsylvania had
ever dreamed, in the bed in her mansion, that she would one
day kneel in the grass of a distant world, a helpless slave
brazenly posed for the assessment of masters.

Tethers were now being tied on the necks of Corinne, Lois, Inez and Priscilla.

"Hopa," said a Kaiila, looking at the red-haired girl. "Waste," said another.

"Hopa," said the mounted Kaiila warrior, approvingly. "Hopa, Wihopawin!"

"Howe," said another.

One of the Yellow Knives standing about put his hand on the hair of the kneeling girl.

Then the lance blade of bluish, chipped flint was at the Yellow Knife's neck. He stood up, quickly, angrily, brushing the lance away, his hand at the handle of his knife, in the beaded sheath at his hip. The lance point, brushed away, returned to threaten him, as easily as a branch, shifted by the wind, might return to its original position. The Kaiila warrior's legs tensed. At a kick backward the kaiila would bolt forward, driving the lance into the Yellow Knife. Yellow Knives and Kaiila, hereditary enemies, tensed.

Corinne, Lois, Inez and Priscilla were pulled by their neck tethers to their feet.

One of the Yellow Knives near the fellow threatened with the lance said something to him. The Yellow Knife at whose chest the lance point was poised then stepped angrily backward. He glanced to the four girls now pulled to their feet. Their tethers were being handed to another Yellow Knife, one mounted. The leader of the Yellow-Knife party said something to the fellow. The fellow then turned away, angrily, and mounted his own kaiila. The Yellow Knives had their share of the loot. Too, because of the recent battle, this area would be, for a time, truce ground.

Urt, or Cuwignaka, Woman's Dress, as he seemed to wish to be called, had been sitting in the grass, breathing deeply and rubbing his wrists and ankles. I gathered that it must be very difficult and painful for him to move his body. He now struggled to his feet and went to the lance, fixed butt down in the turf. He held momentarily to the lance, his head down, keeping his balance. He then unwound the dress from the lance shaft and pulled it on, over his head. He then ripped away the lower portion of the dress, until it hung somewhat above his knees. Too, he ripped it at the left side, to allow himself more freedom of movement. He then uprooted the lance and then, unsteady for a moment, shaken by these exertions, he clutched the lance, supporting himself with it.

"Sleen, tarsks, all of them," said Grunt, in Gorean, looking after the retreating Yellow Knives.

"What were the yellow lances on the flanks of the kaiila of the Sleen?" I asked.

"The Sun Lances," said Grunt, "a warrior society of the Sleen."

"The painted prints on the flanks of the kaiila of the Yellow Knives?" I asked.

"The sign of the Urt Soldiers," said Grunt, "a society of the Yellow Knives."

I nodded. It was common for the members of a given society to take the warpath together.

"Two societies are represented among the Kaiila here," said Grunt. "Most belong to the All Comrades, and one belongs to the Yellow-Kaiila Riders. The fellow in the background, with his war shield in its case, is a member of the Yellow-Kaiila Riders. That may be told by the stylized yellow kaiila print, outlined in red, on the flanks of his beast, over the red horizontal bars."

I nodded. The red horizontal bar, or bars, as the case is, is commonly associated with the Kaiila, the Cutthroat tribe. There were many coup marks, I noted, on the snout and forequarters of the fellow's kaiila.

"That is a prestigious society," said Grunt. "Only tried and proven warriors, with many coups, and many expeditions of war and kaiila stealing, are admitted to it."

"The sign for the All Comrades," I said, "is the heart and lance."

"Yes," said Grunt. "They are sometimes known, too, from the sign, as the Fighting Hearts. The society name, however, more strictly, translates as the All Comrades."

"I see," I said. The weapon ingredient in the insignia left little doubt in my mind as to the sort of enterprise in which such fellows were most likely to be comrades.

"Cheerfulness is indicated by the height of the heart, alongside the lance," said Grunt.

"I see," I said. A heart placed on a horizontal base line, of course, suggested a heart on the ground, or sadness. Grunt had taught me much in the last few days. I could even, now, pick up a little of what was said in Kaiila.

"Let them alone," said Grunt to me, quickly, putting his hand on my arm. Two of the Kaiila were beginning to rummage through our trade goods.

"Very well," I said.

"The Yellow-Kaiila Rider," said Grunt, "is Kahintokapa, One-Who-Walks-Before, of the Casmu, or Sand, Band."

"He is the leader?" I asked.

"It is not likely," he said, "not of a group of All Comrades like this. I think he is more in the nature of an observer, probably sent along to advise and tutor the younger men."

I nodded.

"He is not in the forefront, as you note," said Grunt.

"The leader is the young man, he regarding the red-haired girl?" I asked.

"That, I gather, is the case," said Grunt. "I do not know him. He is of the Isbu Band, the Little Stones."

"You knew the other fellow," I said.

"Yes," said Grunt, "when last I was in the land of the Kaiila, I met him in general council, with Black Clouds, Mahpiyasapa, civil chief of the Isbu."

"You do not anticipate great difficulty with the Kaiila, then?" I asked.

"I do not think so," said Grunt. "It is for Black Clouds, Mahpiyasapa, that I have brought the red-haired girl into the Barrens. For such a woman, sufficiently pleasing to him, he has promised me five hides of the yellow kailiauk."

"I had wondered what disposition you had in mind for her," I said.

"That is it," he said.

"She is to be sold to a chieftain," I said.

"Yes," he said.

"Did you make that clear to our young friend?" I asked.

"Yes," said Grunt.

"Why, then, is she at the paws of his kaiila?" I asked.

"No!" cried Grunt. He then hurried toward the young mounted savage, and the other Kaiila gathered about. Two of them, seeing his angered approach, seized him. Grunt struggled futilely in their grasp. The girl, frightened, on her belly, continued her work, with her lips, her teeth and tongue, biting, and licking and sucking, at the paws and nails of the kaiila.

Words, heated and proud, were exchanged between the two men. Grunt's resolve to conciliate and pacify the savages seemed, in the heat of the moment, to have been abandoned. Then he was thrown backward. Two of the Kaiila drew their knives. I tensed. Grunt, however, had the good sense not to charge them. Suddenly, even in his anger, he realized he might be killed.

The young warrior then spoke to the girl at the paws of his kaiila. "Quick," said Pimples, "stand up. Stand straight. Put your hands at your sides. Press your hands to your thighs. Put your head up. Whatever happens, do not resist."

Quickly the red-haired girl obeyed.

The young savage threw a beaded collar to one of the warriors near the girl.

He approached the girl.

Grunt, at this point, in an excited medley of Dust Leg, Kaiila and Gorean, distraught and angry, entered again into remonstrance with the young warrior.

"Kaiila," I said to Grunt. "Kaiila!"

Grunt then shook his head, gathering his thoughts, and addressed himself, clearly and calmly, in Kaiila, to the youth.

But the young man, clearly, the lance grasped in his hand, high on the lofty kaiila, in his breechclout and paint, was not moved.

The more mature warrior, then, he who was of the Yellow-Kaiila Riders, moved his beast forward. He, too, spoke to the young man. The young man shook his head, angrily. The Yellow-Kaiila Rider then said something to Grunt, and then pulled back his beast, retiring again to the background. I saw that he was not pleased, but he gave little sign of it. It was not seemly, I gathered, for one such as he to enter into dispute with a younger warrior, one of another society and who had fewer coups than himself. Too, it was the young man, and not he, who was Blotanhunka, war-party leader, of this group of All Comrades.

The young man then said something to his fellow near the red-haired girl. Then he gestured to the helpless female, standing naked and straight before him, her head up, her hands pressed tightly to her thighs.

Grunt and I watched as the young man's collar was tied on her throat. She was collared.

Grunt's fists were clenched, futilely.

The red-haired girl looked at her new master in awe. He was tall, and strong, and savagely handsome. Her entire body seemed transfused with fear, and emotion and excitement. It was such a brute who owned her. Too, she realized that tension had been involved in her claimancy. In spite of countervailing considerations, perhaps serious ones, he had decided that it would be he, and no other, who would own her. She knew then that she, a mere slave, was the object of strong desire.

"I do not like it," said Grunt. "It will mean trouble."

"Perhaps," I said.

The young man regarded his new slave, pleasurably, approvingly. She blushed hotly under his inspection, but did not flinch nor turn her eyes from his. Then his eyes grew stern, and she shrank back. She saw then that she could be only his slave, and that she would be uncompromisingly mastered. But even this, I saw, pleased her.

"You have one slim chance for life," said Pimples. "That is to serve him, in all things, and to be pleasing to him, fully, and in all ways."

"I will," she whispered. "I will."

Then the eyes of the young master and the new slave again met. This time, again unable to meet his gaze, she lowered her head. She was very beautiful, her head bowed before her master.

She trembled.

I saw that she was as excited by, and enamored of, her master, as he of her.

"Do not simply stand there, you little fool," said Pimples. "Kneel down before him, and put your head to the grass."

Quickly the red-haired girl obeyed.

I looked at her, kneeling before her master. Doubtless she would be worked hard and used much. She would not be in any doubt as to her slavery, either in his camp or in his lodge.

The young man said something.

"Get up," said Pimples. "Go to him. You may kiss his foot and ankle."

The red-haired girl got up and went to the young warrior. He looked very splendid in his paint and feathers, with the lance, astride the kaiila. She pressed her lips to his moccasin and then to his ankle, kissing him softly. Then she looked up at him, and backed away, his, stripped save for the beaded collar knotted at her throat.

"You have been highly honored," said Pimples to the red-haired girl. "Although you are only a white slave, already you have been permitted to put your lips to his body."

The young man then lowered his lance, until the long point of narrow, tapering, bluish flint was but inches from her

bared breasts. He gestured at her with the lance. "Winyela,"
he said.

"You have been named," said Pimples. "Put down your
head. Put your fingers to your breasts. Say, 'Ho, Itancanka,
Winyela'."

The red-haired girl did this. She then lifted her head again,
to her master.

"Winyela," he said.

"Winyela," she repeated.

He then turned his attention elsewhere, to the trade goods,
mostly Grunt's, through which two of his warriors had been
rummaging. Hatchets, mirrors, knives and cloths, and such,
were now much scattered about, on the grass. He urged his
kaiila to the place. Such concern might seem out of place in
a lofty Blotanhunka. Too, the girl must understand that she is
nothing.

"I have been named," said the red-haired girl.

"Yes, Winyela," said Pimples. I smiled to myself. At last
the red-haired girl had a name.

"It is a beautiful name," said the red-haired girl.

"It means 'Female Animal'," said Pimples.

"Oh," said the red-haired girl, taken aback.

"It is quite a good name, considering that you are a slave,"
said Pimples. "Female slaves are often given names such as
Wasna, Grease, or Cespu, Scab or Wart, until they prove
themselves sufficiently pleasing to have earned a better. I myself was called Wasnapohdi, which means 'Pimples'."

"You are still called 'Pimples'," said the red-haired girl.

"Apparently I have not yet earned a better," smiled
Pimples.

"Winyela," said the red-haired girl. "It is a beautiful
sound."

"Do not forget its meaning," said Pimples. "She-animal.
Female animal."

"No," said the red-haired girl.

"And see that you prove to be a perfect she-animal to him,
obedient, shameless and devoted, in all things."

"A slave," said the girl.

"Yes," said Pimples.

"Do you think he would let me be less," she asked, smiling,
timidly, "such a man?"

"No," said Pimples. "I, too, was once slave among the

Kaiila. I know such men. They will accept nothing less than abject, perfect service from a woman."

"Even if he would permit me less," said the red-haired girl, "I would not want, even of my own free will, to give him less."

I envied the young warrior his lovely, red-haired slave, Winyela. What man, truly, honestly, red or white, would not? But perhaps one must have had a slave, or least once in one's life, to understand this.

"Look at the happy, shameless slave," I said. "She may have been born for that collar."

"Perhaps," said Grunt.

"It may be just as well that your remonstrances proved ineffective."

"She was meant for Mahpiyasapa, Black Clouds," said Grunt. "That lad and Mahpiyasapa are both of the Isbu Band. There is sure to be trouble. Too, I am not getting paid for her."

"That is true," I granted him. "What did the Yellow-Kaiila Rider say to you," I asked, "after he had spoken to the youth, before he had returned to his place?"

"That the youth was within his rights," said Grunt, "that he could claim her, under the circumstances, by right of slave capture."

"Which he did?" I asked.

"Of course," said Grunt. "Would you not have done the same?"

"Perhaps," I smiled.

"At any rate, it is done now," said Grunt. "She is in his collar."

That was true. The collar had now been tied on her neck. She was now, completely, the young man's property.

I looked at her. I saw that she was prepared to serve him well.

I noted, suddenly, looking about, that one of the two warriors who had been busying himself in the trade goods was now reaching for a certain bundle on my own kaiila. It was that in which, rolled, was the story hide and, also, the translator I had brought from Port Kar, that acquired from Kog and Sardak, the Kurii, in the abandoned tarn complex, in the delta.

"Do not," said Grunt to me.

But I was at the side of the kaiila and, firmly, I took the

hand of the warrior from the bundle, and put it to the side.
He looked at me, startled.

Our hands darted to our knife sheaths.

The lance of the young warrior interposed itself between
us. We stepped apart.

I pointed to the goods on my pack kaiila. "Mine!" I said,
in Gorean. Too, I jerked my thumb toward my body. This, in
sign, signifies "I," "Me," or "Mine," depending on the context.

"Howo, Akihoka," said the young man to the fellow
squared off against me, he whose hand I had taken from the
packing on the kaiila. "Howo, Keglezela," said he then to the
other fellow. He then slowly brought his kaiila about and
walked it, slowly, to where the red youth, Cuwignaka,
Woman's Dress, whom I had freed from the stakes, clung,
supporting himself, to the Kaiila lance. He had donned the
white dress of his own accord. He had shortened it earlier,
and torn it at the side, to permit himself more freedom of
movement in it. The lad seemed weak, clinging to the lance.
He had not, however, in the presence of the other savages,
deigned to eat or drink. They must be aware, I supposed, of
this gesture on his part. They would doubtless respect that.
He, in spite of his garb, was showing them that he, in this at
least, could be Kaiila. The two fellows, Akihoka and
Keglezela, followed the young warrior. I adjusted the packing
ropes on the kaiila, securing the goods firmly in place. It interested me that the young warrior had interposed his will as
he had. In this, for some reason, he had protected me. I did
not know him, however. I had never seen him before. It
made no sense to me that he had acted as he had. I was
puzzled. Why had he done this?

The young warrior had now ridden his kaiila about until
he faced Woman's Dress. I noted that his men, too, took up
positions either at his sides, in lines, or rather behind him.
They were drawn up, a few feet from Woman's Dress,
fanned out, almost as if readying themselves for the charge.
Woman's Dress looked up at them, still holding to the lance,
that he not fall. He showed not the least fear before him. I
went to stand near Woman's Dress. Grunt, too, was near to
us. Winyela and Pimples stood to one side.

The young warrior, very clearly, began to speak. This language, to those unfamiliar with it, seems fraught with unfamiliar phonemes and intonation contours. There are many

husky and guttural sounds in it, rasping and sibilant. It is very fluent and expressive. Sometimes it seems almost as though it were exploding into sound, particularly when the speaker speaks rapidly or is excited.

" 'Who has freed you?'," translated Grunt. " 'I am free. It does not matter.' "

The young warrior spoke rapidly to Woman's Dress who, boldly, and in an almost fiery fashion, responded to him. It seemed to me incongruous that Woman's Dress, weakened, in the remains of the dress of a white female, should carry on so stoutly and resolutely with the young warrior. Both, of course, were Kaiila. I wondered if both knew one another, from somewhere before. Woman's Dress, I saw, was a man.

"What is going on?" I asked Grunt.

"The young fellow wants to know who freed him, and Woman's Dress is protecting you."

"I freed him," I said to the young warrior, stepping forward. "Translate that," I told Grunt.

"I do not think that would be in your best interest," said Grunt.

"Translate it," I said.

Reluctantly, Grunt complied.

The young warrior regarded me.

"He is not surprised, of course," said Grunt. "It is what he would have suspected."

I nodded. I would surely have been the prime suspect in this matter. I was obviously not one familiar with the Barrens. I could speak only a smattering of Dust Leg and Kaiila. Presumably, then, it would have been I who, in foolishness, or not knowing any better, would have had the temerity to cut the thongs.

"Canka," said the young warrior, striking himself on the chest with his fist. "Akicita hemaca. Isbu hemaca. Kaiila hemaca!"

" 'I am Canka, Fire-Steel,' " said Grunt. " 'I am a warrior. I am of the Little Stones. I am of the Kaiila.' "

"Tal," said I, "I am Tarl Cabot."

"Wopeton," said Grunt, pointing to me. "Hou, Hou, Kola." Then he turned to me. "Your name would be meaningless to them," he said. "I have called you 'Wopeton,' or 'Trader' or 'Merchant'. That may serve as a name for you, unless you want another. I have also conveyed your greetings."

"I understand," I said.

In the following I will give the gist of the conversation that then ensued. Understand that Grunt, or Woman's Dress, upon occasion, acted as interpreter. Understand, too, that more than this was said. Certain points only are here conveyed. There were additional exchanges which took place between Canka and Cuwignaka, between Fire-Steel and Woman's Dress.

"It is as I thought," said Canka to me, "it was you who freed this callow prisoner."

"He has survived, and he is strong," I said. "He, like yourself, is Kaiila. Respect him."

"He was the slave of white men."

"Now he is free," I said.

"He would not carry arms," said Canka. "He would not take the warpath."

"I had no quarrel with the Fleer," said Cuwignaka.

"We put him in the dress of a woman and called him Cuwignaka," said Canka.

"I had no quarrel with the Fleer," said Cuwignaka.

"You shamed the Isbu," said Canka.

"I had no quarrel with the Fleer," said Cuwignaka.

"When again we went against the Fleer we gave him the opportunity to join us, the right to wear the breechclout and be a man. Again he refused. We then bound him in his woman's dress and sold him to the Dust Legs."

"I had no quarrel with the Fleer," said Cuwignaka.

"The Kaiila have a quarrel with the Fleer, and you are Kaiila," said Canka.

"The Fleer have not injured me," said Cuwignaka.

"Your grandfather was killed by Fleer," said Canka.

"And we, too, killed Fleer," said Cuwignaka.

"How is it that you have dared to return to the Barrens?" asked Canka.

"He was brought," I said. "The white soldiers brought him. He could not help it."

"They brought me," said Cuwignaka, "but I would have returned anyway."

"Why?" demanded Canka.

"Because I am Kaiila," said Cuwignaka, "no less than you!"

"Do you think you are a man?" asked Canka.

"I am a man," said Cuwignaka.

"You do not wear the breechclout," said Canka.

"It is not permitted to me," said Cuwignaka.

"Because you are a woman," said Canka.

"I am not a woman," said Cuwignaka.

"If you return to camp," said Canka, "you will live as a woman. You will wear the dress of a woman and do the work of a woman. You will scrape hides and cook. You will gather kailiauk chips for the fires. You will tend lodges. You will please warriors."

"I will not please warriors," said Cuwignaka.

"I think that I will give you as a female slave to Akihoka," said Canka.

"I will not please warriors," said Cuwignaka.

"That is the first duty of a woman," said Canka, "to obey men, and be pleasing to them."

"I am not a woman," said Cuwignaka.

"You do not wear the breechclout," said Canka. "And these others, too, do not," he said, surveying Grunt and myself.

"A yard or two of cloth," I said, "does not determine manhood in my country."

"In his country, and in mine," said Grunt, "one might wear the breechclout and not be a man, and one might be a man and not wear it."

"That is apparently not the way of the Barrens," I said. "Here, in your country, it seems all that matters is whether a certain garment is worn. If that is the case, in your country, manhood is cheap, costing no more than the price of a strip of cloth."

"That is not true!" said Canka.

"Be careful," said Grunt to me. "Be careful, my friend."

"The breechclout does not make manhood," said Canka. "It is only a sign of manhood. That is why we do not permit those to wear it who are not men."

"Cuwignaka is a man," I said, "and you do not permit him to wear it."

"It is fortunate for you that you are not a warrior," said Canka.

"Akicita hemaca!" I said angrily, in his own language, striking myself on the chest. "I am a warrior!"

"Be careful," said Grunt. "Do not put yourself within the coup system."

Canka sat back on the kaiila. "I do not know if you are a

warrior or not," he said. "But it is perhaps true. You did free Cuwignaka. You are thus, at least, a brave man. You have the respect of Canka."

I was puzzled. I had not expected this attitude on his part.

"Was it you," I asked the young warrior, "who staked him out?"

"It was Kaiila," said Canka, carefully.

"It was Hci, with his fellows of the Sleen Soldiers, of the Isbu, the son of Mahpiyasapa, civil chieftain of the Isbu, who did it," said Cuwignaka.

"It was not Canka, then, and the All Comrades, who did it?" I said.

"No," said Cuwignaka. "But it was Canka, and Hci, with the All Comrades and Sleen Soldiers, who first put me in the dress of a woman and later bound me in that dress and took me to the country of the Dust Legs, there selling me as a slave. That was on the decision of the council of the Isbu, presided over by Mahpiyasapa."

"Canka," I said to Cuwignaka, in Gorean, "does not seem to be displeased that you have been freed."

"No," said Cuwignaka.

"You wear the dress of a woman," said Canka to Cuwignaka, suddenly, angrily. He said this, personally, emotionally. It was as though he, somehow, found this personally shameful.

"I am Cuwignaka," said Cuwignaka, defiantly.

"You hold to a lance of the Kaiila," said Canka. "Surrender it."

"It was you yourself who, when you found me staked out, placed it unbroken beside me. It was you yourself who took the woman's dress which Hci had thrown beside me and wrapped it about the shaft of the lance."

Canka did not respond to this. Such an action, of course, had served to mark, and conspicuously, the place where the lad had been fastened down. The location had been marked, almost as though with a flag. Grunt and I had seen it almost immediately upon coming to this portion of the field. And even had there been none to see it, at least none of our common world, that marker, the unbroken lance, the cloth wrapped about it, might have seemed to have served some purpose to he who had placed it there, perhaps standing for some measure of recollection and respect. This it might have mutely symbolized, if only to the grass of the Barrens, and to the winds and clouds, and perhaps to those of the Medicine World, should they exist, who might have looked down upon it, and pondered it.

"Surrender the lance," said Canka.

"No," said Cuwignaka. "You put it beside me, and it is unbroken."

"Surrender it," said Canka.

"I will not," said Cuwignaka. "If you want it, you must take it from me."

"I will not do that," said Canka. Then he said, "You were freed. Someone must pay." He was looking at me.

"He is my friend," said Cuwignaka.

"I am Blotanhunka," said Canka. "Someone must pay."

"I will pay," said Cuwignaka.

"What is owed here," said Canka, "it is not yours to pay."

"I will pay," said Cuwignaka.

"It is not you who must pay," said Canka. "It is another who must pay."

"I am a warrior," I said to Canka. "I demand the right of combat."

"I do not wish to kill you," said Canka.

This startled me. It seemed to me that Canka had shown me unusual solicitude. He had protected me with Akihoka and Keglezela, in the matter of the trade goods. Now, it seemed, he had no wish to enter into combat with me. He was not afraid of me, of that I was sure. I had little doubt but what he thought he could kill me, if such a combat were joined. As a red savage I had little doubt but what he regarded himself as the superior or equal of any white man in single combat. White men, on the whole, did not even count as being within the coup system. Similarly, he had explicitly professed his respect for me. Thus it did not seem that his disinclination to fight with me was motivated by any supposed indignity or shame in doing so. He was not refusing to fight with me as the larl might refuse to fight with the urt.

"I do not understand," said Grunt to me, in Gorean.

"Nor do I," I said.

"He does not seem to bear you any hostility," said Grunt.

"No," I said.

"Someone must pay," said Canka.

"Then we must fight," I said, stepping back.

"I cannot fight you, for a reason which you cannot understand," said Canka, "but these others, my friends, the All

Comrades, do not have this reason." Several of his fellows, at
these words, grasped their lances more tightly. Their kaiila
moved under them, sensing their excitement.

"Set a champion against me," I said. "I will fight him, and,
if successful, each of the others, in turn."

"I am Blotanhunka," said he. "I will not risk my men in
that fashion."

"It is then all or none," I said.

"Yes," said he.

I stepped back, further. "I am ready," I said.

"Do not fight," said Grunt. "These are Isbu Kaiila, All
Comrades. There are seventeen of them. They, each of them,
are skilled warriors. All have counted coup. You would be
doomed."

"You would fight, would you not?" asked Canka.

"Yes," I said.

"Tatankasa," said Canka.

" 'Red Bull'," translated Grunt.

"It would make my heart heavy to have you killed," said
Canka. The kailiauk bull is 'Tatanka'. The suffix 'sa' designates the color red, as in 'Mazasa', 'Red Metal', 'Copper'.
The expression 'Kailiauk' is used by most of the tribes for the
kailiauk, which is not an animal native to Earth. The expression 'Pte' designates the kailiauk female, or kailiauk cow.
It is also used, colloquially, interestingly, for the kailiauk in
general. This is perhaps because the "Pte" is regarded, in a
sense, as the mother of the tribes. It is she, in the final analysis, which makes possible their hunting, nomadic life. Like
many similar peoples, the red savages have generally a great
reverence and affection for the animals in their environment.
This is particularly true of the animals on which they depend
for their food. The useless or meaningless slaughter of such
animals would be unthinkable to them.

"I am ready to fight," I said.

"Do not be a fool," said Grunt.

"I am ready," I said to Canka.

"There is an alternative," said Grunt. "Can't you see? He
is waiting."

"What?" I asked.

"The collar," said Grunt.

"Never," I said.

"Please, Tatankasa," said Canka.

"Please," said Cuwignaka.

"Please," said Grunt.

Numbly I unbuckled my sword belt. I wrapped the belt about the sheaths, the sword sheath and the knife sheath, and handed the objects to Grunt. I was disarmed.

Words were spoken. One of the savages, he at the left of Canka, Akihoka, leaped to the ground. Canka threw him a collar. It was tied on my neck.

I regarded Canka. I was his slave.

The hands of Akihoka fastened themselves in the collar of my tunic. I was to be stripped naked before them.

"No," said Canka.

Another warrior approached me, with thongs and a rawhide rope. Another jerked my hands behind me. I was to be bound, and put on a tether, like the mere animal I now was, only a slave.

"No," said Canka.

The warriors then withdrew from me, puzzled, and remounted their lofty beasts.

Canka then turned his kaiila about. He looked over his shoulder at me. "Follow us," he said.

"Very well," I said.

"Howo, Winyela," said Canka to Winyela. He pointed to a place in the grass near the left flank of his kaiila.

"Quick," said Pimples to Winyela. "Run to the place he has indicated. It is the place for you to follow his kaiila, the place of a slave."

Swiftly Winyela ran to her place beside the kaiila. There she stood with her head down, submissively.

"Good," said Pimples.

"Winyela," said Canka.

She lifted her eyes to his.

"Winyela," said Canka, again. In this context he was not saying her name so much as reminding her of what she was.

"Say, 'Ho, Itancanka,' " said Pimples.

"Ho, Itancanka," said Winyela.

"Good," said Pimples.

Canka, then, in good humor, set his heels to the flanks of his kaiila and, slowly, the beast walking, took his way from the place. The girl, stripped and barefoot in the grass, her throat tied in his beaded collar, hurried along beside him, taking care to remain exactly in her place.

"I am ruined," said Grunt.

"You are ruined?" I asked. "I am a disarmed slave."

"There is something strange about that," said Grunt. "You have not been stripped, or tied. I do not understand it."

"Winyela, too," I said, using her new name, "has not been tied." We looked after the retreating warriors. Winyela was hurrying along at the left flank of Canka's kaiila, a girl's running place by the beast of her master.

"Have no fear," said Grunt. "In the collar of Canka the red-haired beauty will learn her slavery well."

"You still have most of your trade goods," I said.

"And I am among them, Master," said Pimples. "Surely I am worth something."

"Lie on your belly," said Grunt.

"Yes, Master," she said, immediately complying. She had spoken without permission.

"The red-haired girl," said Grunt, looking after the warriors, "was for Mahpiyasapa, civil chief of the Isbu. Last year when I was in the country of the Kaiila, he put in an order for such a woman. Such a woman was on his want list, so to speak."

"Doubtless when Canka returns to the main camp he will surrender her to Mahpiyasapa," I said.

"Do you think so?" asked Grunt.

"No," I said.

"I am thirsty," said Cuwignaka, sitting down in the grass. "And I am faint with hunger."

These were the first signs of weakness which he had showed. How shamed and foolish I suddenly felt. How little consideration, how little attention, we had given him.

I hurried to the pack kaiila and fetched from it the water bag. Grunt, from his own stores, brought forth some dried, pressed biscuits, baked in Kailiauk from Sa-Tarna flour. We watched him eat and drink. We did not feel that his stomach would be ready yet for the meat of kailiauk. We had some from the Dust Legs. It was in sheets, cut almost as thin as paper, dried in the prairie sun, layered in a flat, leather envelope, a parfleche, originally sealed with a seam of hardened fat. By confessing his need for drink and food before us Cuwignaka had, in his way, honored us. This was the sort of thing that a Kaiila warrior would be likely to do only among those whom he considered his friends and comrades.

"Meat," said Cuwignaka.

Grunt and I exchanged glances but, in the end, we fetched Cuwignaka some of the strips of dried kailiauk meat.

He sat, cross-legged, in the grass, and ate some. "It is enough," he said. He thrust back the remainder to Grunt, who inserted it in the opened parfleche.

"I am now ready to go to the camp," said Cuwignaka.

"You are in no condition to travel," I said.

"I am ready," he said.

"You will ride," I said.

"I can walk," he said, rising unsteadily to his feet. He picked up the lance, using it as a staff to maintain his balance.

I began to remove my things from my kaiila, with the exception of the bridle, the saddle and saddle blanket.

"What are you doing?" asked Grunt.

"I am preparing the mount for Cuwignaka," I said.

"Do not be foolish," said Grunt. "This is your opportunity to escape. Ride westward, like the wind. Flee."

"I do not understand," I said.

"Do you not see, my friend?" asked Cuwignaka. "They have given you this chance to escape."

"They could doubtless follow me, tracking me, with strings of kaiila, until my own beast played out," I said.

"Doubtless," said Cuwignaka, "but I do not think they wish to do so."

"They are letting you go," said Grunt.

"Go now," said Cuwignaka, "for, later, in the main camp, others may not be so lenient."

"Go," said Grunt. "You would then have a fine lead on others, in the main camp, days from here, who might wish to follow you. Make good your escape now. It is doubtless their intention."

"But why should they permit me this?" I asked.

"I do not know," said Grunt.

"I was told to follow," I said, "and I said that I would do so."

"It was necessary that such a command be given," said Grunt. "None expects you to follow."

"I said that I would," I said.

"They will not expect a white man to keep his word," said Grunt.

"Your word is respected in the Barrens, is it not?" I asked.

"I think so," said Grunt.

"Then so, too, will be mine," I said.

"Run," said Grunt. "Do not be a fool."

"What are you going to do?" I asked.

"I am going to the main camp of the Kaiila," he said. "I have come to this country to trade."

"You have business in this place?" I asked.

"Yes," said Grunt.

"I, too, have business in this place," I said.

"You are mad," said Grunt.

"Perhaps," I said. But I had not come to the Barrens to turn back now.

"Get up," said Grunt, kicking Pimples lightly in the side with the side of his foot. "We have work to do."

"Yes, Master," she said, rising, and smoothing down the skirt of the tiny slave tunic with the palms of her hands. She was the only one of the girls whose clothing had not been taken by the red savages. The red-haired girl, Lois, Corinne, Inez, Priscilla, the others, had all been stripped. Canka had permitted her to keep the garment, such as it was, to draw a distinction between her, who could speak Kaiila, and the others, who could not.

To be sure, there is a controversy as to whether or not it is more humiliating for a woman to be put before masters in such a garment or merely stark naked, save, perhaps, for a brand and collar. Surely slave tunics leave little to the imagination. Among the girls, of course, there is little disagreement in practice, though some in theory. The girls, commonly, treasure even the tiniest rag which can afford them some shielding, however pathetic, from the imperious gaze of masters. Too, from the point of view of the masters, the little that might be left to the imagination, small as it is, by such a garment, is often found to be intriguing and stimulating. It encourages them to her stripping. Too, giving a girl a bit of clothing, tends to give one more control over her. For example, will she be told to remove the garment, or will it be taken from her, and if so, publicly or privately? It must be understood, of course, that a slave, having no rights, does not have the right even to clothing. That a girl is wearing even a rag is usually a sign that she has pleased her master, and quite significantly, too. Often the garment of a slave girl does not come easily to her. In private, of course, even rags are often dispensed with. The slave is the property of the master, and, in the privacy of his quarters, she is done with, totally, as he pleases.

"Take care of the things which were mine," I said, "if you would."

"I shall," said Grunt. Slaves, of course, own nothing. It is they who are owned.

"I think it is time to follow Canka," I said to Cuwignaka.

"Ride from here. Escape," said Grunt.

"Mount up," I said to Cuwignaka. He stood, unsteadily, clinging to the lance, as though to a staff.

"I will walk," said Cuwignaka.

"You are weak," I said.

"I am Kaiila," said Cuwignaka. "I will walk."

He took two or three faltering steps, supporting himself with the lance. But then, suddenly, his legs buckled. For a moment he held himself up with the lance, but then, heavily, fell to the side. Painfully, with the lance, hand over hand, he pulled himself again to his feet. He took another two or three faltering steps, supporting himself with the lance, after Canka and the others, but then, again, fell heavily in the grass. I moved to go to him, but Grunt's hand on my arm stopped me. "No," he said. "Do not demean him. He is Kaiila."

Pimples, too, I noted, had not moved to aid him. I nodded.

Cuwignaka struggled to a seated position in the grass. He sat there, cross-legged, angrily, the lance beside him.

"I have decided to rest," he said. "I will sit here for a time. Then I will get up, and go."

"Very well," I said.

"He may not be able to walk for days," said Grunt.

"In a day or two," I said.

"Perhaps," said Grunt.

"He is Kaiila," I said.

"That is true," said Grunt, smiling. Then he turned to Pimples. "Busy yourself, Girl," he said. "Pack our stores. A trail awaits."

"Yes, Master," she said.

I lent my assistance to Grunt and Pimples, and, in a few Ehn, we had secured the goods about either on the travois attached to Grunt's pack kaiila or on my own pack beast. Pimples put the discarded coffle chains, and the manacles which had bound the Hobarts, on the hides of the travois, fastening them about one of the tie ropes.

"I wish you well," I said to Grunt.

"I wish you well," said he to me.

I watched Grunt and Pimples, with the three kaiila, his

mount, the kaiila drawing the travois and my own pack beast, wending their way away, through the tall grass. They turned and waved, and I waved back. Then, after a time, they were in the distance, following the trail of Canka and his party. I could see the smoke of evening fires in the distance. That was presumably the Kaiila camp. Canka had not tethered Winyela. He had let her run free at the flank of his kaiila. That seemed an unusual courtesy to be extended to a new girl. I smiled to myself. I suspected the young warrior might already care for the red-haired slave. I did not think he would be eager to surrender her to Mahpiyasapa, his chieftain.

"What are you thinking of?" asked Cuwignaka.

"Various things," I said.

"If you are not going to flee," said Cuwignaka, "perhaps you should follow Canka, now."

"I will wait for you," I told him.

"I may sit here for a little while," he said.

I smiled. "I will wait," I said.

"The lot of a slave among the Kaiila, as among our peoples generally," said Cuwignaka, "is not an easy one."

"I do not suppose so," I said.

"At least you are not a female," said Cuwignaka. "The Kaiila, as others of our poeples, do not treat their white beauties with gentleness."

I nodded. I supposed not.

Total pleasingness, at all times and in all ways, and instant, and complete obedience, to the least whim of the master, is standardly required of Gorean female slaves, incidentally, not merely of those who wear the collars of red savages. I had little doubt but what there were many in the cities who could instruct even the red savages in matters pertaining to the utilization, management and control of female slaves. If anything, I suspected that the lot of the female slave in the Barrens might be a bit easier than that of her imbonded sister in the smooth corridors and ornate palaces of the high cities. Each street and each square in such a city is likely to have its tether posts and whipping rings.

"Canka did not even tether Winyela," I said.

"Let her displease him even in the least thing," said Cuwignaka, "and she will quickly discover that she is a slave and that he is her master."

"Doubtless," I said. I thought that this might be good for

the former Miss Millicent Aubrey-Welles, the former debutante from Pennsylvania. Such girls thrive best when kept under a strict discipline.

"I was not stripped and tethered," I said.

"No," said Cuwignaka.

"I do not understand that," I said.

"It is not so hard to understand," said Cuwignaka.

"Why were such things not done to me?" I asked. "Why
was I not attacked? Why was I permitted an opportunity to
attempt escape? Why have I been treated with such lenience?"

"Can you not guess?" asked Cuwignaka.

"No," I said.

"Canka," said Cuwignaka, "is my brother."

"What are you doing?" asked Cuwignaka. I had fetched
my kaiila. "What are you doing?" he asked. I lifted him
gently to the saddle.

"I can walk," he said.

"No, you cannot," I said.

"In a few moments, I shall be able to do so," he said.

"Ride," I said. I then handed him the lance from the grass.
It was metal-bladed, with a long trade point, some nine
inches in length. It was riveted in the haft at two places and
reinforced with rawhide bindings. The nature of these bindings and the three lateral red marks near the head of the
shaft marked it as Kaiila. The binding was traditional; the
marks were an explicit convention, signifying the Kaiila, the
Cutthroat tribe. Other marks upon it, which might have sig-
nified an owner, had been scratched away, probably with the
edge of a knife. No feathers were attached to the lance.
Never as yet, it seemed, had it touched an enemy.

Cuwignaka swayed in the saddle. I steadied him.

I looked out over the prairie. Somewhere, out there, somewhere, was Zarendargar. I had come to seek him. Others, too,
had come to seek him. Kog and Sardak, with some compan-
ions, and at least one other Kur, as well, whom I had seen
earlier, threatening the Waniyanpi, had survived the recent
action. I did not doubt but what they would press ahead in
their grisly mission. The Kur is tenacious. These Kurii I did
not think would be in great danger from the red savages.
Several of them had departed from the scene of battle un-
harmed. Such beasts were unfamiliar to the red savages. Sus-
pecting that they might be denizens of the Medicine World

red savages might be likely to give them, wherever possible, a wide berth.

They would have no such reservations, of course, pertaining to a lone white man wandering about in the Barrens. Such might be, I supposed, even hunted down for sport. Alfred, the mercenary captain from Port Olni, I supposed, must now be making his way back to civilization, with his men. I expected that they would be successful in this endeavor. Few tribes, most of which are usually dispersed in scattered bands, would be likely to wish to, or be able to, bring a force against them, some three or four hundred mounted men. Doubtless, too, the soldiers, now, would keep careful watches. The lessons of their foolish arrogance had been harshly learned; those who have survived such mistakes seldom trouble themselves to repeat them. I did not expect to see Alfred, or his men, again.

I glanced back, down into the shallow valley. I could see Pumpkin, and his Waniyanpi, down there, still clearing the field. Behind one of the partially burnt, abandoned wagons would be she who had once been the proud Lady Mira, an agent of Kurii, of the resort city of Venna. She was now naught but a stripped, luscious, yoked slave, tethered by the ankle to a wagon axle. She had been found with the soldiers. She had, in spite of this, after having been stripped, to determine if there might be any interest in owning her, been given a slim chance to save her life, prostrating herself and performing intimate acts at the feet of a master's kaiila. She had apparently licked and sucked well at the toes and nails of the beast, making clear to all, saving perhaps herself, her aptness for slavery and the suitability of its collar for her fair throat. Then, after having performed these foul and degrading acts, so fitting for a slave, and doubtless having been passionately aroused by them, she had not been, as she had doubtless expected to be, ravished at length by imperious masters, but bound and given over to Waniyanpi. What a rich joke was this played on the aroused and tormented woman. How cruel could be the tortures of the red savages! She had been found with soldiers. Stripped, and forced to reveal herself as a slave, and aroused, she had then been given to Waniyanpi. She would be taken to one of their compounds. They would respect her. She would be called 'Turnip'.

"I think I am ready now," said Cuwignaka.

"Can you travel now?" I asked.

"Yes," he said.

I glanced once more, then, over the prairie. It seemed open. The horizons were broad.

I then, leading the kaiila, on which Cuwignaka rode, slumped forward, with the lance, set my feet in the tracks of those who had preceded me, Canka and his party, and Grunt and Pimples, toward the smoke of the evening fires, toward the camp of the Isbu Kaiila.

In a few moments Cuwignaka straightened his back. I was pleased to see that he now held his head up. He was strong. He was Kaiila.

"A trail awaits," said Cuwignaka.

"Yes," I said.

Presenting JOHN NORMAN in DAW editions . . .